# Doretta's Damnation

A Novel

Harald Lutz Bruckner

**Books by Harald Lutz Bruckner**

*The Blue Sapphire Amulet*

The Birken Saga
A Trilogy

Book 1. *Escape on the Astral Express*
Book 2. *A Wanderer on the Earth*
Book 3. *The Born-Again Phoenix*

*Harald's Garland*

*Lighthouse Mystery*

*To Doris and Lynne*

# Chapter 1

HER screams were echoing down the marble stairway. Fernando charged out of his offices and rushed up the highly polished steps, nearly taking a spill in his stocking feet. He pushed open the doors to their private quarters in the palatial home of his ancestors, only to find his mother, Señora Esmeralda Garcia Lopez, and Doretta's personal maid, Valentina, bent over Doretta, who appeared to lie prostrate in their marital bed.

His mother fanned Doretta's face while Valentina wiped away the perspiration on Doretta's brow and applied cold compresses. Doretta was mumbling outbursts in German, although it was well known that her Spanish skills had markedly improved since her arrival in Santiago in April of 1963, now more than five years ago.

She seemed visually pleased when she glimpsed Fernando approaching her. "What happened? Did you have another nightmare?"

"I must have heard the marching of the guards outside.

The sound took me back to events buried deep in my subconscious mind. You've been with me close to ten years and know how often the past invades my dreams."

Esmeralda Garcia Lopez touched her mantilla, pushing it slightly off her face. "When I walked into the room, she was yelling 'Momma, Momma, hold me, hold me!' I could tell she was having another nightmare and summoned Valentina to assist with the care of your wife."

"Thank you, Mother."

Fernando touched Valentina's arm. "Why don't you see my mother back to the breakfast table? I'm sure my father wonders what's happening. Please assure him that my wife is just fine, and that she suffered with another bad dream. We'll be down in a while."

Valentina held out her right arm to Señora Garcia Lopez, who in a state of excitement had failed to carry her trusted cane. The mild stroke she had experienced two years earlier resulted in a slight limp on her left side but no further impairment. As soon as Valentina closed the doors gently behind them, Fernando turned to Doretta.

"Tell me what happened that frightened you so deeply? Was it the same dream? I'm always amazed how you can recall and speak of the events that torment you in your sleep."

"I found myself in the arms of my mother in that primitive bomb shelter under our house. Moments earlier, three Nazis had dragged my father out of the house, practically beating him to death with their billy clubs and calling him a stinking Jew. There was blood everywhere. When I looked up at Mother, her dress was covered in blood spatters. I screamed for her to hold me as the sirens kept blaring, and the sound of bombs striking near us frightened me to death. It was all so real. No matter how often those scenes play out in my nocturnal adventures, I never seem to be able to free myself of their impact on my existence. It's more than twenty-five years since I lived through those events."

"I try to understand, although I never suffered such trauma. Perhaps Dr. Rodríguez Amado was right when he advised you to write down some of these experiences in the hope that committing your thoughts to paper might ultimately free you of them. With your well-practiced typing skills, it shouldn't be too much of a challenge. I will arrange for you to have total privacy in the office next to mine. Don't worry about style or writing a masterpiece; just put your thoughts down as you recall the happenings that plague you.

"It's a beautifully appointed room with lots of natural light and a pleasant view into our gardens were you to pause as you looked up from typing. I'll bring in a designer and have the room changed to your liking, perhaps making it a bit less masculine.

"You know there is no need to worry about the children. As much as you love Mario and Alona, they will be well taken care of by servants. You can spend much time with Mario when he is free of his tutor in the afternoons, and you can always step away from what you are doing to peek in on Alona in her room. She won't mind stopping whatever she is doing. What do you say?"

"Let me think about it. I need to take a shower and make myself presentable before I can join you and the others at breakfast."

She kissed Fernando lightly on his lips and let her vision follow him out of the room. Doretta freed herself of her negligee and stepped into the shower. She closed her eyes as she let the warmth of the water soothe her tormented body. When she opened her eyes to reach for the lavender soap, she could only scream in desperation. She was covered in blood from head to toe. Fernando rushed in, seeing his wife shaking like an aspen tree in late fall and dissolved in tears.

"Don't come near me and don't touch me. Turn off the blood and hand me that old blanket from the closet. I don't want to ruin your mother's precious towels."

"What are you talking about? What do you mean by turning off the blood? All I see is you in your wet nakedness." Fernando stepped into the shower and, in spite of Doretta's protestations, enfolded her in his strong arms, trying to make her feel safe.

"There, there. Just let me hold you. You are not covered in blood. Your imagination just ran wild with you. Please try not to let your nightmares invade your daily life. Come back to me; be the woman with whom I fell in love when we first met in Zürich ten years ago. I loved our walk-up apartment on the fifth floor of the old building. Walking all those steps up and down kept us in good shape, especially me, since I spent most of my days sitting in study halls exercising only my brain and doing little to stay vital. How I treasured making love to you in our cozy bed. You remember those days? How happy we were without all the trappings of my heritage."

"Thank you for holding me. You brought me back to reality. Don't frown on your heritage. Your family, other than your mother, has accepted and welcomed me and our children into your world of wealth and well-being. It's a world I never knew and certainly never expected to have and surround me. I've learned to love your parents, especially your father. Your mother has a much harder time showing her love for me.

"Mario and Alona were the ones who opened her heart. Perhaps we should think about having another child; perhaps another boy, a second heir to the estate? Your mother often voices her concerns to me that something could happen to Mario. What would happen to the Garcia Lopez line? She regrets never having been able to conceive another child after she gave birth to you. The way she often speaks to me, I wonder if she is attempting to place her guilt on me."

"Let's not worry about Mother. I want you to be happy. As to making another baby, I'm all yours. You want to give it a whirl?" Fernando freed himself of his shirt and trousers and nudged Doretta back into the shower.

# Chapter 2

DORETTA Garcia Lopez walked into her newly designed office space. Fernando had lived up to his promise of creating an environment that would make her feel at ease and comfortable in the isolation she sought from the world that surrounded her. No expense was spared, much to his mother's chagrin. Esmeralda Garcia Lopez had envisioned this German woman as someone who would produce numerous heirs rather than the complicated individual she turned out to be. And now her son was encouraging his wife to write an account of her life rather than seeing her involved with her growing children. Esmeralda decided to confront her daughter-in-law.

"What makes you think you know how to write? Who do you expect to read such drivel? You hardly speak proper Spanish! How dare you even conceive of the idea of writing and wasting your time and our money?"

"I will write for the purpose of healing myself. It was Dr. Rodriguez Amado and Fernando's idea and not mine. I am not writing for anyone but myself and certainly would not be presumptuous enough to attempt writing in Spanish. It was you who insisted that Mario and Alona be raised by servants that met with your approval. You didn't want our children to be exposed to my inferior command of Spanish and, God forbid, to the German language.

"I hate to disappoint you; both children someday will be trilingual. Their father speaks to them in Spanish; when they are with me, they are exposed to both German and English since I'm fully in command of both languages. How else can I respond to your verbal assault? I would prefer that you leave me to enjoy this wonderful day in the pleasant room your son has created for me."

Esmeralda struck the leg of the table with her cane. "Perra!" [bitch] was all she uttered numerous times before she walked out, slamming the heavily carved wooden door behind her.

Doretta knew what she called her and opted to ignore it. She'd made up her mind to deal with more pressing matters than appeasing Esmeralda. *I will let Fernando handle his temperamental mother*, she mused as she sat down to write.

I was eleven years old when my father was taken away from us by the Nazis. I can still see him being beaten by those men as they dragged Father out of the house. We had no idea where they were taking him, and we never saw him again. Mother often wondered what might happen to her half-Jewish offspring. She adored my father, Emanuel Abraham Osram. He had been a successful attorney and provided well for my mother, my younger twin brothers, and me. I was always very much loved by my family but especially by my father. Seeing him forcefully removed from our lives left me emotionally scarred for life.

The last year of the war was the worst. Mother was in constant fear for us. She was afraid we would be taken from her and she herself placed in a camp for no other reason than having married a Jew and producing three bastard children. That was how we were viewed by the ruling powers. To shelter us, we rarely left the house and always sought protection in our basement during the many bomb attacks. The sounds of falling bombs put the fear of God in me. I became almost paranoid and traumatized with angst during these dark nights of terror visited upon the city dwellers. Toward the end of the war, we saw much destruction even in broad daylight. We were in our basement when our house took a direct hit during the last attack on the city on March 11, 1945.

We were fortunate to survive it. When the cacophony of falling bombs ceased, Mother kept striking a heavy copper kettle with a cleaver, alerting those on the outside to our existence under the rubble of the collapsed house. I remember questioning Mother: "How come you have those things in the shelter? Don't they belong in our kitchen?"

"Of course, they should be in the kitchen, but I wanted to be prepared in case we were caught in the cellar. And you see, Doretta, it's a good thing I had foresight."

And she was right; after hours of being trapped,

a neighbor heard Mother's banging on the kettle and alerted a crew of men who dug us out from what was left of our demolished home. We had lost everything but our lives.

Mother was in tears when she beheld us and the heap of refuse that had been her home since she married in 1931. Three years later, she would not have been allowed to marry my father. Unions between Jews and Christians were no longer sanctioned under the rule of the Nazis.

Mother held us by our hands. "I have no other choice but to take refuge in the public shelter. The neighbors who remained friendly toward us lost everything as well. Fortunate for them, they have family who may house them for now. I don't have that option. The only one left, God willing, is your grandmother, Welter. I have no way of getting in touch with her. She lives too far from the city, and there's no longer any transportation. The bomb shelter it is; with a little luck, we'll be given some food and hopefully blankets to keep us comfortable. There have to be good samaritans among our fellow man."

Mother hugged us. My brothers were chewing on the tails of their shirts. "I know you are hungry and thirsty, boys. I'll do my best to find someone to be charitable to us. Please be patient with your ailing mother. I'm sick in my heart."

As we were walking down the many concrete steps leading us to the deep underground bunker, we became aware of the chill and dampness surrounding us. The only light in this dank place was given by sporadically hung bare lightbulbs suspended from the cold concrete vaulted ceiling. Mother finally located a vacant bench where no one had chosen to sit. "Let's grab these seats before others as desperate as we claim them. Doretta, you stay here with Lutz and Lenny. I'll search for something to fill our empty stomachs. Whatever you do, do not move and do not vacate the spot we finally found and will have to call home until this nightmare is finally over."

Neither my brothers nor I spoke. We listened to the muffled voices of others huddled near us. I couldn't help detecting the steady drip-drip of water coming off the concrete vault above us. I wasn't certain how Mother would handle the dampness of the place with the severe case of arthritis she had battled for the past few years. I don't know how often she expressed the wish that she and Father had fled with us to Spain while they still could have. Now it was much too late. More likely than not, Father was long dead.

My brothers and I couldn't believe our eyes when we saw our mother approach after what seemed to be an eternity. The boys were literally running towards her. "I garnered two loaves of *Kommissbrot* [army bread] from the old baker on the corner. He wasn't proud of his product, telling me it was more filler and sawdust than anything else. He told me to eat it as fast as possible while it is still warm and much softer than it would be in a couple hours. Cooling would turn the bread literally to stone. The kind lady at the fruit kiosk sold me a few of her apples. Sorry, there's no margarine or cheese—just dry bread and apples."

The boys had relieved Mother of one of the loaves, tearing pieces from the treasure Gisela Osram had secured. "Boys, eat slowly; we can't have any of us choke. Take a bite from your apple between bites of bread to get a little moisture. I have to get back to the stairway. There was a nurse in a Red Cross uniform giving people clean water to drink. I will have to see if I can find an empty beer bottle or some other vessel in this hellhole since we have nothing from which we could drink. We have to learn to make the best of what we have left. Walking back, I saw an abandoned large quilt lying on the ground. If it is still there, I'll grab it. It's quite dirty, but I don't care. Neither will you when it gives us much-needed warmth. Be thankful you wore your shoes when we sought shelter in our cellar. Just imagine walking on this dirt and gravel with bare feet."

She turned her face, not wanting us to see that she was crying. Mother wasn't exaggerating when she called the bunker a hellhole. We were condemned to live in hell for nearly two months. Now and then, when the all-clear alarm was sounded, Mother allowed me to take my brothers for a short walk to the outside. It hurt our eyes when we would finally see sunlight. Our eyes were conditioned to darkness and the miserable low light in the caverns of the bunker.

On the morning of May 7, one of the bunker guards entered the space with a bullhorn. "The war is over. Germany has surrendered to the victors of this debacle. They tell us the Führer is dead. Germany has been defeated. You are safe and may leave this place for good."

People around us hugged each other, very much "unGerman" in character. There was hardly a dry eye among mostly women, children, and old people who had shared the bunker for months. Mother decided to leave the dirty old quilt and other wraps she had fetched for our comfort during our confinement in the hellhole—even we young'uns kept referring to our very temporary home in that unflattering term.

Mother faced us as soon as all four of us had adjusted to being in broad daylight. "We have a challenge ahead of us. But I've made up my mind. We will go on a very long walk. If Grandma and her house have survived this nightmare, then we will have a place to stay until I can come up with a better idea. That is the only solution to our homelessness I can envision at this very instant. I know you can do it. It may take us at least two days to get there, but get there we will. Hold on to your drinking bottles; we'll find bread and water somewhere. There will be little else to be had along the way. It's too early in the growing season for us to find anything edible in the many fields we'll be crossing.

"I want you to kneel on the ground and pray with me: Dear God, we give thanks for having spared our lives. We hope Papa made it to heaven when he was condemned to death by the powers that ruled our country. We give thanks for the defeat of our rulers and pray you protected Grandma and her home. Shield us from evil and danger as we start our trek to safety on this sunny May day. Thank you for your grace, oh Lord."

Mother rose to her feet and hugged each of us before she led the way in a southeasterly direction out of the city. "Be strong, children. God willing, we'll turn a new page at your grandmother's home."

# Chapter 3

Mother had been correct in her assumption that it would take us close to two days of walking. When night fell on the seventh of May, she gathered her gumption and knocked on the door of a dilapidated farmhouse. Greeted by an old woman, Mother confessed to our situation and begged the woman to allow us overnighting with the animals in the barn. The lady was kind enough and permitted us to do so. Even better, she asked us to join her and her invalid husband and partake of their humble soup supper and warm homemade bread. All of us thought we hadn't heard correctly. Just the thought of something warm in our stomachs made us smile with deep appreciation.

While enjoying this blessed meal, we learned that all three of the elderly couple's sons were killed during the war. None of them were married before they were drafted into service to their country. There would be no heirs in this family.

Mother crossed herself before she took part in

the meal, thanking God for her children and begging for continued blessings on all gathered in this home. I was going on thirteen, and Mother encouraged me to act like an adult and help with the raising of my twin brothers. She made sure I understood my responsibilities in holding our little family together. I was fully aware that none of my father's relatives survived the Holocaust. The only family who would be able to rescue us was my maternal grandmother.

When we finally arrived at Grandma's home late in the afternoon on May 9, Mother and I took a breath of relief when we saw the little house still standing in the distance. The small dwelling survived the nightmare with only minor blemishes.

Walking up the muddy path to Grandma's house, we saw a small figure emerging on the porch. To us, it was a miniature castle standing proudly high on a hill. At first glimpse, Grandma wasn't certain who was approaching her humble home. And then she realized who she was beholding. She rushed toward us. There were tears of joy flooding her eyes. She reached for my mother and enfolded her firmly in her arms.

"My God, child, you are alive. I thought I would never see you again." And then her loving arms held my brothers and me. "Thank God, you are still among the living. Didn't Emanuel come with you?"

"Sorry, Mom, the Nazis took him away from us in 1943. More likely than not, they killed him in one of those camps if he even made it to one. They practically clubbed him to death the day they came for him at our home—our home that is no more. It was totally destroyed during the last major bombing in March. The children and I were in the cellar.

"It is a miracle that we survived the destruction of the house. Neighbors eventually heard my desperate signaling by banging on an old copper kettle. They heard our pleas for help and dug us out of the rubble. The children and I lived for close to two months in the underground bunker. There was no other place for us to stay."

"Well, you are safe now; this will be your home for as long as need be. Gisela, you can share my bed. It was always plenty big for your father and me; may he rest in peace. Lutz and Lenny, you two can share one of the beds in the guestroom, leaving the other bed for your sister."

Her glance fell upon me. "My, my, Doretta. You are almost a young woman. You've gotten to be so tall and slender. You are even taller than your mother. You must be taking after the Osram tribe."

While Grandma had never approved of Mom marrying a Jew, she learned to love my father for the kind man he was and never uttered a negative word about him around us. She was fully aware of our feelings toward our father and especially how I missed him being the oldest.

On that very first day, all of us came to recognize the treasure we had found at the end of that endless trek. Quarters were humble and tight, but Grandma surrounded us with her love and made us appreciate what we had. She liked nothing better than us sitting around her dining room table liking what she prepared no matter how meek a meal she was able to eke out of the tight rations.

"How long has it been since any of you have graced a school bench? Even our country school has been closed since early 1943. There are hardly any children left in this neighborhood. Those who were of school age at the time were all sent away to other parts of the country. I'm surprised they didn't ship you off to somewhere."

"Mom, I have to confess. After they arrested Manny, I knew I had to hide the children. When some of the neighbors asked what happened to them, I lied and told them they were in a camp in Czechoslovakia."

"Good girl, Gisela. I knew I hadn't raised a dummy. I don't know what I would've done if they had taken you and the children. What a terrible time we've been through. Lord knows what we'll learn about the horrors committed by the great Führer and his supporters. Here and there, I've heard of people who came back from those KZ camps (concentration camps). No one really wanted to talk about it for fear they might be sent back."

"Mom, you realize none of Manny's relatives survived. They were all taken to the camps between 1937 and 1944. I was fortunate to have my dear husband for as long as I did. I still shudder when I look back to the day when they arrested him. Doretta suffers terrible nightmares reliving that day; she sees herself covered in her father's blood."

"Oh, no! That poor child. Did she have to witness that? How awful a memory of the man she loved so dearly."

Grandma reached out to me wanting to hug me.

"Come to your grandma's loving arms. I hope you'll never have to experience anything like this again."

Grandma and Mother were thrilled when school resumed in the fall of 1945, giving mother and daughter a few hours of peace and quiet. Lutz and Lenny were a challenge at age eleven. Grandma gave them a well-deserved licking when she caught them smoking a smelly stogie in the back of the house. After she punished them with her fist full of switches, she made the boys smoke the stogie until they barfed all over her garden. She wanted to make sure they never forgot their offensive behavior on her property.

# Chapter 4

I never forgot the first day my brothers and I set foot in a school after being deprived of that privilege for well over two years. We didn't realize how much schooling we had missed until our new teachers began to ask questions or sampled our abilities with nothing but negative outcomes. We were given old textbooks that had seen much use through the years.

Lutz and Lenny were given opportunities to catch up and were able to enter a track that would lead them eventually to higher education. For me, the gap was far too great to make the leap. I finished Grundschule [basic school] and was, at best, trained to become a good wife and mother. On my own, I studied English and actively pursued shorthand and typing. I excelled in all three subjects and pleased my mother and grandmother when they found me looking for gainful employment in 1950.

"How did your interviews go in Düsseldorf? Did you

have any difficulties passing the tests they gave you?" asked Grandma.

Mom was all ears as were my brothers. I was the first in the family to earn a living wage; the family was living on social assistance, restitution funds paid to my mother for the loss of her husband during the Nazi era, etc. Grandma collected my grandfather's state pension.

I did very well on all my tests, particularly with my typing and the ability to read and write in English. "I was offered my first job. I'm starting to work next Tuesday, November 7. My starting pay is one hundred and ten DM monthly. I'll find myself a room in the vicinity of Graf Adolf Strasse, which will be in easy walking distance to Backhoff & Backhoff, a legal firm."

Grandma opened a bottle of Mosel Riesling. "We must have a toast to our newest breadwinner in the family."

All, including my brothers who were sixteen, lifted their glasses and said "prost." Only my mother spoke softly, saying "L'Chaim." She was speaking for my father, who would have spoken like his ancestors—the Jewish toast "to life"—which touched me deeply. I had to turn away from my well-wishers, not wanting to spoil their joy of celebrating my achievements. It was that night that I had my bloody nightmare for the first time in many a month. It seemed whenever I was reminded in some manner of my father, I would relive those moments of his ill treatment by the Nazis and seeing him covered in his own blood. I feel like he shed his blood to save us from the evil we were privileged to survive. I often feel guilty that I was allowed to live and he found himself murdered by those brutes.

I loved being on my own. The job was all I could ask for; I received many compliments from the men for whom I worked and was periodically rewarded financially. While Mom liked being close to Grandma and would forever feel indebted for her generous welcome in 1945, the time had come for her to be on her own. She was young enough to think about finding another partner in life. I encouraged her to seriously consider the rest of her earthly days and living them alone. And then the opportunity presented itself. One of the young partners in the law firm in Düsseldorf met a young woman from Essen. I couldn't wait to tell Mother when I visited the following weekend. We talked at length the first opportunity we had when Grandma took her constitutional nap in the afternoon.

"Mr. Brecht just got married; he and his wife, also an attorney, are opening their firm in Essen and have asked me to take a position with them. It's a substantial increase in my salary, and I have accepted their offer. I've given Backhoff & Backhoff a month's notice and will be moving to Essen in early November.

"I'm planning to search for an apartment in the *Wasserturm* [water tower] area. It won't be easy, but Erna Brecht has connections. I'm hopeful. How would you feel about my getting a place large enough to accommodate all of us? I'm sure Grandma wouldn't mind not having lanky Lutz and Lenny under her feet. They'll be able to finish their Abitur [comparable to an Associate degree] in Essen, and I presume they will be going on to university studies. I know Lutz has told me he wants to follow in Father's footsteps," said I.

"He's told me as much too, and I'm all in favor of it. The money is certainly there, and he will also qualify for all sorts of government support. Lenny wants to finish his Abitur but first take a break from studying. He's eyeing a job in auto sales at some high-end dealership in Düsseldorf. We are talking Maserati, Rolls-Royce, Bentley, etc. I'm not about to discourage him; let him get it out of his system and then return to studying when he's ready for it. Sometimes I can't believe those two stem from the same source.

"Now to your idea of getting an apartment for us in Essen. If you are lucky enough to find what you have in mind for the four of us, go for it. I suppose, you and I could share a large-enough bedroom as could the young men. Lutz is viewing Göttingen for his studies. If that comes to pass, he certainly wouldn't be commuting. Knowing Lenny, he would want his own place in Düsseldorf.

"What I'm trying to tell you is to simplify matters; don't go looking for anything larger than a nice apartment with two bedrooms and a bath and a half. That's all we'd really need in the immediate future. Give me plenty of time to let Grandma get used to the idea of an empty nest for the second time in her life. Personally, I believe she is ready to let us fly. She's been wonderful to live with, but I'm ready to try something new," was all Mother added.

"Did you mean a new place to live or a new man in your life?" asked I.

"Both if you want me to be truthful with you."

"That's great, Mom." I hugged my mother, needing to feel that parental connection. I was still missing my father terribly but didn't blame Mom for trying a second time at being happy and having someone with whom she could share the rest of her days.

I found the perfect place in an ideal location right after the Christmas holidays and was glad no longer to have to live in just a room for rent. Mom hopped on a train to Essen. I met her at the Hauptbahnhof [main railway station], and we took a streetcar to the Wasserturm. Mom approved of my choice and had no difficulty signing the rental contract in her name. Mother moved by mid-August of 1952 to our new abode. The boys opted to finish the school year in Garath and would then transfer to Essen and complete their studies toward obtaining their Abiturs. Grandma was happy that the change to the empty nest would be a gradual affair.

# Chapter 5

FERNANDO stepped quietly into Doretta's domain. She was staring out of the large picture window, her hands momentarily resting on top of her typewriter. She was totally unaware of his presence. As far as she was concerned, he had this terrible habit of sneaking around on sleek marble floors in his stocking feet. He disliked shoes, and hated slippers even more. He didn't mean to startle her.

"You didn't sleep well last night, did you? How long have you been slaving away at your trusted friend? Sorry, I didn't want to interrupt or, even worse, scare you."

"I woke shortly before dawn and made my way down here not wanting to disturb anyone, especially not your mother. She told me in no uncertain terms what she thinks of my wanting to write. I told her I wasn't attempting to create the epic of the century and that you and Dr. Rodriguez view my writing as therapeutic."

"What'd she have to say to that?"

"She didn't respond to my explanation but called me 'perra'

as she stomped out of the room. I thought she began to like me after she met Mario and fell in love with Alona, who resembles her strongly. I don't deserve to be called 'bitch or slut' but will continue to respect Esmeralda because she's your mother. She made it quite clear that she expected me to be a breeding machine presenting you with many more sons to assure the longevity of the Garcia Lopez line."

Fernando was fully aware of Doretta's fragility. He lifted her chin, directing her gaze toward him. "Don't let her get to you. It will take time for her to understand the issues that continue to haunt you. She still doesn't know that your father was Jewish and that you are often traumatized by reliving that day when he was removed from your life in such a brutal manner. My mother has lived a very sheltered and indulged existence and has little empathy for others living outside her world of affluence and ease. She has never wanted for anything. I will speak with her and hope she will change her attitude toward you. But no matter what, you are my wife and the mother of our children; you are a vital part of the Garcia Lopez line, and don't you ever forget it." He bent down to kiss her gently and sneaked out of the room as quietly as he had entered.

Fernando decided to speak to his parents rather than to his mother alone. Both he and Doretta knew that his father's attitude toward Doretta was totally different from that of his mother. With that in mind, Fernando knocked three times on his father's office door, signaling to him that it was he who wanted to see him.

"Come in, Fernando. What's the matter and causing that frown on your face? Is Doretta okay? I have hardly seen her during the day other than at mealtimes. She seems to enjoy that writing business to which your mother made reference a few days ago. If I'm reading your mother correctly, she doesn't approve of Doretta's serious approach to the matter at hand."

"I would like you to summon Mother to your office and let's have out whatever is plaguing her. I'm hoping to enlist your support in this discussion. I'm not what some would call a male chauvinist, although mother would like nothing better were I to show such tendencies toward my wife. I spent too much time in Europe and have learned to drift away from that typical Latin male role model."

Don Carlos, as his father was known in the community, rang a bell on his desk. Valentina appeared promptly. "Please ask Señora Garcia Lopez to join us in my office." The servant nodded and backed out of the room silently.

Within minutes the door opened and Esmeralda entered her husband's very private space, totally surprised to see her son sitting across from his father. Of course, as soon as she made her entrance, both father and son rose from their chairs. Fernando immediately assisted his mother with getting seated. Esmeralda looked from her son to his father and back at their son.

"Do I dare ask what this is all about? I don't like to be called away from my morning prayers."

"Sorry about that, Mother. I was the one who asked Father to have you summoned to his office. I believe it is high time we have this talk. We probably should have settled certain issues when Doretta, Mario, and I arrived from Switzerland five years ago. I'd like to remind you, we are speaking of my wife and our children, your grandchildren. How dare you call my wife a bitch, or worse, a slut? She is a decent woman and has done nothing but tried to bend to your unrealistic rules and expectations.

"You haven't got a clue what this woman experienced as a

young girl. I hope to God our children will never see me being dragged out by a bunch of hoodlums beating me bloody and half to death." Fernando had to swallow and reached for the glass of water his father offered him. He could see the hurt in his son's eyes. Esmeralda just stared into space, living up to her reputation of being the "Ice Princess" on the hacienda, but it was she who responded first to her son.

"Why would anyone want to drag her father out of his house and beat him half to death? I thought Germans were more civilized than that. Are you stepping back in history and making reference to an event in Doretta's childhood?" She gasped and clutched her mouth.

"Oh, my God. I get it. She's not only German, she's Jewish! How could you do this to our bloodline? Now I have partially Jewish grandchildren."

Don Carlos stepped in. "Esmeralda, you are being totally out of line. I do not want you to mention one more word about the impact on our pedigree. You are beginning to sound like some fascist talking about pure Arian lineage. I happen to love my grandchildren and don't give a damn what kind of blood flows through their veins. They are part of your and my flesh and blood, and I expect you to treat their mother with civility and respect. If you ever again make use of a label the likes of which you bestowed on our daughter-in-law, you will rue the day you do so. Do I make myself clear?" Esmeralda just nodded, confirming that she accepted her husband's reprimand.

"No wonder your wife has nightmares," added Don Carlos. Have you considered analysis with Dr. Rodriguez Amado?"

"He's trying to avoid regular sessions at this time. It was he who recommended that Doretta commit her experiences to paper in the hope that writing about the events might ultimately resolve her issues. He's talked about discussing her nightmares with her under hypnosis. For now, let's see what happens. I'm pleased to report that she hasn't had another episode since she started writing. Maybe Doc Amado is onto something. So please, Mother, try to be a bit more empathetic toward my troubled wife. I love her very much, and she is a wonderful mother to our children. Thank you."

He winked at his father as he backed out of the room. His parents just stared at each other, neither adding another word.

# Chapter 6

"BUENOS dias, Madame," was Valentina's soft-spoken greeting as she faced Doretta.

"Buenos dias, Valentina. What brings you to call on me?"

"Señor Don Carlos asked me to keep a closer eye on you. He wants me to look after you at all times of the day; and if needed, I'll be there for you during the night. All you need to do is ring my bell. I'm honored to be your personal attendant.

"When your dear husband was born, I was his nursemaid. I practically raised him. My husband, Juan, is one of the chauffeurs. He'll be at your service anytime you wish to get out of the house. Our daughter, Juanita, works with Alona, as you well know. My family has been linked to the Garcia Lopez family for several generations. When I was younger, I was in alterations at a department store in Santiago for a short while, but it's so many years ago, I can't remember when I didn't work in this house. My grandmother, may she rest in peace, raised Señor Don Carlos and his siblings."

"Thank you for telling me. I should make more of an

effort and become familiar with all people who are part of my extended family. You understand, it often was the language barrier and the initial very cool reception afforded to me by Donna Esmeralda. You know very well how things stand. I'm still hoping that one of these days we'll become closer. It's not in my nature to be so detached."

"May I bring you some coffee or tea or some freshly pressed juices? Anything to start you off on this lovely fall day?"

"A glass of orange juice would be fine, Valentina. I still have a hard time dealing with fall in the sunny month of May. The hemispheric topsy-turvy situation is something else I've never quite gotten used to."

"It will grow on you, Madame. Some things in life take getting used to." Always having a positive disposition, Valentina smiled.

*I don't know what's wrong with me. Most of the time I feel closer to the servants than to Fernando's family. I suppose having wealth gives you certain airs. I just wasn't bred that way.* Her mind fled halfway across the globe. *Mother will be cutting lilacs in her garden any day now; pretty soon snow will spread itself over our beautiful gardens here. I should be adjusted to my different life after five years of being in Fernando's world.*

Doretta turned toward her typewriter, trying to collect her thoughts. She couldn't help herself, carrying on a conversation with a machine as she faced the typewriter. *Okay father confessor. I do wish you were a person I could just talk to. That would be so much easier. Maybe I should give some thought to and arrange for analysis with Dr. Rodriguez Amado. Well now, where did I leave off?*

I loved my work at Brecht & Associates. What I loved even more was the peace and harmony Mother and I appreciated in our new place. Neither of my brothers chose to reside with us for any length of time. By early September 1952, Lutz was off to Göttingen and Lenny was living in Düsseldorf, dreaming of owning one of those fancy cars he was successfully selling. We enjoyed seeing the twins for short visits but treasured our time together when it was just the two of us.

My life changed completely when I met Hektor Birken serendipitously in fall 1952. He introduced me to dear friends of his who had shown him a different world than what he was used to. We discovered similar likes and especially loved dancing. Hektor and his friends invited me to join them on a winter vacation in the south of Germany in February 1953.

A week before we left for Oberstdorf, I attended a dinner at his parents' home where we became acquainted with an old boyfriend of Hektor's mother who was visiting from the United States. It was this stranger who planted the seed that ultimately would change both Hektor's life and mine.

Both Hektor and I fell in love with the magic of the winter wonderland that surrounded us, and we fell in love with each other. It was in Oberstdorf that Hektor wrote the fateful letter to this total stranger asking him to become his sponsor. We made love for the first time the night he wrote the letter. Our fate seemed to be sealed.

When Hektor sailed out of Hamburg in late April of 1954, I had no idea what life held in store for me. All I knew was I couldn't wait for him to return to me as soon as he had seen enough of the New World. We became officially engaged on my birthday in October. He mailed me a golden ring and proposed to marry me during a very brief transatlantic phone call. It was all so romantic. His plan was to return to me in the spring of 1956.

We wrote to each other at length at least twice a week. And then, the totally unexpected happened. Hektor's last letter to me was dated in late August of 1955. I frantically leafed through the daily mail without finding an envelope with the familiar handwriting. After two weeks of moping, my mother wanted to know what was bothering me. I was nearly testy with her.

"Haven't you figured it out for yourself? I haven't heard from Hektor in over two weeks. As tenuous as my relationship is with his mother, I called her. I thought he might have written to her directly for a change. For most of the time he's been gone, I was his messenger and conduit. He didn't feel like writing the same thing twice. She assured me she hadn't had a letter from her son in months. Where does that leave me?"

"Have you considered calling Hektor? He might be ill. For all you know, he might be dead. Didn't you tell me that he mentioned in his last letter he was planning to visit distant relatives in Long Island in early September? Isn't Long Island close to New York City? God forbid, if something happened to him in his travels. If it was I, I wouldn't be that nonchalant about it. I realize it would be costly, but I would be more than willing to share in the expense. Give it some thought."

"I see your point, Mother. But who would I call? I know he is rooming with a couple called Shelves, but I don't have their phone number. And if I did have a way of contacting these people, I can assure you, they wouldn't speak German were I to call them. I suppose, I could attempt speaking in English. That would be a lot of money poured down the drain. I just have to hope for the best. I'll call Helena, his mother, again in a couple of days and see what she advises me to do."

When I did call her, Helena was fearful, frantic, and furious about her son's silence.

"I don't know what has gotten into our son. His father wonders if he was taken ill or worse. I asked my sister to consult her card layer and her astrologer, although I put little stock in the occult. Sometimes I think we made the biggest mistake by letting him sail off into the New World. He should have stayed in his homeland. Sorry, Doretta. I have no way to help you. All of us have to just wait and see." She left me hanging on the phone, which had gone dead.

In early November, I received "My Dear Doretta Letter," letting me know that he fell in love with another woman and was calling off our engagement. My world was shattered once again. I saw myself as battered, beaten, and hopeless. My mother was clearly shaken.

"What are you going to do? What do you intend to tell people? First, this crazy idea of becoming engaged by long-distance phoning. Now, calling the whole thing off with a little note. I don't know any longer what to think of Herr Birken. He's lucky an ocean separates us. When I spoke with Grandma and the boys, they were ready to make the Birkens' lives miserable."

"What good will that do? They are innocent in this drama. They are just as angry at their son as am I."

First I was terribly sad, and then terribly angry. While the Birkens were totally in agreement with my view of the situation, that didn't change the outcome. Helena told me about the barrage of phone calls visited upon their business phone by my family.

Although Hektor attempted to speak with me when he visited Germany in spring 1956, I made it clear to his mother that I did not want to see him. I didn't tell her I didn't care to see him ever again. I knew, if I said so, she would have agreed with me and fully supported my stance toward her ill-mannered son, whom she was ready to disown. She kept referring to her future daughter-in-law as an illiterate Polack with red shingles. I'm glad I never wound up on the wrong side of Helena Birken; she might have called me some kind of dirty Jew.

Hektor entered into marriage with a woman called Georgia and realized even before their vows were spoken that he was making the biggest mistake of his life. The disastrous marriage ended four years later. How did I know all that was happening to Hektor? His mother kept in touch and shared every sordid detail

of her son's failed marriage with me. We talked last by phone when I left Brecht & Associates in 1958 and took a job with Schrift & Schreiber in Zürich, Switzerland. It was a total change, but I loved the world of publishing.

# Chapter 7

Fernando walked into Doretta's writing emporium, or should he have called it her confessional? It was just before dusk. Before she could pull her last written page from the Remington Rand, he glanced at it quickly.

"My goodness! What good timing! This ought to make for some interesting late-night page turning. And best yet, I'll be Prince Charming and the star attraction of the show." He reached for her and gave Doretta a lingering kiss. He would have loved nothing better than to carry her upstairs and make passionate love to her. He knew that had to wait until later. He had no intention of upsetting the parental applecart. His mother would have had another one of her hysterical fits had they not graced the table at the daily family dinner. His father would have understood, but his mother—never. No wonder the servants so often spoke of her in hushed tones as being the "Ice Princess."

Doretta couldn't resist. "What makes you think you are the star attraction in my scientific epistle?"

Fernando laughed out loud. "You mean to say that I went through all this expense for you to produce a nonfiction epic? I was looking forward to reading all about Señora Chatterley's sexual adventures and outpourings."

"You are wicked! You hold on until we retire. I'll show you Señora Chatterley. You just wait, Fernando Leonardo Garcia Lopez. You haven't got a clue!"

Doretta was seated to the right of Don Carlos, who sat at the head of the long table; Esmeralda was seated on his left and Fernando next to her. The arrangement was the same whether it was the four of them dining or twenty other guests seated with the family. The servants always ate in their kitchen. Her father-in-law touched Doretta's left hand lovingly.

"How are you doing, my dear? Did you enjoy this sunny fall day? Fernando and I loved touring the estate in Maipo Valley. The Cabernet 1968 will be delightful. The grapes look remarkably healthy and blessed by this year's sunshine. This is my favorite time of year. You should get out of this house once in a while; the fresh air would do you good."

"It makes me smile to hear what a great day you spent with your son, touring your grape arbors. It's been a few years since I visited the estate for the first time. Fernando drove me to your winery and showed me the place with pride. It must have been right around the same time of year in 1963. Mario was born in March, and we arrived in Santiago the last day of April.

"What still astonishes me to this day is that your family

has operated this winery since the sixteenth century. Do I dare ask, are there any Incas mixed up in your bloodline? I've read that many lived in this area hundreds of years ago."

Esmeralda glared at Doretta but didn't respond, deferring the answer to her husband. "Actually, there was an Inca princess given to one of my male ancestors. They didn't trade her for wine but for a dozen barrels of beer, which the Inca chief cherished. She bore my ancestor three handsome sons. If you walk through the family portrait gallery, on the right-hand side near the end of the hall, there is a painting depicting the father and his three adult sons looking unmistakably of Inca ancestry."

"That makes me feel a little better about having contributed some Jewish blood to the ancestral bloodline. Looks like Fernando and my offspring are a regular United Nations."

"Absolutely right; that's why we are such handsome people, a good mix of healthy, unrelated creatures. And, of course, Esmeralda is of noble descent." Don Carlos tried very hard to include his spouse in the conversation, but she chose not to participate in what she referred to as common conversational drivel and instead to rise above such matters.

"Don Carlos, actually I'd prefer to call you Papa, I'd love to go with you and be part of the harvesters. It always looked like so much fun when I watched the vintners doing the harvest along the Rhein, Mosel, and the Ahr. I was always particularly fond of the red wines grown along the Ahr."

"That shouldn't be too difficult for your husband to arrange. You could be working side by side with him; it's been one of his favorite things to do since he was about Mario's age. There's an idea; take your young man with you. No better time than breaking him in young. A little dirt and fresh air won't do him any harm. My dad had me sit on his shoulders while he cut down the grapes efficiently. I can still hear that motion of the knife parting the grape clusters from the vines," said Don Carlos.

"When may Mario and I join you?" asked Doretta with excitement in her voice.

"We'll start harvesting next week. It will give the tutor a break, and we'll have the boy all to ourselves. Let's not make it too confusing for the kid between Spanish, German, and English instructions. How about just sticking with Spanish to keep it simple? It will also be easier on the help working the fields," said Fernando.

"Love it! Can't wait."

"I suggest you wear some of my special gloves," said Esmeralda. "If you don't wear gloves, your hands will never again seem the same. Trust me."

Doretta was thankful that Esmeralda at last made a positive contribution to the table conversation. She winked at Fernando when Esmeralda looked down, studying the large emerald ring she was wearing on her left hand. Fernando took the hint.

"I believe it is time for us to retire." He walked around the back of his father, wishing to help Doretta out of her chair. They walked up the marble staircase hand in hand and couldn't wait to be alone.

"I got the message, sweetheart. It was high time for us to leave those two to themselves. There are situations when I wish we were back in our own little nest in Zürich or in our own home nearby. Of course, you realize that will never happen. It just isn't done in our circles. It's an ethnic thing; young and old, sometimes four and more generations, live under the same roof. The younger generation is always expected to look after their seniors. Thank God, there are many rooms in this mansion, and we have our quarters away from my parents."

"I really don't mind. I remember well the days when Mother was thrilled to be taken in by my grandmother, having my brothers and me in tow. Of course, we weren't taking care of Grandma, she was taking care of us. I just wish I could find a way of endearing myself to your mother; she's not as distant as she was in the early years, but she never lets me quite forget that I was raised on the other side of the tracks. Maybe you should have found yourself some Chilean princess and made her happy. I'm glad she seems at least to love our children."

"Speaking of children, how about a little attention to that matter?" She squeezed his hand as they closed the door to their boudoir. Valentina already had turned down the bed, and the nightlights were burning softly next to their sumptuous bed. Fernando quietly set the lock on their bedroom door; he didn't want any unwanted interruptions tonight.

Doretta knew how to please her man. He liked it when she slowly unbuttoned his shirt and freed his bronzed chest of any covering. He himself shed his trousers and skivvies and stood in front of her in all of his manly beauty. He reached for her and held her tightly as he kissed her softly, his lips trailing down her throat. It was now Fernando's turn to fully undress her. Standing next to their bed, their tall, naked bodies cast long shadows across the silken sheets waiting for them.

He laid her down gently and gazed into her laughing eyes. "I love you and always will. Thank you for sharing your life with me and my family. I want us to have more children, and I want us to thrill in the moments of the creative process." His lips left hers and journeyed to her taut breasts, her nipples begging to be moistened by his sensuous mouth before he explored her body in its entirety. As she moaned with pleasure, he sought to be ever so close to her and brought them both to total fulfillment. He kissed her gently on the lips. "What do you think it might be this time? A girl or another boy?"

She smiled. "Guess we'll have to wait and see. We might have to test the waters a few more times to get it right. Remember, you are bedding down with Señora Chatterley."

He pulled her tightly toward his recovering manhood. "Only too happy to oblige, Madame. Señor Fernando Garcia Lopez at your service." He entered her with extreme pleasure written all over his face. Doretta just smiled.

# Chapter 8

THEY were still holding each other tightly as dawn awakened them. Doretta slowly opened her eyes and beheld her handsome husband close to her. She whispered into his ear: "I love you, Señor Fernando Garcia Lopez. Wake up. We have work to do—and I don't mean writing. I need a break from all that. Although the next few chapters will be recalling what I'm experiencing even more vividly at this very moment in time. I love being your wife; I've been reborn."

"What's the rush? I was contemplating Act III to this wonderful play we both seem to be enjoying. I'll make you a deal. I'll have you all to myself in that fancy shower Dad insisted on installing in our bedroom. He considers his the height of luxury and didn't want to deprive us of having the same pleasure. I doubt he'll ever get an invitation to the dance from his 'Ice Princess.'"

"Please, don't call her that. I hear the servants whisper that name on occasion, but I try to ignore them. I'm aware they are saying those things for my benefit. I don't know how often I heard '*la princesa de hielo*' after I arrived on the scene. At first, I didn't grasp what it meant until I consulted a dictionary. When I questioned Valentina, she quietly told me it was referring to your mother and not me. Let me try and see if I can melt that frozen heart in time."

He reached for her and hugged her fiercely before he nudged her out of the comforts of their bed and into that luxurious shower. All covered in generous suds of lavender soap, he seated Doretta firmly on his manhood, eliciting cries of pleasure as he found release in their extreme closeness.

Don Carlos was enjoying the generous breakfast set before him and spotted Fernando and Doretta descending the circular marble staircase holding hands. There was no question in his mind that his children were happy. Fernando's dark hair was still glistening with moistness, and Doretta had that casual look about her. "Looks like you two enjoyed that fancy shower I insisted on installing in your boudoir, am I right?"

Doretta kissed him on the forehead. "You are indeed correct in that assumption, Papa. We loved it—and I mean *we* loved it. Thank you, Papa." She rarely called him Papa in the presence of Esmeralda, who thought it presumptuous and disrespectful on Doretta's part. Don Carlos adored his daughter-in-law and loved her from the moment he laid eyes on her. There was nothing pretentious or standoffish about her. He took her into his heart when he first met her at the Valparaiso seaport.

"Papa, as soon as we have finished breakfast, Doretta, Mario, and I will head out to the vineyards. It looks like a perfect day to get 'my crew' started on harvesting grapes. That's why my gal is wearing these tight jeans and a simple blouse. I've cautioned her not to wear anything that isn't easily washable. You know yourself how often we're decorated with red grape juice when we come home after harvesting."

"Good thinking. I'm glad you are spending this day together. I wish I were young and spry enough to join you, but harvesting is no longer an option for me. I might drive out later and have lunch with you at the cantina. They always have quite a spread prepared for the folks taking a much-needed break from working in the vineyards."

They got up from the table. Doretta offered to fetch Mario from his playroom. Fernando packed needed supplies into the van he was driving. Anything else they might need was either on-site or had been hauled to the vineyards by the hired help. Most of the harvesting crew had worked for the Garcia Lopez family for a number of years. The same men and women, mostly men, returned to their employers year after year. Many had met Doretta at the *Grape Harvest Wine Festival in February 1964.*

Arriving at the vineyards, they were greeted as señora and señor with a generous sprinkling of buenos dias. Fernando grabbed a couple of very sharp cutting tools and showed Doretta how to harvest grapes. "These baskets woven from willow will catch the grapes as you cut them. When the basket is filled, one of the guys will carry it away and empty it into a collection vessel onboard those small trucks you see flitting around. Here let me show you. It takes a little practice, but you'll feel it when you are doing it correctly. Hold the cluster of grapes in your left hand, firmly holding on to the stem. With one swift motion downward of the cutter in your right hand, you separate the cluster from the stem. Listen to the sound it makes when I do it. Once you hear that certain sound, you'll have mastered the harvesting of the grapes. Here, try it."

She knew exactly what he was talking about. Her first two or three attempts were too timid, and she didn't hold the grape cluster firmly enough. The stem was too limp to properly respond to the sharp instrument. By the fourth try, she could hear the sound. "I think you've got it," was Fernando's praise. "Go for it, girl. I'll look and see what our young man is doing. He traipsed off with Hernando, an old pro at this. They've become fast friends."

Two hours later, Doretta discovered why these hardworking men surrounding her were hinting at "aching backs." But every time one of the young bucks was hauling away another wicker basket filled to the brim with clusters of deep purple grapes, she was proud of her achievements and her part in the harvesting of the fruit. After all, she was part of the family now.

Lunch at the cantina was a well-deserved break. She was delighted to see Don Carlos waiting for them. He beamed when he saw the three of them entering the place. "Hey, how is the hardest working crew in the vineyards? All of you look like the grapes are perfect for harvesting—a little juice here and another little splotch there. That's my special crew. Mario, come here. Give Grandpa a kiss. He loves you very much."

Mario hopped into his grandfather's generous lap and gave him a real smacker. There was no question about it; grandfather and grandson loved each other very much. Don Carlos melted when little Mario would look up at him and say in his finest Spanish: "abuelo, te amo."

Fernando took charge. "Back to the salt mines. We've got not quite three hours before sunset. We must use every possible minute to get these grapes harvested. There's talk of the possibility of frost in less than a week. We can't afford to lose any of these beautiful grapes. Mario, Doretta, Hernando, who else? All hop in the van; it'll get you there quicker than walking."

As the sun began to set, Doretta knew she had done a good day's work. She laid her hand on Fernando's shoulder. "That shower will feel wonderful, and I don't want any company tonight—I mean in the shower. I'm totally unwilling to share that spray of hot water. My body will need every little pin-pricking drop of moisture it can get to revive it. You can have it to yourself when I'm done. Deal?"

"Got yourself a deal. You deserve it, Señora Doretta Garcia Lopez. I like that; it has a nice ring to it." She loved it when he extended his hand to help her down from the van.

# Chapter 9

"WHAT are you smiling about? You mind sharing with me?" Doretta loved Fernando's gentle voice instead of the ring of the alarm waking her on this hectic morning at the mansion.

"I had the most delightful dream, and it was all about you, believe it or not."

"Tell me about it. Did we have fun during this mysterious encounter?"

"It wasn't mysterious at all; and yes, it was fun for both of us.

"I was doing research for Herr Heinrich at Schrift & Schreiber at the Zentralbibliothek on Zähringerplatz when you stepped up to the desk where I was working. I had no idea who you were and what you might want from me. I thought you looked exotic, certainly not Suisse or even German. I glanced up from my stack of papers and gave you a hurried onceover. You spoke first: "'Hola! Hablas español?'

"I wasn't sure what you asked me, but assumed you were wanting to know if I spoke Spanish. My first and correct inkling was to say, 'No, I don't, but I speak German and English.'"

"Mein German and English are terrible. I will try mein best. My Namen Fernando Garcia Lopez. Ich komme von Chile. Ich studiere vinificación."

"What is that? I have no idea what you are saying."

"I think you say, 'make wine.'"

"Oh, now I understand. You are studying oenology. Very interesting. My name is Doretta Osram. I'm doing research for a publisher. Would you like to learn German? I could help you."

"Can you have eat with mich?"

"Are you asking me to have dinner with you?"

"Si, Du understand richtig. [Yes, you understand correctly]

"'It's almost time for the library to close. Let me pack up my papers.'

"You weren't quite certain what I said but grasped the idea by watching my actions of calling it a day. You offered your right arm for me to hold onto you and carried my briefcase. I had a real surprise when you walked me to your car. I discovered on the day I met you, you weren't some poor student. That silver and black Mercedes sports number wasn't what the average student was driving. I believe you were trying to tell me it was *just* a Mercedes 190 SL.

"No big deal to you. Do you remember how I reacted when you opened the car door for me? I loved the feel of the elegant black leather seats."

"Not really. You might have said something like 'WOW,' but to tell you the truth, I don't remember anything about your reaction to my car. I was so used to having it. What I do remember is that I fell in love with you on first sight when I spotted you in that dusky and stuffy library. I'll let you write about our blooming romance in your next chapter. This has been fun to wake up remembering how we first met ten years ago."

"Hope you won't mind; I'm taking a break from working in the vineyards today. You're on your own. I might have Juan drive Valentina and me into Santiago later. I do need to get a few things. I want to look my best when Mother and her new husband fly in from Germany next week. I can't tell you how happy I am for her. She was too young and vital to remain alone for the rest of her days. Mom's only in her fifties; she was just twenty when I was born in 1932 and was widowed for more than twenty-five years. I don't want to think about my father; it only upsets me when I recall those horrible scenes. Aren't you pleased with the progress I've made? I just need to concentrate on the positive."

They quickly showered and got dressed. Don Carlos and Esmeralda had been wondering what took them so long after they heard footsteps upstairs much earlier.

"I've instructed Rosalinda and Émile to prepare the bedroom, bath, and sitting room in the east wing for the arrival of Doretta's mother and her new husband," commented Esmeralda. Doretta let me know they are visiting for a month. She doesn't believe her mother wants to make the long flight too often."

"I can certainly understand that. Can you imagine being on a plane for close to twenty hours? Thank goodness, they have one stop along the way where they can stretch their legs. Fernando insisted on upgrading their accommodations to First Class," Don Carlos said.

"Don't you think that's a bit generous? He hardly knows those people, and certainly we don't."

"Remember, he's our only son, and that is his German

family whether you like it or not. He can well afford to please his wife. Try to remember what that poor woman went through, and let her enjoy this visit. Please try for once to put a good face on matters; that's all I ask of you. I do not want this to be discussed any further." The subject was closed for Don Carlos. Esmeralda knew he meant every word of what he said; she knew when she had met her match.

*Buenos dias* was the greeting all around. "Did you sleep well after the work you did yesterday in the vineyards?" asked Don Carlos.

"The shower last night felt great, and I did sleep like a baby. Upon waking, I was telling Fernando about a wonderful dream I had. He laughed when I recalled for him the events of the day when we first met."

Esmeralda was tempted to make a snide remark but opted to abide by her husband's pronouncements. Instead, she was curious what plans Doretta might have for the day.

"I'm taking a day off from the vineyards. I shared with Fernando that I would like to have Juan drive Valentina and me into Santiago. She suggested for me to visit Falabella's. She told me that it is the store you frequent the most, Esmeralda."

"True, other than numerous boutiques I like in town. Are you sure you would not want me to come along? We found some suitable things for you to wear the last time you and I went on a shopping spree."

"Thanks for offering, Esmeralda. This time I want to see a bit more of the city and do a little shopping for my mother and Andreas, her new husband. I'm sure you have plenty to do in terms of planning for their extended visit. I'm hoping my family won't be too much of an imposition. Both Fernando and I were pleased to know that the grape harvest will be complete by the time they arrive. It will be fun for them to witness the Grape Harvest Wine Festival while they are here. Is there anything you might need? I'd be more than happy to do any shopping for you."

"Thank you for asking. I've instructed the kitchen staff and my maid to take care of any shopping that might be needed. I'm not particularly fond of going into the city these days. It's not the same as it used to be when I was young. I hear of too many unpleasant situations occurring in Santiago lately."

"Mother and I shall mind the home. We'll enjoy quiet time with the children. They are growing up too quickly. Mario is such a nice boy and so mature for his age. I'm pleased to see him speaking flawlessly in three languages. It must not be easy to be that disciplined with growing children, but it is evident that it can be done. The way the world is moving, my grandchildren will do well being multilingual, especially with their English skills."

"Thank you for your compliments, Papa. Fernando and I try our best. Valentina and I best be off on our errands. Don't work too hard in 'them there' vineyards." With that, she planted a kiss on Fernando before rushing out to meet Valentina and Juan, leaving Esmeralda agape when she heard Doretta calling Don Carlos *Papa*. She was still of the opinion Doretta had not earned the right to address her father-in-law in such a familiar and affectionate manner. In her mindset, she never would.

# Chapter 10

"JUAN, let's make our first stop at Falabella's. It's the store where Valentina and I probably will spend more time than at any other. I don't expect you to sit around and wait for us to finish what we came for." She glanced at her watch.

"It's just before ten. Why don't you park the car in the underground and find something to do that pleases you. As a matter of fact, if you want to visit anyone you know in the city, please do so. You may use the car, by all means. Meet us back here at one o'clock. We'll have lunch in their lovely restaurant. They won't mind your uniform; don't worry about a thing. You best be off and let us handle our tasks at hand." She gave Juan a big smile. He gave Valentina a quick kiss before he sauntered back to the car.

"Let's check out the better dresses on the second floor. That will be a good place for me to start. Esmeralda insists on taking my parents to the *Teatro Municipal de Santiago,* and I have nothing that she would deem suitable for the affair. You've got a pretty good feel for what she wears on such occasions. Years ago, I attended a few operas with my first love, Hektor Birken. Needless to say, what I wore at that time has all gone by the wayside. Here we are. Please tell the elegant lady approaching us what we are looking for. I still feel somewhat intimidated in these situations, always wondering if I'm saying things correctly. Thanks for coming with me, Valentina, and being my interpreter. This would never have worked with Señora Esmeralda.

"Si," was all Valentina dared to answer. She advised the clerk in very descriptive language and gestures as to my needs, and we were asked to make ourselves comfortable in a smartly appointed sitting area near the dressing rooms. Within a few minutes, three models were taking turns showing the selections made by our clerk. They were all elegant dresses but only the second and fifth numbers would suit my taste. I rose from my chair. "I would like to try on numbers two and five. They are different from anything I've seen Señora Garcia Lopez wear, right, Valentina?"

"Si, señora. I especially like the peacock blue and green one. It suits your coloring." When Doretta stepped out of the dressing room, wearing matching shoes and the dress pinned on her by the seamstress and fitting to perfection, there were several "wows" escaping the lips of the observers.

"I believe that means 'yes'—we'll take that one for sure. I would like to try the orange-red one as well. It's beautifully styled and in a color range I used to wear a lot when I was younger. With all the entertaining and visits to affairs in the capital, I can use two formal dresses. I do appreciate the attention paid to detail. Having fitting shoes without having to stop at a different department is quite the service, too. We'll take both of these dresses. When might you be able to deliver them to the house?"

"If Madame has other shopping to tend to, all can be in readiness in a good hour."

"Oh, that will be wonderful. I do need to look at a couple of suits and daytime dresses in your better dress department. You couldn't by any chance help me with those as well, or could you?"

"Certainly, ma'am. At Falabella's we are trained to work with a given client throughout their desired shopping experience. No need to be dealing with different personnel if you are comfortable and pleased with your first contact in our establishment. Please step over here; I have a pretty good idea what you have in mind."

Two hours later, Doretta concluded her personal shopping needs to her satisfaction. All would be ready by the time they finished their lunch. "I would like to find some unusual ties for my father, and my mother loves exquisite scarves. Might you be able to help us with those as well?"

"No problem at all. We'll just take the elevator over there to the first floor, and I'll show you around. The fall collection of men's ties arrived just recently. I'm particularly fond of the colorful abstract Jerry Garcia creations. They are a touch out of the ordinary. You can't beat the beauty of the Mehta brocade silks from Varanasi. I'm sure your mother will love them. Come, let me show you."

It didn't matter what their clerk, Isolda, touched or handled, she did it with grace and charm and in such a way that the items sold themselves. Doretta was extremely pleased with her shopping adventure. After paying for her purchases, all items were attractively packaged and held at the cashier's desk until Juan was ready to pick them up and carry all to their vehicle. They met him promptly for lunch, which turned out to be a delightful experience for Doretta and her caring servants. She knew this would never have happened in the presence of Señora Esmeralda. Doretta didn't care; she was Señora Doretta Garcia Lopez and could do as she pleased. She had her husband and Don Carlos on her side.

※

They arrived back at the hacienda before dusk. Esmeralda greeted them anxiously as Valentina and Doretta made their way into the house. Doretta turned toward Valentina: "Please have your husband take all my purchases up to our quarters, except for the package wrapped in the blue gift wrap paper. Thank you." She took the lovely gift and presented it to Esmeralda, who appeared to be caught totally off guard.

"Open it. I couldn't resist getting it for you. It was just your taste. I hope you'll like it."

Esmeralda took her time unwrapping the package. When she beheld the Varanasi scarf, she blushed with embarrassment. Never had she expected Doretta to reward her with something so beautiful in return for her ugly behavior. It was not easy for her, but she finally said, "Thank you, Doretta. That was thoughtful of you. This brocade in grays, black, and silver will look stunning with the black dress I'm planning to wear to the opera. Thank you again, it's lovely."

"I'm glad you like it. It was fun finding something that was so completely you. I hope you'll like the things I selected for myself. I would model the evening dresses for you, but I'm bushed. On second thought, I'll keep you in suspense until the night of the opera attendance. I'll need to take a rest before I face all of you at the dinner table. Please make my excuses to Don Carlos. Thank you Valentina for all your help; and thank you to Juan for doing such a fine job of chauffeuring us around." She smiled, walking up the marble stairway to her quarters.

Esmeralda mumbled to herself. "Will she ever learn? They are paid servants and paid well for what is expected of them."

# Chapter 11

"How was your Santiago shopping adventure? Did you have fun and find some beautiful things? Did they treat you well at Falabella's?"

"Well, my dear husband, I spent a lot of your money but had fun doing so. I bought lovely things and was royally treated at Falabella's. The place lived up to its reputation. Valentina shined as my interpreter, and Juan did a great job of chauffeuring us and attending to our every need." She whispered into his ear: "They deserve something extra when you pay them next time."

"Will do."

Esmeralda was wondering what Doretta had said so discreetly to her son.

"And how was your day in the vineyards? Was it a good and successful one?"

"It couldn't have gone better. Father was very pleased that we were able to finish the job and bring in the last of the *Spätlese* before we have our first frosty night. He's always delighted when we don't have to resort to the use of torches and the Wind Angels to shield the grapes from freezing. You look puzzled; have you never heard us speak of doing that?"

"No; I have no clue what you are talking about. Torches and Wind Angels?"

"If and when, God forbid, we have to resort to doing that, you have to come with me and see it with your own eyes. It is actually one of the most beautiful events you will ever witness. The men set large kerosene torches every few meters between the rows of the grapevines. And then the women walk up and down the rows moving large white fans resembling angel wings strapped to their arms. They move them gently, spreading the warmth from the torches onto the grapes and shielding them from the claws of the invading frost. While the women are moving, they are intoning softly sung prayers to the gods asking for the protection of their and our livelihoods. It is absolutely beautiful to hear and see."

"That is strange. I've never heard you or anyone talk about it as long as I have been here."

"Come to think of it, we haven't had to resort to doing it in seven or eight years. Our falls and winters used to be a lot tougher on our business," said Don Carlos.

"Fernando is right, if and when we have to enlist the help of the Wind Angels, it is indeed a thing of beauty to behold. Perhaps, one of these years you will have the opportunity. It won't be this year. We've been spared. Now, we'll look forward to the Grape Harvest Wine Festival and learn if our grapes are among the ribbon winners for the 1968 vintage."

The help and all family members in the room applauded Don Carlos. Mario clapped the loudest. "Grandpa, Grandpa, tell me all about the Wind Angels. Are they real angels? You know I believe in them. I'm sure it was angels who brought me to you."

"Come here, my very special boy. Do you have any idea how much your grandfather loves you?" He picked him up and sat him down on his right knee and then hugged him firmly.

"Now let's talk about the Wind Angels. They are not real angels, but we call them angels because so often they have saved our beautiful grapes from being bitten by the harshness of an early frost and turned them to useless mush. When our grapes are destroyed, there's no money to be put in any bank; even your piggy bank would suffer. There wouldn't be money to pay the help. Do you understand, Mario?"

"Are you saying if the frost had bitten our grapes this year, Valentina, Juan, Juanita, Hernando, and all the other friends of mine would be let go and sent away? That wouldn't be nice, Grandfather. I love them all and they love me."

"True, that would happen at many a place but not on this hacienda. Grandpa learned from the Bible to store up during abundant years and leave something to deal with the lean years. Do you understand me?"

"I think so, Grandpa. You put more into your piggy bank when you don't know what to do with all the money you have and rob the piggy when there is little or none to put in it."

"I knew I had a smart grandson. Give Grandpa another kiss. He loves you, too. Now, to come back to the Wind Angels. Come look at this photo album. Fifteen years ago, long before you were born, your father took these beautiful photographs of the event. You won't have the experience of the sound, but you'll get a feel for why we call them the Wind Angels. Isn't that a beautiful sight to witness? Go, show the photos to your mom. I can tell by her face she's eager to see them."

Mario carefully carried the album to his mother. "Look Mom, Daddy photographed the Wind Angels just so that you and I can see them. Don't they look *agraciado*, the way they use their arms and those elegant fans?"

"Oh, yes. Your grandpa is right, you are one smart boy. Who taught you that word?"

"Daddy did when he talks about you. Very *agraciado!*"

"You better head for the kitchen and have Juanita feed you dinner along with your sister. Next year, when you are six, you'll be allowed to sit with the adults at Grandpa's dinner table. You'll be seated next to Grandma Esmeralda or me, and we'll teach you how to properly eat and behave when eating with adults. Won't that be fun?"

"Eso es debatible! [That's debatable!]

"Hop to it. You're not only smart; you're also a little smart ass." Grandpa gave him another hug before sending him off to Juanita. He was lucky; Mama probably would have given him a not-so-gentle touch on his behind.

# Chapter 12

APRIL 14, 1968, had finally arrived. Don Carlos instructed Hernando, his personal chauffeur, to drive the family limousine to the front of the mansion. There was ample room for all of them and the house guests they were about to meet at Santiago de Chile International Aeropuerto. Don Carlos and Fernando were totally cool, Esmeralda apprehensive, the children excited, and Doretta, with a stomach filled with butterflies, not really knowing what to expect. She was thrilled to see her mother for the first time in more than five years. She wasn't quite certain how to conduct herself toward the new husband. *I won't call him Father, Dad, or Daddy. I just can't! I won't call him Herr Meyer. Perhaps just sir or señor? No, that won't work either. I'll just call him Andreas.*

Mid-April to mid-May was a perfect month for the German visitors. It would be the heart of fall. Processing through customs and Chilean immigration was involved and lengthy. At last, Doretta spotted Gisela, who was virtually clinging to Andreas's right arm. When she recognized Doretta, she let go of Andreas and ran, high heels and all, toward her long-lost daughter. She embraced and kissed her heartily, ignoring all others. Tears of joy on both their faces were touching to the onlookers. Fernando extended his hand in typical European fashion to greet Gisela and Andreas, and then changed his mind as he approached Gisela. He gave her a friendly hug. "Welcome to Chile, welcome to my home country and my family." Gisela responded with a broad smile; it was her first face-to-face encounter with Fernando. She had seen photographs of him and spoken with him by phone while Doretta and he had been together in Zürich.

Esmeralda and Don Carlos merely stood by watching the family principals testing the waters of getting acquainted. Don Carlos held Mario and Alona in his arms. Gisela suddenly realized that her grandchildren were there as well, to welcome her and her new husband. Don Carlos whispered into Mario's ear. "Go and give your other grandma a kiss of welcome. Go; be a good boy. She's been waiting for this moment for a long time." With a gentle nudge, he pushed Mario into Gisela's arms. She was only too delighted to free him of the bouquet of flowers he wanted to hand her.

"Thank you for this special floral welcome. I'm sure your mom and grandmother had something to do with it. Thank you, they are lovely."

"Willkommen in Chile, Oma." That little outburst in German was completely spontaneous and a surprise to all. "Danke schön; das ist aber lieb von Dir." [Thank you; that was very thoughtful of you.] It was deserving of another hug. Gisela finally made the rounds and cuddled little Alona, not wanting to part with her. In some ways, she reminded her of Doretta when she was going on three years, although she bore a certain resemblance to Esmeralda. The introductions among the men were met with less formality. However, the meeting of the two mothers was another story.

Esmeralda's stance was nearly standoffish and condescending. She viewed herself cut from a distinctly different bolt of cloth. She extended her right hand in greeting with a certain degree of hesitation. She looked down on Doretta's mother, appearing to be waiting for a curtsy from the German visitor. Gisela simply shook the extended hand and smiled and said "angenehm," a haughty means of saying "nice to meet you." Gisela was not to be put down by Esmeralda's less-than-sincere welcome. Of course, she was fully aware of the woman's attitude toward Doretta before she and Fernando were even married.

Don Carlos more than made up for his wife's lack of social graces. He embraced Doretta's mom and the new husband with South American charm and exuberance. "Bienvenidas, bienvenidos," as he hugged Gisela and Andreas, respectively. They could feel he meant every syllable of what he tried to convey.

"Let's head for home where we can truly welcome you. You must be exhausted after the long flight?"

Andreas finally was able to speak. "Thanks to your family's largesse, we are actually not as tired as you might expect. We slept for close to ten hours in comfort and were royally treated by the crew. Singapore Airlines provided excellent service. He winked at Don Carlos and Fernando: "Thank you for allowing us to travel in style. It made all the difference in the world. I don't believe my wife would have survived nineteen hours in less comfort."

Don Carlos spotted Hernando resting against the limousine by the curb as they left the airport. As soon as all were seated,

Don Carlos popped the first bottle of champagne. Doretta and Fernando extended crystal flutes to the visitors. "Willkommen in Santiago. We hope you will learn to love this land and its people." Doretta touched her mother's and Andreas's glasses before she connected with her in-laws and her husband. Upon arrival at the Garcia Lopez Hacienda, the visitors were warmly greeted by the house servants. Doretta caught Valentina and Juan's attention.

"Please take my parents to their quarters, and make them as comfortable as you know how." She then spoke to her mother and Andreas.

"Relax for a good hour and refresh yourselves. Dinner will be served at seven tonight. Try to stay awake at least until ten; that way, you will adjust a lot faster to the drastic time change. Tonight will be casual; other evenings, we may dress more formally in keeping with Señora Garcia Lopez's preferences for evening dress." She carefully mouthed to her mother: "When in Rome, we do as they do in Rome." Gisela read her lips on the first trial and winked back at her daughter. She had no intention of making things more challenging for Doretta than they appeared to be.

With her vision following her visitors up the stairway, Doretta said, "I want to know all about Grandma and the boys tomorrow. Love you, Mutti. Again, welcome, welcome." She clung to Fernando. "A special thank you to you for making my family so welcome." She couldn't help hugging her husband as lovingly as she did.

Gisela and Andreas descended the stairway gingerly, both

having their arms filled with wrapped presents for everyone. Mario was not shy and was fully aware of what was about to happen. "Santa Claus is coming early this year. May I open my packages first?"

"What makes you think Santa brought anything for you? Have you been a good boy?" teased his smiling grandfather. Mario was thrilled with his collection of models representing the best in European race cars.

"Abuelo, abuelo, come look. One is just like Daddy's and another is red and white. Wow! These are fantastic. Danke schön. Danke schön! Oma." He ran and hugged Grandmother Gisela.

Doretta held up hand-knitted clothes to Alona, who couldn't care less. She had just celebrated her third birthday on March 31. She was most interested in the wooden jumping jack Oma Gisela had selected for her. Before long, Esmeralda admired a stunning alligator purse, Don Carlos repeatedly inhaled the tempting odors of a special Cuban cigar, and Fernando admired a set of Montblanc silver pens. Doretta's was a gift from her grandmother, an antique diamond and sapphire broach she had always admired.

Andreas loved the Jerry Garcia ties, and Gisela fell in love with the Mehta silk scarves from Varanasi. The pre-dinner gift exchange was a decided success all around.

Don Carlos gestured toward the dining room. "Let's gather around the table; Esmeralda is responsible for the seating arrangement." She made sure Andreas was seated next to her. The hostess was all ears wanting to learn what made Gisela's husband tick. Before she could spring her first question, he cut her off.

"I'm a retired university professor in chemistry. I enjoyed

my academic career but treasure my current emeritus status very much. Gisela and I enjoy our home and love to travel when the opportunities present themselves. And no, I'm not Jewish. Tell me about yourself."

He was almost blasé in his comments, having figured out his hostess from the moment he first laid eyes on her at the airport. He was fully informed that Don Carlos had been born into wealth and abundant landownership on an estate in his family for generations.

Her eyes were on fire. "I am Esmeralda and am a direct descendant of the Marquis de la Pica. The title was bestowed upon my ancestors on July 8, 1684, by King Charles II of Spain." Andreas thought for a moment that she expected him to get on his knees and kiss the ring on her extended hand. Even Doretta had not observed such a display of arrogance before. She was fully aware of the origin of Esmeralda's condescending attitude toward her from the moment she had learned of Fernando's dalliance with her in Zürich. None of that mattered any longer. She was Señora Doretta Garcia Lopez with all rights and privileges, and there wasn't a thing Esmeralda could do about it.

# Chapter 13

"COME in, come in, Mutti. This is where I hide and do my so-called therapeutic writing. I have to admit it's helped me greatly. I guess Dr. Rodriguez Amado knew what he was talking about. I've had some minor relapses but none of the terrible nightmares that terrorized me in my sleep almost nightly.

"Let's sit on this comfortable loveseat and tell me what's happening with the boys. My God, I shouldn't call them boys any longer; they are thirty-four-year-old men. What's happening in their lives?"

"Well, Lutz received his law degree and is now practicing in Düsseldorf. Lenny is still with the automobile dealership. The difference is he is now a partner in the business, and business is booming. Neither of my young men are married yet and decided two years ago to buy a nice condominium overlooking the Rhein. They could well afford a place large enough to accommodate their personal needs. They share one very large room with a huge double desk for their office. I'm so happy that they get along as well as they do. I'm still hoping to have some grandchildren living closer to me, but I'm not holding my breath. The young people today are not as quick to get married as were your father and I. Times have changed."

"How's Grandma doing? She's really getting up in years, isn't she?"

"Grandma will be eighty-five and is doing very well. Her arthritis gives her fits at times, but mentally she is still very much her old self. She loves having Lutz and Lenny living so close to her; they make every effort to see her often. I guess her great cooking is always a drawing card for them, who love a good home-cooked meal now and then. Eating most meals away from home becomes a bore after a while.

"Let's talk, while we have a chance, about your situation here. I get the distinct feeling that you are not on the best footing with your mother-in-law. That scene with Andreas at the dinner table last night told the whole story. She really does act as if she's better than the rest of us. I didn't want to believe what you mentioned several times in your letters, that she is known among her people as the 'Ice Princess.' I'm inclined to share that perception after our encounters with her yesterday."

"Don't let her bother you; I've gotten used to it and know how to handle Esmeralda. One thing I'm sure of, Don Carlos absolutely adores our children and me and that means a lot. He's been a very loving and generous force in my life since I arrived in this country. Some days I pinch myself, wondering if it is indeed I who's living at this place."

"I do miss you and wish you didn't live half a world away from me, but be assured that I understand. You and the children belong here with Fernando. He's obviously very generous with you, and I still can't fathom that he had us fly First Class at his expense. I don't know if I'll be able to handle another long flight like that, even flying in such luxury. Just being confined for almost twenty hours does something to my psyche. Perhaps, one of these days, when the children are a little older, especially Alona, Fernando might consider a visit to Germany. Wouldn't it be great if he could establish a business connection through their winery?"

"Don't think that thought hasn't crossed his mind. He loved living in Europe. I'm not sure if it was Europe, me, or getting away from Esmeralda's controlling influence. He's never said as much, but there are times when I can read in his eyes what's going on in that head of his. He's too loving a son to come right out with it. She has her moments, even with me. When I surprised her with that beautiful Mehta scarf, she was pleasantly shocked. And as far as Fernando is concerned, he can walk on water. It's just having me, Orphan Annie, brought into her plans that has clearly thrown her train off the track. Don't worry; I can handle her, and with Don Carlos's love for me, I've got the right person in my corner.

"I was pleased that Andreas wanted to come with you. Meeting someone in person is so much more realistic than admiring them in photographs from a distance. He seems to be a very nice man—and I'm glad he's in your life, especially with all of us gone. I was proud of him the way he confronted Esmeralda. That sure took the wind out of her sails."

"That surprised me too. I guess he hasn't forgotten how to act like a professor. I understand he was very good at what he did. You don't know yet how we met."

"Yeah, how did you meet? That whole affair was kind of quick."

"Actually, what I did was to answer his ad in the lovelorn column of the WAZ. We met at the Weinstuben for a drink, and the rest is history. My friends thought I had lost my mind, but I have absolutely no regrets. He was lonely after his wife of forty years died. They didn't have any children, and many of his friends had moved away or passed on. One of his *Skat* [German card game] buddies suggested he put the ad in the paper. Lucky me, I was the first to call him. We were married a month later."

"How do Lutz and Lenny like him?"

"Neither had any objections when we married. They like Andreas. He takes the train to Düsseldorf once a month and meets them in the *Altstadt* [old town] for a couple of pints, and then they have dinner. All three seem to enjoy each other's company. When he comes home, he always goes on and on about our boys. He's developed a genuine affection for both your brothers—which makes me happy. I'm more than over-joyed to have Andreas in my life and that my children have accepted him.

"Although, almost ten years older than I, he pleases me in every respect. I like that he still has that joie de vivre. Having been a widow for almost twenty-five years didn't make me look for a sex partner, but for someone who could complete my life in many other ways. If sex was part of the deal, all the better. I'm not complaining. Andreas fulfills me in all aspects."

"That's wonderful news. I hope you two are comfortable in your quarters, and that you will have an enjoyable time with us while you are visiting. You want to come to our bedroom? I would like to show you what I'm planning to wear to the opera next week. If need be, we can make a run into Santiago and find something suitable for you. I don't want to give Esmer-alda any cause for criticizing you. Don Carlos and Fernando are wearing tuxes. If Andreas didn't bring one with him, he can rent one in Santiago."

"You mentioned the opera visit on the phone. Andreas was smart enough to pick up on that; he did bring his tux, and I like the way it looks on him. Now let's see if I have to buy another formal dress."

Doretta rang the bell for Valentina, and she appeared promptly in her and Fernando's bedroom. "Thank you, Valentina. I would like to model for my mother the two evening gowns I bought and need your assistance with getting in and out of them quickly. Let's try the orange-red one first." With Valentina's assistance, she had easily slipped into the first dress.

"I like it; it's a color that has always looked great on you. Well, let's see the second one." Doretta stepped behind a large screen and changed into the other formal. When she stepped out, Gisela was speechless.

"There's no contest. You'll be the talk of the town. And those shoes! How can you even walk in those heels? But they work with the dress. You are stunning; that's what you need to wear. Has Esmeralda seen this on you?"

"Are you kidding? No way! I want her to be surprised."

"That she will be. May I try that orange one on? We are still pretty close in size. You mind?"

"No, not at all. Valentina, would you mind helping my mom into the first dress? Thank you."

When Gisela stepped out from behind the screen, there was no choice but letting her wear it." Valentina made the correct observation.

"Ma'am, I'll take up the hem just a little more than one inch and it will be perfect for you. Without the very high heels your daughter is wearing, the dress is too long on you. We wouldn't want you to trip at the opera house, would we?"

"Certainly not," agreed Doretta.

"As a young girl, I worked with a very nice German lady at Falabella's in their alteration department. She taught me all the tricks of the trade. Taking up a hem is a cinch. I could probably do it blindfolded. I moved back to the Garcia Lopez Hacienda when I married Juan. My family has worked for the family for many years. Juan had been with them for quite a while when we met. The next time we go shopping at Falabella's, I would like to see if the German lady is still working there. She can't be old enough to be retired. Just slip out of the dress, and I'll take care of it right away. No worry about anything, por favor."

"Isn't she wonderful, Mom? Don Carlos insisted on making her my personal maid. There've been days and situations where I wasn't sure I could have survived without her. Well, now that we have all that figured out, let's join the others for lunch. Don't breathe a word about our little masquerade party upstairs. I want her totally in shock when we step out for the evening at the Teatro Municipal de Santiago. It's the kind of thing she often succeeds in doing to me; I'll relish the thought of having my own little revenge."

"Well, here you are. I've been looking all over the place for you," said Fernando when the ladies came down the staircase. "I was wondering if you cloistered yourself with the Remington Rand. Glad to see you spent time with your mother. I took Andreas for a ride to the winery. We actually did a little sampling of the new wines, and he seems to be quite relaxed."

"Did you succeed in getting my husband inebriated?"

"No. I just loosened his tongue a bit; he'll have a fine time dealing with Esmeralda at lunch."

"You wicked man," said Doretta. Don Carlos understood most of what was said. He couldn't help smiling to himself. He was proud of Fernando and how he handled some of the obstacles Esmeralda created for his wife and her family. Her attitude toward Doretta was utterly objectionable to him and represented behavior alien to all that he stood for. There were days when he considered divorcing her, which she knew would never happen because of his devout adherence to the doctrines of the Catholic church for his wife's sake. Unlike her, he wasn't wearing his religion on his sleeve. He often made reference to the fact that he considered himself an atheist.

They were all peacefully seated around the large table. Even Mario was given special permission to join the adults for lunch. Dinner was out of the question until he was six years old. All eyes were on Andreas as he kept smiling between burping and glancing at his nemesis seated directly next to him. Esmeralda finally couldn't resist: "My good man, are you drunk in the middle of the day? How dare you come to the table and sit next to me?"

"I had nothing to do with it. It was your son making me taste all that wonderful new wine. They should have given me something to eat in between pushing those delightful samples at me. Brrrp! Excuse me, Your Highness! Brrrp!" All, even Mario, burst out laughing. It was too funny. Esmeralda got up and stormed out of the room with a barrage of Spanish expletives filling the air.

# Chapter 14

DORETTA didn't sleep well after an evening of discussing events in Germany during WWII. Andreas led the charge with his personal experiences during the era. Only to be followed by Gisela's accounts of what had happened to her first husband and her and the children. It was the kind of conversation that would settle into Doretta's mind and carried the tendency for her to relive those unpleasant experiences in her nocturnal traumas. She decided to get up quietly and retreated to her secluded room where she would feel safe. Rather than typing and possibly disturbing anyone in the mansion, she grabbed a pad and pen and began to write.

Fernando was a breath of fresh air in my existence. Strangely, I had immersed myself so completely in my work, a relationship with another man had been the furthest thing from my mind. The last time I had made love to a man was in Hamburg when I was with Hektor before he took off for New York. That was April of 1954. Four years had gone by.

What intrigued me the most about Fernando were his exotic looks, his casualness about everything, and his charm in mixing languages and doing a fantastic balancing act of juggling between Spanish, English, and German. It was his sincere smile that endeared him to me.

When he walked me out of that library and put me in that spiffy little number of a car, I was toast. Our tête-à-tête at the little bistro where we celebrated our first meeting over Raclette and enjoyed a good bottle of wine was the start of a wonderful friendship, the start of a new life for me as a person and as a woman. He drove me home that night but merely kissed me lightly on the mouth. There was just a hint of a sexual overture. He asked me for the location of the offices of Schrift & Schreiber, which I was only too willing to share with him. After that first encounter, I knew we would meet again.

I wasn't at all surprised to see Fernando leaning against his Mercedes 190 SL, having the biggest grin on his handsome face, when I left the office shortly after five o'clock the next evening. He didn't budge an inch but lifted his elegant hat to greet me. "Care for a ride, young lady. Fernando Garcia Lopez at your service," as he bowed deeply from the waist. "Have you been indoctrinated into the culinary mysteries of Switzerland? You like fondue? I know just the place, Le Dézaley; they've been in business in Zürich for more than fifty years."

"Got yourself a deal; I'd love nothing better." He helped me into the car and leaned closely enough for me to give him a quick peck on his smoothly shaven face. I couldn't help detect a pleasing aftershave lotion. I hate to admit I was aware of stirrings in my sexually starved body. Fernando treated me like a lady. It was a delightful meal, and we talked about our respective backgrounds. He shared with me his upbringing in Chile, didn't hide or minimize the fact that he was financially well endowed, had a wonderful father and a bitchy mother, and was expected to return to Chile after completion of his studies in Switzerland to marry the right kind of girl and produce beau coup male heirs. I wasn't exactly sure if I was the girl he or his family were envisioning. For the moment, I didn't care since I felt safe in having him interested in just me—whether a right or wrong kind of girl.

I shared with him that my father was Jewish, and that he was practically killed in front of my eyes when he was taken from us by the Nazis at the time of his arrest and was never heard from again. He shuddered when I related my fears during the bombings and living in an underground bomb shelter for months until the end of the war. The march to find Grandma and living with her for a considerable length of time and my affair with Hektor Birken rounded out my confession. None of it seemed to perturb him.

That night he drove me home and parked the car in the inimitable European fashion—half on and half off the sidewalk. Without any qualms, he walked up all those darn steps to the fifth floor of the old building.

We were both slender and young and didn't mind the exercise. Neither of us were winded. He took a good look around the place and then plopped himself into a semi-comfortable plush chair. He crooked his right index finger at me, suggesting that I join him on the chair. Well, actually he pulled me down and seated me in his lap.

When he started kissing the back of my neck, I knew we were entering a stage of delightful foreplay. It was perhaps twenty minutes into this fascinating game of give and take that we beheld each other in total nudity. At last he spoke: "Would you like to have me all soaped up in the shower, right here in this chair, or would you prefer for me to bed you in this boudoir of yours? It's ladies' choice at this first dance. Which shall it be?"

I was so taken by him, I decided to dare him. "Can I have more than one choice? How about all three? Let's start right here; have Act II in my bed, and make it the curtain call in the shower. Are you up to it?"

I thought he was going to lose it. "Hmm, a regular Madame Bovary."

With that final remark, he began to tantalize my mouth and throat, sampled my breasts, and languished with lingual pleasures wanting me to be thrilled. I had forgotten how great it was to be with a man. He ravished me as I was straddling his strong legs, welcoming his manhood as he tried lifting his body in that terribly uncomfortable chair. When we succeeded in fulfilling one another, the right arm of the plush chair gave way and broke off. Both of us landed in a sweating heap on the hardwood floor. The neighbor down from us must have thought the house had been struck by a bomb.

We laughed a lot between Acts I and II. Taking the shower together after the curtain call, all Fernando could say was: "What a delightful and entertaining play. Theatre sounds like a lot of fun. May I get us season tickets?"

We decided to be practical. Fernando gave up his room at the university and moved in with me. First thing he did was to replace that ugly chair and bought a new queen-sized bed, mattress, and all the trimmings. His choice would have been a king, but there wasn't enough room. We compromised and were happy with our selections.

We were madly in love, and time flew by. He hated using any kind of protection, and I went along with the idea devil may care. I did watch my cycles but tried nothing else to prevent me from getting pregnant. Deep in my soul, it was something I regretted for four years that I didn't have a child with Hektor. I didn't want this to happen with Fernando.

Fernando informed his parents of our relationship and tried to pave the way for his eventual return to his homeland with a German wife. Esmeralda called repeatedly, imploring her son to abandon me and not to pursue this affair any longer. She told him were he to go through with marrying an unsuitable wife, he would be disowned and disinherited. Most of these phone calls ended by Fernando slamming the phone in his mother's ear. Then there would be peace until she persisted with further bombardments.

By July of 1962, I knew I was with child. Fernando was thrilled to learn that we had succeeded in making a baby. He was like a kid in FAO Schwarz, the famous toy store in Manhattan, and treated me like a queen. I made up my mind, no matter what would happen, I would not give up this child. As much as I wanted to be with Fernando and become his wife, if he opted to bow to the will of his mother, the child was not going to be sacrificed to appease her.

In December of 1962, I received a letter from Hektor. At first I couldn't believe it when I saw the return address. I read the letter at least three times before I shared its content with Fernando. I was terribly saddened as I read the lengthy letter recounting the disastrous marriage to his wife Georgia and how it all ended. He pleaded for my forgiveness and insisted on needing to see me eye-to-eye. When I discussed the matter with Fernando, he encouraged me to have Hektor come and visit us in Zürich. I offered to meet him at the airport in early February.

When Hektor arrived, I was more than eight months pregnant. He was surprised when he discovered that it was Fernando who met him at the airport; I didn't dare handle all those steps any more than I had to. For that reason alone, I had resigned from Schrift & Schreiber in November of 1962. I didn't have to worry about finances. Fernando took good care of me.

When we met, it was a tearful but meaning-ful reunion. I had forgiven Hektor long before this. I expressed my hopes for his finding the right woman someday. Obviously, he and I and he and Georgia were not meant to be for each other. Fernando, Hektor, and I spent a most enjoyable evening together in my five-story walk up. Our farewell the next morning was heartrending and touching for all involved. We wished each other well for our futures in the New World. When we finally parted on that bitter-cold and gray morning in Zürich in February of 1963, none of us realized what the fates had in store for us.

# Chapter 15

THE excitement at the Garcia Lopez Hacienda seemed palpable on the day of the planned opera attendance. Actually, the opera itself was secondary to the anticipated show before, during, and after the performance. One attendee in the group was actually looking forward to the opera itself; for some of the others, it was a question of seeing and being seen on the red carpet at the Teatro Municipal de Santiago.

Valentina was entertaining the children in the playroom. The adults were to gather in the foyer for a champagne kickoff of the event. Esmeralda made sure it would be an elegant production for the purpose of impressing her visitors from Germany. She wanted to be certain they discovered that residents of the Garcia Lopez Hacienda, and people in South America as a whole, weren't living in a *Hinterland* by comparison to Europe's glamorous lifestyle.

Gisela and Andreas were the first to appear and were lavishly greeted by Esmeralda and Don Carlos. Esmeralda looked stunning in her full-length black silk Balenciaga, complemented by the Mehta silk creation Doretta had brought back from her visit to Falabella's in Santiago. She carried an elegant cane heavily embossed with silver, no longer feeling the need to conceal her minor handicap. The men shook hands and admired each other's looks in their tuxedos. Esmeralda complimented Gisela on the evening gown she was wearing; she had no idea it was one Doretta lent her.

At last, Doretta and Fernando came down the marble staircase, she looking breathtaking in her peacock green and blue von Furstenberg creation perfectly draped across her slender physique. Esmeralda almost choked as she watched Doretta, a picture of grace walking in her six-inch heels that blended flawlessly with the exquisite gown. Fernando's tux in midnight blue was a welcome change from the otherwise elegant black variety of evening dress for men.

Don Carlos lifted his glass in greeting and toasted all: "Bienvenidas, bienvenidos to a wonderful evening. I hope you will enjoy Esmeralda's choices. I'm not much for opera and was happy to learn that she had not chosen an evening with Herr Richard Wagner. I believe it is Puccini's *Tosca* we'll be seeing tonight."

Doretta smiled; it was one of her favorites. She loved all of it but especially the scene in the second act when the villain Scarpia gets his comeuppance. Doretta never cared much for any form of violence but, for some reason, Floria Tosca defending herself and succeeding in killing her nemesis appeared to be justified action in her mind.

Don Carlos signaled Hernando to bring the limousine around to the front of the mansion. "We have dinner reservations at Confitería Torres, the oldest restaurant in town; it was founded in 1879. I hope it will be to your liking. The place oozes with antiquity and South American charm."

As Hernando pulled up in front of Confitería Torres, the liveried doorman rushed out to open the doors of the limousine and to assist the ladies in exiting the car. "Bienvenidas, bienvenidos to Confitería Torres." The ladies smiled at each other and waited to be accompanied by their respective spouse into the restaurant. Don Carlos had his own idea; he had asked his son to accompany his mother, and he wanted to enter the place with Doretta on his right arm. Everyone appeared to be pleased, especially Esmeralda. *I'm glad he assigned the honor to my son and not that Andreas character*, thought Esmeralda. She still had neither forgotten nor forgiven being seated next to the "drunken German" as she saw him. Don Carlos and Fernando couldn't help laughing out loud recalling the scene at the dining room table.

Esmeralda, knowing the *maître d'*, had arranged for a secluded roundtable for six with a perfect view of the activities on the avenue. As expected, beef selections chosen by all were perfectly prepared and expertly served. The presentations were exceptional and pleasing to everyone's culinary expectations. The closing act, an array of spectacular desserts, could not be topped by anything.

Hernando and his favorite chariot were waiting for the company to be taken to the opera house in time for their appearance on the red carpet. Esmeralda graciously encouraged Andreas and Gisela to lead the way with Fernando and Doretta entering last. As they moved through the crowd, Doretta couldn't help hearing some of the whispered comments aimed at her gown. Fernando leaned into her: "I keep telling you, you are more than beautiful. I do have to agree with those jealous ladies, that gown is gorgeous on you. And those heels! I'm glad I'm as tall as I am." He tried to tickle her.

They were shown to their private box in the first balcony with the front seats reserved for the ladies. Opera glasses were located in front of each comfortable chair. As soon as they were seated, champagne was served by the attending ushers. Doretta and Gisela were impressed and nodded toward each other. *Must be the way those on the other side live.*

When the lights finally dimmed, Doretta's eyes were glued to the stage. She gloried in Puccini's music and was fully engaged. She didn't dare have another glass of champagne during the first intermission. She couldn't wait for the dramatic ending of Act II.

Doretta knew the words in her head and mouthed them with Floria Tosca: "And, yesterday, trembling Rome lay prostrate at his feet!" She totally understood how this woman felt celebrating the triumphant moment of revenge. Gisela reached for a pretty handkerchief in her tiny purse and passed it over to Doretta. She didn't want Doretta's tears to spoil the elegance of her gown.

The evening was over all too soon. Everyone smiled at Esmeralda as they emerged from the Teatro Municipal de Santiago. "Wonderful evening. Loved the dinner and especially your choice of opera. Thank you, Esmeralda." Doretta flashed a genuine smile toward her mother-in-law. For once, Esmeralda's response appeared to be sincere. After sitting through the opera, she had to balance herself on the cane closely held to her long skirt.

"You looked lovely, my dear. It pleased me immensely that you were so very much touched by the opera. It shows you have soul. I could tell you loved it as much as I do. I'm so glad we've discovered something we truly seem to have in common. You and I should get season tickets. Our men could make it an evening of poker while you and I enjoy our opera fix. We'll talk about it after your family leaves. I would love that." Doretta thought she wasn't hearing correctly but smiled inwardly at having broken the ice.

# Chapter 16

ON the day they were taking Gisela and Andreas back to the Santiago airport for their late-afternoon flight to Düsseldorf with a first stop in Frankfurt, Doretta was certain that she was expecting another child. She chose not to say a word to anyone. Doretta believed Fernando deserved to know first without any outside interference, suggestions, or commentary.

When she skipped her second cycle, she was almost certain she was carrying another child. No wonder that fabulous dress had felt just a tad snugger than when she was first fitted with it six weeks earlier. She remembered well the night Fernando had rescued her after that last horrible nightmare. Now she couldn't wait to say farewell to her mother and Andreas and share the good news with her husband.

The night before their departure, Gisela asked to stop at Falabella's before departing for the homeland. Valentina had talked about this German woman at the store, and Gisela was anxious to meet her and perhaps have her consult in a purchase she desired to make.

Juan was the chauffeur of the day. Valentina was delighted

to accompany Doretta and her family to Santiago. Fernando had a busy day at the winery, and Don Carlos and Esmeralda opted to make their farewells at the hacienda.

"We have so enjoyed meeting you; it's been such a pleasure having you with us in our home." Don Carlos hugged both Gisela and Andreas. Esmeralda was her conservative self and decided to shake hands; however, she was not unfriendly toward her departing guests. She was pleased she had the opportunity to discover something in Doretta she'd been totally unaware of until the night at the opera. It might never have happened had it not been for the visit by her mother. She smiled graciously as Juan drove away from the house.

Gisela was all excited. "Are you sure this German lady is still working at the store? I would so much like to meet her." Valentina explained to Doretta that she had called Fallabella's and asked if Frau Flott still worked in the dress department. She was assured that Lottie Flott was still active at the store and hopefully would be for many more years. "That was good news to me. As I mentioned, I wasn't really certain of her age. She must be younger than I thought her to be," said Valentina.

Doretta conveyed to her mother that Frau Flott was still at Fallabella's and was expected to remain there for years to come. "Das ist wunderbar!" Gisela burst forth, momentarily forgetting where she was.

Juan dropped the ladies off at the store. Andreas decided to have a pint with Juan. He had gotten to like "Austral"—a tasty Chilean beer and invited the friendly chauffeur to join him. Gisela's shopping adventure had little appeal to him.

The ladies took the elevator to the second floor and met Lottie Flott in the better dress department. Her hair showed signs of graying, but her complexion was still flawless. She recognized Valentina immediately and approached her with an extended right hand. "How nice to see you again, Valentina. I had no idea you were still in the Santiago area." They shook hands.

"My husband and I work on the Garcia Lopez estate and have done so since I left here. I'm so glad you are still enjoying your work with Falabella's. She turned toward Doretta. "Allow me to introduce my lady, Señora Doretta Garcia Lopez, and this is her mother, Frau Gisela Meyer, visiting from Düsseldorf."

Frau Flott extended her right hand toward Gisela Meyer. "Freut mich! Willkommen in Santiago." [It pleases me! Welcome in Santiago.] "How may I help you? Is there anything in particular you are looking for?"

"I would like to buy a dress for my daughter. She was kind enough to let me have one of hers for a special occasion while we were visiting." Doretta responded quickly.

"Mother, there's no need to do that. I was so happy to let you take that dress off my hands. I truly didn't need two elegant ball gowns. The one I kept will do me more than fine. Please, this is silly."

Gisela looked at her daughter pensively. There was something different about her looks, but she couldn't put her finger on it.

"Doretta, would you ask Frau Flott for her business card? Perhaps in the future I could contact her and have something sent to your house. It would be so much nicer for me to have a contact in this city. Just in case; one never knows. And at least I could speak to her on the phone or write. Please take one of my cards, and ask her if she would mind keeping it on file for future reference."

There were smiles all around and obvious agreement to accommodate Frau Meyer's wishes. "Kein Problem; mach ich gerne!" [No problem; I'll be happy to do that!] They shook hands and nodded their goodbyes. "You come and see me again, Valentina. I'd love to talk to you some other time," said Frau Flott.

"I will," affirmed Valentina as the others were headed toward the bank of elevators. Doretta reached for her mother's arm.

"Mutti, there was no need for that. I told you I was more than delighted for you to take that dress. Fernando didn't mind; he liked what I kept much better. But I'm glad you came up with the idea of the card exchange. She'll be a wonderful contact for you to have. Now let's see if we can find our two men. I had asked Juan not to stray too far from the main entrance and to be back no later than one o'clock." She looked at her watch. "He'll be here in five minutes. I've never known him not to be punctual."

With that she spotted Andreas, waving at them as they approached. "Hey, mission accomplished? I don't see anyone carry any packages. Couldn't you ladies find anything you liked?"

"No, I convinced my mother that I didn't need another fancy dress and certainly not just now." She caught herself the last second, not wanting to break the news and having her mother leave worried about her daughter's well-being.

"She met the nice German lady at the store and that was a positive experience for both. We better be off to the airport. Your flight takes off in less than two hours. Thankfully, the immigration officers are a bit more speedy when people are leaving. Coming into the country is always a lot more hairy, especially these days. How well I remember the circus when we arrived at the port in Valparaiso. Flying is so much easier than what we did. But you know that story well enough. I wrote about it in detail five years ago."

Juan had them at the airport by two o'clock. Their flight was leaving at three-thirty. After checking their luggage and processing boarding and passport control, they were taken to a lounge for First Class passengers. There were all kinds of liquid and edible refreshments that helped pass the time. Doretta found a nice table that could accommodate everyone. She insisted on Valentina and Juan sitting with them. Doretta didn't care about certain looks she and her entourage were given. Valentina and Juan were like family to her.

It was finally time to say goodbye, which was always hard for Doretta and her mother. They were thankful for the ability of speaking on the phone periodically in spite of the horrendous price ticket for calling. Of course, no one ever knew if there would be a "Wiedersehen" when one lives that far apart and in different worlds. Doretta hugged her mother firmly, not wanting to let go. Neither of the women made an attempt at hiding their sadness. She hugged Andreas.

"Thank you for coming with Mom, and thanks for taking good care of her. I loved meeting you and spending time with you in our home. See if you can convince her to travel again. You heard what Fernando said; he meant every word of it and will always be able to help with your financial arrangements." He hugged her back, trying to hide his own tears.

They were called to their gate and quickly disappeared from sight. Doretta, Valentina, and Juan stepped onto an outside balcony and watched the plane take off. They waved, not knowing if they were seen by those on the departing airplane.

Doretta couldn't bring herself to leave until the plane was finally lost in distant clouds. Tears were flooding her eyes: *Lord knows if we'll ever see each other again?* She had no premonition of what the future held for her and her loved ones.

Doretta thanked Valentina and Juan for their moral support and words of consolation and encouragement during the short journey back to the Garcia Lopez Hacienda.

"I'm glad you could be with me as I was sending my dear mother back to the homeland. We've always been very close, especially after I lost my father. Andreas, her new husband, turned out to be a likable man. I hope she will have many happy years with him. It was very hard for me to see them off; I doubt very much that they will make a return trip to Chile. It's just too long a journey for them. But, thank you again for standing by me. Your kind words and expressions of empathy made me feel loved."

"De nada. De nada" both spoke in one voice.

"I would like to retire for a while to our quarters until my husband returns from the vineyards. Please convey to the Señor and Señora that I need to rest for a while but that my husband and I will attend dinner later. Thank you for assuring me privacy."

Doretta ascended the staircase and softly closed the door to their bedroom. She was relieved to be alone with her thoughts and made herself more comfortable by shedding all pieces of clothing but her beautiful undergarments. Before she slipped into a silk robe, she gently touched her abdomen. *Whoever is in there, you're not quite ready to spell early communications, are you? I'll just have to learn to be patient. But I know, you're in there,* pondered Doretta.

She drew back the heavy bedspread and laid down on the

silky sheets and pillow covers. It didn't take long, and she was sound asleep. The sun was setting when Fernando quietly stepped into the room. He beheld his beautiful wife and decided to wake her with a gentle kiss.

"I'm home at last. How is my lovely wife? I understand from Juan that you had a difficult time saying farewell to your mother and Andreas."

"Thank you for being so considerate. I loved being awakened by your kiss. Some other guy probably would have jumped first thing into the shower, not giving a damn about his sleeping wife. That isn't you, thank God. I love being married to you. But now take your shower and then, get with me under this wonderful silk duvet. I feel so spoiled."

"Is everything okay with you? Why this need for being so close to me? Won't my parents be wondering what's going on?"

"We've got a good hour before they expect us at the dinner table. I just want to be close to you for a few moments. I need you more than I need food right now. So go and get into that wonderful shower and relax. And don't bother to put on anything; I want you naked next to me."

"Is this an invitation to a dance? I know things haven't been quite normal during the last month. I'll be more than happy to accommodate you by being first on your dance card."

He stripped off everything and rushed for the shower. Soaping himself from head to toe, he began to detect stirrings in his groin. Doretta undressed herself completely and kept watching Fernando through the fogged glass enclosure of the shower. After drying himself, he approached his waiting lover, the large terrycloth towel firmly wrapped around his waist. Doretta thought, *is he ashamed of showing his manhood?*

Before Fernando could kneel down on the bed and give his

wife another inviting kiss, she reached for the towel and deftly freed him of his moist cover. "My, my. What do I have here?" She touched him firmly with her left hand as she drew him closer to her with her right arm drawn around his masculine neck. "Come closer to me; I want all of you, and I want you now."

"Señor Fernando Garcia Lopez at your service," and as he took her in one swift move, Doretta responded with great joy."

"Do I feel any different to you?"

"What do you mean by different? I love you just the way you always were? You didn't by any chance have that crazy doctor of yours talk you into having one of those damn IUDs inserted? Tell me you didn't? Some guys have told me they can feel those things at the tip of their penis as they ejaculate. I surely didn't feel anything like that just now."

"Be at ease, my dear husband. No one but you has inserted anything into me for the last ten years. And guess what? With a certain result. Don't you get it?"

"Are you trying to tell me, I'll be a father again?"

"I didn't think I needed to draw you pictures! Yes, we'll have something popping out of there in about seven months. It probably will be at least another month or so before it will start kicking away in my tummy. Did I leave you speechless? Why aren't you saying anything? Sorry; I didn't intend to deflate you."

"That you did. I'm thrilled." Fernando drew her closely to his broad chest and held her ever so tight. "What a wonderful piece of news. Have you told my parents or anyone?"

"No. No one knows about it but you. I purposely didn't breathe a word to my mother and Andreas or Valentina and Juan. I believed it was prudent not to make the farewell any sadder than it was and to have them wonder about it all the way home on that long plane ride. They'll know in plenty of time when we learn a little more about the little bundle of joy. And furthermore, I firmly believed that it should be you to know first."

"Thank you again." He released her gently onto the soft cushions. "I think it's high time for another shower if we don't want to wind up at the top of Esmeralda's special list."

"Absolutely not, especially in view that I have risen in her perception of me ever since the fabulous night at the opera. I've no intention of undoing that new and improved relationship with your mother. So let's get a move on, as you tell me so often." She nudged him out of bed and toward the shower and followed him in close pursuit.

They walked into the dining room all smiles. Esmeralda spoke up as soon as she saw Doretta and Fernando. She waved her cane at Doretta. "Tonight I would like you to sit on my right and my son across from us. Don Carlos may still play his favorites by having you close to him on his left. He'll just have to vie for your favoritism and compete with my attention to you."

*What's wrong with this picture?* It was the first thing to cross Doretta's mind, but she decided not to challenge Esmeralda and went along with her scheme. Don Carlos and Fernando looked just as puzzled. All decided to put a positive face on a confrontational situation.

"How did things go for you today, Doretta? It had to be difficult for you to bid farewell to your mother and Andreas. I do hope they enjoyed their visit with us," said Esmeralda.

"I believe you and Papa did everything to make my mother and her new husband as welcome as possible. They did have a wonderful time. Nevertheless, I doubt they will return to Chile. It has nothing to do with your hospitality. Mom has a hard time dealing with the confinement on a plane for that long a time. It's as simple as that.

"Perhaps there's a surprise that might change Mom's mind. Fernando and I want to share something relating to a future event with you."

"Oh, and what might that be? Are you planning on flying them over here in a private jet or by some other extravagant means?" posed Esmeralda.

"Mother, give Doretta and me some credit for having half a brain. For God's sake, we are having another child in about seven months. What do you say now?" There was deafening silence for a few seconds. Don Carlos hugged his son, and Esmeralda reached out for Doretta. It was obvious they were taken totally by surprise.

"That's wonderful news, Doretta. Have you discussed this with Dr. Rodriguez Amado?" asked Fernando's mother.

"No, not yet. I hadn't told anyone until I shared my good news with Fernando after he returned from the vineyards this afternoon. I did not want my mother to leave with a heavy heart."

"You did right by that," added Don Carlos. "There's plenty of time for them to reconsider making another journey to see us all. At this moment, I'm the happiest Papa in the world." He leaned closer to Doretta and embraced her lovingly.

"Be certain to have Dr. Rodriguez Amado recommend a different ob/gyn. There was no need for you to suffer for three days in labor the way you did with Alona. We are lucky both of you survived the ordeal. I certainly would not go back to that impossible man," was Esmeralda's comment.

"We won't." Fernando sadly recalled the unpleasant situation. "I'll speak with him first thing in the morning. For the moment, let's celebrate."

Doretta declined having any kind of alcoholic drink. "I'll be happy with Perrier. You all enjoy the Dom Perignon. I'm not taking any chances." With that, Don Carlos let the champagne cork fly. There was so much joy in his tear-filled eyes. For once, Esmeralda was completely in agreement with her husband.

# Chapter 17

SHE was wide awake long before anyone in the mansion was stirring. Not even the cook was to be seen in the kitchen. Doretta walked down to her secluded room and closed the door, trying to avoid any noise. She collected her thoughts; and for a moment, she wasn't certain where she had stopped in her account of their happy days in Switzerland. And then she recalled:

✕

Right after Hektor left for Germany, on the morning of February 9, 1963, Fernando sprung his big surprise on me. I was taken totally aback when he spoke.

"When I took Hektor for our little spin of the town yesterday while you were taking your well-deserved nap, I discussed our future plans with him. He tried to impress on me that we should get married before the baby is born. This will come as a surprise to you as well. I didn't want to contradict him or get into a lengthy discussion for obvious reasons. I never was sure which language to use.

"Anyway, I didn't share with him what I'm about to tell you. We will be married in a civil ceremony on Valentine's Day. I started the lengthy process of the marriage application right after the first of the year; having been told that it could take up to five weeks, I needed to do some planning and have foresight. Your passport is in order and no problem for getting you into Chile. The baby won't need one, and mine is obviously just fine.

"We won't breathe a word about our civil marriage to my family. When we finally get to Chile, you will need to attend some instructional classes in the Catholic faith, and we'll get married in the church to please my mother. Eventually, she will find out that the church ceremony was just icing on the cake; we won't be able to hide the fact that we are already married from the priest. But don't fear, he's a good friend of mine.

"Furthermore, I have no intention of sharing with anyone that you are Jewish. It's none of their business and would just add fuel to the burning fire. By the way, I've been in touch with Hapag Lloyd regarding our sailing home whenever that might be. It will depend on the arrival of our little one. As soon as he or she is born, I'll put that in the works."

I was stunned. I had no idea Fernando wanted to get married in Switzerland, but was thankful that our child would have legal parents before he or she would be born. One of my former colleagues, a gal at Schrift & Schreiber, offered to be my witness, and Fernando's school chum, Alfredo, did the honors for him. Once the paper war had been sufficiently fought, the ceremony itself at the city hall was quick and easy. While it was chilly and gray, at least it wasn't raining or snowing as we emerged from the old building. We took our witnesses out for lunch and enjoyed a few laughs and the convivial conversation. Our friends wished us well in our future adventures. I was happy when I managed to climb all those stairs in our building.

※

In the early hours of March 15, we knew it was time for me to be rushed to the closest hospital. No way was Fernando going to see me deliver our child in our little apartment, our love nest in the sky. Worse yet, he wasn't going to be physically involved in the event. Home delivery might be something done at his parents' hacienda in Chile with nursemaids and midwives on hand, but this situation was somewhat more challenging. When my water broke, Fernando enlisted the help of a young neighbor. Between the two young men, I was able to let myself be more or less dragged down all those darn steps. I nearly passed out when they tucked me into the little sports car. Afterward, Fernando chided himself for not having called an ambulance to take me. But we survived.

Mario was born at high noon on the Ides of March. He was a healthy nine-pound baby who decided to present himself most favorably and thus made his entry into our world relatively easy on me and himself. He was a handsome little boy without a bruise anywhere. Fernando could not have been happier when he beheld me and his little boy. He had this big grin on his face, letting me know how pleased he was to have survived the birth of his first child. When he spoke, he had me chuckle. "To be honest with you, when your water broke in that apartment, I was scared shitless for a moment. No way could I have carried you by myself down all those steps. I still don't believe I didn't call for an ambulance. That was so stupid. Let's make sure our next kid will arrive in a more convenient location."

When I saw Fernando next, he carried a beautiful bouquet of spring flowers. He knew how I loved the fragrance of hyacinth. I could tell by his bleary eyes that he had abundantly celebrated the arrival of his son with his poker buddies. After he kissed me and the baby, he shared some more interesting news with me. I had anticipated this development for several days, knowing that Fernando refused to fly; he was deathly afraid of being in the air. Actually, it wasn't fear of flying; he didn't like that a stranger, an unknown pilot, was in control of his fate.

"I've been on the phone with Hapag Lloyd. There is a freighter sailing out of Hamburg on April 5. Its cargo will be nothing but Mercedes and BMWs. There are only two stops slated until we reach Valparaiso. They will unload some cars in Casablanca, and we'll head straight for the Panama Canal. The second drop off is in Lima, Peru, before we sail all the way down to Valparaiso. We are supposed to arrive on Tuesday, April

30. There'll be only six other passengers aboard ship. I traveled by freighter when I came to Europe. I loved the accommodations and the service, and all our meals were exceptionally good. And of course, I'll be able to take my car home with me. We must think of the important things, right?" he winked at me.

His little spitfire was shipped by rail to Hamburg. The three of us and our few suitcases were nicely accommodated in First Class on the Rheingold Express from Switzerland to Cologne, where we switched to the Cologne-Hamburg Express. We stayed for two nights at the Hotel Süllberg which I absolutely adored. I had told Fernando I would stay anywhere but the Reichshof where I had been with Hektor and his mother in 1954. I just couldn't go back there.

Remembering the small cabin on the MS Italia Hektor shared with two other guys, I was surprised to see our accommodations on the freighter "Hamburg Ahoy." The bed was ample in size for the three of us and everything was spotless and clean. There weren't balconies or large windows, but the two portholes allowed plenty of light to brighten the room. I was thankful for the minimal bathroom facilities and the tiny loo. Showers had to be taken in more public areas, so to speak. Fernando enjoyed the joviality of showering with members of the crew; I wound up taking a lot of sponge baths in our cabin. It worked; I hadn't completely forgotten the days of living for months in the underground world of cold concrete under the most primitive conditions.

Moving up the Elbe out of the port of Hamburg,

I could imagine what Hektor must have experienced when sailing for the first time toward the New World. My last conversation with my mother was heartbreaking. She was sorry not to have met her first grandchild or ever having laid eyes on Fernando. Perhaps someday she would have that pleasure visiting us in Chile. She told me she was again on speaking terms with Helena Birken and that they were consoling one another.

I was pleased to learn that Mother had finally made peace with the woman who had always been in my corner; she had been as angry with her truant son as my family and I were in the beginning. I was glad that he had come to see us in Zürich and that we had a chance to talk and the men had an opportunity to meet. When we said goodbye on that cold morning, we were honest in wishing each other the best for the future.

There were a few times with rough days at sea. I don't know what it was that prevented me from becoming seasick. I liked to think that nursing Mario kept me on an even keel. Hearing him suckling at my breasts, with utter contentment reflecting on his beautiful face, might have done it for me.

We were happy to walk on solid ground after we made port in Casablanca. It was a welcome stop for both Fernando and me. Once we entered the South Atlantic and headed for the Panama Canal, the worst of the sea voyage was behind us. Mario was the star of the whole show; all the guys on the crew were nuts over him. They couldn't do enough to make us feel as comfortable as possible.

After a week on the freighter, I needed to wash my hair; I had had one sponge bath too many. Fernando arranged for me to have the shower for an hour all to myself without any peeping toms, the captain assured me. I thought I had died and gone to heaven and luxuriated under the streams of hot water rushing over my body.

The transfer through the canal was exciting for the men; personally, I wouldn't call it one of the wonders of the world. I was thankful that it was there for us rather than having to circumnavigate the Horn. The full-day stop in Lima was a gift from heaven. We didn't have access to the baby carriage, but neither of us minded taking turns carrying Mario in his little papoose.

We walked off our feet, but it felt just great being able to walk to our hearts' content. There were a few rough spots sailing south in the Pacific, but we managed. When a timely arrival for Valparaiso was predicted, I sent a quiet thank you in a heavenly direction. I didn't think Fernando was a practicing Christian, but I was pleased to hear him utter a few words of grateful appreciation on the morning we pulled into the Valparaiso harbor. He wasn't quite sure what to expect. Neither was I.

The crew understood and made sure Fernando's car, our belongings, and we were the first off the ship. There were heartfelt hugs and goodbyes among many best wishes for us and especially for the littlest sailor of them all. They never had had the experience of having a brand new baby on board. It wasn't too difficult for

Fernando to spot his father; Don Carlos was a large man—not fat, he was just very tall and a big man.

The first one he hugged was Mario. He lifted him high above his head eliciting the biggest smile. It was love at first sight. Don Carlos was thrilled to greet his first grandchild. I was next in line; and of course, he had a big hug for his dear son. They had not seen each other in years. Phone calls and writing are okay, but there is nothing like that personal interaction between fathers and sons.

Hernando assisted with stashing our luggage into the limousine. Esmeralda had purposely stayed behind, not knowing how much space would be needed in the car. While Fernando would drive his own car from Valparaiso port to the Garcia Lopez Hacienda, the baby and I and Don Carlos would ride with Hernando in the limo.

It was a good hour's drive through lovely wine country before our arrival at my new home. I had no idea how I would be received by Fernando's mother and the staff who were all waiting for us as Hernando pulled up to the front entrance of the giant house. It never had looked that big in the photographs Fernando had shown me.

What I never realized was the overall shape of the house. It was basically designed as a giant octagon with different wings. There was a wing for the seniors and their staff, a wing for support staff, a wing largely designed to accommodate children with nurseries, and study halls for older children. The kitchen, the laundry, the landscaping needs, and a large workshop were housed in two additional wings. Teachers and tutors and their families could be housed in another section of the structure, and then there was the wing where Fernando and I were to be living. Last, there was a wing for visiting guests.

All of these wings functioned on three levels, a lower level, the main floor, and the second floor. The house would be classified as a timber home where all posts and beams were joined by wooden pegs rather than nailed. The timber frame was what gave the building its external and internal beauty. The central focal point of the house was the spectacular Carrara marble staircase leading to the second floor.

Walking slowly toward me, relying on the support of her elegant cane, I met Esmeralda. I could tell she was looking me up and down. She was actually much more diminutive than I had expected. However, there was nothing diminutive about her demeanor toward me. I knew instantly she was a force to be reckoned with. Her head was covered in a lacy mantilla, probably created by loving hands working fiercely away at tatting in some cloistered shelter in a faraway place. There was a distinct aura of elegance as well as haughtiness about the woman who was my mother-in-law.

With the help of Don Carlos, I got the message that she wished not to be called Mrs. Garcia Lopez, and God forbid, Mom, Mutti, or Mother. It was to be Esmeralda or Señora, and nothing else. She barely laid eyes on the baby who was smiling at her with a toothless grin from the little papoose in which he happily hung from my neck. She gestured to a servant to take the child from me. Apparently, my carrying Mario in that manner was not becoming to the status of her son's future wife. I wondered how she would've acted had she known we were already married; I decided to let Fernando deal with his mother.

The servants were directed in staccato-spoken Spanish by their mistress and acted promptly upon the commands fired at them. A middle-aged woman touched me by my left elbow and directed me to follow her. She didn't introduce herself or say anything.

Everything was done through touching, gestures, and pointing. It was almost like being among deaf people; everything was visually orchestrated. Eventually, the woman kept pointing at herself, repeating the word "Valentina"—until I finally caught on that she was trying to tell me her name. I smiled and she smiled back. She chose to call me Señora Doretta. That worked for me, certainly at this very awkward moment in time.

Valentina guided me up the marble staircase and walked ahead of me to open the door to my boudoir. It wasn't just a bedroom, it was indeed a boudoir. It was a very far cry from our apartment in Zürich, our cabin on the freighter, and for that matter, any place I'd ever lived. There simply was no comparison to the glamorous room Esmeralda had created for her one and only son and whoever would be the future mistress of the Garcia Lopez Hacienda. Of course, the latter turned out to be someone totally different from the woman

Esmeralda had envisioned to be bedded in silks and brocades covering the elegant four-poster.

That very first day I learned from my husband that Valentina would probably be my personal maid and would do all unpacking. Mario would be taken care of by Juanita, Valentina's daughter. I was still allowed to breastfeed my baby; but otherwise, I was not to be involved in taking care of the child.

I was encouraged to read and listen endlessly to recordings of conversational Spanish in the hopes that I would learn to communicate in the native language of my new family. In time, a personal Spanish tutor was assigned to me. This was all so different from what I had pictured for myself. Don Carlos and Fernando were my crutches and support in dealing with life during the early days on the hacienda. I couldn't wait to feel Fernando next to me and assuring me of his love.

I wasn't there for quite two weeks when I became more closely acquainted with the Catholic church. "Monsignor Elvillo will take you under his wings and teach you something about our religion. In the process, you will hopefully learn a lot and be able to improve your Spanish," smiled Esmeralda as she introduced me to the impressive gentleman.

"Monsignor Elvillo will guide you in preparation for marriage. My husband and I envision the wedding to take place in July during the height of the social season. Fernando is our only child, and we expect our son to be properly married and recognized as such by his peers in Santiago society. There's nothing that I can do about your son being born out of wedlock. We'll discuss certain options with the Monsignor." She turned away from me, not even giving me a chance to respond.

I couldn't wait to be alone with Fernando. "Your mother treats me worse than a leper. She positively hates me. And our child, he's being reared by servants; all I'm good for is to feed the boy. This is not what I expected. You need to speak on my behalf; I want to play a much greater role in the raising of our son. And if you won't, I'll simply invade the nursery and take him wherever I feel like taking him. The other thing is our marriage arrangement. Esmeralda is trying to lay guilt trips on me with reference to our bastard son. She didn't say that, but she implied it. I suggest you have a chat with Monsignor Elvillo and your parents and set them straight. How do you say? Pronto! They need to know that I am your wife and desire to be treated accordingly."

Fernando knew I was serious. He asked Esmeralda to invite the monsignor for cocktails and dinner in the hope of building bridges between all who were concerned about certain relationships. The informal arrangement met with my approval.

We gathered in the dining room and were formally dressed, at least in my opinion. I quickly had learned what that meant. Don Carlos opened the first bottle of

Dom Perignon, and all were ready to raise their glasses in a toast. I wasn't quite certain what or who we were toasting. I didn't have to wait for too long to get the answer to my question. My husband took charge of the situation. He raised his glass as his vision swept across those who were looking at him.

"Let's start this process all over again. I would like you to meet my wife, Señora Doretta Garcia Lopez. We were married at the city hall in Zürich, Switzerland, on Valentine's Day. And our son, Mario Carlos Garcia Lopez, was conceived in love and is no bastard. I proudly gave him my name the day I married this wonderful woman. My wife will attend your instructional classes. We will bow to the wishes of my mother and have a Catholic wedding at the Basilica of Lourdes and become joined in marriage to please her and her adoring public. As far as the three of us are concerned, we've been a holy family since February 14 of this year. Salute!"

Don Carlos was the first to embrace me. Monsignor Elvillo politely shook my hand. Esmeralda merely glared at me in total shock and disbelief. When Fernando toasted us with "Salute," I quietly said "L'Chaim" under my breath. To say the dinner conversation was subdued or polite would decidedly be an understatement.

# Chapter 18

Esmeralda saw me emerging from the writing room. She looked up at me and smiled. "How's the writing coming along? Are you making any progress? Lately it seems, you've been spending less and less time in seclusion. I like to think that is a good sign toward recovery."

"I'll be frank with you. I just finished recalling my early days at the hacienda and how you and I had a pretty rough start. I'd like to think we've come a long way since those days five years ago. You have no idea how pleased I was with the way you spoke to me after attending the opera. That evening I recognized for the first time that you had learned to like me or to like something about me. Am I correct in that assumption?"

"Indeed you are. We come from different worlds, and our lives took us along totally different paths. I know Don Carlos loved you from the moment he first met you. To me, you were the stranger who had stolen my son. I had such highfalutin plans for him before he left for Europe. Yes, I wanted him to be well educated and become all those things possessive mothers wish for their sons—be famous and wealthy, perhaps enjoy a glamorous career in politics, become a movie star or a race-car driver, marry a woman known in society. You name it.

"Instead, he meets an ordinary German Jewish girl in Switzerland, gets her pregnant, and finally marries her at City Hall. But you know what? It doesn't matter any longer.

"I've seen how much my son loves you and how much you love him and your beautiful children. Today I recognize that the things I wished for our son weren't important to him. He is and, God willing, always will be a wealthy man. His ancestors have seen to that. What he was looking for was a loving wife and companion to share his life. And those are the things he saw and found in you. I want you to know I may not always show it. It's against my nature and the way I was raised, but I've learned to like you and love you. You are very special to my son, and your children adore you and you treasure them. It shows in all that you do. It makes me terribly sad when I realize what you went through as a young girl and the hate and destruction you had to witness and suffer. I hope to God I never have to see you again coming out of one of those nightmares. It broke my heart."

Doretta reached out to Esmeralda and hugged her firmly. Esmeralda was glad for the steadying effect the cane had for her. It was a beginning. There might still be days when Doretta's mother-in-law couldn't help being what she was; perhaps it would never be a loving relationship, but at least they had learned to be civil to one another and to respect each other's role in the family constellation.

"Don Carlos and I couldn't be more pleased with the good news you shared with us last night. Let's plan on going into town and do a shopping spree. I want you to have some attractive things to wear when you begin to show. Men don't think those things are important. I do.

"My husband is busy with managing our money, and Fernando loves nothing better than being up to his neck in grapes and juices. When it's not that, then he likes to ride his tractor through the vineyards and make sure the pruning and binding of the grapevines are done correctly. He knows this business inside out and is proud of his heritage. And that's the way it should be. As you have discovered, this is a man's world. We women are left pretty much on our own. We want for little since it's always there. What we do want now and then is some attention and recognition of our own worth."

"I see your point, although I don't feel totally ignored. That may have to do with the difference in our ages. At this point, I don't see myself as neglected. Perhaps as we mature, I might see it your way.

"I like your idea of Juan or Hernando taking us into town and doing some shopping. I've never really been a clothes horse and seem to wear things that I like forever. Since it's more than three years since Alona came along, I would like a few new things. There's obviously no great hurry, but let's plan on it. It will be fun doing it with you since my mom is so far away.

"I'm so glad she got to meet Mario and Alona; they are her only grandchildren. My brothers don't seem to be interested in marriage or having children. They have their share of girlfriends, and mother even refers to some as their paramours; but none seem to be prospective daughters-in-law. Gisela is truly disappointed. Andreas and his wife didn't have any children. So if Mom wants to have grandchildren close to her, she needs to start working on those two sons of hers. They are only two years younger than I. And look at us, we are working on number three. I'm glad Don Carlos and you are all for having grandchildren."

"Not to change the subject, I've subscribed for the upcoming season at the Teatro Municipal de Santiago. Starting in October, there will be at least six operas and some ballet. I'm so pleased that you will want to join me on these evenings. I was lucky if I could persuade Don Carlos once a year. He never cared for anything involving music. Sometimes I wonder if he is tone deaf."

"I'm looking forward to it. Spring will be a nice time to spend evenings in Santiago. If there are any performances by the time I'm close to delivery, you may have to find a friend to accompany you. More likely than not, this baby will be a Christmas present."

"Not to worry, the theater season doesn't extend beyond November. As you discovered last month, the Teatro is very comfortable, and I love our box. It's one of my passions, and I'm pleased that Don Carlos doesn't have a problem indulging me. You realize it's not the Teatro Colon, La Scala, or the Metropolitan Opera, but Santiago does a fine job and brings in some internationally known stars in the world of opera.

"I know you will like it—and I love it that I've found you to share in my pleasure. We'll make a day of it and do a little shopping, enjoy a good meal, and feast our ears and eyes on the operatic productions. Juan or Hernando will make an evening of it as well. While we are at the opera, they find numerous ways of entertaining themselves. On occasion, I've encouraged them to bring their wives along for a city fix."

"That is thoughtful of you. Most people on the staff are very pleasant and accommodating. Lord knows, I've learned to appreciate all the help they've given me with mastering a new language. Talk about patient. Valentina is an absolute saint. Thank you for letting her be my personal maid. Juanita is wonderful with Alona. That child is getting to an age where I would like to spend more time with her. She speaks well in Spanish, but I do not want to neglect her German and English. Fernando is in total agreement with me. He discovered in Switzerland that he should have paid more attention to his English and German teachers in school."

"I do need to apologize to you. In that respect, I was short-sighted by insisting the children learn primarily Spanish. In this day and age, other languages, especially skills in English, should not be neglected. Fernando often makes that clear to his father; he believes greatly in the importance of a global economy and the impact of the English language. So you are right. You've done a wonderful job of teaching Mario, and it shouldn't be different for Alona. Girls need to be able to function in today's world as much as boys. I promise you I won't stand in your way."

"Our men are probably wondering what happened to us. I saw Valentina helping with clearing the breakfast table. I don't really feel like eating much this late in the morning. How about some freshly pressed juices, a croissant, and a good cup of coffee?" said Doretta.

"That sounds just right for me. I've never been one for big breakfasts. Looks like another thing the two of us have in common. Sometimes I wonder how Don Carlos and Fernando can eat all they do. Won't they be surprised to see us walk in arm in arm? With that limp of mine, I do appreciate your support when I'm walking. Thank you, daughter." Those were words Doretta never expected to hear spoken to her by Esmeralda. She couldn't help smiling to herself.

# Chapter 19

AT the end of the day, Fernando was always joyful and whistling a tune. Unlike his father, he thrived on music. Often one could hear his radio in the car blaring away some popular tune and Fernando singing along in karaoke style. He actually had a pretty good voice and could carry a tune. Workers in the grape arbors would hear him from a distance and stop working momentarily to applaud Señor Fernando as he whizzed by. That was all the encouragement he needed to entertain everyone along the way. Sometimes, the audience would yell out one of their favorite tunes of the day. Fernando would turn down the radio and accommodate their requests by singing a capella.

Doretta could hear him as soon as he drove into the courtyard. She rushed out to greet him, wanting to share with him her good news. "I had a wonderful day. I called Mom and Andreas, and we spoke for a few minutes. They were delighted to hear what I had to say and wished us well. Their return flight was even more comfortable, and they kept saying over and over how thankful they were to you and Papa for making their pleasant travels possible. Mom is, of course, sad that she won't be with us when the baby is born. When I told her, more likely than not, it would be a Christmas present, she started to cry.

"More good news is that I had a meaningful exchange with your mother. I had written for a couple of hours when she watched me escape from my cocoon. She inquired how my writing was going, and I shared with her that I had reached the point in my writing where she and I first met. I let her know that I believed we had come a long way in the past five years. The resulting conversation was nothing but delightful and positive. I thought I wasn't hearing correctly when she called me "daughter"—something I never dreamt of hearing your mother say to me.

"Having a more amicable relationship with Esmeralda will make my life around the hacienda a lot easier and pleasant. For five years I always felt I was walking on hot coals. Often you didn't realize what my daily trials and tribulations were; you left early in the morning, put on your blinders, and became immersed in your work and your business. When you came home at night tired, you didn't want to hear of the way my day had gone. And I could understand how you saw things. This will make all the difference in the world."

"I'm truly sorry I wasn't fully aware of how you felt. I'll try my best to rectify that situation," was all Fernando was capable of offering in reponse as Doretta continued.

"How often I wished I could go away with you and work in the grape arbors. The few times I did, I truly enjoyed doing it and loved being tired from having done something productive. Mental pressure can often be more tiring than hard physical labor. Now that you succeeded in getting me pregnant again I will be on my best behavior and not plague you with my silly wishes and desires. I'll be the good wife and stay home with mother." Fernando laughed one of his freeing laughs and hugged her.

"When you are in your second trimester, I'll take you with me for a day or two each week. I don't expect you to be physically involved, but it would be good for you to be out and about in the fresh air and get to know some of the people with whom I deal every day. They often ask how señora is doing. Some comment on how much they enjoyed having you work with them side by side.

"I assured them that they will have that opportunity again after you have our third child. They are all looking forward to Christmas. The gals were tickled when I told them how much you and Mario enjoyed the story I told about the Wind Angels. Should the occasion arise in future years, I'll make darn sure that you and the children will experience it. It truly is a sight to behold. If it does happen, it will be more likely in April or May. Those are the months when we might get an early and unexpected frost. When it does happen, it can be scary and costly to our business, but the rescue effort by the Wind Angels is worth the risk. I know you will love it.

"Next time you come out to the vineyards, I'll show you the shed where the ladies carefully store their beautiful wings. There must be at least two hundred of them to accommodate the ninety plus women who work in the arbors. The wings are suspended from heavy oak beams mounted on the ceiling, and each wing is separated from its neighbor. They want to make sure they are always dry and not subject to moisture that would cause rotting. Being made of pure silk, allows for the strength of the lightweight wings."

"That sounds exciting. I can't wait to go out there with you.

There's so much to see and so much to learn. One thing I want to be sure to do again, sometime in late February or March, is to be part of the Grape Harvest Wine Festival. And I would like us to participate in it as a family. I know Mario would have much fun. I can't believe that boy will be six next year."

"Have you started your German and English lessons with Alona? I'm so pleased to hear that Mother has finally seen her way in accepting the importance of our children learning languages other than Spanish. This is especially true as far as your family is concerned. I wouldn't have any problem sending our children to Europe, and particularly to German-speaking countries, if this is where they would like to study. My years in Switzerland certainly allowed me to see the world from different perspectives. Of course, the biggest bonus of that education was meeting you."

"That's sweet of you to confess. Truthful? The thought never crossed my mind to spend the rest of my days in Chile when that handsome dog stepped up to that desk in the Zürich public library."

"Am I still that handsome dog, young lady?"

"Well, come up and see me sometime; let me check you out in my boudoir."

They walked up to their quarters holding hands. Don Carlos and Esmeralda were watching them as they ascended the stairway.

"I'm so proud of our son and Doretta. Just think, another grandchild. I'm hoping for another boy. Don't get me wrong, Alona will be a beautiful girl and a little sister might be fun for her too. Actually, the girls would be closer in age. Well, whatever. We'll take whatever may come," said Esmeralda.

"I'm pleased to hear you talking that way about our

children. I often wondered why you couldn't bring yourself to love that girl. She's certainly made our son's life complete. He seems to be thriving. Who cares if she's German? It doesn't even hurt my feelings that she's got some Jewish blood in her. Who knows what's in ours? None of us are purebloods. Personally, having grown up with animal husbandry, I'm a great believer in mixing up the bloodlines. It makes for healthier people."

"Oh, you with your breeding philosophies. Let me tell you what endeared her to me. The way she reacted to *Tosca* that night, I knew she had a soul. It was almost like a spark that made me look at her differently from the moment I saw her reaction to the tragic plot. Now I understand why she has these terrible nightmares. For a girl that age to see her father practically beaten to death must be almost indelibly branded in her mind. It's those images that one never completely forgets. We've been so fortunate never to have experienced anything remotely like it, and I pray to God every day we never will."

Don Carlos reached for his wife's hand. "You keep praying. I'm glad you gain your strength from your faith. Sometimes I wonder if our fervent wishes reach the man upstairs. Perhaps he's gotten old and doesn't always hear us."

"Don Carlos! That is blasphemous! Don't ever say such things to Monsignor Elvillo. He had a hard enough time swallowing our son's outburst five years ago. I did a lot of praying and talking to him to perform their marriage properly. He finally came around when he realized how sincere Doretta was about the whole thing. It sure wasn't easy for that girl. As far as religion is concerned, she must be all confused. Between her mixed-up experiences in Judaism and Protestantism and now

Catholicism, she must often wonder to whom she is praying or who is interceding for her."

"That's your domain. You know that I'm an atheist deep in my heart. I've lived too long and have seen too many ugly things happening in this world for me to believe that there is a loving Almighty up there somewhere who permits all of these horrible events to be visited on mankind. End of sermon."

"Well, my dear, atheist or not, I shall continue to pray for you and all whom I love. It may not help you, but it gives me peace of mind."

Fernando had seen his folks sitting in the parlor downstairs as he glanced over his right shoulder on his way up the stairs. "I wonder what they are thinking or even talking about?" said he.

"Your father is probably wondering where to invest his next million to make a few more, and your mother is certainly talking about the discussion she had with me. All I know is that I'm relieved to have the air cleared and to be on a better footing with your mom. I've never lived so closely with anyone before where I thought I was so strongly despised. I recognize we are very different and had totally different backgrounds and upbringings; nevertheless, it was hard for me to swallow that intense dislike shown to me. Enough of that. It's over and done with—and that is very good." Doretta reached for his belt and unbuckled it, letting it drop to the floor; and ever so slowly, she unbuttoned the fly of his jeans.

"What have I got here?" He reached for his gaucho hat and landed it with a perfect toss on the top of his coatrack.

He pulled his grape-juice-stained plaid shirt off his torso as Doretta slipped down his blue jeans and skivvies.

"Don't be afraid. You won't harm what I carry inside of me. Remember our lovemaking when I carried Mario or Alona didn't do any harm to those two. They turned out just fine. There will come a time again when you cannot have me any longer the way you prefer to love me; but as we've discovered, there are other ways for us to please each other. We've had a little practice in this, haven't we?"

"You are wicked! I've told you this before, but I love it when you want me, dirty jeans, shirt, and odoriferous all wrapped up in one."

"I love the whole package. And what's so much fun is the unwrapping. You don't stink, and your body isn't dirty. You just smell like my man, and I love it. Having you like this at this very moment is what I want and what I need. So take me, and make me feel like a woman."

Fernando carried her to their bed and entered her immediately; he was fully aware that she didn't need to be foreplayed. She was ready to have him with abundance. When they found their release, they slept for a good hour in each other's arms.

It was about six o'clock when there was a loud knock on the door. Everyone in the house knew their bedroom was off limits. Valentina knew when she could make the bed or turn it down, but never would she have come anywhere near the boudoir when its doors were closed.

"Who is it?" boomed Fernando's voice.

"It's me, Mario. I wanted to surprise you just this once. I got a package from Nana in Germany. Can I open it?" Doretta slipped on a silk robe.

"Go get in the shower. Don't be too harsh on the boy. I'm

happy he is so excited about a package from his grandmother in Germany. He's just a little boy. Try to think back to when you were five years old. Did you ever get excited?"

"Yeah, when I walked in on Don Carlos making love to Esmeralda."

"You are bad. I want to hear more about this one later." She tightened the sash on her robe and walked over to the door. As she opened it, she smiled at Mario.

"Let's take it downstairs. I think your sister might enjoy opening the package with you. I'm sure there's something for both of you inside."

"How come? It's addressed to Señor Mario Garcia Lopez. That's me. It doesn't say anything about Alona."

"Well, we shall see about this." Mario carried the package proudly to the playroom where Juanita was reading from a book to Alona.

"Come sit on Mutti's lap. *Wir haben ein Paket von Nana in Deutschland.* [We have a package from Nana in Germany.] With Doretta's help, the package was opened at last. She could tell by the shape that several gifts were books. There were *Grimms Märchen* and *Der Struwwelpeter* for Mario. *Alice in Wonderland* was for Alona, with lots of German cookies and marzipan and a card addressed to Mario and Alona written in German. Doretta translated:

Dear Alona, Dear Mario,

It was so nice being with you. I hope the books Andreas and I selected will be to your liking. Mutti will have to help with the translations at first. In time you will read and write good German and English and learn to like the stories most German girls and boys love as they grow up. The cookies and marzipan are for you to share with your Papa, Mutti, Oma, and Opa. You all have a wonderful time now.

Much love,

Oma Gisela; Andreas sends his hugs and kisses!

"You two, these are great stories. I promise I'll spend a few hours with the two of you starting in a week. I have a little project of my own I need to finish. Next time Oma Gisela and Andreas come to visit, you'll be able to converse with them in German. They'll be so proud of you, and so will we, all of us grown-ups around you. The other thing we'll start tonight is a reading of one of the tales before you go off to sleep. Maybe some night Daddy can read for you, too. Won't that be fun?"

"Yeah, Mom."

"Now, be good and let Juanita give you your supper. I'll see you before you go off to sleep." She rushed up the stairway and closed the bedroom door tightly.

"It's my turn at that shower. I'll be out in five. I don't want to keep your folks waiting again. The children loved what Mother sent. You'll get to read to them here and there at night. I know you will remember some of the *Grimms Märchen* and *Der Struwwelpeter*—the latter is especially funny and yet very poignant and full of great messages for growing boys and girls. I'm so glad Mom thought of sending them books."

She enjoyed the luxury of the shower and made it a real quick one. A silk jumpsuit did the trick for dinner tonight.

Doretta recalled Esmeralda saying they were going to be casual for a change. They were welcomed with a laugh from Don Carlos.

"Just under the wire. Hope you two had fun." They smiled at each other.

"We did, but then we always do. You know what they say, Dad: Practice makes perfect!" He winked at his dad as he helped Doretta with her chair.

Dinner was a delight. The table conversation centered on the grandchildren and the excitement of sharing with them the tales grandma Gisela sent from Germany. Don Carlos pulled out his pocket watch.

"If you want to read to those children, as promised, you better get a move on. It's close to the time when Juanita turns off their lights. I've gotten there too late a couple of times. Maybe for nights to come, you should have story time before you come to dinner. That may not be quite the pre-dinner fun you two seem to enjoy, but you always have your nights together. It's your choice. We certainly don't mind eating at eight instead of at seven-thirty, right Esmeralda?"

"Oh, absolutely," said she.

Fernando charged for Mario's room, and Doretta walked into Alona's. Alona looked like she was almost ready to meet the sandman. Doretta opened *Alice in Wonderland* and pointed at some of the beautiful, colorful illustrations in the book. Perhaps five or six pictures later, Alona had succumbed to sleep. Doretta kissed her goodnight and made sure all covers were firmly in place. She said a quick prayer and then walked over to join Fernando doing his thing with Mario.

Mario had chosen the story of *Hänsel and Gretel*. It was one of his all-time favorites. He knew it pretty much by heart. There were certain parts he always wished to discuss with whoever the reader was.

"Daddy, I'm glad you are rich and don't have to send my sister and me off into those dangerous woods looking for food. I like being rich and never want to be poor. Just think about being kept by that ugly witch fattening those kids and then roasting them for Sunday dinner in an oven. That must have been a pretty big oven."

"I'm glad to know you think we are rich. And no, Mommy and I will never send you into the woods to gather food for us. But you see, Daddy is rich, as you say, because I work hard in the vineyards. The reason they are doing so well is because Papa Don Carlos and his Papa worked very hard and made something of the place, and they handed it down to me. Do you understand what I'm telling you?"

"Yes, Daddy. Grandpa Don Carlos explained inheritance to me."

"Now you got me; I knew you were smart but not that smart. Why am I reading *Hänsel and Gretel* to you? I should borrow Grandpa's *Wall Street Journal*."

"Oh, no Daddy. He talks about that all the time. Those stories are boring. I like what the kids did to the witch. That sounded like fun."

"Well, the next story I'll read to you is about *Die Heinzelmänn-chen* [*The Elves of Cologne*]. I know you'll like it."

"Daddy, why do you work so much? You've got all that money in the bank. Why don't you just spend some of it? It's fun to buy presents."

"The reason I work so many hours in the grape arbors is so that someday I can pass all of this on to you and your brothers and sisters. Mommy tried to tell you the other day that by Christmas you will have a brother or another sister. That baby is growing in her tummy right now. When you are a little older, Mommy and I will explain how all this happens. Deal?

"Deal."

"Mommy and I will kiss you goodnight, and then it's off to slumberland for you. You want to be bright-eyed and bushy-tailed for your tutor in the morning."

Doretta laid her hand on Mario's forehead and then kissed him. She closed her eyes and began to sing the evening prayer from Engelbert Humperdinck's opera *Hänsel and Gretel* in German. Fernando hugged his wife with all that was in him. The scene touched him to the core, and tears were streaming down his handsome face.

# Chapter 20

THEY were behind closed doors. Fernando still dealt with the touching scene he observed between his son and the boy's mother. Mario hardly had heard any part of it before he fell asleep. Fernando was very much moved, especially when Doretta translated the meaning of the prayer to him.

"I had never heard that before. That melody and the words just tore into my gut. I'm not even sure if I want to share with you my "tale of surprise" I alluded to earlier when Mario paid us his unannounced visit after you and I made love."

"It can't be that *risqué?*"

"Well, parts of the story would fall into that category; and part of it is very sad and you haven't heard about it. It's hardly ever discussed around the table any longer. The risqué part is funny."

"Now, don't be shy. I'm a grown woman and have been around the block a few times."

"I was thirteen and beginning to discover the wonders of sex. At school I had gotten nothing but straight A's that spring.

When I came home with my super report card, I couldn't wait to brag about it with Mom and Dad. I ran up to their bedroom and stormed in without even knocking."

"Your son at least knew how to knock first."

"He's five and I was thirteen. Here stood my dad in all of his manly glory before me— stark naked. Mother was on her knees about to give him the royal treatment. What was so shocking to me was that mother was naked as well and more than eight months pregnant. You've never seen anyone back out of a room as quickly as did I. I had to stuff a fist in my mouth not wanting them to hear me laugh out loud."

"That is funny and not so funny. We better learn to lock our bedroom door in November and December," was Doretta's assessment of the situation.

"But now to the really sad part. Esmeralda gave birth to my brother Alphonso a month later. He became terribly ill within six months after birth. I believe it was meningitis. They lost him and were devastated. Esmeralda became pregnant several more times but never again carried a child to full term. The many miscarriages took the starch out of her. Perhaps now you understand their desire for us to have more than two children. The loss of that boy has always been in the back of her mind as she sent me off into the big wide world. We could not have made them happier the other night when we announced the impending birth of another grandchild."

"Now I really feel a strong bond to your mother. Why didn't she ever confide in me? Talking about such things often helps to deal with your inner turmoil. Why do you think I'm putting my thoughts on paper? To free my conscience—not to write the epic of the century."

"I realize Mom comes across as haughty and standoffish. It's her defense mechanism. Basically, she is a very warm person. My parents have a wonderful marriage these days and adore each other. Okay, father sometimes makes his cracks; but he wouldn't know what to do without her. Neither would she without him being around."

"Well, my dear, let's try our very best to make them as happy as we possibly can. I'm game to give them as many heirs as possible—within reason. I am thirty-six years old. I suppose it's not just for the having but the trying that matters."

As Fernando reclined on his pillow and closed his eyes, Doretta hummed the melody of Humperdinck's prayer. He was soundly asleep in seconds and softly snoring, leaving Doretta smiling at her sleeping prince.

# Chapter 21

DORETTA arose early, having the need to continue her story. She made certain the door to the office was closed tightly before she began typing.

My first lesson in Catholicism came two weeks later. Hernando, Don Carlos's personal chauffeur, drove me to the parsonage of Monsignor Elvillo on the outskirts of Santiago. Hernando was instructed to wait for me until I emerged from my first encounter with the Monsignor—no matter how long a wait it might be. I had no idea what to expect since I had met the man under most unpleasant and challenging circumstances.

I rang a bell at the entrance which announced my arrival. A young man in a white tunic over a black cassock greeted me and ushered me in. He walked ahead of me saying nothing except his initial "follow me." He knocked at an impressively carved door and pushed it open after being told to enter. Monsignor Elvillo merely rose briefly off his chair and nodded in my direction, indicating for me to take a seat in the chair across from his desk. Once I was seated, the young man backed out of the room, which appeared to be a library filled with thousands of books.

"I'm pleased to see that you consented to take instructions in Catholicism under my tutelage. After that confrontation with your husband, I wasn't certain you would go through with it since you obviously do not need the church's blessings to live legally with young Garcia Lopez. It is highly unusual for Jewish persons to convert to Catholicism."

"Actually, I wasn't aware I was converting; I understood that I would receive certain instructions prior to receiving the blessing of our marriage from the Catholic church."

"That is a misconception on your part. If you wish for me to perform a marriage ceremony in our church, you must first be baptized into the Catholic faith and accept its doctrines and live accordingly. It is my understanding that your children are to be raised and educated in our faith, is this correct?"

"I assume this to be the case if this is what Señora Esmeralda Garcia Lopez suggested I do."

"That is indeed the case. You and I shall have four meetings during which I will familiarize you with Catholic doctrine. At the conclusion of this indoctrination, I propose that you be formally baptized into the Christian faith, specifically into the Catholic faith. Being baptized in our faith means that you shall renounce your adherence to Judaism. Do you understand what I am explaining to you?"

"Yes, I do."

"If this is convenient for you, I can meet with you twice each week during the next two weeks, and we could schedule the marriage ceremony to be held on a Saturday three weeks from now. I will perform your baptism at the Basilica of Lourdes during the ten o'clock mass on the Sunday before your wedding."

"I believe the arrangement would suit Señora Esmeralda for sure. She wishes for us to be married with the church's blessings as soon as possible. Unfortunately, she views us as living in sin and not wanting to recognize our civil Suisse marriage as binding and legal. Of course, you must know this is not true."

"That is true in the eyes of the church and those of Señora Esmeralda but not as far as the State is concerned. After looking over your documents, I must concur with your husband that you are indeed married. Señora Garcia Lopez is a devout Catholic and a staunch supporter of our diocese. It is for this reason I agreed to perform this highly unusual ceremony. I believe our meeting today is concluded. I will see you in three days for your first indoctrination."

This time, he got up and walked around his desk and extended his hand. I shook it and nodded in agreement. With the ring of a tiny brass bell, the young man who had greeted me was summoned to escort me out of the parsonage. I was glad to see Hernando waiting for me.

Being a professional chauffeur, he was not inclined to ask any questions, and neither did I volunteer anything that had transpired during my meeting with Monsignor Elvillo. Hernando was my trusted driver for the next four scheduled meetings. Among many other issues bothering me, I had a difficult time accepting that the Pope is God's direct representative on earth. But if I wanted to live a peaceful life on the Garcia Lopez Hacienda, I had to abide by the rules and doctrines of Catholicism. As promised, I was baptized at the Basilica of Lourdes in front of my entire family—servants and all.

The wedding was scheduled at eleven o'clock for August 10, 1963. Esmeralda insisted on my wearing her wedding gown, which needed to be altered to fit my considerably taller figure. The creamy dress had slightly darkened with age, which did not particularly bother me or Esmeralda. Under the circumstances, a pure white dress would have been deemed inappropriate. The top layer of the dress was lace that had been tatted in a cloister in Seville. I was thankful that the wedding took place in late winter; I would have died under the weight of it all during any other time of the year. I wore a simple veil under a crown of white orchids and carried a simple bouquet of calla lilies. Fernando, of course, was in white tie and tails. All in the family were elegantly attired for the affair. We were glad when the ceremony and photo sessions were finally over.

Fernando and I were prepared for the traditional pelting with rice and confetti. Not so at this affair. As the portals of the Basilica parted, there were cheers from the crowd and even the Monsignor. What was even more startling was the cordon of all one hundred Wind Angels decked out in their wings, which were gently moving in the breeze; at Fernando's instruction, they were humming the prayer from Humperdinck's *Hänsel and Gretel*. There wasn't a dry eye in the crowd. No one had ever heard or seen anything more beautiful. Even Esmeralda was moved to tears; she probably was the only other person, besides me, who was familiar with the haunting melody.

No expense was spared for the celebration at the estate. Food and drink were of the finest anyone could imagine. Sedate music was presented by a string quartet during the dining experience, and a dance band took over at ten o'clock. In the end, nothing could top the performance by the Wind Angels. It would always remain the highlight of my experience with Catholicism.

# Chapter 22

DORETTA awoke. Her husband was long gone. There were pressing matters at the winery that needed Fernando's attention. Don Carlos accompanied his son on this chilly July morning, having the need to keep a hand in the business. He was always pleased to reconnect with many of the men and women who had labored for years in the vineyards of his family. He loved it when the children of the vineyards' crew rushed up to him, wanting to shake his hand or even be picked up by him to receive a generous hug.

Walking into the processing plant, Don Carlos turned to his son. "It looks like you are getting ready to test and bottle the 1966 vintage. I like the new stainless steel vats you've installed. Son, I'm truly impressed by the cleanliness you've brought about with the modern equipment. I see from the books that you've hired twenty more men to work in the winery. It shows. I'm particularly pleased with the new label you've created. It ought to do well in the U.S. market."

"Thanks for the kudos, Dad. It's a lot of hard work, but

I enjoy what we are doing these days. By the way, I commissioned cooper Antonius to deliver thirty new and some previously used oak barrels. They will be a much-needed expansion in our wine-processing arsenal."

"You do as you see necessary. I've got complete trust in your abilities. They taught you well in Europe. I hope you don't mind, I need to sit down someplace. My legs aren't used to standing and walking this much anymore. Your mother is correct when she often tells me to get off my duff and get some exercise. But don't forget, I'm past that seventieth mark. The old man isn't what he used to be."

"Go sit in my office. I'll have one of the guys set up a little tasting for you.  Share with me what you think."

Perino, one of Fernando's trusted associates in the business, set up six long-stem glasses in front of Don Carlos. "Buenos dias, señor."

"Buenos dias, Perino."

"Fernando asked me to have you sample the 1965 vintage of different Cabernets we've created and are about to start shipping. Let us know which you like best. We respect your discriminating taste in wines."

Perino poured the first sample. Don Carlos, who was well versed in the art of wine tasting and its importance, held the glass up toward the light. "Good color." He swirled the glass wanting to inspect its legs. His nose took a healthy whiff of the aroma, which he found pleasing. At last, he looked forward to tasting the wine. His pronouncement said it. "Excelente, exquisito, señor!"

"Gracias, muchas gracias, Señor Don Carlos. But that was just the first one. Try this one next." By the time he lifted the sixth glass toward the light, he was glad he would be chauffeured back to the hacienda. He approved of all of the selections, but was still most enchanted by the first he had tasted.

"Perino, in future presentations, serve numero uno at the conclusion of the event. You should always save the best for last. Now, help me to a WC; I have need to relieve myself. Don't disturb my son, but have Hernando bring the car around to the front, please. It's been an enlightening morning. I'm glad I came, but it is high time for my afternoon nap."

Doretta made her way to the ground level and made a quick peek in the nursery. Alona smiled when she saw her mom checking on her. "Mommy, Mommy, can you show me some more pictures? I like my new book Nana sent from Hermione."

"No, no honey. That's the name of the new young girl Grandma Esmeralda hired for the kitchen. Nana Gisela lives in Germany. That's where I grew up. Someday you'll learn all about it. Is your brother next door with his teacher?"

"Yes, Mommy. He told me he wants to study the *Struwwelpeter*. He said I was too little to understand."

"Maybe you are, and maybe you are not. You are a smart girl; don't let your brother tell you such stories just because he's two years older than you are." *I will need to speak to that boy. He shouldn't be putting her down just because she's a girl.*

"Mommy will see you a little later. I'm about to have breakfast with Nana Esmeralda; she's waiting patiently for me in the dining room. Be a good girl and give me a kiss. Thank you; that feels so much better, Alona," as she walked out of the nursery.

She looked back at the room. *We'll need to get Alona's room fixed up and the nursery updated for the new arrival at holiday time.*

Esmeralda looked up and smiled. "You look pretty this morning. I like it when you take care of yourself."

"I had all the time in the world. I don't know what time Fernando took off, but it was early for sure. I actually put on a little makeup."

"If I'm not mistaken, they left shortly after sunrise, about seven o'clock. Don Carlos went with him. He was curious about all that's happening at the winery. Your husband has made so many changes Don Carlos has never seen. He doesn't very often venture off the hacienda anymore. He's become far too sedentary in the last few years. Ever since you arrived from Switzerland, he's been more than willing to let Fernando grab a hold of the company's reigns."

"It pleases me that Fernando is so happy in his work. That's not always the case when sons are expected to take over a family business. There are often internal conflicts between young and old and even more so when those of the previous generation are regular know-it-alls," said Doretta.

"Oh, I know whereof you speak; I've seen it a few times in my life. As a matter of fact, I'm guilty of such behavior myself. Just think back, how I treated you? I'm truly sorry for all the nasty sticks I placed in your path, and I'm overjoyed that we have found the positive in our relationship."

"Maybe I shouldn't mention this, but Fernando shared with me just recently the sad story of having Alphonso later in life and then losing him so tragically at such a young age. It saddens me greatly that you were never again allowed to have more children. For the first time it sunk in why you were advocating so strongly for us to produce more heirs. May the good Lord be with us and our children."

Esmeralda reached for Doretta's hands. "No need to apologize. I'm glad to be aware that Fernando let you know about the sad experiences Don Carlos and I had. Fernando dealt for years with the facts of this sad chapter in our marriage. Perhaps now you understand why I've acted so protectively toward our son. We, and especially I, wanted to be certain he would marry properly and with our blessings. Obviously, we thought we failed when our son presented us with a fait accompli, announcing that he was marrying a German woman pregnant with his child. You can well imagine my initial reaction.

"All of this has changed. While initially shocked when our son informed us of your civil-service marriage that evening, at the infamous meeting with Monsignor Elvillo, I had to admit to my proper self that we had indeed raised a responsible human being. He did the honorable thing by marrying you when he did and giving our first grandchild a name of which he can be justly proud. As the bard said many moons ago: 'All's well, that ends well!'"

"Thank you for saying it, Esmeralda. My inner hope had always been that one day we would learn to like each other. Strife and discontent are not really in me. Oh, life has taught me to fight for what's right, but I've never been known for my confrontational nature. Knowing what I know today, I can accept and respect your initial attitude toward me. You live in a different world than the world in which I was raised, and I don't mean that in comparing differences in financial security and social status. We are talking hemispheric, cultural, and linguistic cataclysmic differences that needed overcoming. I firmly believe we are on the brink of no longer stepping off insurmountable precipices. I wholeheartedly agree now with Dr. Rodriguez Amado and the importance of venting and talking to one another. We may not always like what we hear, or are even forced to hear, but a good thunderstorm usually clears the air."

"Amen girl," said Esmeralda. "I'm glad Hermione caught my signal when I instructed her to hold the warm dishes for breakfast. There's nothing worse than a cold omelet or chilled eggs over easy. Let's enjoy our fruit plate while they heat the croissants and pour us some fresh coffee. I've so enjoyed this morning and talking with you."

"So have I."

"How's the tummy? I'm so pleased that you're not suffering with morning sickness the way I used to. That's a real blessing."

"I had a couple minor episodes with Mario and none that I recall with Alona. I count my blessings indeed. So far so good with this one. I'm pretty close to the point where I might feel some life. That's always been such a wonderful experience when it first happens."

"How well I remember those days with Fernando and later with Alphonso. It was tragic that we lost him so soon. He was a strapping boy and so healthy. He was the spitting image of his father; we were looking at a photograph of Don Carlos taken in 1897 when he was close to age two. Fernando has a lot of his looks from my side of the family. We have no idea how Alphonso was exposed to meningitis. I still have a hard time dealing with his death." Her eyes had filled with tears. Doretta got up and put her arms around her mother-in-law. Her heart ached for the dear woman and the loss of her son.

# Chapter 23

It was four o'clock on the morning of August 10, 1968. Total darkness enshrouded the Garcia Lopez Hacienda. The incessant ringing of the large bell located in the center court of the mansion awakened those who were still soundly asleep. Fernando and Doretta were the first to jump from their four-poster and ran to see what was happening. The flashing lights of an ambulance approached from the west. Fernando spotted Juan and Hernando standing next to a covered body settled on the ground.

"What's going on? Who's under the blanket?"

"We are sorry to tell you, it's Señor Don Carlos. It was the night watchman who found him. He was barely breathing, and he appeared to be shivering from the cold. He was too heavy to lift for any of us. So we made him as comfortable as we could. It was Adolpho, the watchman, who called the hospital to send an ambulance and then began to ring the bell seeking help."

Fernando got on his knees next to his father. "Dad, can you hear me? It's me, your son." There was no immediate response, but he could feel a gentle pull on the sleeve of his pajama top. The ambulance crew was momentarily on the scene.

"Everyone please step back while we triage the patient." All did but Fernando, wanting to know if his father was still alive. The EMTs carefully removed the blanket from the top of Don Carlos and attempted to listen to his heart. They knew he was alive and exhibited extremely slow and shallow breathing. Within seconds, he was on a gurney and slipped into the ambulance. One of the EMTs gave mouth-to-mouth resuscitation. Don Carlos opened his eyes but could not respond to any verbal demands for answers.

Doretta had helped Esmeralda into a running suit and pulled one of her furs from the closet. She herself was clad in warm slacks, a sweater, and a heavy alpaca ruana. She had torn a heavy jacket from the closet and handed it to Fernando, who drove one of the station wagons and followed the ambulance in hot pursuit. Shortly before five o'clock, Don Carlos was being examined by a team of doctors at the local hospital. The chief of staff addressed the anxious family within minutes.

"Señor Don Carlos suffered a major CVA; that is, a catastrophic stroke to his left side. He shows little comprehension and is unable to respond to any verbal commands. He appears to be severely paralyzed on the impacted side. We will do everything to make him as comfortable as possible. The EMTs medicated him in the ambulance according to their assessment that they were dealing with a stroke patient. However, the impact was of a nature that our prognosis for recovery is extremely guarded. We recommend that next of kin remain on-site until we have done further studies. He will be in room #1 in the ICU. Please have only one visitor at a time stand by him. And please do not interfere with medical personnel attending the patient."

Both Fernando and Doretta took turns consoling Esmeralda. She was the first wanting to be by her husband's side. It was a long night and day. All realized quickly Don Carlos's hours to live were few. He passed away peacefully on the morning of the twelfth of August. He was surrounded by his wife and his only son and family.

Seated in the limousine with her loved ones, Esmeralda touched Doretta. "No need for either of us to rush out and buy black funeral attire. It's always been my favorite color to wear. Perhaps in the back of my mind, I always wanted to be ready for such a sad event. I'll wear one of the heavily laced long creations, and I'm sure you'll be pleased with the one I would like you to wear. With minor alterations by Valentina it will fit you just fine. It is elegantly draped around the waist and will be perfect for my motherly daughter. You are beginning to show a little, as you well know. I'm so sorry Don Carlos didn't live to see this new grandchild born.

"Fernando, for you and the men, there are hundreds of black armbands I stored after Alphonso's funeral. You may want to hand them out to the men to wear at your father's service. I suppose, you'll wear your tails and dad's black silk hat. While we are having the service at home, I want us to make the proper appearance. I just cannot break with my Castilian upbringing."

✕

Señor Don Carlos Garcia Lopez was embalmed and coffined before being transported to the Garcia Lopez Hacienda. His coffin was closed; it was draped in the red, white, and blue national flag and was displayed in the center courtyard of the family mansion. The service was conducted by Monsignor Elvillo. Don Carlos had expressed among his last wishes the service be held among his family and all who labored on the estate rather than at the Basilica. This was the home where he was born; this was the place where his ancestors had labored, loved, and lived for generations. This was the place where he wanted to bid farewell to this world before being laid to rest.

As Monsignor concluded his final words of consolation to the family, the Wind Angels entered from the back of the court-yard and surrounded Don Carlos's coffin. As they gracefully swayed their silken wings, they began humming the haunting prayer from Humperdinck's opera.

Esmeralda held unto Fernando and Doretta's hands; Mario and Alona stood closely between their parents. Their vision swept over all who paid their final respects to their master; most people's eyes shone with love and sadness.

According to his will, his body was taken to the Cementerio General de Santiago where he wished to be buried in his family plot next to his other son, Alphonso. His longtime private chauffeur Hernando had been chosen to drive the hearse carrying Don Carlos to his final resting place. Hundreds stood by the roadside in silence as the funeral procession moved slowly down the long-winding road.

# Chapter 24

Esmeralda was seated in the backseat of the limousine; all were deep in thought reliving in their minds the burial of Don Carlos. He left them all much too soon.

Mario and Alona were giggling, trying to tickle Juan's neck and playfully pulling on wispy curls that escaped from underneath his driver's cap. He went along with the innocent fun these two had teasing him. Only momentarily taking his eyes off the busy road, he winked at the children, encouraging them to continue their silly prank that seemed to distract the all-too-serious adults in the backseat.

"When will Grandpa return from this trip? I thought that was a strange-looking go-cart he was driving. Why was that guy in the funny outfit and pointed hat talking about a long journey home? I hope Grandpa won't be gone too long," said Mario.

Doretta and Esmeralda stared at Fernando. Doretta spoke at last. "This one *you'll* have to explain."

He tapped Mario on the shoulder. "Son, look at us. We are all still crying. Your Grandpa is indeed gone on a very long journey, but it's a journey from which he will not return to us. Your grandfather died. He's in a deep sleep from which he will not awaken. That long box you saw, it's not a go-cart; it's called a coffin. And a coffin is sort of like a fancy bed from which people can't get up. They have to sleep in there forever—and that is a long time."

"Well, if he knew he was gonna be gone for so long, why didn't he kiss me goodbye the way he always did?"

"Oh Son, you're making this very hard for me. Your grandpa took very ill during the night. They took him by ambulance to the hospital. He didn't have a chance to kiss any of us goodbye. God took him by his hand, and he walked away from us to a better place."

"I don't think I like God. That was mean even if he wanted to take Grandpa to a nicer place. I always thought he loved his home and all of us?"

"He did. But now you have to trust your father; he knows best. In a few years when you are older, I'll explain it all to you."

Esmeralda smiled at her son, her eyes brimming with tears. She didn't have to say a word; he read her mind loud and clear. Just then Doretta winced and leaned into Esmeralda. "Put your hand on my tummy. I felt it the first time when we were waiting to hear from the doctors at the hospital. I didn't want to distract anyone. It feels so different. Can you feel it?"

Esmeralda took Fernando's hand and put it next to hers on Doretta's tummy. After a couple minutes he spoke.

"It is different. To me it feels like two heartbeats. Might you be carrying twins?"

"I suppose that is possible since I have twin brothers."

"You better make an appointment with Dr. Rodriguez

Amado; he'll know where to send you. If we are indeed correct with our diagnosis, won't that be fun?"

"I'm not sure about fun, but I will be thankful for all the help I'll have from you." There was a twinkle in her eyes as she looked in Fernando and Esmeralda's eyes. She would be happy with the support she would have from Esmeralda and the servants at her disposal. She still had a difficult time finding herself surrounded by helping hands who were viewed as servants. *I don't think I'll ever get fully used to calling them servants; in my mind that concept died generations ago.*

"I'll be sure to see the doctor right away and put your minds at ease. Don't rush off quite yet and buy beds, buggies, and booties for twins. Let's first make sure the diagnoses by Doctors Garcia Lopez were correct."

The momentary distraction was welcomed by all. There were smiles fleeting across everyone's faces. While Juan was helping the ladies out of the limo, Fernando rushed off to the nearest phone and dialed Dr. Rodriguez Amado's number.

"Dr. Amado's office. How may I help you?"

"It's Fernando Garcia Lopez. On our way home from my dad's funeral today, I learned from my wife that she suspects she is pregnant with twins. I would like her to be seen by the good doctor as soon as possible to put our minds at ease."

"I see that he had a cancellation tomorrow morning at ten. Could you bring her in then to see the doctor?"

"Yes. Put us down for ten. We'll be there for sure. Thank you."

He greeted Doretta with the good news. "I've got a ton of work waiting for me at the winery, but this is more important. I'm taking you into town tomorrow morning to see Doc Amado at ten. I want to hear what he has to tell us."

"Thanks, dear. That's a load off my mind. I had visions of having to wait for an appointment. I'm glad you called; that appointment nurse often gives me a runaround. She claims she cannot understand me. Right now, I'm ready for a nap. It's been a full program since Papa left us. I hope you understand, Esmeralda?"

"Of course, I do. You go and lie down. It will give Fernando and me a chance to talk. There's so much that will need tending to. Go on, dear. You just worry about yourself and the baby— or should I say, babies?"

"Wouldn't that be a surprise?" Doretta whispered as she ascended the staircase. Fernando guided his mother into Don Carlos's office.

"Mom, Dad had everything in very good order. Everything is left to you at this point, and that's the way it should be even though I could ask for my share of the estate right now. I see absolutely no need to press you for anything. I have my trust fund and an excellent income from the estate and believe I'm well compensated for my services to the company.

"Someday, when something happens to you, our children will equally inherit their respective portion of the remaining 50 percent; Doretta and I will be the recipients of the other half of the estate. I see no need to challenge Dad's will and to make the lawyers rich. Does that answer any questions you had?"

"Thank you, Fernando, for being the good son you are. I'm with Doretta. I need to have my rest as well. The service was heartbreaking and the funeral challenging. I'd forgotten how big that cemetery is. I thought the family plot was well taken care of. But now that your father and Alphonso are there, I will make more of an effort to visit regularly. Excuse me, I must rest. Cane or no cane, my hip really bothers me today." She waved the cane in the air as she reached to close her bedroom door behind her. Fernando charged up the marble staircase, anxious to be near his wife. It had been one hell of a day.

# Chapter 25

FERNANDO knew he should have looked in on the children, especially Mario, who seemed utterly disturbed by the death of his grandfather. He would deal with Mario tomorrow. At this very moment, he needed to be close to his wife and she to him.

He was pleased to find Doretta soundly asleep. He undressed quickly, hardly making any sound, and laid down next to her. He couldn't resist placing one of his hands on her abdomen. *I wonder who's in there? Is it another girl? Another boy? One of each? Perhaps even two boys or two girls?*

He marveled at the possibilities. The thought of having twins had never occurred to him, although the possibility of this was obvious. Doretta had those twin brothers, who he, unfortunately, had never met. Fernando was glad Gisela and her new husband had wanted to visit them and his family in his homeland. It was highly unlikely that her brothers would ever consider doing so. That was a mistake he made while they lived in Switzerland. Pondering their situation, he drifted off into sound sleep.

Lying on his back he snored so loud, Doretta thought he

might wake the dead. She finally nudged him gently and got him to turn on his side. "There, there, that's a lot better," as she eased him back to sleep.

She rose and quietly made her way down to Mario's room. "Here you are. Are you enjoying those drawings in the *Struwwelpeter*? I want to talk to you about Grandpa. Do you remember his big dog you liked to play with? He was the big Saint Bernard. He called him Barney, because he loved sleeping in that old barn, the shed, where the wings for the Wind Angels are stored."

"Oh yes, Mommy. I remember. He was so old and could almost not walk anymore. He was always falling over his own paws. Grandpa called the doctor who gave Barney a shot. I thought that might hurt. But he didn't mind and went to sleep. They told me he went to doggy heaven."

"Well, Mario, he didn't go to sleep, he died because Grandpa didn't want him to hurt any longer, and that's why he called for the doctor. And that's kind of what happened with Grandpa. He was hurting a lot, and God didn't want him to be in so much pain anymore. That's why he came during the night and took him to heaven."

"You think maybe Barney was waiting for him?"

"That's a good possibility. You are much too young to understand all of this. Someday you will. I just wanted you to know that God wasn't mean when he took Grandpa away. It was just like with Barney, it was his time to die and go to heaven and not suffer any longer."

"I'm glad they are both in heaven. Where else could they go?"

"We'll save that story for another day, okay? It's time for me to kiss Alona goodnight and then speak with Nana Esmeralda. She's sitting all alone at the dining room table. Be a good boy now, and eat all the vegetables Cook has fixed for you. Don't just eat the hotdogs. Kiss me goodnight. You know how much Veronica likes to spoil you. Be sure to say that you love her."

She kissed him back. "That's a good boy." Doretta peeked into Alona's room, not wanting to surprise or frighten her. She didn't need to fear. Alona was sound asleep; her hand was firmly clutching the copy of *Alice in Wonderland*.

✳

"I just had a good chat with your grandson. I wanted to make sure he understood that God wasn't mean when he took Don Carlos home. I reminded him of what happened with Barney last year. He did remember the dog and what the vet had to do."

"That was a good idea. It has to be hard for someone so young to digest what happens when we get old. They are so full of life that a concept of permanent sleep would be difficult to accept. Thank you for doing that. I could tell in the car that he was challenged by his grandfather's untimely death. Telling him only that he was too young to understand wasn't good enough. Barney was a good analogy. I can see him accepting that since he was with us when the vet put the dog to sleep. Don Carlos wanted him to witness Barney's end of life. Makes me wonder if he had some premonition?

"Well, my dear. Let's talk about life and something more pleasant. Do you really believe that there might be a pair inside of you?"

"I'll find out soon enough. I was pleased that Fernando got

ahold of Dr. Rodriguez Amado and can't wait to hear what he has to say when we see him in the morning. Fernando was sound asleep when I woke up and sneaked out of the room, not wanting to disturb him. Sleep was good for all of us. I presume he'll join us for dinner when he wakes from his nap."

Esmeralda smiled. "Speak of the devil; he's awakened. Give me a kiss before you sit down. You'll have to do double duty in the kissing department now that your father is gone. But you don't mind; you never have. We raised you to be a loving person." Fernando kissed his mother on the forehead and touched her beautiful hair lightly.

"Thank you, that was a loving touch. I needed that tonight.

"I cannot tell you how grateful I was for both of you to have been with me today. I'm not sure how I would have gotten through a day like this had you not been there."

"We are with you on that. I know we've talked sometime about living in a modern high rise in the heart of the city. That would have been fine when we were younger and it was just the two of us. No way would I want to trade what we have here for a place in Santiago. I love the hacienda and all who live here with us. Let's face it, it is one big family. I don't view any of those people as our servants; to me, they are more like an extension of our family," said Doretta.

"Those are attitudes I had to acquire. It took me a long time to feel that way, but the older I get and the more I rely on their daily effusion of kindness, the more I've learned to see them as friends rather than servants. I absolutely agree with you, Doretta. They are part of our family."

Fernando fixed himself a Manhattan up and offered one to his mother. "No thank you, Son. I'll just sample a glass of our own Cabernet. I believe it's vintage 1965, a good year. You are being sensible and are having freshly pressed juice, Doretta. Good girl. Salute." She raised her glass in a toast to the next generation. Doretta decided not to be shy: "L'Chaim!" [To life] she responded to Esmeralda's toast.

# Chapter 26

"GOOD to see you, young lady. You look like the picture of health. Why don't you undress behind the screen and slip on one of these fashionable gowns we provide free of charge," was Dr. Amado's comment.

"You are full of wisdom this morning, Dr. Rodriguez Amado. I believe fashionable and free of charge are oxymorons. I suppose next you'll inquire how my epic novel of the century is coming along."

"I didn't want to bring it up, but Fernando shared with me that you seem to be convinced that the process helped. I was very pleased to learn that you haven't had any of your terrible nightmares lately. In all seriousness, how far are you in your writing? Have you stayed away from books, magazines, movies, discussions, and so forth that deal with the era in your life that troubled you as much as it did?"

"I'm at the point where I arrived in Chile and worked through my initial confrontations with Esmeralda, getting to know the language and the people, converting to Catholicism, and getting pregnant with my second child. It certainly was a time of many positive and negative impressions bombarding me daily. Sometimes I wondered if I made a mistake marrying Fernando and entering his world, which was totally different from what I was used to. It wasn't just different, it was downright alien toward me. Today I can honestly say I have no regrets and have found happiness in the New World."

"That sounds very encouraging. I'm glad you took my advice and stayed away from counseling. You helped yourself; that's all that matters. I have no problem with counseling; however, in your case I was convinced that you would be able to work through your issues on your own. I believed you needed to find yourself. It also looks like you and Fernando are getting along fine. Now that I talked you into being completely relaxed, let me take a closer look at the latest developments. You look in great shape for being more than five months pregnant."

He examined her with his well-known gentle touch and then listened to the baby's heartbeat. When some noticeable kicking commenced in Doretta's abdomen, he sort of backed away to get a better look at the activity.

"I hope you won't be too upset if I confirm your diagnosis. You were correct in your assumption. You will be delivering a set of twins in December. From what you told me, it should be very close to Christmas. My wife and I often travel that time of year; however, this December is an exception, and I will be around to deliver these two precious bundles."

"Would you call in Fernando and let him in on your assessment of the situation. You can't tell what they might be? Or can you?"

"From the activities I've observed and the strength of the heartbeats, my first inclination would be to say we are looking at two males. That is as far out on a limb I'm willing to go. I could arrange for an ultrasound examination at the University Clinic, if this is what you would want."

"I won't make that decision; I'll leave it up to Fernando. Why don't you bring him into this conversation. Is it okay for me to get dressed? I know you are enchanted with this gown, but it's not quite my interpretation of a Christian Dior."

"Oh, come on now. Humor me; I particularly find the rear view very seductive." He laughed out loud as he went to get Fernando from the waiting room.

"Come in Fernando. Your wife is full of good news."

"Well, were we right, is it double trouble or not?" laughed Fernando.

"I'm not sure about double trouble, but there are twins for sure. I'm speculating it's a set of boys, but that's just a hunch based on the strength of the heartbeats and the kicking activities. As I told Doretta, I could send her into the city and have an ultrasound done at the University Clinic if this is what you want. Just let me know, and I'll set it up for you."

"What do you think, Doretta? Are you that nosy, or would you like all of us to be surprised? Personally, I like the idea of speculating what the outcome might be; there are at least three possibilities: two boys, two girls, or one of each. Shall we have a betting pool? That might be fun for the staff."

"You are impossible, but since you are asking me for my consent, I like the idea of a mystery and a surprise. Let's wait and see until they decide to emerge. At least now we know that we need to be prepared for two new members in the Garcia Lopez constellation. Thank you Dr. Rodriguez Amado."

"We've known each other for many years; why don't we skip the doctor bid and make it Diego."

"Thanks, Diego. That's less of a mouthful, especially for

me," replied Doretta. "I had to get used to being called Señora Doretta Garcia Lopez. I always thought we got carried away with long handles in Germany, but this beats them all."

"I would like to see you on a monthly basis until the time of your delivery. Please set up your appointments with my secretary before you leave. Of course, if there are any signs of complications, call me immediately any time of day. As I said earlier, you are in great shape. Keep up the good work." He gave her a quick hug before he shook hands with Fernando.

"Good work, Nando." He slapped his back firmly. "Sorry about your dad; he would have loved to be around for the coming attraction. I guess it was his time. Again, I'm so sorry you lost him."

"Thanks, Diego. You missed a great service. But I understand. Baby deliveries don't wait for anything or anyone. That's the way it goes sometimes in life. It's a coming and a going!"

⚶

Fernando helped Doretta into the car. "Be sure to always wear your seatbelt now that you have such precious cargo on board."

"Don't worry, I always do. While I never worry when you, Juan, or Hernando are driving, one never knows what the other drivers can cause. The traffic in the city has gotten so much worse.

"Remember, your mother and I are going into the city sometime next week. It's the first opera of the season. She's so excited about it. It will be good for her to look forward to something she truly enjoys. She's already made all sorts of plans."

"That's good. You two should make a day of it."

"Her first stop is planned for Falabella's, where she insists on buying some more attractive maternity clothes for me, including an evening dress for the opera. She's made standing reservations for a perfect dinner table for two at Confitería Torres for all six events, and she's assured me I didn't have to worry about missing anything because of the upcoming attraction. The opera season will be over by the middle of November."

"I can't tell you how happy I was the way things turned out at the last opera visit," said Fernando.

"I agree. I don't know how things would be today if it hadn't been for that serendipitous discovery of our mutual love for opera. It was like magic how differently she treated me from that moment on. It's not your cup of tea, but I'm so thankful that your mother and I found each other at last. I'm not sure what the opera will be next week. Somehow I recall it to be *Madama Butterfly*. I have a good recording of it and should listen to it again before we see it."

"I know some of that music and love to listen to you when you hum it or sing it sometimes. Speaking of humming, I still cannot get the image of the humming Wind Angels at our wedding and at Dad's service out of my eyes and ears. I thought it was an unforgettable experience. I mentioned to Diego that it was too bad he had to miss Dad's service. He told me he had an emergency call that morning.

"Well, I hope you and Mom have a wonderful day in the city. I may quit early that day and have some of my buddies over for a session of poker in memory of Dad. That's what he and I did most of the time when Mom took off for Santiago and the Teatro de Municipal."

# Chapter 27

*I don't know when I will find time to write once the twins are born. One thing is for sure, I won't have a nursemaid and, with two of them, they'll probably have me nursing around the clock. Thank goodness, Alona is long beyond that and enjoys eating anything Verona prepares for her.*

Fernando and I enjoyed the evenings and nights we had together. Mario loved being around his father who spoiled him every opportunity he had. Esmeralda wasn't much better. I was glad to be able to spend as much time with my growing boy as I did. That probably would not have happened in Europe if I had returned to a position with Schrift & Schreiber in Zürich. Having access to help and lack of financial worries made life definitely much more pleasant. I thanked my lucky stars whenever I took the time to pray, not always knowing if I should pray to the God of Abraham, Mother Mary, or to the God of Martin Luther.

Looking back, I was thankful that Esmeralda insisted on hiring a tutor for me after I was in the country for a few months. She and Don Carlos spoke neither German nor English and found it challenging to have me around. My early attempts at Spanish were pathetic and challenging for someone as sophisticated and educated as my mother-in-law who spoke flawless Spanish.

I had lessons five days a week for two hours each day. Once we were past the elementary levels of communicating, my tutor took me for drives into the city. He insisted I try my skills shopping in department or grocery stores, ordering in restaurants, talking with children at a kindergarten—all sorts of everyday scenarios that made the use of the foreign tongue so much more practical as well as fun.

When I declared that I was pregnant in late 1964, Esmeralda had the unadulterated nerve to speculate on who the father might be. Of course, my husband knew that it was no one else but he. While my tutor was a very attractive, charming, and young Latin, the thought had never crossed either of our minds to make it more than it was. While the three of us had lots of laughs over the matter, Esmeralda showed no signs of letting it go until one day when her son had a serious conversation with her.

"Mother, you and I need to have a talk. I'm quite aware of your opinions of my wife. We've had this conversation before. Renaldo is doing a great job of teaching Doretta; and by your own admissions, she's come a long way in communicating with you, Dad, the staff, and especially with Mario. While she is very much concerned that the boy learns German and English, she enjoys bantering with him in Spanish.

"As far as your suspicions go, you have nothing to worry about. Doretta and I have a very good rapport in bed, and you have nothing to fear from Renaldo. There's absolutely no doubt in my mind that I'm the father of this child. I had no intentions of telling you this because I happen to know how you feel about such matters; but when Renaldo first started working with Doretta, he shared with me that he has no interest in the opposite sex. He's very much in love with his partner who shares his apartment in Santiago. Now, does that make you feel better?"

Esmeralda just stood there her mouth agape. When Alona was born a few months later, there was no question she was our child; as a matter of fact, the resemblance to Esmeralda in baby pictures was startling and uncanny.

I had been assured by Diego that my delivery probably would be easier with a second birth; that turned out to be not quite true. As easy a time as I had with Mario, and he weighed almost two pounds more than Alona, it was a breech presentation that made her birth more difficult. I don't know what caused her to be breech but don't want to go there again, especially not with twins. Luckily, the attending ob/gyn was able to turn her and didn't have to resort to the use of forceps. Unfortunately, Alona was not without blemishes and not exactly a poster child when I brought her home from the hospital.

Fernando's mom gave her a thorough looking over

and was relieved that she was basically a very healthy child. She was petite by comparison to Mario, which didn't concern anyone. At first, Esmeralda did not want me to nurse the baby since she strongly believed in employing nursemaids; however, both Fernando and I made it clear to her that the use of nursemaids wasn't our choice. I definitely insisted on nursing Alona for the first year.

Unquestionably, Esmeralda tried her hardest to make my life as miserable as she could. There wasn't a day I wasn't reprimanded for one thing or another. If it wasn't my appearance, then it was how I dealt with the children, the servants, how I spoke, my lousy Spanish, etc. She became skilled in selecting times and places for executing her dispensations of criticism or verbal punishment. She wouldn't dare do it in the presence of Don Carlos or my husband but delighted in facing me in front of any servant. Of course, many times I had no clue what she was talking about in her machine-gun delivery of torrents in Spanish. Actually, I didn't have to understand a word, her facial expressions said it all.

Once I had fully recovered from giving birth to Alona, life became more tolerable. What kept me from hating where I had chosen to live was my husband's love for me and our children and the joy I derived from being loved and admired by Don Carlos. He made every effort to compensate for the hateful conduct of his wife. Sometimes, I felt like Cinderella facing the evil stepmother daily.

But those days passed too and things turned more positive for me when Alona was past her first birthday and required less of my constant attention. It was then that I took Fernando and Don Carlos's advice and got out of the house for a few hours each weekday. I went regularly to work with Fernando and enjoyed working side by side with him in the vineyards and the winery. I got to know many on the staff, especially many of the women who worked for the family. It was the strong bond I formed with the women that helped me greatly in improving my communication skills and to learn as much as possible about the family business. I no longer saw myself as an interloper but someone who truly belonged.

I don't know if it was sheer curiosity or a deliberate attempt at psyching me out. When the hacienda was introduced to television in 1965, there were several regular programs that featured the rise and fall of Nazism in Germany. Esmeralda seemed to be taken by the cruelties depicted. She would often question whether these things actually did happen. While I didn't object to being questioned or doubted, it was watching the events again and again that brought the whole trauma back to the fore rather than keeping it buried deep in my subconscious mind.

The results were the frequent occurrences of my nightmares. There were times when I was ready to leave since I had concluded Esmeralda thrived on tormenting me. It was only the love of Fernando, my father-in-law, and the dear women of the staff who kept me going. I was ready to pack up my kids and head for the Vaterland.

I'm glad I stuck it out, only to discover that even

the meanest and most unforgiving person could ultimately be shown to have redeeming value. In my life
and personal experience, no one exemplifies that conclusion more than Esmeralda.

# Chapter 28

I was still sitting at my desk, rereading what I had just committed to paper, when my office door opened gingerly and Esmeralda walked in.

"Do I dare interrupt? I'm so excited; the mailman just delivered our season tickets for the Teatro. You were right; this week's offering is *Madama Butterfly*. I'm thrilled it's Renata Tebaldi in the lead. I've heard of Christa Ludwig as Suzuki. I'm not familiar with the tenor singing Pinkerton. I just adore Puccini's music and especially this opera.

"What delights me even more is that we are doing this together. I'm not sure I would go by myself. Years ago, one of my friends who attended cloister school with me used to join me on occasion. When she died, that was pretty much the end of it. Once in a very blue moon, I browbeat Don Carlos into taking me, but I wasn't very successful most of the time. So this is perfect."

"How soon do you want us to leave tomorrow? I'll arrange for Juan to drive us, and I'm sure Valentina would love it if she could join him for the afternoon. So rarely do those two have an opportunity to do something enjoyable together," was Doretta's observation.

"I would say if we leave here about three-thirty at the latest, that will be just right to do our little shopping spree at Falabella's. Our dinner reservation at Confitería Torres is for six o'clock, which gives us plenty of time with curtain call being at eight. What do you think, Doretta?"

"Why don't we make it three o'clock; one never knows these days what the traffic is like in the city."

"Perfect for me. It will give me plenty of time to get dressed and made up after I take my constitutional nap. I'll leave it up to you to make the arrangements with Juan and Valentina. Don't spend too much time typing. Get out into the fresh air. It's another perfect spring day; Don Carlos's spring flower garden is about to burst into bloom. It will always be such a wonderful reminder of him." She walked around the desk and gave Doretta a loving hug. As she left the room, all Doretta could hear was the tap-tap of Esmeralda's cane fading away as she moved toward her own wing in the mansion.

⋊⋉

Juan dropped them off at the main entrance to Falabella's and then parked the car. Valentina joined Esmeralda and Doretta for a few minutes. She wanted to take the opportunity and say a quick "hello" to Frau Flott, her long-ago supervisor in the better dress department. They were greeted shortly after getting off the escalator. Frau Flott remembered Doretta from the last visit.

"How nice to see you again. Are you still enjoying the beautiful dresses you selected when we last met?"

"I certainly do," responded Doretta. Frau Flott smiled at Valentina and shook her hand.

"Looks like you are still with the family."

"Oh, I am. I wouldn't dream of leaving Garcia Lopez Hacienda. It's indeed my family. I won't stay around. Just wanted to take the chance to see you again. My husband, the chauffeur, and I will enjoy the rest of the day in town and catch up with old friends and his family. I'm sure you'll be able to help these two lovely ladies with anything they are looking for. We'll talk some other time." Valentina rushed away not wanting to keep Juan waiting for her. Frau Flott turned toward Esmeralda.

"Is it something for you, ma'am, or your daughter-in-law, that you are looking for? That black ensemble you are wearing is exquisite."

"Thank you, Frau Flott. We are wanting to select some attractive maternity clothes for the young woman. My daughter-in-law is expecting twins in December. Those stunning dresses you sold her when she saw you last, they are now resting in her closet waiting to be worn again.

"Actually, it's only the peacock blue and green stunner that's on hold for the moment. The orange-red one, her mother, Gisela Meyer, received as a present from her daughter. You remember the German lady, don't you?"

"Oh yes. She's written to me a couple of times. What a lovely lady. I was born and raised in Essen; I was aware of a certain connection to her when we first met. Writing to her allows me to keep up with my German."

"Thank you, Frau Flott. It makes me extremely happy to know that you've stayed in touch with my mother. These days, we mostly talk on the phone rather than write except on special occasions. She almost fainted the other day when I told her I was expecting twins at Christmastime. I was glad that Andreas, her new husband, was there to catch her."

"Now tell me what you have in mind?" Esmeralda took charge; she knew Doretta would be far too conservative when it came to spending money.

"I want my daughter to have some decent daytime ensembles she can wear to social functions and an occasional church visit. The other thing I insist on is that she has a couple of elegant dresses to wear to the opera. I read in one of the tabloids that Balenciaga designed special maternity formals for one of the European princesses in waiting."

"I know what you are talking about. The dress is designed with an expandable waistline that is most cleverly concealed with an off-shoulder draping, giving the appearance of an Empire waistline. It's available in elegant silk prints or solid crepe Georgette. Copies are available through Hong Kong, and I could have a selection for your perusal shipped here in three days."

"Do you by any chance have any visuals available from which we may select?"

"Of course; I even have some fabric swatches. You are not the first to inquire about formal maternity frocks. I'm so pleased that we are no longer hiding our mothers for several months in a closet. Please step over to my desk, and I'll show you what I have on hand. Señoras Garcia Lopez, please make yourself comfortable in these chairs. I admire you for undertaking this visit in your conditions. Would you care for some espresso or tea? It's all right here. Allow me to rest your cane right by your chair."

"Actually, I would like some Perrier, if you have it. I'm quite thirsty," offered Doretta.

"May I have the same, please. I usually don't drink coffee or tea this late in the day," said Esmeralda. Both women needed the relaxing interlude.

"Now, here are some of the swatches, materials in which the Balenciaga copies are available. Take a look and let me know what you decide. Here comes the girl with glasses and the Perrier." Frau Flott stepped back into the better dress department and selected several items that seemed suitable to what Esmeralda had in mind for her daughter-in-law.

"I realize this one looks a lot like my other green and blue formal although totally different in style. I really love the treatment above the waist, and that neckline has always suited me with my elongated appearance. What do you think, Esmeralda?"

"I like it very much. For a second choice you might consider the royal blue crepe Georgette. I have a stunning necklace of baroque pearls with matching earrings and a watch that Don Carlos gave me when Alphonso was born. Please accept these as an early Christmas present. It would look most elegant with that dress and on you. I always thought the length of the necklace was far too long on my petite torso. On you, it will look perfect."

"Let's see how fast she can have the dresses here. Did she say they would be delivered by air from Hong Kong? I swear that was what she said," voiced Doretta between taking a sip of her water.

"Frau Flott, I believe we've decided on two dresses. As you remember, these are my favorite colors in the print and this style in the royal blue Georgette is the other one we selected. How soon could you have them in the store?" commented Doretta.

"If I call the order in this afternoon, I will have them at the store by next Monday. There's no need for you to come into town. We will send the dresses out to the hacienda along with a seamstress from our alteration department. Any minor alterations could be done on-site. What I would like to do, is for you to stand up just for a moment to allow us to get the correct length of the dresses. I see you are wearing a more sensible medium heel these days. The six-inchers could be a bit too daring in your condition. You better save those for later."

"Oh, I love those heels and have stored them safely for future exposures at the opera house. But this will be the height of heel for now. May we take a look at what else you've selected for us, Frau Flott?" She held up a half dozen smartly designed maternity ensembles. *"Je ne sais quoi? Chique,* indeed," was all Doretta could whisper. Esmeralda echoed her sentiment.

*"Trés-chic!* We'll take all of them in size 10." Doretta almost choked on her Perrier.

"We are a little pressed for time, Frau Flott. Please summon the alteration person to make the necessary adjustments and have these outfits delivered along with the evening dresses you are ordering from Hong Kong. Please write up the invoice for our purchases promptly. I would like to pay you before we leave to meet with our chauffeur."

"Yes, señora! Always at your service." She bowed politely and extracted a calculator from her desk drawer. Frau Flott discreetly presented the invoice to Esmeralda, who opened her purse and extracted the necessary bills in one-hundred Escudos denomination to satisfy the cost of the extravagant purchase. Esmeralda didn't bat an eye. In her world, the purchase amount was chicken feed." She rose from the chair, momentarily feeling some stiffness in her hip. She reached for her cane.

"Could you direct us to the ladies room, please. I'd like to be comfortable during our ride to the restaurant. And thank you for your excellent service, Frau Flott. We'll see you again real soon. Personally, I have all the black dresses I'll ever need, but this young woman needs to update her wardrobe once she has blessed me with two more grandchildren." She couldn't hide her pleasure as she led the way to the ladies room.

Juan and Valentina were waiting for them as they approached the main entrance to Falabella's. Doretta held Esmeralda closely to her. Both were fearful of tripping and falling on thick carpeting or oriental rugs. They much preferred the smoothness of hardwood or marble flooring these days.

As they maneuvered the last of the steps, Esmeralda greeted Juan in a most friendly manner. "Thank you for always being so punctual. If the traffic isn't too bad, we might only be late for our dinner date by a couple of minutes."

"No problem, ma'am. I'll have you there before six o'clock. Did you tell me to be back by the opera house by ten forty-five?"

"Yes, *Madama Butterfly* runs for not quite three hours."

"I'll pick you up at the restaurant at seven-thirty which will get you to the Teatro in plenty of time. Enjoy your dinner. We know it will be lovely. Don Carlos treated us once a few years ago when he was here for a business meeting."

"I'm glad he did that. He was a dear. Well, here we are,

Doretta." Juan assisted both ladies out of the limo and turned them over to the waiting doorman. They were guided to their reserved table by the *maître* d'.

"Thank you, sir. That's a lovely table. It's exactly what I asked for. May we see the menus right away. We are off to the Teatro shortly after seven-thirty."

"Would you care for a cocktail or a glass of wine before dinner?" inquired the waiter.

"Thank you kindly, but no. Neither of us would care to imbibe before the opera; not my daughter in her condition, and I because of my advanced age. I need to be totally sober to enjoy the opera." Doretta smiled; it was the second time Esmeralda referred to her as daughter rather than daughter-in-law.

"I understand completely, señora. Do you have anything specifically in mind for dinner?"

"How is your *Churrasco* and *Chacarero*? I would like my guest to try something typically Chilean."

"They are both excellent, and we are well-known for the quality of meat."

"How would you feel about trying both? I'm sure there's no problem with having half of each arranged on our plates. Is that correct, sir?"

"Absolutely, no problem at all. Señor Orlando, at your service." He bowed deeply to Esmeralda.

Dinner was an absolute delight and more than satisfactory to their palates. Both enjoyed the ambiance and their quiet conversation. As they were guided out of the restaurant, Juan rushed toward them to be helpful in getting two of his favorite ladies into the limousine.

As he pulled up in front of the Teatro, he wished Esmeralda and Doretta a wonderful evening at the opera. "I will be here promptly at ten forty-five." He removed his cap in courtesy to his señoras. His eyes swept over the crowd entering the Teatro on the red carpet. He was certain they would have a delightful experience. How well he remembered Esmeralda's joyful accounts after most performances she had attended over the years.

"Let's take the elevator to the second floor. From there, it's just a few feet to our box. I was always thankful to my dear husband for indulging me so generously. It's been one of my greatest pleasures throughout the years.

"Here we are. Looks like we may be alone tonight. That doesn't bother me. We'll splurge just a tad. I'll have one glass of champagne after the first act, and you order whatever tickles you. After all, it is opening night of the 1968 opera season. When I think about it, it brings tears to my eyes. I can't wait for the love duet by Butterfly/Pinkerton during the first act. It melts my heart. Can't you just hear it?"

The curtain went up and the familiar opening bars of *Madama Butterfly* echoed through the hall. Soon the bickering scene between Butterfly and her notorious relatives was a thing of the past, and the orchestra led into the love duet. The two women looked at each other smiling through their tears. Esmeralda was taken back to an early date with Don Carlos; Doretta's mind went back to 1954 when she attended a performance of *Madama Butterfly* with Hektor. They couldn't take their eyes off the stage.

When the curtain went down after Act I, both women decided they were basket cases. The usher offering champagne and other refreshments was a welcome diversion. The flower duet by Tebaldi and Ludwig in Act II was an absolute delight and would ring in their ears for days to come. Esmeralda almost dreaded the opening of Act III with the incomparable *Un bel di,* the showstopper of the opera, followed by the tragic death of the heroine. Who wouldn't be touched by such glorious music? Esmeralda and Doretta were thankful for the lacy handkerchiefs they carried in their elegant little purses.

Juan spotted them as they walked out of the Teatro, Esmeralda holding firmly onto Doretta's left arm. He could tell from their facial expressions that the opera had been a decided success. "I can see you liked what you experienced. I'm sure Valentina will love hearing all about it on our drive home. We should be there in less than an hour."

"Thank you, Juan. We hope you and Valentina enjoyed your visit with friends and had a nice evening. We were delighted with the opera; the voices were spectacular. I haven't heard a *Madama Butterfly* like that in a long time." Doretta could only smile and concurred with Esmeralda's account of the experience. She sat back in the comfortable leather seat of the limo and listened to Esmeralda telling Valentina all about the exciting evening.

It was almost midnight when they arrived at the hacienda. All the others had retired much earlier. Esmeralda and Doretta wished each other a pleasant night and proceeded to their respective quarters. Valentina offered to accompany señora to her chambers and to assist with undressing, which she politely accepted. At least she didn't have to enter her boudoir alone. Doretta was comforted by the soft snoring she detected as she entered her bedroom. She undressed quickly and enjoyed the warmth of Fernando's body next to hers as she slid under the down comforter. As she drifted off to sleep, the love duet from Act I rang in her ears. Even deep in her first sleep, a beautiful smile graced her face.

# Chapter 29

IT was mid-October when Fernando conspired with his son, who was going on six years of age. "Mario, your mom's birthday is coming up soon. In years to come, I will take her and you and your brothers and sisters on a very special trip."

"What do you mean by brothers and sisters? All I have is one sister."

"But come Christmas, you will either have two new brothers, two new sisters, or perhaps one of each. You will be the oldest of all the kids, and I expect you to become the leader of the troops."

"Are you sure of that? I thought you were in charge of the tribe."

"I am, but both Mom and I will need your help with the growing family. Because of the babies she carries in her tummy, we can't even think about traveling. That's why I want you and I to think of a very special surprise for her. Can you think of anything that would truly please her?" His face turned into one giant question mark; Fernando had never noticed how serious his boy could look. His forehead was marked by strong furrows as he looked up to his dad.

"I know of one thing she would truly love—and so would I. That's probably selfish on my part, but I'm sure Mom would be thrilled."

"What's that, Son? Don't keep me on tenterhooks."

"What's that supposed to mean? My hands aren't hooks, last I knew."

"Son, that's just an expression grown-ups use. I meant to say, don't keep me guessing or waiting for your suggestion. What do you think Mom would like for a surprise?"

"Ever since Barney died last year, she's been missing a dog sitting by her feet when she works away in that room of hers or when she walks into the nursery to talk to Alona. I would love it if you would get us another dog, and I know, Mom wouldn't like anything better for her birthday. Just think of her reaction if we were to present her with a cute puppy. Can't you see the smile on her face? And better yet, the puppy could grow up with my new brothers or sisters."

"Why didn't I see that or think of it? That's a wonderful idea, Mario. We won't tell anyone about it. Next week, you and I will have a father/son day and go into town. Kind of like Nana and Mom do when they go to the Teatro. I'll just fib a little and say I wanted you to have an afternoon with me at the horse track. You'll love seeing the Hipódromo Chile. Nana knows how much I used to love it when Grandpa took me on one of these father/son adventures at least once a year as I grew up.

"At one time, he owned a couple of race horses and loved to show his face among friends when his thoroughbreds were in the running. And when they came in first, or even second or third, he was thrilled and always was very generous with his buddies at the clubhouse bar afterward. When I was old enough to drive, I would be his chauffeur and get the car back to the hacienda. Nana Esmeralda wasn't too happy to have him come home half-baked."

"What's half-baked?"

"That means he had too much to drink. You've never seen my papa or me that way. In his later years, he drank only a glass of good champagne and sometimes tasted our own vintages. He outgrew his taste for hard liquor and minded the doctor who told him to watch what he was drinking.

"But let's keep our minds on getting the puppy. There are two large pet shops I can think of. I'm sure between the two of us, we'll find a puppy all of us will like. What do you say? Do we have a deal?"

"Deal, Dad. I won't breathe a word to anyone. How about next Wednesday? That's two days before Mom's birthday. I'm sure Juan and Valentina wouldn't mind watching the puppy for a day and keeping the big secret." Mario couldn't wait for Wednesday to arrive.

"I cleaned out the little kennel that was sitting in the shed. No one was watching or wondering what I was doing. I bet it's the one they used to bring Barney home when he was a pup."

"Good thinking, Mario. I'll stash it in the back of my car when all have retired tonight. The old blanket I keep in the trunk will come in handy. I'll just throw it over the kennel; no one will have any idea what we are up to. We'll go for the first two or three races and then check out the pet shops."

Mario was excited when they arrived at the Hipódromo Chile; he had never seen anything like it. Sitting on his father's knee, he had a pretty good view of the races. He loved seeing the horses and the colorful silks the jockeys were sporting. "Boy Dad, this is something. I hear people talking about winning or losing money. Did you buy tickets? Could we maybe win enough money to pay for the new puppy?"

"Sorry, Mario. Your grandfather lost so often that I learned my lesson. I work hard for the money I'm paid; I don't like to take chances on losing it at the Hipódromo. I come here to watch the horses and the people. That's all the excitement I need or want. After the next race, I'll take us to the clubhouse, and we'll have a nice lunch. You may order anything you like. I won't even make a suggestion; you know how to read and can order what you want. Is that OK with you?

"Sure, Dad. That sounds like fun. When I go to a restaurant with Mom or Nana, they always order what they think is good for me. This is much better."

When seated at the Clubhouse, the waiter initially handed only a menu to Fernando. "You may give my son a menu as well. He reads quite well for his age. I've told him he may order whatever he wants."

"Si, señor! Right away." Mario practically ran his nose up and down the extensive menu. "Dad, I would like the German brats on a bun with sauerkraut and ketchup. Maybe some potato salad on the side? Could I have some Fanta? They have it here. Nana Gisela talked about Fanta when they were visiting earlier in the year. It must be some drink they have in Europe."

"Listen to my son? A regular bon vivant. Mom is teaching you well. I'm proud of you." Mario chomped a man-sized bite off the first brat.

"Dad, these taste good. Want some?" He pushed his plate toward his father.

"No, you enjoy what you ordered. I'm thinking back to being in Zürich and how I used to like the bratwurst or the Leberkäs on their good buns."

"What's Leberkäs?"

"It literally means 'liver cheese' but has nothing to do with either. It looks like the meat in a hotdog but is baked in a bread pan and served in large, thick slices. Most Europeans know it and love it. I did too. Would you like something sweet for dessert?"

"Not right now, Dad. I'm full! Brrrp," he burped.

"Don't say that in the presence of your grandma or Mom, for that matter. You say: 'No, thank you; I've had more than enough.' And reach for your handkerchief, or better yet, don't burp at the table."

"Okay Dad, will do. May I have an ice cream cone after we find the puppy?"

"That's a good choice. Just what I feel like having later. Well, are we ready to go puppy hunting? You have any idea what kind of dog you might like? Or should I say what kind Mom would like? I hope not another one as big as Barney."

"I know for sure she doesn't like little yappy dogs." Fernando paid for the luncheon and held his son by the hand as they walked to the car.

✹

The first pet shop wasn't exactly Fernando's cup of tea. The place stank to high heaven. They quickly walked by the dog pens and were not favorably impressed by the shabby manner in which the puppies were kept.

"Let's blow this pop stand! I hope we'll do better at the next place. Wouldn't that be disappointing if we came home empty-handed?"

"Don't worry, Dad. I feel it in my bones. We'll find just what we want at the next shop."

"Okay, my wise old man. I'm glad you have such feeling bones." *I wonder where he got all the smarts? Sometimes I can't believe what I'm hearing,* crossed Fernando's mind.

They walked into the second pet shop and could tell the difference immediately. The place was spotless and all animals humanely kenneled and treated. "Daddy, daddy, come here. Look at these blond labs. Count them! There are eleven of them, and one is cuter than the next. Can I have one of these? We don't have to look any further. Mom would love to have one. Gosh, that one over there is a cute boy. May I hold him?"

"Let's see if we can find someone who works here." Fernando saw a girl wearing an apron who looked like she was staff. He raised his hand to get her attention. When she spotted him, she walked over right away.

"May I help you with one of these adorable pups? They just joined us this week. They are nine weeks old."

"Would it be possible for my son to interact with some of these puppies? I always believed strongly about a pup looking for its master rather than the reverse. One can tell a lot by the selection process and how the animal feels toward a human who wants to provide it with a new and permanent home."

"That is extremely perceptive on your part. We prefer *doing* it that way. I'll take you in the back where we can open the kennel and your young man can interact with all eleven of them. Then we'll see who chooses whom? What's your name?"

"I'm Mario, and this is my dad, Señor Fernando."

"I'm Sally. Nice to meet both of you. Just follow me into the back of all the kennels where we can open each one to create a larger running area for each of the groups of dogs. That way interested buyers can truly interact with the animals."

Fernando nodded his approval to his son. He was totally impressed with the cleanliness of the facility. It reminded him of his winery. Same idea. The gates were opened—so to speak. Eleven gorgeous puppies leaped and bounded over each other with excitement.

Mario stepped over the waist-high barrier allowing himself to be immersed in puppy haven. Two females and the male he had spotted before came right up to him and began to lick his bare legs. He bent down to see if they wanted to discover his face and hands. He extended a hand to his three interested friends and began to speak softly, wanting to encourage further interaction. It was the male who was all over him. "Dad, this is the one. I can tell he likes me and wants to go home with us. I just know it. Can we have him?"

"Since you are so sure, let's get him. Not only is he very friendly, I also like his silky coat. Mom will fall in love with him. Let me pay the young lady, and you start thinking about a name for your new friend. He probably has some highfalu-tin name on his papers but that doesn't mean we have to call him that. Come up with a name that's easy to pronounce for everyone involved."

He walked with Sally toward the cash register and inquired as to the dog's price. There were no objections. He was correct in his assumption; the dog was a pure breed and did come with papers. His official name was Filius Oberdank V. "I can assure you he will remain in name only on paper, not at our home. It's cute but not practical on a ranch and with four kids eventually."

The young lady smiled and let it go. "He's yours to name. I can tell he'll be very much loved, which is most important to us when we give our animals into the hands of strangers."

Fernando went out to the car and retrieved the kennel. It was perfect in size for their find. "That's great. You came equipped. We like that." Sally placed Filius Oberdank V lovingly into his traveling home.

"Well, young man, have you come up with a name of your own or is it going to be just Filius?"

"His name will be Pablo, if that's OK with you Dad?"

"Pablo it is, unless your mother has a different idea. Remember, it's her birthday present. Actually, I like your choice of name. It fits Nana Esmeralda's taste and interest in modern art. Picasso always was one of her favorites."

It was well after dusk when they arrived back at the hacienda. Juan stood by one of the garages as Fernando pulled up in front of the main entrance. He rushed over to open the door for Fernando.

"Buenas noches, señor. You want me to park the car?"

"Yes, and be sure to leave the windows open. When you are certain Señora Doretta is seated at the dinner table, take the little fellow into your quarters and don't breathe a word to anyone but Valentina." He pointed to the kennel in the backseat; "It's a birthday surprise for my wife. When he needs doing wee-wee or poo-poo, make sure you take him outside through your backdoor. By the way, Mario named him Pablo and I like the name he chose. You understand all that?"

"Yes, señor. We will all be happy to have another dog around. We'll take good care of Pablo. I like his name, señor."

Doretta was already seated at the dining room table with Esmeralda. They were chatting away and weren't even aware of Fernando and Mario's arrival. Fernando insisted on bringing the boy in to say good evening to his mother and grandmother before he retired to the kitchen and a late-evening snack with Juan and Valentina. "Give your mom and grandma a kiss, and tell them what a wonderful time you had at the races. He cannot deny that he is Don Carlos's grandson. He wanted me to bet on some of those horses in the worst way, but I taught him that one can have a lot of fun just watching the races at Hipódromo Chile without losing one's shirt."

"I wouldn't have minded losing my shirt; it's old and the sleeves are getting too short. But Dad wouldn't fall for my ploy. And yes, we didn't waste any of his hard-earned money, had a great meal at the clubhouse, and had lots of fun. I would love to have another father/son outing soon. I even had a lesson in table etiquette."

"What's that supposed to mean?" asked his grandmother.

"He's just being a little smart ass. I taught him not to say 'I'm full,' and to use a handkerchief to cover his mouth when needing to expel air when seated at a dinner table."

"You mean to say my grandson burped in a restaurant?"

"Exactly, Mom. He knows better now; at least I hope so."

"You had a good lesson, Mario," said his grandmother. Doretta thought it was high time to end the little lesson in table manners.

"Now, kiss Grandma and me goodnight and look what goodies Valentina is holding for you in the kitchen. I believe Cook fixed one of your favorites for you."

"You mean she made me a pizza?"

"Yes, and it doesn't have anything green or fungi on it; it's all sausages and different cheeses, just the way you like it. Off to the kitchen, and then to bed you go. It's been an exciting day for you."

*And you don't know the half of it, Mom. Won't you be surprised?* He was chuckling to himself as he made his way across the courtyard to the kitchen wing.

# Chapter 30

FERNANDO and Juan hatched a unique way of presenting Doretta with her special birthday present. A wine crate for the 1963 vintage, which normally would hold twelve bottles of wine, was chosen to be the kennel for little Pablo. Valentina had cleaned it thoroughly and then lined it with thick and absorbent paper padding. A colorful piece of silk would be its covering. When Fernando would ring a little brass bell at their bedroom door, it would be the signal for Juan to set the crate at the bottom of the marble staircase.

Pablo would be comfortable for the short period he would have to suffer in any kind of kenneling. In the two days of taking care of him, Valentina and Juan discovered that Pablo was a free spirit and liked to roam. And so the morning began. It was about eight when Fernando decided to wake his bride, the birthday child, with a gentle kiss.

"Time to face the reality of turning thirty-six, my dear. Happy birthday and many more." She was still half asleep as he spoke to her.

"Did you have to wake me? I had such a wonderful dream,

and it wasn't about turning thirty-six. You just wait until your birthday comes around. You'll have a rude awakening. Is it okay with you and the others if I shower first and make myself somewhat presentable?"

"Of course, dear. It's your birthday, and you may do whatever pleases you. There's no rush to do anything. I have nothing urgent at the winery this morning and left my calendar open just for today's event."

Doretta headed straight for the shower when she realized what time it was. She usually had breakfast with Esmeralda no later than nine o'clock. Often she got up much earlier and secluded herself in her writing room. After her last confessions, she believed she was close to being caught up to the present and might just make journal entries when she had the need to do so.

Fernando sat by his desk and was glancing through the morning papers. He was disturbed when he learned that certain individuals suspected the United States CIA to be entangled in Chilean politics. He decided he didn't even want to think about government-related issues. He was an apolitical man and perfectly happy with his life and the lives of all who lived at the Garcia Lopez Hacienda.

He folded the paper and tossed it into the recycle bin. *Good riddance!* He opted instead to help his wife with getting dressed. "You are beginning to more than show; it's becoming increasingly evident that you are carrying more than one child, and we have two months plus to go. Are you feeling OK?"

"I've never felt better, other than finding a comfortable position to sit or lie in bed. But this too shall pass. And just think of the rewards—two for the price of one. Esmeralda, more likely than not, would want me to continue to have children.

If you don't object, and we'll keep this just between the two of us, I would like my tubes tied after I give birth to these two unless there is some health issue with our latest offspring. Do I have your word on this?"

"I concur; you will have your hands full with seeing to the raising and educating of four children. But as you suggested, we won't discuss this with my mother. I'm quite aware of her Catholic attitudes in such matters." He coughed for a moment.

"That morning dress you selected looks beautiful on you. You need help with your hair? Personally, I think it looks just fine. A touch of lipstick and you are ready to enjoy the day. Shall I go and let Esmeralda know you'll be right down?"

"By all means. I'll be more than ready in two minutes." Fernando stepped through the bedroom door and closed it softly. He reached into his pant pocket and rang the little bell as planned. Doretta opened the door and looked somewhat puzzled.

"Did I just hear a bell ring or was that my imagination?"

"I didn't hear any bell. Are you still dreaming?"

"No, I'm not dreaming. I'm wide awake and ready to face the world come what may."

Lately, she had gotten into the habit of holding onto the rail with her left hand and to look at every step she'd take as she descended the staircase. She spotted the little crate sitting at the bottom. What caught her eye was the colorful silk covering it. For a split second she thought she had seen the piece of fabric move. *Must be some problem with my vision.* She could see the label 1963 embossed on the crate in letters of gold.

"You know I won't have any alcohol while I'm pregnant. That was very thoughtful of you to present me with this special vintage. I realize it was the last year Don Carlos was in charge of the winery before you took over. Maybe we should just store it in the wine cellar until next year. Perhaps we can have some of it for our New Year's celebration if my delivery is on time."

"Well, here we are. Why don't you at least take a look and see what else might be under that lovely cover."

Fernando could tell she was hesitant to bend down and peek under the silk square. He reached for it and pulled it away with one swift motion. "Ta-dah! Ta-dah! Happy Birthday." There was applause by all standing in the back. Esmeralda held onto Mario and Alona, and Juan and Valentina and some of the other staff were watching as well. Fernando picked up Pablo and put him into Doretta's waiting arms. She was absolutely shocked and speechless.

"Say hello to Pablo. Mario picked him out from a litter of eleven pups. It was he who came up with the new name. Somehow Filius Oberdank V didn't work for him. I had to agree. Yes, we had a wonderful time at the racetrack, but the main purpose of our father/son adventure was to find the puppy. I believe the whole family was ready for this joyful occasion. Cat got your tongue?"

"I'm indeed speechless. Thank you, Mario. I'm in love with your choice, and I love the name. Thank you, Fernando, for my wonderful present." She kept snuggling Pablo who couldn't get enough of licking her face. There was no doubt in anyone's mind that the birthday child and Pablo had bonded at first sight.

And then it was Mario's turn to show off his prized birthday present for his mother and share Pablo with Nana Esmeralda and his sister.

"What do you say, didn't Dad and I do a great job of picking a meaningful present for Mom? Wow, did I have a hard time staying away from him while he was in Juan and Valentina's care for the past couple of days. Now and then I could hear him yapping a bit and was hoping Mom wouldn't hear him."

"Mario, I love the dog, and his name is perfect. Thank you. You made your grandma a very happy woman. When we had to put Barney to sleep, I thought we would never have another dog in this house. Pablo will be a wonderful addition to our family. I love the color you chose.

"I had been wondering about your father/son adventure in the city. I was well aware that your father wasn't big on the Hipódromo and couldn't imagine you spending a whole afternoon at that place. Of course, now we all know what you did. You take good care of Pablo. I'm sure when he is housebroken and a little older, he'll come to see me on his own. You can be certain, Pablo will always be welcome at Nana's place."

She had opened her arms wanting to hold him. Fernando wasn't certain his mother could handle the dog with just one hand.

"Mom, why don't you sit down and I'll put Pablo into your lap. That will be easier for you. He does weigh close to twelve pounds, and he won't get any lighter. Look at the size of his paws; he'll be a good-sized dog when he is fully grown. You'll love him; you never were fond of little yappers."

"That I wasn't and never will be. Barney was as big a dog as we ever had. Years ago I had standard poodles; they were well-behaved dogs and so smart. Pablo will be different. I've never had a Labrador, but this one just about steals my heart. He's got the cutest face and such alert eyes. Pablo and I will become good friends, I'm sure. Now, enough of this dog talk. I'm ready for some breakfast and a little adult conversation."

She gestured toward Mario to take the dog before she

attempted to rise from her chair. Esmeralda was always fully aware of her handicap but handled the situation with grace. When she walked away supported by her elegant cane, there was no doubt in anyone's view that she was the Garcia Lopez dowager.

On this special morning, both Mario and Alona were allowed to sit at their grandmother's dining room table and partake of the breakfast being served. It was not necessarily food to their liking, but as long as they were given the honor of having breakfast with the grown-ups, they were not given dispensation to say "I don't like this" or "I don't like that"— they had to at least make an effort to try it first before they declined eating it. Those were Grandma's rules, and there was no deviating from the plan.

After they were all properly seated, Grandma toasted the birthday child and the others with her glass of champagne. Everyone had juice except Grandma and Fernando.

"Son, you and I will finish this excellent bottle later thanks to that German champagne bottle stopper you brought back with you five years ago. I don't know how often your father made reference to the liking of that particular stopper."

Esmeralda rose from the table and walked over to the credenza. She picked up a little package and placed it in Doretta's hands.

"Open it. It's something I was given by my grandmother on my thirty-six birthday. From the time I was eighteen years old, I always received a unique piece of jewelry for my birthdays from Grandmother until she passed away."

Doretta handled the package with care. When she opened the box, she discovered a beautiful broach with sapphires and diamonds tastefully set in platinum. "Thank you, Esmeralda.

It is indeed beautiful. Are you sure you wish for me to have this?"

"Yes, my dear. I've treasured it for many years, but now it is time to part with my precious jewelry. I can wear only so much, and what good does it do sitting in the safe? Enjoy it, Doretta, and let me see you wear it. When my time comes, it will all go to you anyway. I wasn't meant to have a daughter, and now I have found you. Thank you for making my Fernando and his children so loved. I'm so sorry for letting all those years go by in such meaningless ways. I'll try to make it up to you in the time I have left."

Fernando pinned the broach on Doretta's morning dress. She walked over to Esmeralda to give her a hug in appreciation of what she had said, much more so than for the valuable present bestowed upon her.

"Fernando meant well, but it deserves to be worn with something more appropriate in elegance. Thank you for the precious gift, but even more for the kind words spoken. I'm very happy that we've moved beyond our differences and have learned to like each other. It means a lot to me." She confirmed what she said by hugging Esmeralda's frail stature firmly.

# Chapter 31

IN the early hours of December 15, Doretta awakened Fernando. "Wake up, my good husband. It's time for you to take me to the hospital. I started labor over an hour ago. I want to get out of bed and be ready for the ride. I'm thankful, my water hasn't broken yet. To be safe, have Juan cover the backseats in the car with a protective shield. I want him to drive and have you sit with me in the back of the car. I need your physical support and strength until I'm safely ensconced at the hospital and in Diego's presence. I'm hoping he's delivering me and right with his predictions this time."

Juan brought the car around. Doretta declined Valentina's offer to accompany her for the delivery. "I'd rather you be there for Mario and Alona when they wake up and find me gone. I'll be OK in the company of my husband and in the competent hands of Dr. Rodriguez Amado. Don't look so worried; I'll be just fine. Come here, give me a hug, and wish me well." They hugged briefly and then Doretta was off for the thirty-minute drive.

No sooner was she checked in, when Diego and a nurse stuck their heads into her private room. It was by no means a temple of elegance and modernity but clean and functional which was all she was looking for.

"How are you faring, young lady? Fernando, would you mind stepping out for a moment? I would like to do a quick check and see where we are. I'm surprised your water hasn't broken yet. When did you say you became aware of the first labor pains?"

"I looked at the alarm by our bed at three o'clock when I was awakened by the first shooting pains. It was close to five when I awakened Fernando. So looking at the time now, I'd say it's been a bit over three hours since I went into labor."

"You just relax and let Fernando help you with the breathing exercises I gave you. Signal the nurse when your water breaks. They'll summon me promptly. I'll start on my rounds right away. I've an idea you'll go to the delivery room in less than two hours, at least by what I can determine from your dilation."

Elijah Avraham Garcia Lopez and Eduardo Emmanuel Garcia Lopez were born at 10:35 and 10:47, respectively, on December 15, 1968. The deliveries went without any complications whatsoever as predicted by Dr. Diego Rodriguez Amado, although they were slower in coming than he had anticipated. Both boys weighed just under seven pounds and measured twenty-four inches in length, slightly longer than the average newborn. They were identical twins except that Elijah bore a tiny white birthmark on his left cheek just below the ear.

Doretta and Fernando had discussed names for the boys before she had to be taken to the hospital. Doretta felt strongly that she wanted her father's names to be carried on if one or both newborns would be boys. Mario bore Don Carlos's name as his middle name, although he was never called Mario Carlos unless he was in any sort of trouble. To this day that had rarely been the case; he was an absolute delight to everyone.

When Alona was born, Fernando insisted on calling her Alona Doretta and would not concede to naming her after his mother. At the time, he was too conflicted with his mother's attitude toward his wife. Had one or both of the newborns been female, Doretta would have gotten her way of honoring Esmeralda. The gods didn't grant her that wish, but she was thrilled to hold a pair of healthy boys in her arms when Esmeralda walked into the hospital room on the arm of her proud son, Fernando Leonardo. He carried the name of his grandfather.

Esmeralda was a vision in black silk, proudly wearing the Varanasi scarf, a brocade creation in grays, black, and silver, that Doretta had presented her earlier in the year. She walked gracefully toward Doretta, discreetly using her silver-embossed cane. Her face lit up with a smile, rarely seen on her these days, as she reached out to touch her newest grandsons.

"You are presenting me with something I never expected to see in my life. I long to hold my boys close to my breast. Fernando Leonardo, please fetch me a chair and place it close to my daughter. I want you to hand me the boys and place them in my arms." He knew she was serious in her demand; she only called him by both given names when she meant business.

When Fernando succeeded in accommodating his mother's

wishes, her vision took in her children and grandsons; tears of joy flooded her face and gently touched the countenances of Elijah Avraham and Eduardo Emmanuel.

"Thank you for my beautiful grandsons, thank you for honoring your beloved father, Doretta. May he have found peace in the arms of our Lord." She bestowed the sign of the cross on all of whom she spoke.

Esmeralda couldn't wait to get back to the hacienda and share her good news with her other grandchildren and the staff. She firmly believed that the arrival of the two new grandsons was a gift from God. There hadn't been a night since the day of Alphonso's death when she didn't end the day without pleading to the Almighty to protect Fernando and to bless him with many sons. She looked up to heaven as she walked into the house. *Thank you for listening to my fervent prayers.*

Doretta, Elijah, and Eduardo were greeted by thunderous applause by all at the Garcia Lopez home as they emerged from the limousine on Christmas Eve. It would be an evening long remembered by those who were privileged to witness the scene. It was truly a blessing none had the gift of clairvoyance.

On Christmas Day, the phone rang. It was Gisela and Andreas calling. Fernando handed the phone to Doretta, having said *Frohe Weihnachten.* He remembered that much German. "You'll be really surprised," he said to his wife, still teasing her by holding on to the receiver; he was pleased to know that they cared enough to call.

"Hello, this is Doretta."

"Hallo, this is your mother; Frohe Weihnachten and congratulations on a job well done. How are the boys? I was thrilled with the good news when Fernando called last week."

"Frohe Weihnachten to you, too. I was wondering when I would hear from you. Elijah and Eduardo are doing well. They surely love to eat and keep me on my toes. We are still up half the night with feeding and changing diapers. I'm grateful to have Valentina and daughter Juanita helping with the care of the children. I do need to confess, I have it a lot easier than you did with Lutz and Lenny.

"You and Andreas ought to give some serious thought to making another journey south. Perhaps not right away, but keep it in mind in a year or two when the twins are beginning to communicate. That might be fun for you to be with all your grandchildren. From what Fernando told me, there are still no brides on the horizon for my brothers in Germany. Well, you think about it."

"Thanks for planting the seed, but I really will have to think about this one. You know how I feel about being cooped up on a plane for that long. Andreas, of course, would love it. He's always got sand in his shoes. Have a wonderful Christmas. Here's Andreas; he wants to congratulate you. Love you."

"Hallo Doretta, Fröhliche Weihnachten and hearty congrats on the successful delivery of the twins. Gisela loves the names you and Fernando have chosen. It's a nice tribute to your father."

"Thank you, Andreas. That was thoughtful of you to say. I was pleased that Fernando agreed with my choice of names. I asked Mom to give some thought to another visit. I would appreciate it if you would do a little pushing. You know how hesitant she is when it comes to flying."

"I'll do my best. Again, enjoy those babies and the holidays, and enjoy the sunshine. It's gray on gray and bitterly cold around here. Talk to you soon. Hugs to all. Aufwiedersehen."

For a few seconds, Doretta just sat quietly, still holding the receiver gone silent. In her mind she was with them in gray on gray and bitterly cold and visualized the festively decorated Christmas tree in the living room. At times, she still had difficulty swallowing the hemispheric differences.

# Chapter 32

DORETTA was the picture of good health and her children were thriving. Mario learned to enjoy being seated next to his father at the dinner table for adults in his grandmother's wing of the hacienda. The boy had reached the honorable age of six to do so. He had been properly taught how to eat with a fork and knife and how to conduct himself appropriately in the presence of his elders.

These were rules of etiquette strictly imposed by Señora Esmeralda. She was determined to see her grandchildren raised in a style of conduct acceptable to the highest echelons of social behavior in the country. Doretta learned to recognize that her mother-in-law wasn't a snob but simply could not jump over her own shadow of hereditary appropriateness; it was in her blood.

Fernando made the announcement at the dinner table. "Our family will be honored in the Grape Harvest Wine Festival on Valentine's Day. All but Elijah and Eduardo will be in traditional Chilean festival dress and will be riding in the parade. It is a great honor for our family and staff to be selected by the Festival Board." Mario raised his hand.

"You have a question, Son?"

"Will I ride my own horse, Father?"

"That you will indeed. Alona, Elijah, and Eduardo will ride with Grandma and Mom in the decorated limousine surrounded by the many who work with us in the vineyards, the winery, and the Garcia Lopez Hacienda."

"Are we going to wear anything different for the festival? I've heard Juan and Valentina talking about the festival in years past. He talked about wearing Gaucho something. I had no idea what he was referring to."

"Juan is correct. All males in the parade, and that includes you and me, will wear a Gaucho poncho and a typical Gaucho sombrero. The ponchos may be very colorful or of subdued colors; the Gaucho sombrero is almost always black. Females will wear all sorts of dresses with colors primarily being red, white, and blue representing the Chilean flag."

⋊⋉

Early in the morning of Valentine's Day, Fernando drove his Jeep to the winery in Maipo Valley and had asked Mario to join him. "Before the parade, there will be a wine stomping competition, a rather messy but very fun affair. I want you to be part of the competition. Many of our men will be stomping with us."

"Tell me a little more about this messy fun experience. I'm well known for not liking messy jobs."

"I'm fully aware, Son. But in this one I want you to take part. Your participation is dictated by your heritage. The men in our family have done this for generations. There will be a series of large vats from different vineyards competing in the event. The vats will be filled with a certain weight of grapes. Some wineries have only females doing the stomping; others use only males; and others use both male and female stompers. You and I and all the guys in our vat will wear old short pants and a white T-shirt and have bare feet."

"Bare feet? You must be kidding. I get the idea. You want me to crush those purple grapes with my bare feet? They'll never get clean again."

"Yes, they will. And you will have fun. First, we'll start singing and dancing, holding onto each other and moving in one direction. Then we move in the opposite direction, move ever faster and faster, and stomp harder and harder. The whole idea is to get as much juice out of those grapes as is humanly possible and to have fun doing it.

"The crowd standing around and watching cheer on each team in the competition. The vat that produces the most juice is awarded the winner trophy. If you look in Don Carlos's office, you'll see a few of our trophies collected through the years. So do your father the favor of wiping that frown off your face, and have fun with me."

"Okay Dad, I'll try. I'm glad you have a decent shower at the winery. I wouldn't want to get dressed and sit on my horse covered in grape juice and slimy purple skins. Just the thought of it gives me the willies. But I'll do it to make you happy."

Hordes of festively dressed visitors watched the shenanigans going on in each vat. The noise was cacophonous. Some who stood too close were spattered with grape juice and decided to step back. Too close to the action was decidedly not a good thing. Mario wished he had worn a hat or cap. Juice and slime were dripping down from his hair and face. *How did I ever let my father talk me into this? He might think it is fun; I surely don't.*

After a good hour, it was all over. The measurements were made, and Fernando's vat came in second. "See Son, you didn't have enough fun. That's why we have to do it again next year."

"Oh no. Not this kid. Why don't you put it off for a few years and then do it with Elijah and Eduardo. You'll have four extra feet for your team. And they might like it and have fun."

"Okay Kiddo, I'll take it under advisement. Let's hit the shower and get ready for the parade. We'll have perhaps a better chance of winning a trophy with our 1967 Cabernet."

Fernando and his crew of grape treaders took turns in the shower at the winery. When they stepped out, all of them wore black britches, sparkling white shirts, and brown-beige Gaucho ponchos that were dramatically accented with black abstract symbols. Black boots and black Gaucho sombreros finished their outfits. Riding high on their festively decorated steeds, the Garcia Lopez troupe was a sight to behold.

As honorary participants, Fernando's contingent led the parade. Hernando drove Doretta, Esmeralda, Alona, and the boys in the sparkling black limousine, the hood boasting a floral arrangement in red, white, and blue blooms. They were followed by the Wind Angels dressed uniformly in patriotic colors with the wings swaying softly in the breeze. Fernando and Mario sat resplendent on their stallions, leading the large group of men from the Garcia Lopez Vineyards identically dressed and seated on their horses. Their appearance in the parade was rewarded with generous applause.

At the conclusion of the event, all participants received the blessings of Monsignor Elvillo, who represented the church. It was he who awarded the Golden Goblet for the best of the 1967 vintage to the Garcia Lopez Winery. Fernando lifted the trophy high for all to see.

"Thank you, your Honor, for awarding us this prized recognition. Thank you to all who work with me in the vineyards and the winery. Without your faithful and diligent contributions, none of this would've ever been possible. I thank you from the bottom of my heart on behalf of my entire family."

He bowed gracefully toward the monsignor and the members of the selection committee. Those who stood closest could see the tears in his eyes as he spoke. He was regretting the fact that his father had not lived to see this day.

# Chapter 33

MARCH of 1969 brought distinct changes in the Lopez family. Young Mario faded out of the daily picture when he started attending Lower Prep at the Grange School in Santiago. Both Esmeralda and Mario's father strongly believed that it was critical for the boy to attend one of the best schools available to him. While he would be sorely missed during the school year, he and the family always looked forward to vacation times when he was able to return to the hacienda and familiar surroundings.

Alona attended kindergarten at a nearby facility, allowing Juanita to concentrate her efforts on the twins and to free up time for Doretta. Nursing the babies forced Doretta to be housebound. Nevertheless, she wanted to make a substantial contribution to the business of making and selling wine. Furthermore, staying near the twins gave her the opportunity to spend time with Esmeralda. With these thoughts in mind, she chose to discuss her plan of work with Fernando and Esmeralda.

"I spoke with Diego, and he assured me that one good glass

of Cabernet a night wouldn't do any harm to the twins while I'm still nursing. So treat me nicely and pour me a glass."

Making an attempt at imitating Don Carlos assessing the wine's characteristics, she lifted her glass toward Esmeralda.

"Here's to motherhood," she giggled. "Gosh, have I missed a good glass of wine for the last year. While we are all enjoying ourselves, I would like to discuss with you a certain plan."

"What plan might that be?" asked Fernando. Esmeralda was all ears.

"With Mario gone off to school and Alona spending the mornings in kindergarten, I can't just sit around this place until my breasts are in demand. I've worked all my adult life and need to feel productive in some fashion. I realize I can't work in the vineyards or the winery because of their location. Even if I could establish a regular feeding schedule, I would still spend more time driving back and forth, which I don't view as very productive. Of course, I could do as so many less fortunate have to do; I could haul the twins with me to work. Please spare me the lecture; I wouldn't do that anyway."

"Don't keep us guessing. So what's the plan?" was Fernando's comeback.

"I'm turning my confessional into a functional office. I already have a typewriter, a phone, etc. Perhaps a tabulator and calculator might come in handy. I could take care of a lot of the correspondence, invoicing, etc. You name it. I would like to have a hand in the business. And in between being useful to you and our business, I may spend time with your mother, who leads a pretty lonely existence these days. What do you say to that?"

"I think it's a wonderful idea for Doretta to become involved and keeping her mind sharp. I couldn't agree more with her assessment of the situation. And besides that, I love the idea of spending time with her when it isn't interfering with her work for you. Remember, she did have a responsible job when you met her. She only gave up her work because of being pregnant with your child," voiced Esmeralda.

"I'm not about to pick a fight with the two most important women in my life. If you want to turn the emporium of creativity into an annex of our family business, so be it. I'll do anything to accommodate you and make that possible. I have a good secretary, but there are many days when she is swamped with work and probably would love to take advantage of a helping hand."

"For one thing, you could route many incoming calls of inquiry to me. At this point, I'm pretty much trilingual, which should be of some benefit. You have many companies in German-speaking countries with whom you do business. So take advantage of my skills. Like I said before, I have to have something to keep my mind in circulation other than being numero uno in the mammary department for Lord knows how long."

"Are you sorry we created Elijah and Eduardo? Please don't say yes."

"Let's not even go there. I love the boys. If I didn't have all the help that is at my disposal, I might be overwhelmed having to deal with two infants at my age, and I would look at things differently if I had to be on duty all day and every day of the week. But that isn't the case. Just having to be around to nurse the boys simply is not enough for me to be fulfilled intellectually. I hope you can see my point."

"Doretta is right; men look at life from their point of view and don't realize a woman has other needs than being a good wife and mother. Most of us had a life before we married into our lot. I'm totally in support of what Doretta wants to achieve. So tuck away your chauvinistic attitude, and be helpful in setting up this office for your wife. In the end, she'll be happier, you'll be happier, and guess what? I'll be happier. Doesn't that count?"

"I give up. I know when I've met my match. I'll get things started first thing in the morning. Happy now?" Before another word could be added, he poured himself a second glass of wine.

"I don't dare have another glass although I'd love it. I'm glad you are seeing things my way. Just remember how happy I was working with you in the vineyards and would love doing it again. I have to be practical and accept the fact that it can't be done right now.

"Yes, one of the women on the staff had a baby two days after the boys were born, and she's actually approached me and offered to be a nursemaid. But that isn't what we want. I need to nurse those boys for the first year for their and our sakes. And to be honest with you, I don't want to give up those moments of utter closeness to them for any kind of a job. I like to think that you can see both sides of the coin.

"When I give up nursing our sons, we can revisit my proposal and make necessary changes. For now, I like the idea of taking care of my motherly and wifely duties as I've suggested. And thanks, Esmeralda, for your strong support."

Esmeralda lifted her glass of Dom Perignon: "Here's to us women. We need to stick together."

Doretta's proposal became reality within a matter of two weeks. Amanda, Fernando's secretary, had no problem at all with forwarding any phone calls dealing with inquiries to Doretta. She was particularly pleased when the person on the other end of the line did not hablo español and would start chatting in English. Amanda thought the new arrangement was a marriage made in heaven.

Coming home at night, Fernando would deliver the paperwork for invoices to be typed, which were promptly executed the next morning and posted to the customers. Doretta believed she was making a contribution to the business, and Amanda could concentrate on different issues. It was a good working relationship all the way around.

※

The year flew by and Doretta looked forward to being less housebound. She continued to work regularly, but donated as much time as possible to Mario and Alona when they were not in school. After the initial shock of being separated from his family, Mario made new friends at school and enjoyed his teachers and the subjects he was studying. But right now, he was glad it was early December, and he was home for his long summer vacation. He was looking forward to the Christmas celebration surrounded by his family.

He owned up to his mother that his language skills in English and German came in quite handy.

"Well, I'm happy to know that all those hours of drilling and correcting you are paying off. What are your favorite subjects in school?"

"I love math and English, and I dabble a little in painting. Perhaps next year I would like to take piano lessons, just for something different to do."

"That will make your grandma very happy. You know how much she loves music. She hasn't played her piano ever since she had the stroke. She will love listening to you and perhaps even give you some helpful hints on how to play. It's a shame she doesn't want to try. She told me not too long ago that she really misses it but can't stand the way her imperfect playing sounds to her. Who knows, she might offer to teach you. From what your father tells me, she was very accomplished years ago."

"I like what you are doing for Dad. It's nice for you to keep a hand in the business; but at the same time, you can be there for my brothers and for Grandma. She was so sad after Grandpa died."

"Well, the best thing you and Dad did was to get Pablo for me for my birthday. He's so much company for Grandma and me. She absolutely adores Pablo."

"He's grown into a beautiful creature. I wish I could have him at school. I've actually asked about it, but there is no way they would allow me to have Pablo with me in the dorm. If I were blind or had some other handicap, then I might be allowed to have a service dog. Of course, that is luckily not the case; but unluckily, it would be the only way of having Pablo with me. So you better love him for you and for me. You should have seen him jump right up on me when I got out of Juan's car. He was all over me. I thought he might have forgotten me. Not so. He's one smart cookie."

"You have no idea how much joy Pablo has brought to all of us. He's become a regular member of the family. Alona was a tad skittish around him in the beginning. Now she can't wait for him to greet her with hugs and kisses when she comes home from school. He stands by the window in my office and watches when the school van drives in. I swear that dog can tell time."

"I'm so pleased to learn what an important role my little pup has assumed with all of you. I guess none of us realized how big a part Barney played in all of our lives until he was gone. Grandpa taught me a good lesson when he insisted that I learn about life and death as young as I was. I still remember the lesson you taught me after Grandpa died. Knowing what I know now, I'm glad you convinced me that God isn't mean."

"Come here, my big boy; give your mom a hug and a kiss. I miss you, too, every day that you are gone, but your papa was right sending you to a good school. It pleases me to know that you've learned to like the place. It would be terrible if you hated being there.

"Let's go into Grandma's wing. She's so looking forward to having you home for your long vacation. You've always filled a very special spot in her heart. No question, she loves Alona, but you and your brothers are clearly her favorites. She isn't obvious about it with Alona. Believe you me, she is very generous in buying things for her and loving her. But you boys have done it to her. She might envision Alona becoming a nun; but you boys will always be saints to her, and she can't wait for you to come marching in."

"Well, let's surprise her. I know the tune. Let's sing it together and shock the heck out of her. She'll love it," said Mario.

They did it. Doretta pretended to blow a trombone, and Mario acted as if he was playing a saxophone. Esmeralda didn't say a word; the tears were just rushing down her cheeks as she was watching them march in. She held her arms wide open and hugged Mario fiercely as if it was for a last time.

"Your grandfather loved that tune when Louis Armstrong played it. He always wanted to go to New Orleans and experience Preservation Hall. So many things he wished to do and see and never had the chance. I hope your father will take some time and enjoy his life with his family and travel the world. We lived and saw the world through the movies and now television; you need to see these things with your own eyes.

"But right now, I'm glad you are here with me. And before I forget about it, you must forgive this old woman, but I love my new companion. Thank you for finding Pablo for us. If you go into my bedroom, you'll find him napping on my bed. It's one of his favorite places to be, and I'm so thankful that you picked him. He's my other love."

"Go wash up and put on some clean clothes. Your father ought to be home any minute. He'll be hungry and ready for dinner. Let's not keep him waiting. Things are in high gear at the winery, and his days are full. He'll be very happy to share his day's experiences with you. Although you are only going on seven, he has great expectations for you and is eager to discuss certain issues. He knows how much you loved working in the vineyards with him. He's still laughing his head off when he tells the story of the 'grape-stomping' son of his."

"Don't remind me. I can still feel all that sticky and slimy all over me. He'll never get me to take part in that game again. He's on his own. I loved the parade and everything else; stomping the grapes was the pits. I still don't understand why he thinks that is so funny. Please don't bring up the subject. I want to have a good time while I'm home and not annoy my father. Deal?"

"Yes, Son. I won't bring up the subject. I hear the garage door; it must be your dad."

All eyes were on the entry as Fernando walked in. He placed a large envelope on Doretta's desk and then waved on his way up the marble staircase. "I'll be down in fifteen. I've got to clean my act before I can join you." He closed the door behind him—not too gently.

# Chapter 34

MARIO was the first of his family to rise. Usually, it was Doretta liking to work in her office in the quiet of the day. Her first caller was always Pablo, wanting to be let out of the house for his constitutional. Today, he sidled up to Mario as he saw him walking down the stairway.

"Come on, Pablo. Let's go for a little walk. Did you sleep well on Grandma's bed?" He scratched the dog behind his ears and at all the places well-known to him to be most pleasurable for Pablo. "You like having me home, don't you?" as he picked up his gait.

"How would you like to come with Dad and me to the vineyards and the winery today? Does Dad ever take you? You'll have to ride in the backseat of the Jeep, but you wouldn't mind, would you?"

As soon as Mario mentioned 'Jeep, Dad, vineyards, and winery,' the dog started yapping and waving his tail. Mario realized that smart Pablo understood what he was talking about.

"There's lots of work for me to do in the vineyards. You can come with me and run around to your hearts content. Aren't you glad I'm home for more than two months?" Pablo kept waving his tail. He may not have understood every word, but he was pleased to hear he was going to spend the day with Mario.

Walking back into the house, Pablo made his familiar rounds. First stop was at Doretta's compound, then Esmeralda's quarters, looking for Juan and Valentina, and finally charging up the stairway searching for Fernando. He found Fernando standing in the shower and barked at him.

"Hi buddy, are you checking up on me?" When he stepped out of the glass enclosure, Pablo was watching his every move, here and there giving out yelps of encouragement.

"Are you trying to tell me to get a move on? I know you, buddy. All I need to fetch is my belt to keep these jeans from falling off me and my loafers. There; I'm all set for the day. Are you happy now? Let's go see Grandma. I can smell you've been with Doretta already. No doubt, I can detect a hint of her Chanel No 5. You can't fool me."

Mario greeted his father as he saw him walk down to the central parlor; Pablo was trailing him closely.

"Have you had a discussion with my dog? It wouldn't surprise me if he got across to you what I suggested."

"I know what's coming. No wonder Pablo acted so excited to see me. Did you say anything about the Jeep and the winery? That little devil knows exactly what you were talking about."

"Yes, I dropped those names, and I'm sure he knew what I suggested. You mind if we take him along here and there? I'd love having him with me while working with the crew in the vineyards. I can't get over how strong he's become." He looked up at his dad with the biggest smile on his face.

"Dad, I'm so glad you let me have him. That was a fun day, but the best part was finding Pablo. Thanks!"

"Let's join Mom and Grandma for breakfast before they scold us. Leave it to me. I'll get Grandma's permission to take Pablo with us for the day. She doesn't mind as long as he's riding with me in the Jeep. I realize we got Pablo for Mom, and he is her dog; but Grandma has gotten almost too possessive of him. He fills her days with love and attention, and keeps her warm and protected at night. I don't know why, but lately she often feels insecure. She doesn't like some of the things she reads in the papers or learns from the news on TV. So let's see what she says."

"Buenos dias, guten Morgen, señoras. Did you rest well and are looking forward to a sunny day?"

"Buenos dias, señor. Why so formal this morning? Are you trying to get on my better side, Son? Let's hear what you have in mind."

"Mario is joining me at the vineyards today and would like to take Pablo along. Would that be OK, Mom? He loves that dog and misses him while he is at school. We won't do it every day, but now and then it would be fun for Mario and also be good for Pablo to get some real exercise."

"I understand completely. You take him along; Pablo will love being with you and the men working the vines. How are the grape arbors looking this year?"

"We'll have an excellent harvest. Many of the Cabernet grapes are showing signs of good coloring. We are ready to start cutting the first bunch as we speak. The Pinot Noir vines aren't quite there yet. It will be good to have all the help I can get. I'm pleased with the new men and women who've joined the company. Amanda did a great job of interviewing for the vacancies that occurred. I'm very pleased with the job my wife is doing and that she and Amanda have established such a great working relationship. Sure makes my job a lot easier. Thanks, dear."

"Before I head back to my desk," said Doretta, "I want to speak to Juanita and see how Elijah and Eduardo are getting along this morning. Elijah still fights her when she wants to give him his bottle, but she told me last night he was hungry enough not to resist her any longer. Other than this little quirk, they are both doing fine. I don't feel too guilty about turning the feeding over to Juanita.

"She did a wonderful job taking care of Alona and now looking after the twins. She loves the twin-buggy we got for the boys and takes them for rides almost every day after their morning baths.

"The one thing I've cautioned her about is the road that she likes to take. I tried to explain to her that she needs to walk against oncoming traffic, giving her a heads-up to see what's coming toward her. You may want to talk to her as well; I want to make sure she understands the reasons for my concerns." Doretta's face was marked by worry as she spoke.

"Next Sunday, I'll make it a point to walk with her and will push the pram and physically demonstrate to her what you have in mind. Then there shouldn't be any question about what you want her to do with the children when she takes them for a ride. How does that sound?" responded Fernando.

"Good idea. Be sure to call attention to that segment in the curve of the road where no sidewalk seems to exist. She always dismisses my concerns with being familiar with the road and that her mother used to push her in her pram along that way, and she's obviously survived the many rides without being harmed. That's supposed to put me at ease. I've spoken my piece."

"Don't work yourself into something that will upset you, please? I'll take care of it and will speak with Juanita. You want me to include Valentina and Juan in the conversation? They certainly know what you are talking about. He drives on that road often enough."

"You'll do as you see fit. Thanks," said Doretta.

Esmeralda hadn't missed a word of the conversation and felt wanted to speak to Doretta's issue.

"Doretta is absolutely right in being worried about that girl taking such chances. God forbid, if something should happen to those boys, I'd never forgive myself for not having spoken out. If it was I, I'd tell her to avoid the road all together.

"There are some lovely areas around the estate where she can take the children. It may be a bit harder to push the pram on unpaved roads, but she is young and shouldn't have any trouble doing so. I want you to make this quite clear to her. And if you have a problem with addressing Doretta and my concerns, I would have no difficulties speaking to her myself. I may be an old woman, but most people around here still remember who I was and who I am. I can assure you she won't have a doubt in her mind after I'm done speaking to her," voiced Esmeralda.

Both Doretta and Fernando nodded in agreement. They hadn't heard her speak in that manner for a long time. How well Doretta recalled. However, this morning she was totally of one mind with her mother-in-law.

"Señora, I'll take care of the matter. Not to worry." Esmeralda knew he understood her completely.

⋈

"Well, young man. Let's get Pablo, and hit the road. The vineyards are awaiting. Make sure you wear good shoes. You'll be OK in shorts and a short-sleeve shirt. There are hardly any mosquitoes this time of year. Just make sure you put on some sunscreen. I'll meet you and Pablo by the car."

"Okay, Dad. Will do." He kissed his mother and grandmother and looked for Pablo, who was having his early snooze lying in the morning sun on Grandma's bed. Pablo hadn't gotten the drift of the table conversation and was sound asleep.

As Fernando pulled away from the hacienda, Mario turned to his father. "I've never seen Grandma so mad at any time. She was on fire this morning. Was she serious about what people thought of her? She's always been so nice and loving to me."

"She wasn't really mad at me and just wanted to make sure that I will impress on Juanita the importance of knowing what to do and what not to do when she takes your brothers for a ride. Grandma loves all of you kids very much and doesn't want anything to happen to you. Ever since she lost my brother at such a young age and I was all she had, she's become terribly protective and possessive of me and, now, you kids.

"Grandma could be stern, and some people thought she was very mean; but she has changed in her ways. In her old age, she has nothing but love and concern for all of us. But, not to worry. I'll have a good chat with Juanita on Sunday when I'll accompany her on the walk with your brothers."

Mario was watching Pablo sitting in the backseat, enjoying the breeze and taking in the scenery as it rolled by. Now and then, there would be a woof or two when he spotted something of interest. Otherwise, he seemed to be perfectly content to have come along for the ride. They made a quick stop at the winery to let Amanda know where they were headed. Pablo jumped out of the car knowing he would get a friendly pat from Amanda. They had gotten to be good friends.

"Here's my buddy. Come let me see you. Looks like Mario gave you a good brushing this morning. You'll need it again for sure when you go home tonight." She knew how he loved to roll in the dead leaves and weeds on the ground. He was always ready for a major brushing at the end of the day.

"I gather the men are already working. This morning, I'll stop first at lot fifty-two. I want to introduce Mario to the young man you hired three weeks ago. Did you say his name is Geronimo? I think he'll be a good one to work alongside Mario. Some of our elder workers don't have the patience to teach a young buck. And I can't hang around for any length of time. I need to check on a couple of areas that are on the other side of the yard."

"I believe Geronimo will work well with Mario. He isn't as young as you think; he has a son Mario's age. That should really make it fun for both. So better get going. Mario, you and Pablo have fun today. See you later," said Amanda. Fernando knew when he was being shooed out the door.

They would arrive at lot fifty-two ten minutes later. On the way, they passed the large shed that housed the wings for the Wind Angels. Pablo barked as they were passing by. "He knows that place. I let him take a peek at the angels' wings a few weeks ago. He was really intrigued when he saw those things move in the wind. You would have thought he'd seen ghosts."

"Well, I think he's not far off the mark. First time I saw them, I got scared. They are eerie looking hanging from the ceiling. If it was just a few of them, that wouldn't be so impressive; but more than two hundred hanging and moving the way they do gives me the creeps. One of these days, I want to see them in real action. The way you and Grandpa talked about the wings and the torches burning in all those rows of grapevines must be quite the sight."

"I cannot make any promises, but we never know. If it will occur this year, it could be while you are on vacation. It can happen in October and sometimes in late February and early March. The weather gods can be very fickle."

"What do you mean by that?"

"I meant to say the weather is very unpredictable. Living so close to the high mountains, anything can happen almost anytime. We've had heatwaves in the middle of winter and snowstorms and hard frosts in the middle of summer. It's for that reason, that your grandfather and I were always happiest when the grapes were safely harvested, properly stomped, and fermenting in our oak barrels. Nothing can go wrong there other than something stupid committed by man. And that happens too now and then."

Mario just listened. He wasn't about to seek verification on the stomping process done properly or not. Fernando drove off the gravel road and parked the Jeep near lot fifty-two. He spotted Geronimo and walked up to him with Mario and Pablo close in tow. He extended his right hand in greeting.

"Buenos dias, señor. This is my son Mario and his buddy Pablo." Pablo was already taking his first roll in the leaves and weeds.

"Nice meeting you, Geronimo." Mario shook hands with the man. "My dad's secretary mentioned you have a son my age. What's his name?"

"My son's name is Carlos. He goes to a special school; he was born deaf. Maybe someday you'll get to meet him. He's a hard worker when he's given the chance. I like your pal; what a beautiful lab. He'll be fun to have around. Have you done any work in the vineyards before?"

"Yes, last year. My mom and I worked at cutting grapes for a whole day. That was a lot of fun. This year, my hands are bigger, and I've practiced using the cutter. I'm sure I will hold my own. You'll tell me when I'm not doing it right, won't you?"

"I surely will, Mario." They could tell the boss was antsy.

"Well, Son. I've got to get over to the other side of the mountain. We'll be harvesting for the first time in the area where we planted a thousand vines of Pinot Noir. It's an experiment that I hope will pay off. It was Grandpa's idea to try something new. You and Pablo behave yourselves and make me proud of you." He hugged his son and shook paws with Pablo before he literally jumped into his Jeep.

The dust-covered Jeep approached lot fifty-two before four o'clock. Fernando counted five wagons heavily laden with purple grapes. He was pleased with the amount of fruit that had been gathered and would be on its way to the processing plant. Geronimo, Mario, and Pablo were all sprawled on the ground enjoying a well-deserved rest.

"Tired, eh? Looks like you and the crew had a productive day. We are not quite ready to cut the Pinot Noir, give or take a week or two. Are you and Pablo ready to head home? He looks like he's had his fill of fresh air. Did you and Geronimo like the lunch Valentina packed for you?"

"Yes, we did. The lemonade was a blessing. I gave part of our sandwiches to Pablo. That was OK to do, right?"

"Didn't he like his regular food I left?"

"Oh, he did, but when he ate it all and saw us munching on our sandwiches, we could tell he was still hungry. Neither Geronimo nor I could resist those begging eyes."

"That's okay, Son, as long as you didn't let him have any of your chocolate. That wouldn't be a good idea. Of course, you know all about that. Let's get moving. Mario, you and Pablo hop in the backseat. I'll give Geronimo a lift to his bus stop. This way he'll get home a little earlier."

"Muchas gracias, señor; that's very thoughtful of you." When Fernando pulled up by the bus stop, Geronimo lifted his Gaucho sombrero: "Muchas gracias, señores." He firmly shook hands with Mario and his father.

As he drove toward the Garcia Lopez Hacienda, Fernando turned to his son who had moved to the front passenger seat. "That's a real gentleman for you. I hope you enjoyed working with him. How do your hands feel after working for a good part of the day?"

"My hands are okay, but now I know what old men mean

when they talk about an aching back. That hot shower will feel just great, Dad."

"It will. Better yet, you won't feel a thing later. For sure, you won't have any trouble sleeping tonight. How about coming out with me sometime next week to the other side of the mountain? You'll get to know some other people working for the company. They are all anxious to meet you. Sounds like the guys have been talking about you. Just wait until they meet you and Pablo."

"Next week will be good. I promised Grandma I would accompany her into the city one day to do some shopping. She insists on buying me new clothes for the upcoming school year and wants me to let her know what I want for Christmas. Is that okay with you? Juan will drive us into town. She wants to have lunch with me at some fancy restaurant she and Mom go to when they attend the opera. I don't have a problem with what she wants to do right now. I just hope she doesn't expect me to join her and Mom at the opera next fall."

"You and Grandma have fun doing that shopping spree. As far as the opera is concerned, she might ask you to meet her and Mom once or twice during the season. Do me a favor. Be a good grandson, and make Grandma happy. We don't know how long we'll have her around. When she does ask you, tell her to invite you on an evening when it isn't an extra-long or tragic opera. She'll understand. Some of the lighter fare, oper-ettas, can be fun. They are almost like musicals, which you like."

"Good advice, Dad. I'll keep that in mind if she should bring up the subject. For now, let's let sleeping dogs lie."

※

They arrived shortly before sundown and were greeted by Esmeralda. "Looks like we've had a full day of hard work. My, Pablo, Juan better brush you right away. You cannot jump on my bed as dusty as you are. And you two better get into a shower. I'll tell your mother that you are home from the hills." She walked to Doretta's office, her cane punctuating every step she took.

"Our gentlemen have returned from work. They and Pablo look the part. I've asked for Juan to clean up and brush Pablo and have sent our men to their respective showers. Are you almost done for the day?"

"Just about. I finished answering several inquiries from Germany regarding our last three vintages of Cabernet. They found our price line for these quality wines attractive and may buy some if shipping costs won't be too harsh on their bottom line."

"I'm so proud of you the way you've gotten involved in the company. It's something I was never given an opportunity to do. You do it well, and I know Fernando appreciates all you take on. He should. What's absolutely the best is that I have you close to me, and you can look in on the boys anytime you want. Did I hear you tell Valentina that you watched Elijah trying to get on his feet?" asked Esmeralda.

"I did. I was totally surprised. And Eduardo was closely observing his brother. He'll probably try it next. I can't believe we are having their first birthday party in a few days. Where does time go?"

"I'm glad not to be the only one saying that. I make that statement at least once a day. In your case, time has gone by swiftly because you are living life to the fullest and feel productive and fulfilled when you put your head down at night.

You have children who adore you and a husband who loves you. And without wanting to beat my own drum, you also have me, who has learned to love you and to appreciate everything you do," was Esmeralda's reply.

"Thanks, Mom. How well I remember when you didn't want to be called anything but Esmeralda or Señora Garcia Lopez, or just plain Señora. We've come a long way in almost seven years, haven't we? I couldn't be happier the way things turned out."

Esmeralda bent down and hugged Doretta. "Let's have a drink before our men join us. I'm aware, he's only a boy, but you wouldn't know it, the way he works, talks, and conducts himself. Don Carlos would be so proud to call him his first grandson.

"I feel adventurous; I'll have a glass of our best Cabernet with you. Diego always tells me it's good for my health." Doretta poured the brilliantly colored wine into two of Esmeralda's favorite crystal goblets. As they lifted the glasses toward each other, they spoke in one voice. "L'Chaim." Doretta smiled broadly; she'd never heard those words spoken by Esmeralda.

# Chapter 35

"Buenos dias, Juanita. I would like to talk to you while we are taking the boys for a stroll. Let's stay on the left side of the road and walk against the traffic."

"Buenos dias, señor!"

"Isn't it a lovely morning? I thought I'd catch you before you and your parents leave for the Sunday morning mass. Both my wife and my mother are very much concerned about you walking with the pram on the busy road."

"But the paved road is much easier and nicer to walk."

"That may be true, but the danger of you and the boys getting into an accident is much greater, especially in that curve where the pathway is so narrow and partially broken."

"I always watch and am careful."

"Nevertheless, these are some changes we insist on. We prefer that you not walk on the paved road after this. On days when we have not had any rain for a while, the walkways around the hacienda are quite maneuverable and shouldn't be difficult for you to handle. If we had rain during the night or the day before, you may take the pram on the paved road but you must walk against the oncoming traffic so that you and the pram can easily be seen by the drivers and you can see what's coming at you. If you have to take the paved road, I want you to go exactly where we are walking now. Do you understand me?"

"Si, Señor Fernando. I'll do as you say. You boss man."

"I'll leave you to your walk and will report our conversation to my wife and Señora Esmeralda. Have a good day."

He checked his wristwatch. *I'll have time for breakfast with my ladies. I don't want to be late for my first flying lesson*, thought Fernando. Doretta and Esmeralda, already seated and chatting with Mario at the dining room table, looked up in surprise.

"Where have you been?" inquired his mother.

"As promised, I had my talk with Juanita. I gave her specific instructions according to your wishes. I believe she understood what I was telling her and will act accordingly. I was polite but firm in what I had to convey to her. Her family has worked for us for many years; I did not want to create any bad blood."

"Thank you for speaking to her," said Esmeralda. Doretta nodded in agreement.

"I want to just grab a quick bite and a cup of coffee before I head to the airfield. I haven't told any of you, but I'm starting to take flying lessons this morning. It is something I've always been interested in doing. There's no better time than now. I'm still young enough to learn and to be issued a pilot's license."

There was dead silence momentarily; it was exactly as he had expected, but he wasn't about to bow to any objections by his mother or his wife.

"What made you decide to do this now?" said Esmeralda.

"Mother, Dad and I talked about it shortly after I returned from Europe. Then I became too involved in the business, and the years went by. Now that we are doing well and everyone is healthy, I don't have to worry about a pregnant wife or financial considerations. I want to follow my dream. Please let's not take this any further. Doretta has known about my passion for some time, right?"

"It's true, Mom. He has often spoken of wanting to do it. I won't stay in his way."

"May I come with you, Dad?" Mario asked.

"You may come with me to the airfield and watch me being taught, but you will not be allowed on the plane during my lessons. Someday, after I have my license, you certainly will get plenty of opportunities to fly with me. I hope your mom will join in the adventure. Speaking of adventure, you and I better be on our way. We'll tell you all about it at dinner."

He kissed Doretta on the cheek and bowed toward his mother. "Come on, young man. Wish me luck!" They rushed out to the Jeep and were on their way to the airfield. Fernando knew precisely where he was to meet his instructor and plane. He recognized the HFB 320 Hansa Jet from a distance.

"That's it, Son. What do you say?"

"My God, Dad. That's a jet plane. Are you sure you want to learn to fly a jet? I had visions of a little puddle jumper."

"Grandpa and I looked at this aircraft when it was first shown at an air show in 1964. It's for that reason I want to learn to fly on this model. He always encouraged me to follow my dreams."

"Boy, Dad, this is really exciting. I can't wait for you to have your license and to fly with you. Won't that be fun? You have any idea yet where you might want to fly when you are ready?"

"I do. But for now you'll have to wait. It's supposed to be a surprise for you, your sister, and Mom. I doubt Grandma will want to get on any plane, never mind with a freshly baked pilot."

"Good luck with your lesson; here comes your instructor. Have fun. I'll keep my eyes on you." The instructor walked up to Fernando and stuck out his hand to greet his student.

"Señor Garcia Lopez? I'm Walter Hague, your flight instructor. I've flown this jet for almost five years. It's a real beaut. You'll enjoy learning to fly her. Is this your son?"

"Yes, this is Mario. He'll be seven in a few weeks. He can't wait to get on a plane with his papa when he knows how to fly."

"I'll bend the rules. You'll come with us today. You just stay buckled in your seat and just watch. No talking. Your papa has to hear every word I say. Understood? Let's get on this machine."

Mario was speechless and followed the man's instructions. He quickly climbed up the steps and entered the plane. "Dad, this is really cool. Look at those fancy seats and all those buttons, lights, and levers to push and move. Wow! How much does this thing cost?"

"You mean the flight lessons or the plane itself?"

"I mean the airplane. It looks very expensive."

"I believe the cheapest version sells for about one million dollars."

"Did you hear that, Dad? One million dollars?" His mouth stayed agape.

"Grab that seat on the aisle in the first row. From there, you'll have the best view of your dad learning how to fly this wonderful machine."

Fernando and Walter got into their seats, adjusted them to their personal comfort, and buckled themselves in. Both men were wearing earphones to provide superior communication. Walter adjusted his mike, making sure Fernando heard every word. His first instruction was to put the plane into motion and taxi to the runway. So far so good. It didn't take long, and Fernando had them airborne.

Instructor and student nodded at each other with appreciation. The first part of the lesson went very well and was subject to mutual approval. As they approached the landing strip, Fernando wasn't as relaxed as he had been during the flight. The touch down was not quite perfect but not disastrous.

"A bit rough on the landing. We'll work on that next Wednesday. I have another lesson scheduled for you at noon. That will give you time to get your crew started in the vineyards, and we can enjoy a good hour in the air and work on some of the finer points. We definitely want to have a softer landing next time. How does that sound?"

"Sounds great. I'll see you at noon, and I'll be alone.

"How did you like that, Son? Wasn't it fun?"

"Yes, Dad—all but that bump at the end. For a second, I thought we weren't going to make it. But you did well otherwise. Yes, it was fun. And I was happy you let me on the plane, Señor Hague. I hadn't expected that."

"My pleasure. Just don't talk about it in school. Next time you'll get on an airplane, will be with your father being a certified pilot. It will be a while, but he'll make it. He's got lots of potential."

All shook hands before Fernando and Mario headed back to the hacienda in the Jeep. "Dad, it was really neat that your instructor let me on the airplane to watch you fly. It's a cool plane. That's not the one you are planning to buy, or is it?"

"It might turn out to be the one if I can get a good deal. Grandpa left me one million in a special fund to buy my own plane. Grandma knows about the fund, she just doesn't know about it being designated to buy a jet. I'll let that be one of my surprises."

Mario couldn't wait to get to the house and share his adventurous morning with his mom and his grandmother. He ran into the house yelling for them. He found them both seated in his mother's office.

"You won't believe what happened!"

"Where's your father? Is he all right? Nothing bad happened on the plane?" asked Esmeralda. Doretta was just staring into space.

"Grandma and Mom, Dad is just fine! He did a great job of flying the jet. But the best thing was the instructor allowed me to be on the plane."

"Oh Dios mío! Both of you on a jet and your father just learning to fly. How could the instructor permit that? You are giving me heart failure," said Esmeralda.

"Grandma, it was a hoot. Dad will be a great pilot. Remember, the instructor is in control of the jet. I wasn't scared at all. It was so much fun. I wish they'd let me come for the next lesson next Wednesday, but Dad has other ideas."

"What's all this whining about? Nothing to worry. My instructor has been piloting that plane for close to five years.

He knows it inside out. So cool it. I'm good with the instructor; he's a very competent guy. He bent the rules for Mario, but he loved it. And we are both here safe and sound. So no more whining, please.

"Depending on how things go in the next few weeks, I'll have my license by the end of May. Fall will be a great time to do a bit of traveling. And I may buy my own plane. It will give us an opportunity to do some fascinating exploring of the world. That's what Dad wanted me to do, and he made adequate provisions for it. If you've been wondering, Mom, about the special fund he created for me, he intended for me to buy my own flying machine."

"Interesting, he never said a word about it to me."

"When we went to the bank to make the arrangements, he told me it was a father/son thing. I guess he meant it."

"Isn't that close to a million dollars in that account?"

"Yes, it is actually one million dollars plus interest earned. I may not spend all of it on buying the jet. If I have to, the money is there for me to use. I won't use any company funds for my personal pleasure."

"Thank you for being my responsible son."

Nevertheless, Esmeralda couldn't hide the fact that she still had serious reservations about her son's latest flight of fancy.

"I would like our Sunday dinner to be a family affair. I want my entire family seated at my table tonight. Juanita can bring up the highchairs from the nursery, and we can put a booster on one of the chairs for Alona. Juanita can assist with feeding the younger children. It won't be perfect, but that doesn't matter tonight. What's important to me is that I'm surrounded by my entire family."

"What's the matter, Mom? Is there anything wrong with you? Did you have a bad report from the doctor this week?"

"None of it. I'm my usual self. After all the excitement in the last few days, this business with Juanita, and now these flying lessons, I just want you all real close to me and thank the dear God for keeping you all safe. That's all."

"Well, don't you do that every night anyway? I always see you kneeling in front of the little altar in your boudoir."

"Now, now, Son. Are you spying on your old mother? Can't I do anything in private?"

"Mom, I'm not spying—just keeping a watchful eye on you as Dad asked me to do. He may be gone, but his influence is still with us."

"Muchas gracias, Dios mío!"

# Chapter 36

FERNANDO'S flying license was issued on June 1, 1970. He, Doretta, and Mario made a day of it and drove to the airfield in Santiago. Walter Hague had volunteered to participate in Fernando's negotiations for the jet. The plane under consideration was less than one year old. He offered the seller seven hundred and eighty thousand dollars. Walter Hague thought that was a fair offer. An hour later, all papers were signed, the funds expertly transferred, and the purchase duly notarized. Fernando was the proud owner of his own HFB 320 Hansa Jet. With its capacity for ten passengers, he intended to use it for some of his business travel. He would be able to write off certain trips as professional expense.

"Well, all aboard. How about lunch in Puerto Montt? I hear there's a great German restaurant. Game, Walter?"

"Don't have to ask me twice. I'll go to the Club Alemán any time."

With slow traffic on this early winter day, they were airborne quickly. They landed at the Puerto Montt airport not quite two hours later. The German feast was placed before them by two-thirty. And a feast it was. Fernando and Doretta had not tasted the likes of Jägerschnitzel, Knödel, and Rotkohl [dumplings and red cabbage] since they left Switzerland. The dessert buffet had Mario salivating. He was like a kid in a toy store.

"Did everyone like our little adventure?" inquired Fernando as he made a soft landing in Santiago.

There was a resounding "yes" from all passengers.

"We'll do it again real soon. I can't wait to take you to Puerto Natales and an adventure in Torres del Paine National Park. It's one of the finest parks in the world. Natives and foreigners consider it a national crown jewel; and best yet, it's now at our fingertips." There was applause from the passenger section.

⋊⋉

Not having Doretta or Mario close at hand, Esmeralda had ventured into the realm of the nursery. She was surprised to see Elijah and Eduardo trying to move around the room holding onto each other, grasping the hands of Juanita, or performing a balancing act by reaching for chairs, tables, and other low-level pieces of furniture.

"Well, aren't you cute. I had no idea you progressed already past the crawling stage. It won't be long, and I'll hear the first attempts at human communication. The boys don't speak yet, do they Juanita?"

"Actually, señora, when your daughter-in-law enters the room, both greet her by saying 'Mama,' and I've heard Elijah greet your son with 'Papa.' It won't be long before they'll try other words. They are very smart kids."

"I guess I better stop in here more often; they might get to like their grandmother. On another matter, Juanita, I was pleased to hear that Señor Fernando spoke to you regarding the concerns my daughter-in-law and I had about you taking the children onto the paved road. Please don't take the children there. All that traffic on the road frightens me. Thank you for listening to my son." She walked toward Doretta's office as she heard the car pull in. She greeted them with open arms.

"How is Captain Garcia Lopez?"

"Captain, not quite yet. I'm just a pilot and the proud owner of a great plane. Ask my son and his mother what they think of their experiences today."

"Come here, Mario. Tell Grandma all about it."

"Dad did OK flying all the way down to Puerto Montt. We would never have had lunch at Club Alemán today had it not been for Dad flying us there. It was marvelous, Grandma. I mean the flight and the food.

"Flying down there, we could see the Andes Mountains in the distance over our left shoulders, the Chilean fjords and glaciers beneath us, and the Pacific looking over our right shoulders. Dad flew as low as he was allowed. Thus, we could see whales breaching and schools of dolphins leaping in the air. Next time we fly north close to sunset, Dad wants me to look for the Green Flash. He says it's almost as beautiful as the Northern Lights. Grandma, you should have seen it all. I love flying. When I grow up, I want to be a pilot and fly all over the world. I never knew the world was this beautiful."

"I wish your grandfather could have heard you say those words. He always wanted to see so much more of this earth. I'm so happy that you and your parents can experience it now. It must be inspiring to see it all from above, giving you a totally different perspective of things. I wish I was younger and in better physical shape. You wouldn't be able to hold me back." She was heavily leaning on her cane as she spoke to her grandson.

Doretta reached for Esmeralda's right arm. "Please sit down. He'll go on and on about his exciting day. I liked Fernando's flight instructor, and the plane he bought is beautiful. I wish you would be willing to try it but understand your hesitancy at this stage in your life. It is a new experience. I wasn't sure I would like it but am willing to give it my best.

"I was glad when I stood once again on solid ground. Although, as you well know, it wasn't so solid for a few moments late this afternoon. It wasn't a biggie, but there was enough motion for me to almost lose my balance. I was glad it was over in seconds. I don't believe I'll ever get used to periodic earth movements."

"After a few earthquakes, you become accustomed. It's only the devastating ones that are scary, especially in densely populated places or the cities with tall buildings. The hacienda is built in such a way that you are hardly aware of earth movements. That's why I love living here. I feel so much safer all around.

"You had your excitement, and I had mine. I took heart and ventured into the nursery. I didn't believe my eyes when I watched the boys trying to walk. And Juanita tells me they are even beginning to call you and Fernando by name. That is wonderful. I'll make it a point of stopping in more often. They do grow up so quickly. I wish your mother and Andreas could have the experience; they simply live too far away. Of course,

I understand. You would never get me to sit in an airplane for close to twenty hours."

"That's my mother's argument. It's not just the comfort or discomfort; for her, it's the length of time being cooped up in a plane. I don't believe she's claustrophobic, but she feels threatened in confining spaces. I doubt she'll ever make that journey again. Fernando has talked to both of them, but she doesn't even want to think about flying. So photos, telephone conversations, letters, and packages will have to do the trick. There's nothing we can do. We can't do other than offer to make the trip as pleasant as possible. I can lead them just so far; I cannot make them swallow the idea. As they say in English, 'You can lead a horse to water but you can't make it drink.' It's the same idea."

"Let us enjoy the evening. We cannot solve all the problems of the world. I'm so pleased the three of you had such an enjoyable day. I can tell my son has indeed realized one of his dreams." Esmeralda led the way to the dining room.

# Chapter 37

In September 1971, Fernando called for a family conclave. After Don Carlos passed away, Esmeralda assumed the leadership as the matriarch. Only for the last two years had she deferred the honor of sitting at the head of the table to her son.

Doretta was seated to his right; his mother, still being Señora Esmeralda, to his immediate left; her first grandson, Mario, directly next to his grandmother, and his sister, Alona, close to her older brother. Elijah and Eduardo were sitting next to their mother.

At Fernando's request, the house servants closest to the Garcia Lopez family, Valentina, Juan, and Juanita, graced the opposite end of the long dining room table. This was much to the annoyance of Señora Esmeralda. In her mind, servants stood next to the table but would never be seated with the family. However, she believed her son had good reason for including the help in what he had to convey, and Esmeralda had absolutely no intent of challenging him or appearing confrontational.

"My reason for calling this gathering is to discuss an

upcoming extended journey I will be taking with my wife and the two older children. That said, Valentina and Juanita as well as Juan, will be totally responsible for the well-being of my mother, Señora Esmeralda, and our youngest children, Elijah and Eduardo, and of course, Pablo. In as much as I would like to have all of you partake of the adventure, due to age or circumstance, that isn't a possibility. Being in touch with the political atmosphere in our country, I do not wish to postpone our travels and must, therefore, impose these restrictions on who may and may not accompany us.

"We are booked on the M.S. Lindblad Explorer sailing out of Ushuaia, Argentina, on January 8, 1972. We will be sailing for two weeks through Antarctica. Our flight will take us first to Puerto Natales to explore Torres del Paine National Park before we fly to Ushuaia. Our departure from Santiago is planned for December 28. This means you will be on your own for not quite a month. Are there any questions?"

"This sounds very exciting, and I'm pleased that you will realize another of your long-held dreams. God forbid, if there was need, how would we get in touch with you? Neither the phone nor writing would be an option, correct?" as she raised her left eyebrow. Fernando knew his mother meant business.

"We'll need to check in at Torres del Paine and leave personal information. Headquarters would know how to reach us; however, on the ship, you will only be able to contact us by using wireless in an extreme situation. Does that speak to your concerns, Mother?"

"Yes, that is better than I had envisioned. I have no intention of bothering you while you are traveling; I wanted to know how I can reach you were there some matters of critical importance."

"We have three very busy months ahead of us; but with

the excellent help on board, I expect nothing but the best of outcomes. Aside from taking care of business, we'll have to complete serious shopping. I would like to suggest that Mario and I handle our shopping spree since I have a good feel for what we might need—especially for hiking in the national park.

"Doretta, I'll hold you responsible for taking care of Alona and your personal needs. Perhaps Mom would like to accompany you into the city. It will be a nice outing for her."

"I look forward to it," commented Esmeralda. She was ready for an outing into Santiago. "Maybe we could do the Saturday matinee of *Hänsel and Gretel* with Alona? It might be a wonderful way of introducing her to opera. Wouldn't that be fun, Alona?"

"Yes, Grandma. Mom has spoken about something from the opera that she really likes. I enjoyed the story; I've read it a few times in the book Grandma Gisela sent from Germany. It's so worn; we may have to get a new copy for our younger brothers."

"I'll let Oma Gisela know; she's always asking what she could send for you children. Oma has learned not to send any clothes; what we are wearing here is so different from what people wear in Europe," said Doretta.

"Attire on the M.S. Lindblad Explorer during the day is pretty straightforward with very little formal wear and mostly practical and weather-appropriate clothes and footwear. We'll need to be prepared to handle anything from sunny and pleasant to icy and very wintry. I understand we have to learn to be quick-change artists; the weather can turn from one second to the next. But we'll have lots of time to talk about all that," said Fernando, thinking he had the last word.

Elijah spoke up: "It not fair, we not go with you. We be good boys. Why she go and not we?" He pointed across the table at Alona.

"Alona will be almost seven years old, and no children under the age of six are allowed on the ship. So you'll just have to wait your turns. You'll have a lot of fun at home. Grandma and the others will make sure you won't be bored," Fernando responded. Eduardo thumbed his nose at his brother.

"You not do that. I older; Mom says me born first. You better watch out!" All who saw the exchange between the twins broke out in laughter.

)(

"I've ordered the tickets for *Hänsel and Gretel* for October 16. Would you like to have lunch with Mom and Grandma at Confitería Torres, Alona? It's a nice restaurant. Your mom and I go there regularly. I think you'll like it."

"That sounds like fun. I'm sure it will be different from what we get at the school cafeteria. The food's not bad; but week after week, it always seems the same."

"You have become such a well-mannered girl; Mom and I will be proud to show you off at the restaurant. We'll leave right after breakfast with Juan and Valentina. We'll start at Falabella's and look for some of the things Dad suggested you'll need on the trip. But let's not forget, Christmas and your birthday are coming up as well."

"You never forget, Grandma, do you?"

"Sweetheart, Grandma might be limping around like an old woman, but my mind is still pretty sharp. Thank God!"

"Grandma, what's so special about that opera? Isn't it all about those mean parents, the kids getting lost in the woods, and that terrible witch? It's really not a nice story. I like that the kids roast the nasty old witch and find their way home to their worried parents. They learned the hard way; it wasn't a good idea to send those children by themselves to search for food in the dark forest. It gives me the shivers just thinking about it, Grandma."

"You see, the story teaches you something. Out of the bad situation comes something good. That's what most fairy-tales try to teach us. But what your mom loves the most is the *Abendsegen* [Evening Benediction from Act II]. Ask Mom to sing it for you in German some evening. It sounds lovely when you hear it sung in her native tongue. You speak enough German and will understand the meaning of the words. I know you'll like it."

"Now I'm looking forward to going, Grandma. I didn't realize it would be sung in German. It will be a good way of testing what I've learned. Shopping sounds fun too. Is that the place where you and Mom have gotten some of your pretty dresses?"

"It is, and the lady who waits on us is from Essen, the city where your mom was born. She still speaks very good German. Won't that be fun?"

"Grandma, we'll have a wonderful day, just the three of us." Esmeralda kept smiling at her granddaughter, who was quickly becoming a young señorita. Unquestionably, Alona bore a strong resemblance to Esmeralda. She showed early signs of having her grandmother's high cheekbones, the striking forehead and hairline, her beautiful green eyes, and her expressive mouth. Mario was a reinvention of his father, whereas the twins clearly favored the Osram bloodline.

# Chapter 38

LEAVING Falabella's, Juan was loaded down with packages. He was sorry he had left Valentina waiting in the limo. She could have given him a helping hand. "Looks like the señoras had fun today," observed Juan.

"Oh, yes. Grandma was most generous buying dresses and shoes for Alona. I had a great time selecting sweaters, anoraks, parkas, and boots for the Antarctica trip—not to mention flannel shirts, wool hats and scarves, and jeans. Alona didn't care for the silk underwear, but I know she will appreciate what we selected once she gets to the deep south of the world. It may be the height of summer on our calendar; but the sudden and bracing winds and the pelting by snow and hail will teach all of us quickly that we are indeed in Antarctica, the coldest place on earth," said Doretta.

"Grandma, I love the elegant dress you bought me for the visit to the opera. It goes well with Mom's favorite dress. The shoes are cute, too. I'm glad I don't have to wear those high heels that Mom sports with that outfit. She looks great in those shoes. I don't think I could walk in them."

"Someday you will when you are all grown up. For now, the black patent leathers will work just fine for you. How did you get along with Frau Flott? Isn't she a helpful lady? I don't know how I would do all that shopping any longer without her helpful hints," said Grandma.

"She does speak fluent German. I had a nice chat with her. She said she would drop Oma Gisela a note and tell her about our shopping spree today. I guess they write to each other regularly. I think that is nice."

"I agree. She told me that there are a lot of German people living in Santiago, and she enjoys speaking to them in their native language. It makes them feel more at home," said Esmeralda.

"What will Juan and Valentina do when we go out for lunch and to the opera?" Alona wanted to know.

"They usually have a bite at one of their favorite haunts in town. Valentina used to work at Falabella's before she met Juan, who was working for us. It's after they were married that she came to live with us again. She was my personal maid until I started sharing her with your mom."

"Will I have a personal maid when I'm grown up, Grandma?"

"You certainly will; maybe we'll promote Juanita or hire someone new. As I said, they'll visit good friends in town while we enjoy the opera. It's nice for them to have a few hours of not having to worry about their jobs.

"No one needs to feel badly for them; your father pays his help very well. He's a wealthy man. He doesn't like spending money frivolously but is generous with his wealth and love for all who live under his roof, including all who work with him. He learned that from your grandfather. You don't remember him, do you?"

"I remember him as being a big man who often smiled and spoke lovingly to Mario. He'd pick me up and give me hugs and kisses. That's about it."

"I understand; you were barely three years old when he left us. But now you have me, and I love you with all my heart. Don't get me wrong, I'm fond of my boys, but you are my one and only granddaughter—and it doesn't hurt that you are like me."

"Is that good?"

"I hope to God it is! Don't let anyone tell you otherwise. We are very special—you and I." Esmeralda embraced her granddaughter and hugged her firmly.

"Now we better be off for that lunch at Confitería Torres. I know you'll like the elegance of the dining room and the men in fancy dress waiting on us. We don't want to be late for the opera."

※

As they were taking their places in their booth at the Teatro, Alona ran her hands over the red velvet covering of the seats. She spotted the opera glasses at her seat and started to twirl them. She was fascinated by the sounds of the orchestra tuning up and marveled at the abundance of the many different instruments. She had never seen some of the brass and woodwinds and certainly never a harp.

"Grandma and Mom, this is wonderful. Thank you for bringing me. I never dreamt it could be so exciting. I love seeing all those different instruments. They even have two pianos. What's that big golden thing with the large strings on it? That thing is awesome!"

"Oh, that's a harp. It probably will be played by a lady. There are not too many male harpists."

"Is that why Daddy sometimes says: 'Stop your harping!'"

"That's not a nice thing to say. You just wait until the lady plays the harp; then you'll feel differently about the instrument."

The conductor walked to the podium and was greeted by resounding applause. "Why are they applauding? I haven't heard anyone sing."

"He's the man in charge of the players in the orchestra. When he signals them by gesturing with the little stick you see in his right hand, they know what and how to play it. You just wait and watch. But now you must not talk any longer. Just watch and listen to the music and the singing, OK?"

"Okay, Grandma." Alona hadn't figured out how to use the opera glasses. Her mom showed her without saying a word. When the curtain went up on the first act, Alona was spellbound; she listened to every word sung. When refreshments were served during the first intermission, she was pleased to receive cookies and juice. "Those champagne glasses are beautiful, Grandma. Are they crystal? They sound like crystal when you and Mom toast each other."

"Yes, they are the finest Bohemian crystal one can buy. Nothing but the best in the Teatro. They are ready for the second act. Watch Mom when they start singing about the angels. You'll see what I meant when I told you she absolutely adores that passage."

As the chorus began singing the *Abendsegen*, Alona reached out for her mom's hand, seeing that she was dissolved in tears. She wanted to speak to her mother but didn't dare make a sound; she didn't want to incur a reprimand for improper behavior on this wondrous day. Doretta saw her troubled child clearly wanting to express her empathy for her mother. She squeezed Alona's hands lovingly and smiled through her tears. Their souls were one at that very moment. Esmeralda couldn't have been more touched by any other scene; as her vision turned back to the stage, she couldn't hold back her own tears of joy.

Walking out of the Teatro, Alona was full of happiness. "Thank you, thank you both for taking me. I loved it. The opera is so much better than the story. It's the music and the singing that make you forget about the bad things that are happening. And Mom, the *Abendsegen* was the best. I can see why you love it so much. It is very touching between the words and the music. It made me feel close to heaven. Is that where Grandpa is these days?"

"Yes, Alona. That's where Grandpa is right now," said Doretta and Esmeralda speaking in one voice.

"Grandma told me you liked to sing the *Abendsegen* to me when I was a baby. Would you do it again sometime? It would be a wonderful way to fall asleep."

"How about tonight? It would be a perfect way to end a perfect day. I love you!" whispered Doretta as she embraced her daughter.

# Chapter 39

December 15 was a crisp and clear day; it would be a day of celebration at the Garcia Lopez Hacienda since this was the day of Elijah and Eduardo's third birthdays. There would be two identical birthday cakes, each bearing three blue candles; lots of singing; and opening of presents in the nursery. Juanita had done a splendid job of decorating the boys' room.

Early in the morning, Fernando and a couple of his men had gone to the Christmas tree farm and selected the perfect tree to grace the central parlor of the house. In previous years, he'd taken Mario to select the tree. Now that the boy was away at school, he opted to be his own judge for selecting a handsome specimen. As much as he would have liked having Elijah and Eduardo along for the adventure, they were too young for the experience.

He had help fitting it into the fancy stand that was always filled with water for the purpose of keeping the tree fresh. Once the tree was firmly established in its substantial stand, he asked all who were there to lend a helping hand in decorating it.

"Alona, Daddy has to climb to the top on the tallest ladder

in the house. That's the rule. No little people or seniors on the ladder. There are many places on the bottom and in easy reach for you and Grandma to hang your favorite ornaments. Although before you do any hanging of ornaments, I need to string the lights from top to bottom. Next come the strings of dried berries and corn the women at the vineyards created. Then it will be time to hang ornaments. Do we all understand the drill?"

"Yes, señor," said Alona, imitating her older brother when saluting their father, the pilot. A burst of chuckles echoed through the house. Everyone was having fun. Three hours later, all stood back to admire the yuletide masterpiece in which all on site had given a helping hand.

"We'll wait to put the presents under the tree, especially edible presents sent by Oma Gisela and Andreas from Germany. We learned our lesson last year, didn't we? Pablo had a ball ripping open any odoriferous offerings," said Doretta.

"I believe we shouldn't tempt him. There are plenty of areas on the buffets and credenzas in the hall to display those goodies. Let's not torture our otherwise very well-behaved dog. It isn't fair to tease him, and getting into chocolates and marzipan could spell death for Pablo," offered Fernando.

"Is that true, Daddy? Pablo could die if we would feed him chocolate?" Alona asked.

"Depending on how much, that could be the case. If nothing else, he could be a very sick puppy, and that we wouldn't want to have on Christmas, right?"

"Oh no, Daddy. We'll tell Santa to just put non-edible presents under the tree. I'll write him a note in three languages and leave it by the cookies and milk we always put on the windowsill. You think he'll get it?"

"That's a very smart girl. Most santas read English very well, but adding the Spanish and German will help. Maybe our Santa will fly down to us from way up north. You know he's very popular in Germany around the fifth of December. After that, he travels to many other countries. He leaves the delivery of Christmas presents in Germany and other German-speaking countries to the Christkind [christ child]. What do you think of that?"

"I'm sure Santa knows where we live; we put German, English, Spanish, and Chilean flags on top of the house. He shouldn't have any difficulty finding us." When she finally went to bed that night, she insisted her mother sing *Abendsegen* instead of the spoken evening prayer.

Mario was astounded when he arrived from school and spotted the beautiful Christmas tree. There were so many ornaments he had admired since he was barely old enough to stand. Even as a toddler, he loved walking around the tree and carefully touching his favorite decorations. He could tell his father had done a splendid job of putting on the final layer of tinsel. He couldn't get over all presents tastefully arranged under the tree. Some were surely items he chose when he went with his father into town in preparation for the dream of a trip to Torres del Paine and Antarctica.

Come Christmas Eve, he knew the routine. Grandma always insisted all attend the mass at six o'clock at the Basilica. In her younger days, she loved the midnight mass; but these days she preferred to have dinner at a respectable hour followed by the opening of the presents. She knew her grandchildren were too anxious to wait for Christmas morning.

Fernando became misty-eyed as he put Elijah on his shoulders, walking him around the tree. "Isn't this a lot of fun, Elijah? You get to see the tree so much better than just standing next to it. Look at that pretty teddy bear sitting inside the tree."

"Can I touch him, Papa? He looks so soft."

"You sure can. We can do even better. You can hug him for a while, and then I'll put him back where he's sitting now. Deal?"

"Deal, Papa." Eduardo clamored by his pant legs.

"My turn, Papa. I wanna ride too!"

"Glad you spoke up; but Papa wouldn't forget you. You are my last and youngest boy. You are special too." *I don't know what's wrong with me, but I feel like these two really need my attention tonight,* crossed Fernando's mind. He reached for the hanky in his back pocket, wiping away his tears. He nearly stayed home, not wanting the boys left behind with Juanita. They were too young to attend mass with the others.

⋈

All festively dressed, they entered the hacienda after mass. "I thought Monsignor Elvillo led a fine service, didn't you think so, Doretta?" said Esmeralda.

"Yes, I loved the candlelight and the warmth of the church. The crèche was spectacular. The music was outstanding, and I appreciated that his homily didn't go on and on. No one wants to listen to a diatribe on Christmas Eve," replied Doretta.

"I wholeheartedly agree," was Fernando's contribution to the conversation. His mind was on dinner and opening presents. In that respect, he was fully in tune with his growing boys. He was pleased that Esmeralda suggested even Elijah and Eduardo be seated with them at the dining room table for the occasion. Juanita would feed them some of their favorites rather than expecting the young boys to partake of the adult yuletide fare.

"Cook is about to serve our hors d'oeuvres; I suggested oysters Rockefeller and escargot. Fernando, please open a bottle of Dom Perignon. We need a toast to usher in the holiday season, don't you think?" said his mother.

"Here's to a wonderful Christmas, a very happy New Year, a joyful journey, and best wishes to all our loved ones here and beyond!" offered Fernando. Esmeralda eyed Doretta still holding her glass. "L'Chaim," they spoke softly to each other as Esmeralda smiled upon her family.

The perfection of the Chateaubriand, white asparagus, and roasted potatoes was appreciated by the adults. The children couldn't wait for the baked Alaska to be served to all as the crowning touch to the superb dinner. They knew it would be time for presents after dessert. And so it was.

Fernando donned his Santa hat, letting the children know that he was personally chosen by Santa to be one of his helping elves. He was clever enough to arrange the presents in order of the children and the adults. He would start with the first present for Eduardo and end each round of distribution with Esmeralda. They had learned from past experience that letting the children distribute or raid the display of presents under the tree made for sheer bedlam and an unbelievable mess.

The battle of the presents ended at eleven. It was clearly high time for the youngsters to be tucked into their respective beds. Even Esmeralda couldn't help yawning, but she was determined to bestow a very special, last present on Doretta.

"Please open this. It's a piece I was given on Christmas Eve of 1938 by my grandmother. I want you to have it, Doretta. Ever since that night so long ago, I always wore it on Christmas Eve, except tonight."

Doretta opened the elegantly wrapped package. When she lifted the cover, she held her breath for a moment. It was a very large broach in rich yellow gold clustered with rubies and diamonds. It was a masterpiece of jewelry design. She had tears flooding her eyes.

"Thank you, Mom! It is absolutely stunning; I'll treasure it for the rest of my days." The two women hugged, both exceedingly pleased that they had learned to love one another.

# Chapter 40

FERNANDO had Elijah and Eduardo in his arms, giving them hugs and kisses. "You boys really be good and always listen to Grandma, Juanita, Valentina, and Juan. Mommy, Mario, Alona, and I will be back in a little while. I wish you were a little older and could come along. Maybe we'll do such a trip again in a few years when you are allowed to get on the special ship. Papa and Mario will take lots of pictures of the penguins and whales. Won't they be fun to look at?"

"Thanks for showing us pictures of things you will see. Aren't you scared to fly that big bird? Was your teacher good?" asked Elijah.

"Okay, boys. I've had lots of lessons, and my teacher was really good. I have a piece of paper. It says Papa knows how to fly, and it is safe for him to pilot hat big bird. You want Papa to show you?" He reached for his breast pocket and pulled out his license.

"That says Papa knows how to fly and that it is safe for him to operate the big bird. Are you happy now?"

"Yes, Papa. That makes me feel better. You fly good now

and be safe with Mommy, Mario, and Alona in the machine," was Eduardo's comment. The boys kept hugging him, not wanting to let go. Next it was Mommy, Mario, and Alona's turns to kiss them goodbye. Fernando was glad he had some play in his flying schedule. At last, they all hugged Esmeralda.

"I'm not going along to the airfield. I'll stay home with the little boys. You have a wonderful time and be safe. I can't wait to hear about this adventure when you return on January 23. You must forgive this old woman, but I will count the days until we are all together again. May the Almighty be with you every step of this journey. I love you." *What is my inner voice trying to tell me?* questioned Esmeralda. She had to turn away, not wanting to spoil their excitement with her tears.

Hernando was holding the doors on the large limousine. "I managed to stash all the suitcases and bags for the first part of the journey into the trunk; everything designated to go on the ship is in the trailer. It's pretty tight, but I found a spot for every last piece. I'm glad the plane is as big as it is. You shouldn't have any trouble stowing your gear. As per your instructions, I labeled and separated the luggage for the national park from those pieces needed for the ship to Antarctica."

"Good thinking, Hernando. That will help a lot when we land in Puerto Natales. We do have a lot of stuff; I'm glad Mario and I decided not to take our own ski equipment. If we have need for it, we'll rent ski gear. Thanks for your thoughtful input."

Loading the plane was accomplished easily. Fernando was glad the goodbyes took place at the hacienda. As soon as Doretta and the children were buckled in their seats, Fernando shook hands with Hernando and hopped on the plane. He pulled up the steps, secured the door, and got into his comfortable pilot seat. Within ten minutes, he was given the all-clear for takeoff; and they were on their way to Torres del Paine National Park. They were airborne shortly after noon and would arrive just before two o'clock.

It was a day made for flying. Eventually, his three passengers took turns sitting in the copilot seat. Doretta encouraged Mario to be first in line for the special treat.

"Just make sure you are buckled in, and keep your hands close to you. You can look all you desire, but do not touch or move anything. Understood?"

"Yes, Dad. I understand. I'm fascinated by all the meters, switches, and handles. This is really neat. I'm happy to know Mr. Hague was a good instructor. How do you remember what all of these things do?"

"If you do it often enough, it becomes second nature. Look down to your left, and you'll see the fjords. The water is so beautiful. Mom and Alona are admiring the clouds building over the Pacific; and if you look up, you'll see the Andes mountains in the distance just like you did when we flew with Walter Hague to Puerto Montt. Remember that day?"

"Oh, yes. It was so exciting. I don't want to hog this seat; I'll ask Mom to take her turn." Doretta deferred to Alona; she was perfectly happy where she was seated. Doretta wasn't sure if she could handle the frontal view as things seem to move straight at you. She didn't want to test her stamina; being airsick wouldn't be so much fun.

Time flew by, and they were in a landing pattern shortly before two o'clock. Fernando had arranged to be met by a driver from the hotel near Grey Lake where he had secured two rooms with exceptional views of the mountains and the lake.

Doretta and Fernando had discussed the lodging arrangements for the hotel as well as the ship. Being age eight and six, respectively, they believed Mario and Alona could share a room or a cabin as long as they each had their own bed. That might not be a possibility a few years down the road, but both they and the kids were comfortable with the arrangement on the present trip.

Jon, the driver from the hotel, was skilled in handling the luggage. Fernando secured the plane at the hangar and made sure all was in order before they took off for the hotel.

"We are having exceptionally good weather at the moment. Of course, you know that it can change all so quickly. Nevertheless, I would recommend that you take a tour to the glacier first thing in the morning. It is absolutely spectacular, and you should experience it while you are in the park.

"Be sure to layer your clothes, and wear warm headgear and gloves. If you feel comfortable canoeing, you and your son may want to try that while you are near the glacier. We could arrange for the canoe from our vessel that takes you up the lake to the glacial wonder. Be prepared to experience a feast for the eyes. Spectacular doesn't do it justice. Stupendous might be a better way of describing the glacier event."

"Dad, can we do the canoe? I've had a little taste of it when I went camping last year. It was so much fun, and you can get very close to things of interest."

"Count us in, Jon. Will you make the arrangements, please? My wife and daughter will stay on the vessel. What time does the boat leave?"

"We take off before sunrise in order to have the best morning light on the glacier and surroundings. It may be a challenge, but you will be pleased to have done it in the early morning hours. Trust us, we do know what we are talking about. In this case, the morning hour bears gold in its snout. It's an old saying somewhere; don't ask me where? Some foreigner told me about it."

Doretta knew what he was saying. "Morgenstund hat Gold im Mund." How often had she heard her grandma in Germany say that?

"When we get to the lodge, I'll show you where you need to meet the boat at six in the morning."

Alona looked at Doretta and had a quirky grin on her face. "We'll do it, boys!" said Doretta. "Just this once. That has to be freezing at that hour of the day. No canoe for us. I presume there is a warming station on the boat?"

"Yes, ma'am, and they even serve great hot chocolate and cookies. You'll be pretty comfy if you wear the right gear. Don't worry about not canoeing; you'll have a wonderful experience from the boat on which we are taking you."

Checked into their rooms, they gathered for dinner in the dining parlor, a place some might describe as undistinguished. There were many choices, and the food was served in generous portions. Doretta was glad Esmeralda was not along for the ride. All retired at an early hour, knowing that wake-up calls came at five-fifteen. Fernando and Mario settled on what to stash in their backpacks. Watching his father pack, Mario looked over his father's shoulders. "Dad, did you remember to bring your Leica and your special telephoto lens?"

"Is the Pope Catholic? Of course! My camera equipment was the first stuff to land in a side section of my backpack. It's easy to get at. I wanted to be sure to have it on the canoe trip. Watch me get great shots of the glacial monsters." Doretta reminded the kids to be warmly dressed; they were venturing into the world of blue ice.

Starting out in the dark, they sailed up Grey Lake in relative silence. All they could hear was the steady hum of the boat engines and people speaking softly. As daylight broke, they were greeted by icebergs floating past them in various sizes. After a good hour or so, the massive glacier in all its majestic splendor came into distant view. The mountains beyond the blue sculptures were largely hidden by banks of low-lying fog.

"We will be very close to the glacier in thirty minutes. At that point, we will turn off all engines; and the vessel will move slowly only by the motion of the natural current in close proximity to this wonder on earth. Those who are signed up to canoe should go below deck and be prepared to leave the vessel," announced the captain.

"That's us, Mario. Are you ready, young man?"

"Yes. Let's have fun. Did you hear the noise from that calving just now? That was some splash. Now I see why the captain told us to stay at least one hundred or more feet away from the glacial towers," was Mario's take on things. They got into their two-seater canoe with Mario seated toward the front and waved as they separated from the boat.

Doretta and Alona were watching in awe as the stupendous ice show unfolded. The colorful canoes looked like tiny dots of the spectrum against the massive structures, figures, and towers of blue ice. The show went on for an hour, moving about and seeing this wonder on earth from many different angles. All who remained on board the vessel were smiling when those who dared to canoe near the blue spectacle had returned safely.

"Mom, that was awesome!" announced Mario. He had grasped a small "iceberg" from the freezing waters and presented it to his mother and his sister who looked at the frozen jewel undisguisedly.

"That was very pretty, but now it needs to go back into the water. We are not supposed to create puddles on the boat," said Doretta. Fernando and Mario opted for the warmup room and hot chocolate. The cookies weren't bad either. All were looking forward to a warm breakfast.

"After we clean up and make ourselves comfortable, I want to attend the informative lecture about the park and specific hiking tours that the four of us want to do. Is everyone on board for hiking?"

Mario was all enthused; Doretta and Alona were less so. Hiking sounded like a lot of hard work, but they were not about to be outshone by their male company. Fernando registered that his two ladies were not as excited about the hiking adventures he had dreamed about experiencing. Listening to the myriad choices open to visitors of the park, he made his compromising proposal.

"There's a very easy trail, the Fauna Trail, that all of us should aim for tomorrow. Perhaps, the following day, we'll relax by the hot spas and enjoy the beauty of the park from a distance. Rested up, I am proposing to do a hike to the lake at the foot of the Cuernos, the Horns of the Paine. It will take us by a sensational waterfall and a fast-moving glacial river. The walk itself is rated as easy. The worst that can happen, we may run into some very strong winds. If we succeed in accomplishing that, let's get all relaxed and do a driving tour of the park for the next two days.

"I've always dreamt of doing the challenging hike to the base of the Torres del Paine [the blue-gray towers], which is the highlight of the park. Mario, are you up to hiking close to eight hours? It's a difficult hike—not quite twenty kilometers in length. Standing at the foot of these majestic towers will be our reward for the hard work. What do you say, Son?"

"If you think I can handle it, I would love to do it with you. Seeing the images in the slide presentation makes me want to do it. Some of those rock slides we need to conquer during the hike look tough, but I believe I'm up to doing it, Dad."

"Then that's our plan. Are you OK with what I'm proposing, my dear? The two early hikes should be enjoyable for you and Alona, especially with a day of rest between hikes. After that, the two of you will be on easy street. The day Mario and I test ourselves, you two could stay near the hot spas or do a tour of the area."

"It's a reasonable plan. I'm sure Alona and I will enjoy our days at Torres del Paine NP without the risks you are planning to take. I don't want my concerns to be in your way. You are old enough to know what you should and what you shouldn't do, especially with your eight-year-old son. It sounds formidable to me, but you are in charge." She gave him a quick kiss, giving him to understand she really cared about his well-being.

"If it eases your mind, I'll hire a professional guide for the day. It only makes sense to do it that way. I certainly would not want to get lost in the woods or deal with the vagaries of rockslides or whatever else we might encounter on the trail."

"Thank God, that's the best idea I've heard since we

arrived. It's all spectacular but overwhelming for someone born and raised in the flatlands. I do want you to have a wonderful experience and enjoy all there is to see. I know Mario will remember this place for the rest of his days."

※

They were blessed with perfect weather. There were encounters with sudden gusty winds and momentary significant drops in the temperatures; but on most days, azure skies vaulted over the magnificent landscape of the park. Doretta and Alona loved the fields of spring flowers along the hikes they had chosen to do. Seeing the Horns across the lake at the end of their second hike was rewarding enough for Doretta and Alona. Having driven through the park and seen the Torres del Paine in the distance, they were perfectly content with the experiences afforded them. In preparing for their visit to the park, they had been alerted to expect huge crowds of visitors during this most popular time of year. There were many people enjoying the different venues but not the hordes of visitors they were warned to expect.

When Fernando, Mario, and their guide, Tony, returned to the lodge, they were elated. "Mom, you should have seen the Torres; they are indescribably awesome and beautiful. I'm so glad I did this with Dad. I'll never forget the experience." Fernando patted his son lovingly on his head.

"You did okay, Son. I was really proud of you. So was Tony. He was really impressed with how you handled some of those rocks over which we had to climb. That wasn't easy, and you did it and never complained. I think you've earned that hot chocolate and those delectable cookies they offer. Ladies, you have to excuse us. We'll catch up with you at dinner. I believe we are ready for a shower and a well-deserved nap."

Mario couldn't stop talking at the dinner table about the events of the challenging day. Doretta and Fernando concluded that Act I of their adventure of a lifetime had been a resounding success for at least one person in the group. They had to be honest with themselves, it was a pleasure for all; but the achievement of success was simply known to a greater degree by Mario.

# Chapter 41

THE phone kept ringing at the Garcia Lopez Hacienda. *Is anyone going to pick up the darn phone?* Fernando kept tapping his foot. There were three others standing outside the public phone in the parking area. At last, Esmeralda answered her private line.

"Garcia Lopez, Esmeralda speaking."

"I almost hung up on you, Mom. There's a lineup of people waiting outside the booth. How is everything going? This will be our last chance to talk until we get off the ship in two weeks."

"What a nice surprise, Son. I was hoping you would call me before you set sail to the unknown. Everything here is just dandy. The boys have been very good. They are missing all of you but have done their very best to keep me happy. They are right here. When they got up this morning, they decided to come snuggle with Grandma. That was my eye opener this morning. Here, say hello to Elijah and Eduardo."

"Hola Papa! Are you having a good time? Eduardo and me miss you. When you coming home?"

"Hola Elijah! We had a great time at the park. Some day you will do this with your brother and me. Mommy and Alona had fun too, but Mario and I really enjoyed the hikes. Is your brother there?"

"Si Papa, here he is. You have fun with the penguins. Take lots of pictures. Miss you, Papa. I love you."

"I love you too, Elijah!" He had tears in his eyes. *I didn't realize I would miss you so much,* ran through Fernando's mind.

"Hola Papa! I hear you have lots of fun with our brother. Is he good boy like us? You see any penguins?"

"Hola Eduardo! Mario is a very good boy. No, we've not seen any penguins so far. That comes next. I promise I will take lots of pictures. Are you behaving yourselves and not making trouble for Juanita and Grandma?"

"Si Papa, Elijah and me very good boys. We play a lot in the yard. Me, Pablo, and Elijah like the new hiding place in the thing you built. Me forget name you call it. He likes running in the thing. Pablo better than Elijah and me getting back home."

"You be careful in the labyrinth. Papa didn't want you to explore the maze by yourselves. You and Elijah stay out of it until I'm home. We'll do it together, do you understand me?"

"Si Papa. Me good boy. Grandma wants to talk. Adiós Papa. Te amo, Papa."

"I love you too, Eduardo!" Some guy kept pounding on the telephone booth. "Make it quick, buddy. Look at this line of people waiting!"

"Mom, sounds like the boys are having fun in the maze. I'd rather they not play in there until I've done it a few times with them. I've got to get out of the booth. People are giving me a hard time. Until soon. I love you very much. Best from all of us. I'll call you from Ushuaia when we get back from

Antarctica. Again, thanks for everything. Te amo, Mama!" He slammed the receiver not too kindly and stepped out of the booth.

"Go for it! It's all yours." He tapped his Gaucho sombrero in a salute to the guy who had patiently waited during his phone call to the hacienda. He was glad he'd had a chance to speak with his mother and the twins.

Jon had collected their bags and was ready to take the Garcia Lopez family back to the airfield in Puerto Natales. The hearty breakfast was appreciated by all. "I hope you liked your stay with us and that all of you have Torres del Paine in fond memory. You have all you brought with you?"

"Thanks, Jon, we do. And speaking for all of us, it was a good experience. My son and I especially liked the challenging hike to the Torres. Someday, when our twin boys are older, we men will be back. Mario talks about wanting to do the 'W Trek' when we come back."

"That's a great five-to-seven-day adventure in the park. You guys will love it. Good choice, Mario. Keep dreaming."

The car was rolling down the dusty road toward the airfield at Puerto Natales. "I haven't had a chance to tell you. After breakfast, when you all were getting your packing done, I found a public telephone booth. I managed to get through and spoke with Grandma and the boys. They are all doing just fine, and Grandma was happy to learn about our exciting adventures in the park. I was a bit disturbed by the fact that Elijah and Eduardo have discovered the maze. Apparently, they've gotten lost in it a few times. Luckily, Pablo found them and led them to freedom. I've asked them to stay away from it until I can teach them when we are back."

"That was smart. I wish you'd let me know about wanting to make the call," said Doretta.

"I wasn't aware of the existence of the phone booth until I stepped out to catch some fresh air. They have the thing well hidden in an Oleander forest. When I saw a guy step out, I took the advantage. By the time I hung up, there was an angry mob waiting in line. Supposedly, I talked too long. Well, I'm glad I did. The boys sounded like they were really missing us. Grandma was in a good mood. They'd surprised her this morning wanting to cuddle with her in bed. I don't remember them ever doing that before, do you?"

"I wasn't aware they'd ever tried that. Have you two ever cuddled with Grandma?"

"No, never." spoke Alona and Mario at the same time. "We've come to your bedroom, but never to Grandma's. Glad that she's being especially nice to the boys while we are gone," said Alona. Fernando just smiled, still enjoying the afterglow of having spoken to the twins.

⋊⋉

Jon had them at the airfield in good time. He helped carry their belongings onto the plane. "Nice machine you got here, señor. Looks like she's all ready for takeoff. It's great that we have this little airstrip to accommodate private planes these days. Seems your machine is pretty new. How long you've had her?"

"Not too long but wouldn't want to be without her any longer. It's my adult toy; you know what I mean, don't you?"

He reached into his jeans pocket, retrieving an appropriate tip for Jon.

"Thanks, Jon. It's been a real pleasure. See you again someday!" The men shook hands. Jon headed back to the lodge at Grey Lake, and Fernando turned to speak with the attendant at the airfield; he paid him for tanking the plane and for looking after it in their absence. "You think we'll make it in about two hours to Ushuaia?"

"As the albatross fly, it's less than three hundred miles. With this machine, you'll probably touch down in a little over an hour. There are not too many planes flying into Ushuaia. Weather looks good too, today. There's talk about a storm brewing starting tomorrow. The weatherman predicts very strong breeze conditions around the Horn. You headed that way?"

"Yeah, we are picking up the Lindblad Explorer and heading to Antarctica tomorrow."

"Sounds like a fun experience. If you ever come back to the park, be sure to set down here. Nice knowing you, Señor Fernando." Fernando handed the man a well-deserved tip. Both men lifted their hats toward each other in saying farewell.

Fernando got on the plane, making sure all doors were tightly closed and Doretta and Alona were belted in their favorite seats. Mario, his copilot, was waiting for him to start the engines. They were airborne within minutes, and the passengers were waving at the attendant on the ground who was waving back at them.

As predicted, their flight was relatively short and without a hitch. The landing in Ushuaia was smooth and perfect in Mario's opinion. A driver was waiting to take the Garcia Lopez family and their several trunks holding their personal belongings for the upcoming sea voyage to the hotel. The plane, secured in the hangar, would be waiting for them for the return journey to Santiago on January 23, 1972.

They were greeted by the concierge at the hotel. Buenos dias, señor. Do you have a reservation with us?"

"Si, it's a reservation for tonight, January 7, for two rooms under the name Garcia Lopez."

"Oh, yes. Here we are. Your rooms are in readiness. Our men will take your luggage to your accommodations. Welcome to the Destello Verde [Green Flash] Hotel."

Fernando had requested rooms with a good view of the sea and the harbor. He was certain he had spotted the Lindblad Explorer with its unmistakable red paint job as he approached the landing strip earlier. Looking out of their window, he recognized the ship moored not too far from where they were located. Boarding was projected to take place the following day starting early in the morning.

"I'm glad all of you heeded my advice to pack a few things in our handy satchels. That way none of us have to go digging through the overseas trunks. It will be great when we can unpack and stay on the ship for two weeks. You agree?"

"Oh yes, my practical husband. I can't wait to get into my trunk and find something different to wear than jeans and pullovers. Alona fully agrees with me. We needed to be dressed for the activities we pursued at Torres del Paine; the ocean voyage will be a decided change—at least in the evening. Did you remember to pack your tux?"

"Yes, dear. I had Valentina fold it carefully with tissue inserted to cut down on the wrinkling. If worse comes to worse, they'll have services on board. During the day, I hate to disappoint you, you'll be thankful for jeans, silk long johns, sweaters, windbreakers, and whatever else. The guy at the hangar in Puerto Natales spoke of bracing weather heading our way."

"Now you're telling me. Remember, I never was the world's greatest sailor. This will be a totally new experience for Alona. At least our fortitudes were tested during our voyage in 1963. Of course, Mario won't remember. He was perfectly happy rocking in his bed. We'll deal with it as it comes," said Doretta.

Dropping off the trunks at their rooms, one of the men spoke: "Dinner will be served at six tonight, señor. It's a spectacular seafood buffet. You don't want to pass it up. Of course, if you are not a friend of seafood, we also serve the best in Argentinian beef. Enjoy your overnight stay at Destello Verde Hotel." Having collected their tip from Fernando, the men backed out of the room, closing the door gently.

"I've learned to appreciate these men not always slamming the doors," was Doretta's comment. "After this exciting morning, I need a good nap. I'm happy you selected this convenient hotel. From what I read, there's not much happening in the town other than coming and going to and from Antarctica. The harbor is a very busy place." She underscored her feelings by an unladylike yawn. "Excuse me, I'm about to conk out!"

※

Dorian, the driver from the hotel who had met them at the airstrip, was selected to drive the Garcia Lopez family to the Lindblad Explorer. They arrived at the harbor shortly before eight o'clock. The sparkling-white upper decks atop the bright-red hull of the ship were recognizable from a distance. On close inspection, she looked like she had undergone a thorough cleaning after her most recent voyage to the seventh continent. Officer Paulus Swanson greeted Fernando as he stepped out of the hotel transport. Fernando tipped his sombrero in response to being greeted by the young officer. "I presume, Señor Garcia Lopez, your wife, and children? Welcome aboard the M.S. Lindblad Explorer. I'm Officer Swanson, second in command."

"Fernando Garcia Lopez. This is my wife Doretta, our son Mario, and our daughter Alona. Our twin boys, barely three years of age, couldn't join us due to your age restrictions, a stipulation we fully understand. We are pleased to meet you and are looking forward to an exciting adventure."

Officer Swanson waved at two crewmen to help Dorian with the luggage of the boarding passengers. "Please assist this gentleman with taking Señor and Señora Garcia Lopez's luggage to cabins #104 and #106 on the Lido deck. Thank you." A uniformed cadet approached with a tray of champagne glasses. "May we offer you a coming-aboard cocktail? We'll have something nonalcoholic for your son and daughter promptly." He lifted his glass toward Fernando and Doretta: "Again, a hearty welcome aboard the M.S. Lindblad Explorer.

"Have you ever sailed on any large body of water, or is this a first experience for you?" asked Officer Swanson.

"My wife and I sailed on a freighter nine years ago from Hamburg to Valparaiso via Casablanca, the Panama Canal, and Lima, Peru. Mario was a newborn baby at the time. One might say it was a baptism by fire. We weathered stormy and calm seas and mostly enjoyed the journey. I gather the Atlantic and Pacific meet your criteria of having sailed on a large body of water?" Fernando received the response for which he was hoping—good laughter all around. Even Mario thought it was humorous.

Officer Swanson turned to a second cadet. "Please guide Señor and Señora Garcia Lopez and their children to their cabins. Make certain the accommodations meet with their approval and are to their satisfaction." He smiled at Doretta. "I look forward to serving you, Madame. You are invited for lunch at the captain's table at noon. Your cabin steward will provide you with any refreshments you desire. Just call him at his station; the phone number is at your bedside in your cabin.

"You are the last passengers to board. We'll set sail for Cape Horn in less than an hour." He bowed in Doretta's direction and clicked his heels, indicating that he viewed the reception ceremony on board ship concluded.

# Chapter 42

ADVISED by Officer Swanson that they would be seated at the captain's table for lunch, Doretta debated about what they should wear.

"If it was dinner, I might consider dressing up; for lunch, I'll wear a nice shirt and slacks and a puli [pullover] over my shoulders. That's what most guys I see walking around are sporting," commented Fernando.

"That helps. The children and I will dress accordingly. The puli is a good idea. Looking at the water and the sky, we may be in for exciting surprises. I was pleased to learn from Officer Swanson that we can get medication for seasickness at the infirmary. With all the medications, salves, and creams I brought, I completely forgot to pack Dramamine."

"I doubt you'll need it, you never got sick on that long voyage on the freighter. But it's good to know, as far as the kids are concerned, although neither complained on Grey Lake. Mario didn't mind the choppiness in the canoe. We'll see. Cape Horn and the Drake Passage might be more of a challenge.

"I looked at the posted weather forecast and it might be a bumpy ride for the next three days. We should be passing Cape Horn toward evening, at best, late this afternoon. When I was up on deck with Mario just now, he commented that he has never experienced wind like that before. He's probably correct in that assumption. Are we ready to meet the captain?"

The dining room held a pleasant ambiance and was not what might be called opulent. The variety of differently shaped tables allowed the not-quite one hundred passengers to be seated comfortably. At the head of the room stood the captain's table, a large oval table for twelve. The *important* man in his dress blues was standing among passengers, greeting them and facilitating the introductions among his honored guests.

"I'm Lutz Amundson, your captain on this voyage. Please be seated wherever you wish at this luncheon; just save the central chair in the back row for me. That will always be my chair. After this introductory luncheon, I would like to have two different persons seated next to me at each subsequent meal. In other words, I want you to play musical chairs throughout this journey. That way I will get to know each of you, and you'll learn a bit more about me and your fellow passengers. How does that sound to you?" Some affirmed loudly and others plainly nodded, not being sure of the suggested seating arrangement.

"Please introduce yourselves by the name you wish to be addressed."

The Garcia Lopez family opted to speak first.

"This is my wife, Doretta; our son, Mario; our daughter, Alona; and I'm Fernando. Our home is in the wine country outside of Santiago, Chile."

"We are Joyce and Lloyd and hail from Florida."

"Trish and James from London, England."

"I'm Barbara from Williamsburg, Virginia."

"My name is Sharon, and I live in Seattle, Washington."

"I'm Rosita, a fashion designer in Buenos Aires."

"Nice to meet all of you. Looks like an interesting mix of folks. It will be my distinct pleasure to discover something about your varied backgrounds. Please be seated. Our steward, Horst, who comes to us from Bremen, Germany, is about to present the menu. I'm confident there will be something delectable for everyone."

Menus were read studiously as all diners were off in their own worlds. All one could hear were the mutterings of other diners, the clinking of ice cubes being placed into water glasses, and an occasional pop of a champagne cork. "Anything from the bar?" inquired the steward.

"Not at this hour. I need to be steady on my feet to face the wiles of Cape Horn," said Fernando. Lloyd and James agreed. The ladies declined alcoholic beverages at this hour as well, especially since the motion of the Atlantic could be felt noticeably in the dining room.

"I must share my wisdom with you. If you haven't had at least six- to eight-meter waves in this part of the ocean, you can't claim to have gone around the Horn. It just isn't right if you experience it sailing on mirror-flat seas. And I believe you will have the royal treatment. Never fear, you'll be perfectly safe; just roll with the punches," said Captain Amundson. His smiling vision caught all sitting at his table.

At that moment, two cadets came onto the scene, assisting the dining room stewards with flipping up wooden ledges all around each table. "These work very well for us; at least nothing will have an opportunity to slide off the table. It's a necessity on oceangoing vessels, especially in this part of the world," the Captain enlightened them.

Fernando turned to face his daughter. "Are you feeling OK, Alona? Your stomach doesn't feel funny or unusual?"

"No, Dad, I'm perfectly fine. My teacher sailed the seven seas, as he says. He told me not to look out portholes or windows and to watch the movement of the ship relative to the horizon. Also, he said to stay away from juicy or soupy foods. I'm having a steak sandwich and little else. I trust my teacher."

"Sound advice. You must have shared your story with your brother. I see he ordered the same for lunch. After the meal, I want all of us up on deck. Make sure you wear the heavy windbreakers over your sweaters and wear the Scandinavian wool hats we brought. They'll keep your ears and your necks warm in this wicked wind. It's blowing for sure out there. You'll get plenty of fresh air, the best medicine to prevent seasickness. And wear gloves!"

"We surely will. My new hairdo can't wait to face the stormy seas. I'm so glad I had it clipped very short before we left," was Doretta's comment. *Gosh, can you imagine wet and long hair hanging around my face? Some mess that would be, thought Doretta.*

Fernando wasn't certain he could get the door to the deck opened; the wind was that strong. Reportedly, there were gusts between thirty and forty knots. Women, whose hair wasn't covered, looked like trolls with their hair standing straight in the air. People were sliding on deck like pieces on a chessboard. There wasn't another vessel in sight as they sailed by Cape Horn. They barely could make out the land formation as they passed by. Some thought they could see the outline of some sculpture; they didn't, the low-lying fog was that thick.

The passengers on board found themselves in the Drake Passage as night descended. The gusts subsided to more acceptable levels, ranging now from fifteen to twenty-three knots. By dinnertime, those in the Garcia Lopez contingent had adjusted to the rock 'n' roll of the Lindblad Explorer. Captain Amundson was in his white evening dress uniform and jovial as he greeted his dinner companions. "Looks like we've survived the ides of Cape Horn and are entering calmer waters," he chuckled.

"Calmer, is a matter of opinion," was Barbara's reply.

"Even inside, we can feel the wind," she added. "It almost blew our bridge cards right off the table when Sharon, Fernando, Doretta, and I tried to play a few hands before dinner. Thanks to the table guards, they didn't slide into Neverland. You are promising things will improve when we get closer to the Antarctic Peninsula?"

"I can't make promises about the weather in general; but when we sail up the Lemaire Channel in thirty-six to forty hours, things will be much calmer as far as wind is concerned."

"Phew! That's a blessing," spelled Sharon. Joyce and Doretta concurred. Mario and Alona just giggled. "We loved that wind; it was fun seeing all those trolls sliding about on the upper deck."

"Leave it to my kids to see the positive in this adventure," contributed Fernando. They were seated next to the captain, who smiled upon his youngest tablemates with pleasure.

"Hey, how did you two like going by Cape Horn? Wasn't it thrilling having done it in a challenging storm?"

"We were glad it wasn't calm; it would have been only half the fun, and we wouldn't have been able to brag about the adventure when we are back home. At least, not honestly. I've never seen waves that high," said Mario with a big smile on his face.

"I agree. It was a lot of fun. I've never been on any ship before. At least, my brother had the experience as a baby. Of course, he doesn't remember; it was so long ago," said Alona.

"I grew up in Sweden. My father had a sailboat; and therefore, I was on the Baltic Sea from a very young age. I've always loved the mystery of the sea. This is the best job any man can have," was Captain's reply.

"We are glad you like your job as Captain of this ship. My dad likes his job as a vintner. Isn't it good we all like to do different things? I want to be a doctor, at least that's what I'm thinking about right now. I may change my mind," Mario glanced at the Captain.

"When will we see penguins? That's what I came for," said Alona.

"As we are sailing up the long and narrow Lemaire Channel, you may catch site of the first penguins getting a free ride on some of the icebergs floating by; but there will be several islands where you go on land and be so close to the penguins, you might be tempted to touch them. Of course, that's a real no-no. Don't even think about touching any of the animals you encounter, okay?"

"Yes, Captain, my dad told me the same. I can't wait to see my first real penguin!" She took a bite of the bread she had taken from a silver basket being passed to her by the captain. "I like the taste of this bread."

"Good. The ship's baker used my mom's recipe. It calls for lots of fennel. It gives it that unique flavor. Glad you like it. Put lots of that good butter on it. I'll fight you for the heels." Captain winked at her.

Alona tried to get her mother's attention, waving at her across the table. Doretta was carrying on a serious conversation with Barbara, who was sitting next to her. "Mom, try this bread. It's really good. The captain says it's his mom's recipe. Wait until you taste the fennel, whatever that is. I like it. It's a wonderfully different taste."

Doretta signaled Alona in a not-so-subtle manner to pipe down. "Thanks, Honey. Please, not so loud. All the adults are in conversations of their own. Tell me about it later."

"Later would be too late. Captain, is the baker making this bread every day while we are on the ship? What's it called again?"

"The ship or the bread, Alona?"

"Both; the names are strange."

"The ship is the Lindblad Explorer; the bread is called Amundson's Fennel Surprise."

"Thank you, Captain. I won't forget. I'll tell my mom about it later." Alona's voice wasn't exactly sotto voce.

Dinner at the Captain's table was a decided success all the way around. Captain Amundson particularly loved the little discourse with his youngest passenger on board.

Two days after sailing out of Ushuaia, the Lindblad Explorer had safely crossed the Drake Passage and was getting close to the Antarctic Peninsula. It truly was a rock 'n' roll affair, fortunately with not too many seasick casualties on board the vessel. Most of the passengers were seasoned travelers. Officer Swanson reached for his megaphone.

"We are approaching Brown Bluff, which lies on the Antarctic Sound. We are not making landing here but will travel slowly along the coast, wanting to give you your first experience of seeing wildlife in the Antarctic against this giant brown cliff rising toward the heavens. Use your field glasses, and you will see all kinds of Adélie and Gentoo penguins. Don't miss some of the birds that are actively posturing for us."

"Daddy, did the man say there are penguins? Can I see through your glasses?" asked Alona. Mario had his own binoculars.

"Did you spot any, Dad? I see some way off on the right side," said Mario.

"Got 'em. That's quite a colony of them. You want to look, Alona?"

"Yes, Daddy. Are they way too far for you to take a picture, Daddy?"

"Yes, even with the telephoto, they wouldn't show up too well. But there'll be more chances. Where's your mother hiding?"

"She's standing right there, talking with Sharon, one of the other ladies at our table."

"Oh good, I thought she might have gone to our cabin."

The Lindblad kept moving slowly. Soon they arrived at Wilhelmina Bay. Before Officer Swanson could alert the passengers, they were privileged to see breaching whales and an abundance of seals loitering on giant and smaller icebergs in close proximity to the ship. Officer Swanson's announcement was annoyingly disruptive in the pristine world surrounding the vessel.

"We are dropping anchor at this lovely spot. You'll be able to enjoy the whale show until we summon you to dinner and after dinner if you are so inclined. Don't stay up too late. The magic show continues tomorrow morning.

)(

The Lindblad entered the Lemaire Channel shortly after breakfast. The majority of passengers were on the observation deck, all bundled up and keeping their cameras close to their chests for body warmth. Mountains and hills were peeking through the fog in the distance. There wasn't another ship entering the channel. The main engines were turned off; the ship moved largely with the power of a small auxiliary engine and the currents of the channel. There was merely a wisp of black smoke rising from the single chimney. The silence was almost deafening. And then Alona spotted her first penguins close up and leisurely riding alongside the Lindblad on a small iceberg.

"Daddy, Daddy, look at those penguins. Please make a picture; I want to show it to my brothers."

"Okay, Honey, I will. But please, no yelling. If you see something you like, tell me softly. The other people like the quiet of the moment and are enjoying it. You understand, Alona?"

"Sorry Dad, I'll be more careful next time. Did you get a good picture of them?"

"Yes, I'm sure the boys will like it when you tell them about seeing your first penguins close enough for me to take a good photo. You'll see a lot more and different kinds of penguins as we continue on the trip. This part is more about the mysterious landscape, the floating icebergs, and the foggy mood. So, no more outbursts, *please*! You don't want to stay in the cabin, do you?"

"Oh no, Daddy. I'll be a good girl."

They reached the end of the almost seven-mile long Lemaire Channel late in the afternoon. It was nearly an endless day with daylight in evidence almost around the clock.

Their last surprise on this late afternoon was the arrival at the Penola Strait and Petermann Island. Some of the icebergs and ice carvings were spectacular, only to be outdone by another show of the playful breaching by a pod of whales.

※

Fernando and Mario were up at five o'clock. Warmly dressed, they snuck out of their cabins, making sure they had their binoculars and the Leica with them. The sun was high in the sky, greeting all on top deck under a spectacularly clear and blue sky. No matter where one looked, people were showing their utter surprise by beholding the unfolding drama of sailing into the Gerlache Strait. It was like New Year's Day, watching the Rose Parade in Pasadena. There were astounding displays of carved giant ice blocks, one after another; some with graceful arches broken through over time; others as flat as a pancake and the size of a football field; some covered with frolicking penguins and seals; and others providing a landing stage for albatross and many varieties of seabirds.

"Mario, you rush down to our cabin; and let Mom and your sister know what they are missing. Tell them they can catch up on sleep when we are back home. This simply is too beautiful for them to miss. My photos will be great, but there's nothing like seeing something like this through your own eyes."

"I'll be right back. I don't want to miss any of this. If need be, I'll even skip breakfast with the captain. I see they are serving hot chocolate and cookies over there. That would be good enough for me," Mario was shouting to his dad as he was running down the steps to the Lido deck.

People were discussing the immensity of the icebergs, realizing what they were seeing was only 10 percent of what each of these floating structures represented. In spite of the bright sunshine, the prevailing temperatures were pretty nippy. Cadets were passing out wool blankets and hot drinks. The crowd began to thin out when Doretta and Alona made their first appearance on deck.

"Why didn't you wake me before you and Mario decided to explore this white wonder? I would have gotten up. After we drew those heavy curtains and I put on the mask the steward provided, I finally fell asleep. I'm just not used to daylight for twenty-four hours. On the other hand, can you imagine what it is like during the dead of winter? I would find that depressing and probably would become an alcoholic.

"This is beautiful. Look at this giant archway coming straight at us. Can you see all those penguins clambering on the ice, Alona? Come over here and look at them. Be sure to take some photos of that scene, Fernando. The boys will just love it," said Doretta.

The crew was well aware of the spectacle on top deck and that many had no intention of spending time in the dining room. After hot chocolate and cookies, they offered a variety of tasty sandwiches and mugs with piping hot delicious soups. None of the crew could blame their passengers for not wanting to miss any part of Mother Nature's drama playing out in front of their eyes.

When they arrived at Paradise Harbor, the captain ordered the crew to drop anchor. Interested passengers were tendered in small zodiacs for their first landing. Each boat held no more than fifteen passengers, all wearing age-appropriate swim vests in bright shades of orange. The Garcia Lopez family was among the fifteen in the first rubber boat launched.

Fernando assumed the crew gave preferential treatment to his family because of the children.

"What do you say now? We'll be among the first to explore the bayside. Both Argentina and Chile maintain bases at this area. We may and we may not stick our noses into those places. If you were older, visiting the bases would be of greater interest. Let's concentrate on the colonies of penguins. How does that suit you, Alona?"

"Whole colonies of penguins at our fingertips? That sounds perfect, Daddy. I know I'm not supposed to touch them, I heard what the captain said. But we'll be able to get really close to them, won't we?"

They walked by the bases and soon were completely surrounded by penguins. All island visitors discovered quickly that getting too close to penguins has its negative side; none of them had realized how odoriferous these creatures were. Doretta was the first to comment on the situation: "I believe you are calling the child by its wrong name; these birds are not odoriferous, they downright stink. I wouldn't want to get any closer to them than we are, never mind touching them. Personally, I liked them better from a distance." Mario was pinching his nose. Fernando held Alona by his hand after he had sufficiently photographed the penguin colony. "Are you still crazy about seeing penguins, my girl?"

"Yes, Daddy. They may stink as Mom says, but I think they are among the cutest creatures God put on this earth. I just love the way they waddle around and how they seem to communicate with each other. When they take to the air and finally dive into the water, their flight is so graceful. I can't see enough of them. Are we doing other landings, Daddy?"

"I've read about a place called Neko in Neko Harbor, which is on the Antarctic mainland. I'll check with Officer Swanson or Captain Amundson tonight over dinner. That might be the last place for us to land before we arrive at the South Shetland Islands. There, we are supposed to see some of the largest colonies of penguins."

"Yippee, more penguins."

"Don't get yourself too excited at the dinner table tonight. You won't be sitting next to the captain; so please don't yell across the expanse. I want you to be on your most-ladylike behavior, understood?"

"Yes, Father." Fernando knew she had gotten the message.

Captain Amundson was pleased to hear from most passengers how much they had enjoyed the landing at Paradise Bay. "It is a beautiful place, and the scenery is spectacular." Fernando raised a question about the upcoming landing before everyone was seated at the dinner table. "We will make a brief landing in Neko because of its unique location. It might be of less interest to the children. You may consider going alone or with Mario. Your wife and Alona might want to stay on board and just enjoy the whirlpool. Just a suggestion; I speak from past experiences."

"Good suggestion. I'll discuss it with my gals later." When he did explain his conversation with the captain to Doretta and Alona, they were more than willing to enjoy some relaxation on the Lindblad. He and Mario did participate in the landing at Neko Harbor early in the morning. The mountains and impressive glacier walls took their breath away. They were surprised to encounter a large colony of Gentoo penguins. "Let's keep the last discovery under our bonnets. Alona would be mad that she didn't come along."

"Will do, Dad."

Once all were back on board, Officer Swanson made an important announcement. "We are now headed for the Errera Channel, which is tricky and challenging to our navigators. It's a very narrow channel often saturated with icebergs. Watching us maneuver through the channel may be more exciting than the ultimate reward when we get to our landing site, Cuverville Island, which claims to have the largest colony of Gentoo penguins."

"Did you hear that, Daddy? The largest colony of Gentoo penguins. I hope you are planning to take me, stinking or not."

"Of course, that's why you are along on this journey, and I'm not about to deprive you of the largest colony of Gentoo penguins."

The observation deck was packed. Practically all ninety-two passengers were assembled to watch the tricky navigating drama through the Errera Channel. All breathed sighs of relief when anchor was set near Cuverville Island. The crew, well-drilled in handling the zodiacs, assisted those who wished to go ashore. Hardly anyone spoke; they were listening to the sounds emanating from the Gentoo penguin colony. Alona was so enthralled and uncharacteristically whispered:

"Daddy, can you hear the penguins? There must be thousands of them."

"Look at these. This one is feeding its young, and those are carrying their baby piggy-back," observed Fernando.

"Oh Daddy, they are so cute," Alona was in seventh heaven. Mario reminded his father.

"Dad, don't forget to take photos. It's incredible to watch this sea of penguins. I never dreamt there could be this many."

Doretta held onto Mario. "These birds seem so social and friendly, not only toward us invaders but to each other." One of the guides overheard Doretta's observation.

"These Gentoos were bred and born here and do not migrate. They are homebound and very friendly toward each other and other animals. The only time they evidence any territorialism is when it comes to sheltering and protecting their nests and eggs. Gentoo penguins are among the friendliest creatures in this world of snow and ice."

"Mom, wouldn't it be fun to adopt one of these?"

"It would be, but we don't live anywhere near very cold water; and that is what penguins need, Alona. You'll just have to be happy with Pablo. I wonder if he misses us?"

"Don't worry, Mom. He loves playing with Elijah and Eduardo," said Mario.

Sailing away from Cuverville Island, the captain commented on the sea ice. "This is what we fear the most. It is the floating ice that forms from the seawater. Some places it becomes so dense and thick that ordinary vessels cannot move through the thickness of the ice. There are times when even our vessel is trapped and needs to wait for the ice to be softened by the sun. We try to avoid such situations, but it can happen.

"It looks pretty dense right now, but other ships in the area have wired us; it appears we'll be able to make our planned landings at Greenwich Island in Yankee Harbor and Half Moon

Island in the South Shetland Islands in late afternoon. We are blessed with these endless days of sunshine allowing us to land almost any time of day and view Nature's treasures. Reportedly, there are four thousand breeding pairs of Gentoo penguins on Greenwich Island."

"Daddy, can we go? I don't care if we miss dinner tonight. I'm sure they'll have something for us to eat when we return from our outing." Captain couldn't help overhearing Alona's concern.

"No problem, Alona. You don't have to miss anything, and you won't go hungry. Our crew packs nonperishable treats for each person going on a zodiac landing. More importantly, they carry drinkable water and other beverages aboard the motorized rubber rafts. You'll be surprised what you'll get to eat and drink while you are out there close to your favorite animals." He patted Alona gently on the back of her head.

"Thanks, Captain. I can't wait for our next landing."

Greenwich Island was all the captain had promised. None had expected anything that could top the experiences they had had so far. The sunlight had softened, and those going on land cast long shadows as they passed squawking seals dusting themselves with sand. They were taken aback by the scenic beauty of Half Moon Island. All marveled at the snow-covered cliffs in the background providing home to a huge colony of Chinstrap penguins. The air was filled with countless Antarctic terns and other varieties of seabirds. A pair of albatrosses came from nowhere and surprised the human visitors to Half Moon Island.

Alona was fascinated by the looks of the Chinstraps. "They almost look like they are formally dressed in their black and white uniforms. I don't know which are cuter, the Chinstraps or the Gentoo." All the way back to the Lindblad, she couldn't stop talking.

"I'll probably dream about penguins tonight. Thank you for bringing me here. I never thought I could like a place this cold, white, and blue. But it is more beautiful than any picture I saw before we came."

They sailed overnight through manageable sea ice to Whalers Bay at Deception Island and made their landing shortly after breakfast. Fernando was looking forward to a totally different experience.

"Kids, there are no penguins to speak of on this island. It's main attraction is the extinct volcano. That big hole you saw in the photo in the brochure in the ship's library is called a caldera. Part of it collapsed and has formed a lake inside the former volcano. We can walk around the caldera. When you get back home, you can talk about having walked on a volcano in 'Show and Tell.' Won't that be a different story?"

"Dad, this whole trip will be fun to present to my classmates at school. I'm hoping to use some of the photographs you are taking. Like you always say, a picture is worth a thousand words," spoke Mario. Doretta encouraged Alona to talk about her penguin adventures in her "Show and Tell" segment when she was back at school.

After leaving Deception Island, the Lindblad sailed in a northeasterly direction through the Bransfield Strait, the destination being Elephant Island. Their arrival was projected for early evening. Fernando and Doretta spent time in the library wanting to prepare Mario and Alona for the last landing in Antarctic waters.

"There are some interesting facts about this place. First, sorry to say, Alona, there are no penguins on Elephant Island.

If there are any, they are strays. The island is shaped like an elephant and its major inhabitants are harems or herds of elephant seals. They are everywhere. These seals have long-hanging noses that look almost like an elephant's trunk. That's how they got their name. Elephant seals are usually very friendly but make loud, roaring noises, particularly during mating season. While they are reputed to be docile and lovable, fights between large alpha males during the mating season can get bloody."

"When is the mating season, Dad?" Mario wanted to know.

"I understand we are right in the middle of it. You might just see some fighting males along the shores when we get there. They are not exaggerating when they speak of 'bloody.'

"You have heard some of the men speak of a man called Ernest Shackleton. He was a famous explorer of the seventh continent, and he and some of the men working with him died during their last expedition. There is a large sculpture of Shackleton on Elephant Island to memorialize this man, his crew, and their endurance."

"Will we see the statue, Dad?" asked Mario.

"From what I heard, it will greet us where we'll land with the zodiacs. You can read about Shackleton on the plaque of the statue."

Captain Amundson kept his promise. Elephant Island came into view in early evening. Most passengers wished to visit the island and marvel at the primary residents—the elephant seals. There was no question about it; they were pretty noisy critters and could be heard from a considerable distance. Mario's vision was glued to the island, searching the shore for fighting elephant seals with his binoculars. He became more excited the closer they came to landing.

"Dad, look slightly to the right. You'll see a couple of battling male seals. They are huge. That one on the left has bloody fangs. Boy, they are fighting hard." Alona wanted to make a looksee, but Doretta discouraged her from peeking through the binoculars.

"Honey, that sounds ugly. I don't want to see it and neither do you. I've never understood why men like things like this or a sport like boxing. What's so enjoyable about seeing one of God's creatures mutilating another? When we go ashore, you and I will look at the sculpture and then walk among the harems of female and young elephant seals. That will be much more to our liking."

"Okay, Mom. That sounds good to me," agreed Alona.

By eight-thirty all were back on board. They were looking forward to a relaxing late dinner. Better yet, the next day was a day at sea before they would make landfall at South Georgia the following morning.

That night, Barbara and Sharon flanked the Captain and were engaged in lively conversation. The steward had just set down a tray with ten flutes of Dom Perignon when a loud crash occurred that rocked the Lindblad. The champagne glasses tilted just a tad too northerly and their content would have landed in Doretta's lap had she not excused herself seconds before impact, needing to powder her nose.

"Did we hit an iceberg?" asked Mario.

"I don't believe an iceberg, but we may have had a collision with one of our large buddies in the deep blue sea, a whale. It's happened on occasion in these waters. I'm sure one of the divers is already checking out the scene below to assess damage, if any," said the Captain. Three stewards came to the rescue of the captain's table and cleared away the downed glasses and spillage. Within minutes, none of the damage was in evidence and freshly poured champagne was individually presented to the adults. Captain Amundson toasted his guests: "Here's to a successful and poignant conclusion to the first leg of our adventure. I hope all of you have enjoyed your days in Antarctica." There was resounding agreement with the Master of the Ship.

Alona was still thinking about the whale. She knew she was supposed to be quiet when adults were conversing. "Captain, do you think the whale was hurt? That crash was terribly loud."

"I guess we'll never know. Let's hope our ship wasn't hurt; but if we suffered any damage, I would have been informed by now. Our special divers on board are trained to check for damages in these situations." He smiled broadly at Alona as he lifted his glass again to all sitting at his table.

# Chapter 43

AFTER a most relaxing day, the excitement of looking forward to a formal night at sea was palpable in the air. Doretta couldn't be more pleased with her choice of evening dress. Alona's was in similar colors to Doretta's peacock green-and-blue evening gown she had worn to that first opera at the Teatro all those years ago. It still fit her like a glove, and she felt extremely elegant in the von Furstenberg creation.

"My ladies look beautiful. Does this tux still fit me well? It's been some time since I donned it last. I'm glad you found one for Mario that closely matches mine. Pretty sharp, young man," as he reached over to adjust Mario's black tie. He would save the white tie for another affair.

Walking into the dining room, some of the other passengers discreetly commented on the elegant family seated at the Captain's table. Everyone on board looked their smartest this evening. Doretta couldn't quite decide who was more elegantly dressed among the ladies seated with them. The men in their tuxes and their companions in brilliant colors were a feast for the eyes. When Rosita finally strolled in, flamboyant was perhaps the most fitting descriptor. A good friend of Doretta's would have called her tacky elegant. Doretta thought she was more artsy than anything else. Last but not least, the Master of the Ship made his entrance decked out in black pants and a white formal jacket. All stood at the table, having waited for his appearance.

"Good evening, ladies and gentlemen. Welcome to my table on this auspicious evening. Please join me in a glass of champagne. It's a pleasure to have you on board and take part in this magic journey through a part of our world most people will never experience. You are indeed unique travelers." He lifted his glass: "L'Chaim, no other toast says it any better. To Life. Let's enjoy every moment of it. Please take your seats."

After the elegant dinner, there would be dancing in the lounge. Actually, there was a dance competition. "Mommy, may we watch you and Daddy dance?" Alona wanted to know.

"You certainly may. It's been a while since your father and I have danced, but I believe we still can do a mean foxtrot. You just watch us on that parquet floor." They did the trot and won a bottle of champagne for first place. Doretta and Fernando shared it with their friends from the captain's table who had come to watch the dance competition. It was an evening none wanted to forget.

The Lindblad dropped anchor early in the morning at Fortuna Bay. The air was crisp but by no means as chilly as they experienced for the past days after leaving Ushuaia. While South Georgia is still part of the Antarctic ecosystem, the lack of sea ice allows for somewhat more temperate weather. Wildlife photographers speak of the *Serengeti of the Southern Ocean* because of the abundance of wildlife. In South Georgia, one speaks of millions of penguins of various species. Perhaps the most sought after are the encounters with thousands of King penguins making this their home in a landscape of incomparable arctic beauty.

"Speaking of penguins, this is it, Alona. Today you will make the acquaintance of the kings of penguins. There are thousands on this island, and they are all waiting to meet you."

"Daddy, you are funny. How would they know that I'm visiting the island? We've only traveled by plane and ship for days. These penguins don't know me from Adam."

"Of course, they don't know you, Your Highness. I was just trying to add a little levity to the situation."

"What's that supposed to mean? Why are you testing me? I've never learned all those fancy words you are using."

"All right! Daddy was trying to make a joke. But the King penguins aren't a joke. They are some of the most majestic animals you will ever see."

Walking off the rubber zodiacs, they were greeted by several species of seals loudly serenading the arriving visitors. Elephant seals were lazily lounging on the sand; other seals were racing in and out of the water. Albatrosses were flying above their heads, close enough that they could feel the movement of the air on their scalps. And then they were facing them. A garland of King penguins in all their splendor and majesty waited to welcome the visitors to Fortuna Bay.

Alona was speechless. She stared at these magnificent creatures in their elegant white and black dress coats accented with touches of orange on their chests, necks, and beaks. She was amazed by the intriguing sounds made by these giant birds.

"They sound so different, Daddy. It's almost like they are trying to communicate with each other, perhaps trying to communicate with us?"

"I don't know about speaking to us. But I read that the chicks identify their parents by the sound of their voicings; that is, the chicks distinguish acoustic signals generated by their parents. Pretty smart birds, don't you think?"

"Not just smart, they are absolutely beautiful. And just keep looking; there are thousands of them lined up behind this greeting committee. And you want to know something really funny? I don't even smell their poop any longer. Their beauty made me completely shut out that smell of theirs." She watched Mario pinch his nose.

While Alona kept alerting her mom and brother and anyone she had met on the ship to the wonders of the King penguins, her father was keeping his Leica busy. He was beginning to wonder if he had brought enough film with him. Not to worry, the crew on the Lindblad was familiar with such shortcomings of their passengers. They always kept a good supply of fresh film on ice.

As they kept walking, they discovered a fairly well-trod hiking path and decided to take advantage of the opportunity to get some good exercise on this sunny day under an azure-blue sky. Alona kept practicing her numbers by trying to count the King penguins she saw. When she reached three hundred and fifty-five, she decided it was a boring game. Instead, she concentrated on listening to the sounds thousands of these magic birds were generating.

The adults looked forward to the cocktail hour and a chance to exchange impressions of the day. Alona and Mario sat down in the playroom, attempting to capture their recall of the events in paintings. When Doretta discovered them, deeply engrossed in creativity, she was pleased to see what her children had painted.

"These are really good watercolors, and you captured the essence of the penguins." She picked her favorite from each of her children. "May I have these? I love them. I want to brag about you at the dinner table tonight. And they are not for sale!

"Mom has to go back to the lounge before Dad becomes worried. I'm so glad I caught you working at these. I'm sure some of the others at our table would like to take one home as a souvenir. So keep on painting. These two that I have, no one can have. They are *mine*—as you used to say, Alona." She trailed out of the playroom, still looking with a certain pride at the translucent, watery sketches in her hands.

She couldn't wait to show them to Fernando and some of the other guests. "Look at what our kids are doing while we are sipping away."

Joyce took a peek at the paintings. "These are lovely. I hadn't realized we had such gifted artists at our table."

"To tell the truth, neither did I. I knew they were both gifted in the learning of languages. Both are fluent in Spanish, English, and German. Mario does very well in school in math and the sciences. But I've never seen him draw or paint. Alona

I've noticed playing and drawing with crayons and such; but without wanting to brag, these watercolors are really nice. They certainly capture what we were able to glean today."

"It's nice when they are so talented. Both of us are in education. I did secretarial work in a department for communication disorders, and Lloyd was a school principal. We always loved being around young people. Two of our three children are enterprising in other fields; the youngest clung to education. And now, we are admiring the progress of our grandchildren. You'll have to wait a while for that experience. It's really been wonderful having you and your well-behaved duo at our table. I believe everyone, including the captain, has enjoyed having Mario and Alona with us during this amazing journey."

"Thanks, Joyce, that was nice of you to say. Alona can get a bit too excited at times, but she's learned after that first outburst at the table the other night. I guess it's the only way they learn; I can't keep them locked up all the time. My mother-in-law is very strict about table manners and didn't permit the children to eat with us until they were six years old. Mario knows the drill, but Alona only recently was allowed to eat with us adults. She's still a touch rough around the edges. But Grandma will take care of that." Joyce and Doretta smiled at each other, each knowing what the other thought.

At the dinner table, Joyce couldn't resist commenting on the children's artistic abilities. "Doretta, please share with the others at the table the two paintings Mario and Alona did this afternoon while we were having cocktails and discussing the events of the day. They are lovely. Don't be shy; you are allowed to brag at this table. All of us have children except our talented designer from Buenos Aires."

The two paintings Doretta held dear were passed around the table and were widely admired. "These are lovely," said Rosita.

"And just to set the record straight, I do have a child born out of passion. My daughter is eighteen and is considering entering a nunnery. Wouldn't you think that's the pits. Born out of wedlock and becoming a nun?" There was dead silence around the table. *What an interesting way of changing the subject!* ran through the captain's mind.

"These are really nice depictions. You have more of these?" said the captain. Mario saw an entrepreneurial opportunity.

"My sister and I did a bunch. I'll fetch them from our cabin before dessert is served. We would like each of you to have one. The others, Alona and I may consider for sale in the gift shoppe. Is that a possibility, Captain?"

Fernando glanced at Doretta. "That's my son. It's Don Carlos, his grandfather, reincarnated. He would be so proud of him."

"Of course, you may put them into the gift shoppe. There'll be a 10 percent commission to do so. I must pay the help," grinned the captain.

"Got yourself a deal!" Mario and he shook hands and beamed at the onlookers at the table.

※

Overnight, the Lindblad sailed to Gold Harbour. Prepared by on-board lecturers, the visitors were welcomed by another very large colony of King penguins. The day spent on land was a mix of joy and bitter remembrances. Mario and Alona loved their new encounters with the King penguins; the adults visited the Norwegian seaman's church and paid homage to Sir Ernest Shackleton at his final resting place at the church's graveyard. Watching a movie at the Whaling Museum brought back the tragic ending to Shackleton's explorations on the seventh continent. The Lindblad set sail in the early evening, saying farewell to Antarctica. Its passengers were looking forward to two enjoyable days on board as they were headed west-northwest toward Port Stanley and the Falkland Islands.

※

Discussions in the various lounges were lively. "How shall we spend our last days before ending this magical journey?" asked Fernando. He wasn't the only one posing the question.

Mario and Alona didn't want any part of museums or stuffy indoor places. Their preferences were focused on exploring the wonders of Nature. Doretta was inclined to agree with the children. Living close to a metropolitan area, museums were not at the top of her favorite list for things to experience either.

"I saw photos of Macaroni penguins. They look different from any we've seen so far. I understand there are an abundance of albatross and caracaras on the islands; I would like to see them soar into the air. And, of course, I cannot wait to be greeted one last time by a chorus line of waddling King penguins. Those experiences are at the top of my wish list," said Mario.

"Yeah, Macaroni penguins, for sure," echoed Alona.

Landing on the pristine white sandy beaches with their zodiacs, one of Mario's wishes came true. A line of fifteen King penguins, touching each other's flippers, gave the impression of holding hands. "Snap that picture, Dad, please. They are incredibly funny and beautiful at the same time. They are unforgettable."

Just as all in the Garcia Lopez family were still laughing at the humorous display by the King penguin welcoming committee, three albatross were swooping down to the crystalline waters giving the impression of wanting to touch their human invaders. "They are huge," voiced Alona. She appeared almost scared by their wingspan.

Walking away from the sandy beaches, they heard strange avian vocalizations. "What's that strange sound?" asked Doretta. "It's scary!"

"That rattling sound you hear right now is that made by caracaras. They are usually pretty quiet except during mating season," was Fernando's response.

"It sounds to me like someone running a stick along a wooden fence. It's a weird sound," added Mario. Alona finally wanted to have her say.

"I want to see the Macaroni penguins, please. Daddy, help me find some."

"We do have a guide we can consult. Let's find out where the Macaroni penguins are hiding," said her father.

"They are among the most difficult to encounter," said the Nature guide, "and are relatively small in number by comparison to the other four species of penguins we have in the Falklands. I suggest you work your way toward those rocky cliffs and use your binoculars. You may spot them among the Rockhopper penguins. The Macaronis have pink feet, a bright orange beak, and have orangy-yellow head feathers, which give them a very unique look. Good luck finding some."

"Who's game to hike and find these elusive penguins Alona wants to add to her Nature discoveries?" said Fernando.

There were no objections among his troupe. It took nearly an hour to get close to the rocky cliffs the guide had pointed out. Both Fernando and Mario went to work using their binoculars. They spotted a goodly number of Rockhopper penguins, always aiming their focus at the feet and the heads since those two areas had the distinctly recognizable body parts of the Macaroni penguin. Mario almost yelled and then caught himself.

"Dad, look to the right of that black outcropping. I see one with his bright pink feet. Oh, and there is a second one waddling right behind it. You see it?"

"Oh, yes. Now I've got it. Alona and Doretta, come look. You must see these. That's as close as we'll come to seeing these critters." Alona peeked first.

"Daddy, they are beautiful, and so different. Look at them, Mom." Doretta took a quick peek and handed the binoculars back to Alona. "Here, Honey. You enjoy the Macaroni penguins to your hearts content. Maybe Daddy can get a shot with his telephoto lens. If the pictures turn out, you can talk about it with your classmates when we get home. Speaking of home, I'm ready to be there in two days. It's been a wonderful adventure, but I long for home and my loved ones." The others didn't comment.

They spent most of the day truly appreciating their Nature hike, encountering Magellanic, Gentoo, and more King penguins. Eventually, they found a little roadside stand where they had an enjoyable local repast and something to drink. By late afternoon, Doretta called an end to the outing.

"I'm tired, my feet hurt, and I'm dying for a cold drink. Can we find our way back to the raft and get back to civilization on the Lindblad?" Hearing no objections, Fernando led his entourage like the Pied Piper back to the shore and their zodiac. The hot shower never felt better, and the cold beer never tasted so good.

Dinner was a casual affair; that is, the dress code on this evening was casual. The next day was a day at sea and the last evening would be celebrated in high style and elegant dress. It was the crowning piece de resistance and a celebration to remember. Alona already was speculating about which of her dresses she would wear.

X

"Mom, may I wear the black and white dress? It goes perfectly with my black patent leather shoes, and even better, with the white dress and your dark mink stole."

"If that's what you would like, that's what we'll wear. Your father and brother can be all duded up in their black tuxes and do the white tie touch. Your brother has been wanting to go white tie for some time. This will be the perfect occasion. By the next season, he will have outgrown his tux, and Lord knows what he wants in a year. So, good idea. We'll make it a black-and-white affair all around; well, more or less. I'll be mostly white with a touch of ranch mink. I'm sure your father will approve."

Captain Amundson was stunned when he approached his table. The Master of the Ship was in black and white and so was everyone seated at his table for the farewell dinner. "Who organized the dress code for tonight? This has never happened before. I insist we have the staff photographer take photos. I don't believe this will ever happen again." No one owned up to having been responsible for the black and white color scheme;

it was strictly a serendipitous occurrence and the stimulus for lively conversation around the table. Alona opted to speak.

"I was the one who had the idea first. I asked my mom if I could wear my black and white dress, wanting her to show off the white Dior creation she has never worn before. Dad and Mario just had to follow suit. That was an easy choice."

Trish spoke up. "All of us must have ESP or are clairvoyant, don't you agree?" Everyone nodded in concurrence.

The master sommelier served the Dom Perignon in the finest Bohemian crystal flutes. Rosenthal china and sterling flatware by Towle Silversmiths graced the table covered with an elegant Hardanger cloth.

The selections for all courses of the meal were boundless and exceptional, starting with the hors d'oeuvres, soups, entrée, and salad. *Who could resist the Mont Blanc Ice Cream Bombe?* Rosita believed she needed to speak for the group:

"Captain, you and your crew have outdone yourselves. It was a spectacular odyssey, and this evening is the culmination of all any of us dreamt about experiencing. It was a voyage of a lifetime. I believe none of us will ever forget what we saw, heard, smelled, and tasted, never mind what we felt. It was total saturation of all our human senses. Thank you!" All raised their glasses.

"To you, Captain, and your crew, hip, hip, hooray!"

"Thank you; the pleasure was ours to serve you."

While recognizing the captain with any sort of gratuity would have been a violation of etiquette, generous rewards to the crew were deserved and gracefully extended in all instances.

As the dinner guests slowly made their way out of the dining room, discussions relating to their impressions formed during the journey continued. It was pleasant to realize that the ninety-two passengers and crew on board the M.S. Lindblad Explorer had so firmly bonded during these days on land and sea. Tears in many eyes spelled the regret to see this voyage to the seventh continent come to its inevitable end. Contact addresses were exchanged, and there were hugs and kisses sealing the mournful goodbyes. *Who knew if they would ever meet again?* ran through the minds of many on board.

Getting back to their cabins, most passengers were pleasantly surprised to learn that their cabin attendants offered to assist in the process of final packing and getting suitcases and overseas trunks ready to be taken promptly ashore upon arrival at Ushuaia early the next morning.

⋇

Sailing through the night on relatively calm seas, the arrival in Ushuaia in the early morning hours was timely in spite of a very light fog. Most guests were on the top deck observing the landing maneuvers of their ship. Officer Swanson was handed a document by one of the cadets from the communication center of the ship. He looked up, searching for Fernando among the disembarking passengers. He walked up to Fernando and spoke:

"*Señor* Garcia Lopez, this wire arrived just a few minutes ago. It's for you, personally." Fernando, slightly taken aback, ripped open the wire and read:

*Serious problem at the hacienda. Do not delay returning. You are needed ASAP. Your devoted servant, Valentina.*

Fernando took Doretta aside.

"Read this wire. Obviously, there is trouble in paradise. I've got to get to a phone. What I don't understand is why we heard from Valentina and not my mother? You don't think it is she who has a problem? My God, you think she might have had another stroke? I don't know what to think. Don't say a word to the kids. Let me talk to Officer Swanson. He may have an idea where there might be a phone in the harbor."

"Officer Swanson, are you aware of the location of a public phone in harbor territory? I need to make an urgent phone call."

"Yes, sir. There is a phone in the arrival terminal. Do you need change? We certainly can help you with the needed coins." Fernando was pleased with the courtesies extended to him. He was among the first to get off the ship. Doretta and the kids followed him but stayed away from the telephone booth. Mario wanted to know why his father was needing to use the telephone. The transport from the ship to the airplane hangar had been prearranged and was paid for. Mario had spotted the driver holding up the sign with their name.

"You just have to be patient. Your father received a wire from Valentina. We are hoping nothing is wrong with Grandma. If there were any problems at the hacienda, your father and I would have expected to hear from your grandmother."

No one at the house answered the phone. Fernando became concerned. Watching her husband inside the glass cage, Doretta could tell he was angry. She thought she heard him yell: "Why isn't anyone picking up the damn phone?" He inserted more coins and dialed again, having decided to reach Amanda at the winery. The phone was answered on the second ring.

"Garcia Lopez Vineyards and Winery, Amanda speaking; how may I help you?"

"Amanda, it's Nando. Just before getting off the ship, I got a wire from Valentina, of all people. It sounds pretty urgent. What's wrong? Is it my mother? Don't tell me she had another stroke?"

"I don't know how to tell you this. It's not your mother, although she has completely withdrawn and locked herself in her boudoir. It's Elijah and Eduardo. The boys disappeared two days ago, and no one has found them yet. The Carabineros are on the case and have searched the hacienda, the surroundings, the vineyards, and the winery. They have used their own dogs and even enlisted Pablo in the search. So far there isn't a trace of the boys." She began to sob and couldn't speak any further.

"What can I say? I'm stunned. We'll get there as fast as possible. Make sure Hernando is at the airfield by noon. We might get there slightly later since I will need to re-tank in Puerto Montt. I'll tell Doretta but not the kids. I have to deal with my own turmoil. See you as soon as we get there." He replaced the receiver. Fernando had lost all color in his face, and there were tears in his eyes. *Are the gods wanting to punish me for having taken this journey?* he pondered.

# Chapter 44

FERNANDO didn't have to say anything. Doretta realized the seriousness of the situation. "Mario, please take your sister and go to the driver who is waiting for us. Dad and I will be right there." Mario knew something was awry at home; reluctantly, he held on to the hand of his sister and searched for the driver holding the sign with their name.

"I can tell it's bad. You need to let me know. You cannot shoulder this alone. Remember, I'm your wife for better or for worse. What is it?"

"It's not Mom. The boys disappeared two days ago. Carabineros and their dogs and Pablo have been all over everything that belongs to us. They haven't found hide or hair of either of the boys. It sounds like they were abducted." He reached out for his wife and held on to her with all that was in him and began to sob.

"Why did I want to go on this damn trip? It never would have happened had we been home. Someone knew we were gone and took advantage of Mom and the servants. I cannot believe I did this to my boys." Fellow passengers realized something drastically wrong had happened to Fernando and his family. He just shook his head and didn't want to answer any questions directed at them.

"We've got to get home ASAP. I hope to God I'll fly that damn plane safely enough. That's all I need to do is kill the rest of us." He held on to to Doretta's hand and searched for the driver of the prearranged transport to the Ushuaia airfield.

"You are a good pilot and will get us there." She could feel the impact of what Fernando had learned and sensed she had to be his rock. At this instance, he needed someone to lean on. Doretta knew this was a reversal of roles. He was there for her when her life was upended; now she needed to be there for him. Deep in her heart, she was as badly affected by the boys' disappearance as he; but she had to be strong for him. She could do her crying when back at the hacienda and Mario and Alona were safe. *My God, they might be all we have.* She bit back her tears.

Fernando reached for his handkerchief and wiped his face. He pressed a twenty-dollar bill into the driver's hand and whispered: "Get us to the hangar as fast as possible. Our house is on fire. They are trying to save what they can."

"Si, señor. I'll get you to your plane as fast as possible." Within seconds, the transporter was in gear and took off. Neither Fernando nor Doretta took a backward glance at the Lindblad. The experience belonged to the past; all they could think of was the present and their future.

)(

The additional tip had done its work. They arrived at the airfield twenty minutes later. Fernando jumped from the vehicle and headed for the hangar. Walking away, he called out to Doretta. "Ask those guys standing next to that shed to help with loading the luggage. Tell them they won't be sorry they helped."

By the time the plane was rolled out of the hangar, Doretta had lined up the much-needed assistance in getting off the ground as quickly as possible. Fernando paid off the guys and handed an extra reward to the hangar attendant.

"Thanks for having the jet ready for our departure. Do me one more big favor; use that walkie-talkie of yours and get started on getting clearance for takeoff. I'll confirm with them as soon as all are on board, and I'm in my seat. Thanks. It's been a pleasure working with you." He shook hands, ran up the steps, and drew them into the plane. Fernando firmly sealed the door and was in his seat in seconds. Putting on his earphones, he heard the all clear for takeoff from the tower. They were airborne and on their way in ten minutes.

There were no problems landing and tanking in Puerto Montt. Fernando's HFB 320 Hansa Jet safely touched down at the airfield in Santiago at twelve forty-seven on January 23, 1972. Hernando and one of the men emerged from the black limousine, and greeted Fernando; their mien could best be described as woeful. Hernando shook his boss's hand.

"None of us know what to say. We are still all in shock and hopeful that the police will trace and find whoever it was who took Elijah and Eduardo from the estate. It must have all happened in seconds. Señora Esmeralda truly concerns us; she went into shock when the Carabineros and their dogs showed up at the hacienda.

"Valentina had not said anything to her for fear of causing her to have another stroke. Initially, your mother was so frightened and screamed like a banshee at all the servants. She withdrew into her boudoir and slammed the door, locking it securely. No one has seen her since the night before last. They have heard her sobbing and talking to herself. She keeps saying: 'Why did I trust that woman?'

"It appears she holds Juanita responsible for what happened. I learned from Juan that his daughter had been playing with the boys in the maze, and they were seated practically next to the house at their little play table where she was planning to serve them a bite to eat. When she came outside with their snacks and drinks on a tray, they were gone. She ran all around the building calling them by their names, but there were no responses. Juanita became frightened and looked for her parents. Valentina called Amanda, who contacted the police. Your mother must have been watching from her bedroom window. When the cops showed up at the mansion with three mean-looking dogs by their side, Señora Esmeralda lost it. Valentina decided on her own to send the wire."

"Thanks, Hernando for telling me what happened. I don't care that it is Sunday. I want to speak to the head Carabinero in charge of the search as soon as I get to the house. Then I'll deal with my mother. I can't really blame her for being upset." He himself was ready to scream like a banshee.

Up to this point, they had shielded Mario and Alona from the truth. Doretta believed they needed to share with them what might have happened. As Hernando and his helper drove away from the airfield, Doretta tearfully smiled at her children. Fernando had closed his eyes, hoping to shut out the world.

"I'm sure you've been wondering about all the whispering that's been going on since we got off the ship in Ushuaia. Your father still is in shock, and so am I. However, you are old enough and deserve to know what has happened. It appears Elijah and Eduardo were abducted. Someone stole them right from underneath Juanita's face, so to speak.

"The police and their dogs have searched for them for two days, and they have not found a trace of either of the boys. Even Pablo has been involved in the rescue mission but nothing has come of it. Your grandmother is in very bad shape and may have had another stroke. We have no idea. All we know is what Daddy's secretary, Amanda, and Hernando have told your father."

"Mom, did you say someone must have stolen our brothers? How is that even possible? Why would someone want to steal a couple of boys who are barely three years old? It's sick," said Mario. Alona started to sob and wanted her father's attention. Doretta intercepted her. "Alona, let your father sleep. He's been to hell and back. Come here; I'll hold you.

"If there is such a thing as a consolation, at least there is no evidence that someone hurt the boys. The dogs would have found any signs of torn clothes or blood. Maybe it's just a prank, or maybe someone knows your father and grandmother have a lot of money and want us to pay them before they return the boys to us. It's happened before to people who have more than others."

Alona was softly crying against Doretta's chest. "I want my brothers back."

"Daddy will talk to the police as soon as we arrive at the house. Then we'll know more. For now, let's not upset Dad any more than he already is."

Hernando, knowing backroads, had managed to avoid the Sunday afternoon traffic. They arrived at the hacienda in just under forty minutes. To Fernando and Doretta, it seemed like an eternity.

"Doretta, I'll leave you in charge of the kids and the luggage. Let Hernando and his assistant handle all. You simply direct them where to take the different pieces. Some of that hiking equipment from the first leg of our trip can go to the storage shed for now. I'm heading for my office and the phone."

As he entered the mansion, he faced Valentina, who was crying. "Lo siento mucho, señor." Fernando merely nodded in recognition. "Do you have the phone number for the police? Did Amanda give it to you, by chance?"

"No, señor, but the leader of the police handed me this card. It shows a telephone number."

"Thank you; that will do." He closed his office door and dialed the number. On the third ring, a man picked up the receiver.

"Officer Raymondo speaking. How may I help you."

"This is Fernando Garcia Lopez. I understand you are heading the investigation into the disappearance of our twins."

"Yes, I am. So far we have nothing to go by. If there had been any form of aggression and bloodshed, our dogs would have found it. We had our bloodhounds sniff the children's dirty clothes in the hamper, hoping that would lead us to your boys. Unfortunately, that hasn't happened. We told your servant, Valentina, and her daughter, not to touch the dirty laundry, and certainly not to wash it. These are the only links we have to your boys, and we must preserve them. If Elijah and Eduardo are still in the area, this might be the only way we'll be able to locate them. You haven't received any kind of ransom notes, have you?"

"How would I have gotten them? I just flew in from Ushuaia and have been away with my wife and our older children since December 28."

"You might get something in the mail, someone may call you, or someone might be gutsy enough to slide a note under the front door. The latter would be pretty chancy and the least likely."

"None of that has occurred. Where do we go from here? We can't just sit around and wait. What if no one ever gets in touch with us or with you?"

"I have no answers for you. Fearing the worst, your boys might have been taken to a plane and whisked out of the country. Anything is possible in a case like this. Your children might have been sold to the highest bidder. I hate to be so blunt with you, but anything is on the table. We've had public service announcements on the Santiago television stations showing the most recent photos of the boys. So far we've had no leads, none whatsoever. We'll stay on the case and get back to you if we learn anything new. Sorry, señor!" The phone clicked, and he was gone, leaving Fernando emotionally destroyed.

After sitting in his chair silently for fifteen minutes, he knew he had to face his wife and children, but even more so, his mother. He was like the captain of a ship whose sextant and compass were lost at sea. Doretta had engaged the children in a game, wanting to distract them as well as herself. He waved at her, conveying with a hand gesture that he was on his way to see his mother. She grasped the nonverbal message. He firmly knocked on her door.

"Mother, please be reasonable. Open your door. We need to talk. I've been on the phone with Officer Raymondo who is in charge of the case. You and I need to discuss what he had to say. Please open up; we must face this together." He heard the tap-tap of her cane and experienced momentary relief, hoping to have gotten through to her.

When she opened the door with great hesitation, Fernando didn't believe his eyes. He thought he was looking at the ghost of Mrs. Havisham in *Great Expectations.* She was wearing her wedding dress that was literally torn to shreds. Her otherwise beautifully styled whitish gray hair was hanging down, partially covering her face, which hadn't been touched by water and soap and certainly not by any makeup in two days. Shards of the veil were obstructing her vision. Worse than Mrs. Havisham, she was the Madwoman of Chaillot.

"May I come in? We need to talk. I feel as destitute as do you, but all of us must face the facts as they were spelled out to me just a few moments ago. Officer Raymondo gave me very little hope of finding Elijah and Eduardo. Did you or Amanda receive anything in the mail or telephone calls from anyone demanding ransom for the boys?" Esmeralda pushed the torn veil and her hair out of her face.

"No. I cannot speak for Amanda. You must ask her yourself." For a moment Fernando thought he was listening to a voice from the grave. She began to sob when Fernando reached out to her and begged for her help.

"Mom, I know what's happened to you. My soul feels like it's been torched with a branding iron and ripped from my body. I'm totally lost. I cannot accept what happened and what might happen to our boys. Officer Raymondo painted the darkest pictures for me, and I'm not sure I can live and face the reality of those images as I see them in my mind's eye." He openly cried on his mother's shoulders. The scene took Esmeralda back many years when Fernando was just a little boy. Her voice softened.

"There, there, my precious son. I know of which you speak

when you mention your tortured soul. So is mine. How are Doretta, Mario, and Alona doing? She must be devastated."

"She is, but she's been my rock since I first heard this morning that there was a problem at home. We kept it from the children until we were on our way from the airfield in Santiago and learned from Hernando in some detail of what transpired."

"Son, help me get out of these rags. I need to bathe and have Valentina do something with my hair. I can see, you need your mother. All of us must be there for each other and face the realities that may be visited upon us. I couldn't deal with it alone. I saw myself partially responsible for it and worse, blamed Juanita. The poor girl didn't do anything other than what I might have done. Who would expect someone to abduct our boys right from under our noses? That's exactly what happened. I'll cry myself to sleep and pray that whoever stole Elijah and Eduardo will treat them with love and mercy. I know your faith is not as strong as mine, but that is all I have left to sustain me in this hour of desperation.

"Go to your children, and please ask Doretta to come and be with me. We will sustain each other." She hugged Fernando and kissed him on his forehead. He backed away from her ever so slightly, not wanting her to realize how foul her breath was.

# Chapter 45

A week had gone by, and there was nothing forthcoming from the police. Fernando was of the opinion that the Carabineros had given up on the case. Officer Raymondo no longer answered his telephone directly, but had his secretary inform him that the department was not aware of any new developments. Fernando was thankful for Amanda and the crew of capable men working in the vineyards and at the winery. Watching the postal clerk approach the mansion, he would storm out of the house practically grabbing the mail out of the messenger's hands, only to be utterly disappointed not to have found a ransom note. For hours, he sat by the phone for the same reason.

Doretta and Esmeralda became seriously concerned; Fernando's strange behavior suggested that he was suffering with severe depression, and nothing on the horizon was likely to change his totally out-of-character state of mind. Doretta grasped at anything that might shake him into reality.

"I called my mother and Andreas and shared with them what's happened here. I begged them to consider a visit to be with us and the children. Both Mario and Alona will be out of school until the beginning of March. It would be a perfect time for them to be here. I hope you don't mind, but I offered them the same travel arrangements that you made the last time they came. Andreas assured me they would give it serious consideration, especially under the circumstances, and would let me know shortly."

"That's the best news I've had in days. It will be good to have your family with you and the children. Have you mentioned anything to Mother yet? If not, let me handle it," said Fernando.

"As a matter of fact, I have spoken to your mother about the tentative positive response I was given by Andreas. It was actually your mother's thought that prompted me to call Germany and pursue the matter with my mother and Andreas to begin with. She was of the opinion that company and distraction were desirable at this very moment in time. I do hope that Andreas convinces my mother to make the long trip. I will be anxious to hear from them soon."

✼

Outwardly, Doretta appeared to be the steel magnolia. She believed she needed to be strong in view of Fernando's emotional devastation and the trauma inflicted on Mario and Alona and their grandmother. Having survived the initial shock, Esmeralda became Doretta's stalwart support. Every morning, the two women met in Doretta's office and would pray behind closed doors. They discovered that leaning one on the other got them through the day. It was Esmeralda's faith that saw the women through the worst of times.

"I'm thankful there was no evidence of any violence to the boys. I want to think that whoever took them wanted them in the worst way, not for ransom and not to hurt them, but perhaps to possess them. It is my most inner hope that I am right in my assumption and that Elijah and Eduardo are loved and cared for. This has been my prayer since the day Fernando opened my bedroom door and shocked me into reality. I was feeling sorry for myself instead of feeling sorry for my troubled family," was Esmeralda's confession to Doretta.

Pablo was lying at Doretta's feet. He appeared to be sleeping but was carefully listening in on the conversation. His ears would perk up at the mere mention of the children's names, and Doretta could feel the gentle wag of his tail against her leg at such moments.

"Thank you for telling me what you feel and what you believe. I have similar feelings about this nightmare, and thought it was weird that I was consoling myself with the fact that the boys were not found murdered but were perhaps taken by someone who wanted to have children and couldn't have them. Are you and I trying to whitewash this terrible crime? Are we not facing reality the way we should? I have a hard time looking into Mario and Alona's eyes. What must they feel? Are they worried they might come for them next?" asked Doretta.

"Don't think those thoughts haven't crossed my mind. We are totally helpless. Fernando and I talked earlier; he's convinced the police don't care if they find the boys or who took them. Our concerns are sitting on their back burner and are of low priority. A couple kids less in the scheme of the rich folks on the hill. That's all it is to them. I have the distinct impression they are not even considering it a crime, since there was no evidence of any intrusion or anyone getting hurt or, God forbid, getting murdered." Esmeralda wiped away her tears and reached for Doretta's hands. "You and I need to stay strong for the children and Nando. He must get out of that funk. If he were involved with his work and his people, he might find a better way of dealing with his inner turmoil."

"When I cry on his shoulder tonight, I'll remind him of the world out there that is waiting for him to rejoin. His behavior is so totally out of character. I've never seen him act this way as long as I've known him," said Doretta.

"I have. He went to hell and back when Alphonso died, and when I had one miscarriage after another. He never wanted to be an only child."

"Oh, Esmeralda, I feel for both of you, and I feel for myself and Mario and Alona. I do hope Mom and Andreas decide to come. You were correct; all of us could stand a diversion. Thanks for being with me each morning. I want to look in on Mario and Alona. I'm so taken by Fernando's condition that I feel I've neglected my children."

"You haven't. Valentina, Juan, and Juanita are very good to them, and they understand and feel as badly about this as all of us do. I don't always say it, but they are part of our larger family. Go and see the children, and give them hugs from their grandmother. Please ask Valentina to see me in my chambers. I need some fixing up before I face the world today." She picked up her cane and walked away slowly, appearing more bent over than in recent memory.

Doretta followed her. "Come on, Pablo, let's see what Mario and Alona are up to." She didn't need to extend the invitation twice. He was right at her heels as she headed in the direction of Mario's room. His tail was dancing.

"Hi Mom," was Mario 's welcome. And then he spotted

Pablo. The dog was all over him, and Alona could hear the dog's yapping.

"Juanita, may I see my brother for a moment? I hear certain visitors in my brother's room, and I would like to greet them, okay?"

"By all means. I believe it's your mother and Pablo. He seems to be happy to see your brother; I can tell by his bark and the jumping noises he's making. Pablo hasn't been the same since your brothers disappeared." Alona started to cry.

"None of us have been the same since we returned. I wish they would come back. Why would someone just take them?" cried Alona. Juanita wished she had an answer for the child's question. She had asked herself the same question many times since the day the boys disappeared. Deep down in her heart, she felt responsible for the abduction of Elijah and Eduardo.

They were all seated with Grandma at her dining room table for lunch when a phone rang. Fernando immediately jumped from the table and reached for the receiver. While initially disappointed the call wasn't from the police, he was delighted to recognize Andreas's voice. He called Doretta. "It's Andreas. I like to think it's good news for all of us. Tell him Hernando and I will be at the Santiago airport to pick them up."

"Hallo, Andreas. I hope you have good news? We are all so looking forward to your visit."

"I won't keep you on the hot seat. Gisela and I will be arriving on February 16. It was easier to get suitable accommodations in midweek than on the weekend. I hope Fernando isn't too involved with the grape harvest during the week?"

"No, not to worry. We'll talk about it when you are here." She switched to German for a second and whispered. "I wish he was deeply involved in his work. Instead he is sitting around the house waiting to hear about the boys."

"Our arrival is supposed to be close to noon. I had to do some fast talking, but finally convinced your mother of the importance for us to be with you."

"Thanks, Andreas. You have no idea what your visit will mean to all, especially Mario and Alona. I won't keep you any longer. Give Mom a hug and a kiss. I know she doesn't like to talk on the phone, always worrying about spending too much money. Convince her for once to stop fretting about spending money. We'd give away a fortune if we'd get back the boys. See you on the sixteenth. Gosh, that's less than a week away. Fernando will meet you at the airport. Aufwiedersehen." She turned to the others at the table. There were tears in her eyes.

"I'm so glad Andreas got Mom to agree to the visit. And thanks, Fernando, for making it all happen."

"You said it just now. It's only money. I would indeed give a fortune to have our boys back. Who knows, we may have that opportunity yet. It's worth every Peso to have your mom and Andreas with us. We need our family around us." He took Doretta in his arms, holding her firmly. "There, there. Let it all out. Don't be afraid to show the pain you feel every day; I cannot be the only one who can't handle the loss we were made to suffer."

As planned, Fernando and Hernando met Gisela and Andreas at the Santiago airport. Having traveled in First Class made many things a lot easier. They were among the first passengers off the jet, and processing through pass control and customs was speeded up. It also helped this time that they had all met before. Gisela waved from a distance, and Fernando waved back. He hugged Gisela and shook hands with Andreas.

"Welcome to Chile. We've ordered a sunny day for your arrival. We've had some rather cool nights with the winds of winter drifting down from the heights of the Andes. It's close to the time when we have to be watchful of night frosts threatening our grape harvest. Nothing for you to worry about. So glad you decided to visit. We need you here right now. You won't believe how Mario and Alona have grown since your last visit."

Gisela finally had a chance to say something. It was obvious Fernando was trying to make small talk, wanting to skirt the issue that was on everyone's mind. All Gisela could think about were her youngest grandsons, whom she might never have a chance to know.

"We are pleased to be with you and your loved ones. How is Señora Esmeralda holding up?"

"My mother and Doretta have been my backbone in this whole very sad affair. I don't know how I would have handled the last three weeks without them. It was truly a reversal of roles; those two women have sustained me where I used to be the one who kept things on an even keel since Don Carlos has been gone."

"That's sweet of you to admit. Many a man, especially German men, would have a hard time admitting that their mother and wife pulled them through a difficult situation. It had to be earth shattering for you to make the discovery that Elijah and Eduardo were abducted while you were gone. I cannot imagine what I would have done if something like that had happened to Lutz and Lenny when they were three years old." She put her arms around Fernando; she could see he was close to breaking down.

"I'm so sorry for your loss, Son." It was the first time she had called him that. He knew she was truly empathetic to his plight and pain. Hernando tried his best English communicating with Andreas; his German was nonexistent.

"I've got all the luggage in the trunk. We'll be at the hacienda in not quite an hour. Traffic gets pretty bad in the afternoon." Andreas just nodded. He thought he understood what Hernando was trying to tell him.

Fernando helped Gisela into the car and made sure she was seated behind Hernando, making it easier for them to converse. He hadn't needed to be concerned about conversation in the limo. No sooner had Hernando driven out of the parking lot, then Gisela and Andreas had fallen victim to jet lag and were sound asleep. It made the whole situation more tolerable.

Doretta and the children rushed out of the house to welcome Oma and Opa Meyer from Germany. Doretta hugged her mom fiercely and cried unashamedly. Gisela patted Doretta's back. "I don't know how you did it. You must be devastated. You haven't heard anymore from the police?"

"No, Mutti, not a word. It's like nothing has happened; the boys have just vanished. The police chief implied, in speaking with Fernando, that the boys might have been sold to someone out of the country. I can't even talk about it. Those boys were such a joy. It's so sad that you never got to meet them." Alona came to the rescue. She carried a lovely bouquet of flowers to welcome her German grandma.

"Willkommen, Oma." She presented the bouquet to her

grandmother and then raised her arms, indicating that she wished to hug Nana Gisela. Mario shook hands with Andreas and then welcomed his German Grossmutter with a firm handshake. It was obvious to all that the family dynamics had fallen victim to lengthy separations in time and distance. Hopefully, spending time with Mario and Alona would aid in the repair process. Esmeralda and the servants stood back until it was their turn to welcome the visiting family from Germany. Pablo was sitting patiently at Esmeralda's feet. As she stepped forward to greet her guests, Pablo was right beside her cane.

"I'd like you to meet another new member in our family. This is Pablo. You'll learn to love him." Gisela and Andreas both loved dogs. Andreas grinned from ear to ear.

Esmeralda was gracious when greeting Gisela. Both women understood and felt the pain their children were experiencing. After hugging Gisela, she spoke softly into her ear: "Thank you for undertaking this long journey; our children need both of us." They beheld each other just for a moment; their moist eyes spoke volumes.

The greetings concluded, Valentina took Andreas and Gisela to the guest quarters. "Madame wishes you a pleasant rest. If you are so inclined, family dinner will be tonight at seven o'clock. Señora Esmeralda purposely planned dinner an hour later than usual affording you a few hours of rest. Please ring this bell if you need anything. Bienvenida en chile." She bowed and walked away.

Andreas and Gisela joined the others for dinner and were

pleased to see both children at the table. There was a different atmosphere than there had been during their first visit four years earlier. The delightful presence of Don Carlos was still sorely missed. Señora Esmeralda graced the head of the table on this auspicious occasion and she was charm itself. Andreas had her differently in his memory. He never quite forgot their first encounter.

Both he and Gisela had commented in their quarters what a different person Esmeralda had become over the years. Mario was pleased to be seated next to Oma Gisela. The next evening it would be Alona's turn. They would trade places on alternate evenings. Doretta thought it would be a good way for the children to become better acquainted with their German grandmother. She and Andreas were pleased at both children's efforts to communicate with them in German. Doretta and the private tutors she had hired did a fine job of teaching the children. Of course, Mario was continuing his German studies in school these days.

While dinner was delightful and the conversation lively, Gisela and Andreas had an excellent excuse for retiring early. Anyone who had been on an airplane for close to twenty hours had indeed the right to long for a good night's rest in a bed. The typical exchange of presents would be deferred until the next morning.

Doretta fell into Fernando's arms when they were alone at last. "Thank you for making Mother and Andrea's visit a reality. I just wished they had done it last year. But, as it stands, I need them right now; and I'm glad they are here. Your mother seemed to be pleased to have them with us as well, didn't you get that impression tonight?"

"Absolutely! I'm glad they came. Andreas is really a good man. So pleased that he and your mother got hitched. Come here. Let me hold you tight. Are you chilled? Should I close some of those windows?"

"That's probably not a bad idea. The last few nights have carried the chill of fall in the air. I hope I'm not getting a cold or worse."

"I have something to tell you. Perhaps it will warm your spirits. I made a decision tonight at the table. I'm going back to work tomorrow and would like to take Andreas with me. Obviously, not to work in the vineyards but to show him around the winery. I thought it would be of interest to him, he being a retired chemist. What do you think?" Doretta was all smiles.

"You couldn't say anything better. Honestly, you need your work and your people around you. It will give your mind something to dwell upon other than what befell us as a family. Whoever did this to us is inhuman and deserves to rot in hell. Your mother would probably scold me for using such language. I am thankful for her prayers and her support. I couldn't have weathered this storm on my own." She kissed Fernando, and he returned her kisses fervently, promising each other new beginnings.

# Chapter 46

PABLO had already jumped in the backseat of the Jeep. All he had to hear from his master at breakfast was that Fernando was heading back to work on this sunny morning. The signal to leave was when Señor reached for his Gaucho sombrero in the lobby and gestured to Andreas to grab the passenger seat in front.

"I don't remember if we ever took you to our winery and vineyards, or did we? It's quite a spread and the source of all that is Garcia Lopez. It's been in the family for generations. I know Mario doesn't want to become the vintner next in line. I had high hopes for the twins. Obviously, that dream was taken away from us." He squinted into the sunlight.

"Fernando, to tell you the truth, I can't remember if I or we came to see the vineyards when we were here four years ago. If my memory doesn't fail me, we were here in the dead of winter. However, I distinctly recall sampling wine at the winery. I'm sure your mother hasn't forgotten the drunken German. Well, I won't remind her of that unfortunate episode. I like being here in the fall; the days are a lot cooler and more pleasant."

"The long-range weather forecast speaks of much cooler-than-normal temperatures overnight in the not-so-distant future. It's something that hasn't happened in several years. Perhaps, you may witness the nocturnal dance of the Wind Angels. Neither Doretta nor the kids have ever experienced it. If it does look like it may happen, we must take a ride out into the wine country and have you see it with the family."

"Tell me what's it all about; it sounds so mysterious."

"It's not really all that mysterious; it's just beautiful to watch. When they talk about hard frosts lasting for an hour or so during the night, the men among our crew set kerosene burners every so many feet in all the rows of grapevines. Then we have about one hundred or so women who don silk wings strapped to both arms and walk up and down each of the rows, trying to fan the rising warmth from the kerosene torches onto our grapes, preventing them from freezing. The women hum a pleasant tune while they are activating their wings. We call the women Wind Angels. Mario and Alona can't wait to see this happen. You and Gisela will love it too."

"Fascinating. I've never heard of such a thing."

"Down the road, I'll pull over where we store the silk wings. It's a pretty substantial shed. When not in use, they are suspended from a heavy oak beam. The keeper of the wings is very particular how they are stored; she wants to make sure there is no moisture on them for any length of time to prevent dry rot. When I stop, Pablo knows where to take you; it's one of his favorite places to go. He must smell something he really likes."

"You are not just a beautiful dog; you are also very smart. I can tell by that expression on your face, buddy," said Andreas.

He couldn't resist petting Pablo's head. Pablo was only too willing to accept the attention he was getting from the stranger.

"See that gray shed ahead? That's where I'll pull to the side of the road. Pablo will do the rest. Just be sure to replace the wooden beam that locks the gate to the building. There's no lock to speak of. Nobody but our own people are ever found on this land." *Is that really true?* Fernando questioned his thought.

As soon as Fernando stepped on the brakes and shut off the engine, Pablo leaped from the Jeep and looked from one man to the other as if to say—"get your butts moving." Andreas followed Pablo closely. Andreas lifted the closure beam and opened the gate. There were the two hundred or so wings gently swaying in the soft wind. Pablo kept moving his head side to side as if he was trying to tell Andreas something. "I see, Pablo. They are beautiful," he managed to say. "Let's get back to the Jeep; Papa is waiting for us." He must have understood Jeep and Papa since he charged toward the waiting vehicle. He was in his favorite seat by the time Andreas returned.

"You are not exaggerating; that is a sight to see. Now I want to experience those things in action."

"Well, you'll have to hope for a frosty night. We might have to get you out of bed at three or four o'clock in the morning if you want to see those Wind Angels in motion."

"That would be worth the effort. Don't worry about getting us out of bed. Even Gisela would want to see this."

When they walked into the winery, all were smiles to see the boss back. Amanda walked away from her desk and gave Fernando a big hug. "You remember, Andreas, Doretta's stepfather, so to speak, don't you?" said Fernando.

Amanda smiled as she extended her right hand to greet

the visitor. "Of course, I remember Andreas; your father introduced us a few years ago. He made such an indelible impression on your mother, if I recall correctly." There were chuckles all around.

Andreas had to get used to the informality of being introduced by his first name. In Germany, it might have been Herr Professor Doktor Andreas Meyer. Andreas worked just fine for him in Chile. He enjoyed seeing all the changes that had occurred since his first visit.

A tour of the wine cellars was in order. The processing plant with giant stainless steel vats used for the pressing of the grapes to the bottling and packing areas were a vision in ceramic tile and stainless steel—speaking of pristine cleanliness and functionality. The coolness of the vaults where the oak barrels provided a resting station for the wine was a pleasant surprise.

"This is where I hang out on really hot summer days. Anyone looking for me knows where to find me. If you take a peek around the bend, you'll run across a good-sized desk. That's where you'll find me working in the dead of summer."

"Nice arrangement."

"Listen, there have to be some advantages to being the boss. Why don't you have a smoke and look around. I just need to have a short conference with my secretary. I don't know what I would have done without her the last few weeks. She pretty much ran this show."

An hour later, they were still talking fast and furiously. "I've ordered some lunch. It will be here in a few minutes. Sorry, this is taking longer than I anticipated. Too much piled up during my unplanned absence."

"You take your time; I'm enjoying reading all about the

making of wines. I find it interesting that everything is presented in four languages: Spanish, English, French, and German. One of these days, they'll have to add Japanese and Chinese. We have a whole section of Japanese businesses in Düsseldorf. They call it 'Little Tokyo.'"

"Is that so?" Fernando acknowledged. Lunch was a tasty little surprise. He was offered a sampling of Garcia Lopez wines but declined, not wanting to drink anything alcoholic during the day. Neither Fernando nor Doretta were aware that Andreas dealt with heart issues.

Feeling good about being back at work, Fernando offered a Jeep tour through their various vineyards. Andreas learned about the sources for Pinot Noir, Cabernet, and Chardonnay. While he understood much of wine processing, wine growing and cultivating were not in his repertoire of knowledge.

"This looks like a lot of backbreaking work." Fernando had to agree. He did some of the jobs but had learned through the years that there were people to fulfill the needs of certain occupations.

"Have you seen enough? I'm ready to head home. A shower and a nap before dinner sound great. What do you say, Andreas?"

"I'm ready, too. I won't need to take a shower, but a nap sounds awfully good. Remember, I'm an old man and on top of that, I'm still dealing with jet lag."

"So noted," said Fernando and stepped on the gas.

Fernando was anxious to share the experiences of his first day back at work with his family. He was as giddy as a little boy.

If it hadn't been for Gisela and Andreas standing in the lobby waiting for him to join the rest of the family, he would have slid down the curved bannister. *How many years has it been since I did that last?* Fernando wondered. Instead, he walked down the staircase with grace and aplomb. Esmeralda approved of his conduct and appearance.

"You are looking well. Did the day at work agree with you? It must be so, from the happy face we are seeing." His mother stood closest to him and decided he deserved a hug.

"I had no idea how much paperwork accumulated on my desk; but it was a pleasure to work through the details with Amanda. Sorry, I took so much time, Andreas."

"No problem; it's your business, and it should come first. I enjoyed myself and was pleased to become acquainted with the story of the Wind Angels. Very interesting!" He nodded toward Gisela, suggesting he would share his news later.

Doretta gave Fernando a quick kiss on the cheek. "I'm happy things went so well for you today and that you discovered you were still very much in demand. I look forward to picking up with Amanda where we left off before we went on the trip. It's good for me to have matters that keep my mind occupied. Let's enjoy our company and assemble around Mom's dining room table."

Gisela made a mental note of what Doretta had said. Apparently, Señora Esmeralda and Doretta had become much closer over the years. She couldn't help smiling at both of them with pride.

The children went to their respective rooms after dessert. Alona was anxious to model her new clothes from Germany for Juanita. Mario was excited and wanted to read the instructions that came with the Leica camera and the special lenses he received for a present. His parents realized immediately the value of the gift and weren't certain if such generosity was age-appropriate. Fernando opted to address his concerns.

"Why did you elect to be so excessive in your choice of a present for Mario? Both Doretta and I are very much aware of the amount of investment that was involved in this purchase. The boy isn't even ten years old. Yes, he's an excellent student, a hard worker when he wants to work with me in our business, and I have nothing but praise for him in terms of his behavior. We just think you went overboard in your selection."

"It was my idea," said Andreas. "I had hoped we wouldn't have to discuss the matter with you and certainly don't want to cause any more pain than you've had to deal with in the last month. First of all, you've been exceedingly generous in making our travels to see you as comfortable as possible at great expense to yourselves. Lord knows, we still hope Elijah and Eduardo will be heard from again sometime in the future. However, as it stands, Mario is our only grandson, and this may perhaps be our last time that we will set eyes on him and appreciate the joy our present will bring."

"What about Alona? She's your only granddaughter; wouldn't she deserve equal treatment?" asked Doretta.

"Very true. You really don't believe that we would show such blatant partiality to your children, or would you? Your mother and I have chosen a special piece of jewelry to be given to Alona when she is thirteen years old. It is equal in value to the camera equipment we selected for Mario. We wish we would be around when this precious gift is bestowed on Alona, but we doubt that will happen. You two will have to do us the honor."

Gisela unveiled a red velvet box and handed it to Fernando.

"Please open it. It's not anything we've purchased. It is a voice from the past and one of the very few things that survived the life of Doretta's father, Emanuel Abraham Osram. It was in his family for generations. If my first husband would have had a sister, it would have been she who inherited the priceless jewel. He wanted Doretta to have it and left it in the care of her grandmother at the outbreak of the war. I was totally unaware of its existence until my mother presented it to me before we left on this journey. My mother will be ninety on her next birthday and fears she may not be around for too many more years. It was she who designated Alona to be the recipient of her grandfather's legacy, the emerald amulet." There was stunned silence in the room. Although even Esmeralda was caught off guard, she was the first one to speak.

"That is indeed a priceless and treasured gift from the past. Having been given many valuable pieces of jewelry by my grandmother, I know firsthand what meaningfulness and memory represent in the circle of life. When Alona will become the rightful heir to this valuable treasure, she shall learn the full story of her inheritance. I accept your generous gift on behalf of my family and assure you that Alona shall wear it with pride and dignity until the time comes for her to pass it on to the next generation. Thank you, Gisela and Andreas, and be sure to convey our gratitude to your mother, the keeper of the amulet for all these years." Neither Fernando nor Doretta were inclined to add to Esmeralda's pronouncement. Doretta reached for her lacy handkerchief that all so long ago had wiped the tears of Esmeralda's grandmother.

# Chapter 47

It was four-thirty in the early-morning hours of February 26 when the sirens at the Garcia Lopez Hacienda kept blasting the "SOS" code. Gisela and Andreas were startled out of their deep sleep. Mario and Alona stumbled from their beds and were crying. Doretta reached for Fernando, who was already half dressed when she recognized him standing against the dim light cast from his wardrobe. All others knew what caused the alarm to go off. The signal had been sent from an automated temperature reader at the vineyards. The alarm spelled F R O S T. Fernando took charge.

"Our vehicles are leaving in ten minutes. Anyone who is interested in joining Hernando, Juan, and me better be warmly dressed and ready to go. It's the night of the Wind Angels. It hasn't happened in almost ten years, but tonight is the night."

Valentina assisted Esmeralda with getting properly dressed and ready to leave. Doretta had jumped out of bed and helped her mother and Andreas to be cloaked in warm slacks and alpaca ponchos. Juanita had seen to the children. It was in less than ten minutes before the limousine and the Jeep were set into motion heading toward the vineyards.

They could see the hundreds of torches burning from a distance; the sky was warmed by a glow of reds, oranges, and yellows, giving the appearance of signaling an untimely sunrise. They reached the vineyards, and Hernando and Juan parked the vehicles at a slightly elevated point, allowing all to see the magic unfolding before them.

As discussed in hushed voices during the short ride, Valentina and Doretta emerged from the Jeep and headed straight for the well-known shed. "Good, not all the wings are taken. I'm glad," said Doretta. "Please help me with getting a set properly mounted on me. I, in turn, will assist you. I can't wait to get out there and join them."

Doretta could not have pictured in her wildest imagination anything quite so touching and beautiful. She couldn't decide what was more impressive, the coordination of the graceful movement of the wings or the soft humming of a familiar tune. When Valentina and she caught up to the tail end of the Wind Angels, Doretta was recognized by many as the boss's spouse. Some remembered the day of their wedding at the Basilica of Lourdes and Don Carlos's funeral service.

As soon as the chant of the Chilean hymn faded away, the Wind Angels began humming Humperdinck's *Abendsegen*. So moved, Doretta joined them singing the familiar German words in her clarion soprano voice. The women closest to her nodded with approval and encouraged Doretta to keep singing as long as the Wind Angels did not tire of sounding the familiar tune. There was hardly a dry eye to be seen anywhere.

Gradually, morning dawned in the East; and the first rays of the sun touched man and Nature alike. The threat of damaging frost had abated and the magic show of the Wind Angels ended slowly as, one by one, they stepped up to the ashen-gray shed. The keeper of the wings carefully handled each angelic appendage as she freed the women of their silken wings.

Esmeralda sat almost frozen in time and space, staring at the scene that now was transformed from the nocturnal magic to the reality of daylight. Gisela was still spellbound, and Andreas relived in his mind what he had just witnessed. It was the children who were most excited and outspoken.

"Papa, you never exaggerated. It was magic, and it was beautiful. We loved it!" Mario and Alona said in one voice. "The women gracefully moving, the humming, and Mom singing along with them made it even more thrilling." Esmeralda awakened from her spell and spoke at last.

"I'm so happy this happened while you were here. Even I was very much touched by the magic of the moment. It has been so long since we were privy to experience the saving grace of the Wind Angels. The occurrence is obviously a two-edged sword. The frost could do great damage to our well-being, but the rescue effort of the angels is the magical antidote that is balm to our souls." Fernando concurred with his mother.

"She's right. That hour or so of a hard frost could have undone a year's worth of work. The wings of the angels saved us. The days ahead will be filled with the harvest of the grapes. Only a very few, destined to be *Spätlese*, will remain on the vines. I doubt there will be another spectacle for you to witness during the remainder of your visit."

"It was indeed spectacular to view. Gisela and I were

pleased to see Mario using his new camera trying to document the event. He told us he would like to become a photo journalist and that we could not have given him a more meaningful present. We were astounded when he informed us that he wants to create posters with photo enlargements of Elijah and Eduardo and post them in strategic locations in Santiago. He said he would enlist the help of classmates and teachers at Grange School as soon as he returns in early March," said Andreas.

"That's news to us too. He's never said much, but we knew he was deeply affected by the disappearance of his siblings. Thanks for sharing your observations with us. We will certainly encourage him in his endeavors to find his brothers," replied Fernando.

"He's a typical kid; last I heard, he wanted to become a medical doctor," continued his father.

Fernando and Hernando took the Jeep and headed for the winery. Juan drove the others back to the hacienda by limousine. One might have thought Juan was driving a funeral hearse; the silence in the vehicle was pervasive.

After a change of clothes and freshening up, all were ready for a delightful breakfast to be served by Valentina and Juan. Mario began to speak excitedly about the photos he hoped to have captured at the event and to share for the first time his plans to search for his missing brothers. Esmeralda and Doretta were all ears.

"That's a wonderful idea, Mario," commented Esmeralda. Make sure you have enough posters printed to have some of them distributed out in the country as well. Make certain that our home address and telephone number appear in large print at the bottom of the posters." *Why didn't the police think of doing that?* Esmeralda shook her head still in total disbelief.

Shortly before their visit to Chile was to end, Gisela discussed with Doretta her plans for a visit to Falabella's. She wanted to be sure to reconnect with Frau Flott at the store. She had the idea of making it an all-ladies affair; that is, she wanted Esmeralda, Doretta, Alona, and Valentina to join her on the Santiago splurge. Juan was allowed to come along as their chauffeur.

Frau Flott was delighted to see her German acquaintance once again on Chilean soil. "How nice of you to come and visit me. I was shocked that the children were missing when I watched the news at the time. I was wondering if you would be with the family after that disastrous experience a few weeks ago."

She extended her hand in greeting to Gisela, who replied by whispering in German, "We better not go there. The family still has a hard time dealing with their loss. It was terrible. I want today's visit to be a happy occasion and memory." Frau Flott grasped immediately what Frau Meyer was conveying to her.

"How can I be of help today? Is there anything of particular interest to you? I suppose it's too early to think about the upcoming opera season. Something for the young lady?" She was nodding in Alona's direction.

"Exactly. My granddaughter needs some new clothes for school. She's looking forward to returning to her classes and being with her friends. I would like her to select some attractive, everyday practical things and at least two dressy outfits she might want to wear to elegant affairs or to the Teatro. I understand she had a most enjoyable time attending her first opera with my daughter and Señora Esmeralda."

※

Two hours later, Alona and her entourage smiled happily at Frau Flott and thanked her for a most productive interlude of spending money. Casual clothes and school frocks had been carefully placed in colorful shopping bags bearing the name Falabella. Two party dresses were carried in hanging bags by Valentina.

Alona particularly loved a pale green organza creation by Givenchy that Grandma Gisela insisted on buying for her. It was Grandma Esmeralda who spotted a stunning Mehta scarf of silk depicting colorful peacocks on a royal blue background.

"This will look beautiful with your new dress and complement the one your mother refuses to retire. Of course, I understand why. It still looks most attractive on her; and she has a difficult time relinquishing those six-inch heels. If I envy her anything, it's the ability to wear those gorgeous shoes. Heels used to be my passion. And look at me now? I'm an old woman with a fancy cane. Forget about wearing heels, never mind six-inch heels." Everyone joined her in a moment of laughter.

Riding down the escalator, Alona spotted Juan waiting for them. "We are all done shopping. It was a lot of fun, but now I'm ready for some food. And I love the place where Grandma Esmeralda is taking us. Confitería Torres, please!"

"Aren't you the smarty. Wouldn't you be surprised if I chose a different place for a change. But you know your grandmother. It is Confitería Torres, indeed, where we want to go. Gisela and I insist that you and Valentina join us today. I've requested a table for six. After you drop us off, please park the car and join us for lunch."

Juan was pleased that he wore a dark suit and tie instead of the usual chauffeur's livree; he might have seen himself out of place being seated with Señora Esmeralda and her luncheon guests. Alona's grandmothers smiled at each other. The outing had been a decided success and was a welcome change after so many gloomy discussions dictated by the dreadful abduction of Elijah and Eduardo. Both women heartily wished they could speak more freely in a common language, since Esmeralda spoke only limited German and Gisela floundered in Spanish. All had to rely on Doretta and Alona as translators in any conversation. There were many moments when a gentle smile or a hearty laugh had to say it all.

Driving home to the Garcia Lopez Hacienda, *muchas gracias* frequently echoed in the vehicle bearing the happy shoppers. They were welcomed by Andreas and Fernando, who had enjoyed a jovial hour of male conversation after Fernando's return from a productive day at the winery. Gisela was shaking a finger at Andreas when she saw him holding a wine glass in his hand. "I let Fernando do the heavy drinking; I'm just tasting the Pinot Noir, first of the 1970 vintage they just bottled recently. It's good. You ought to sample it. I know you prefer red wine."

"I will, but remember, it is just one glass for you. Doctor's orders." Alona, full of juvenile exuberance, hopped on her father's knee. "Daddy, just wait until you see all the things Grandma Gisela insisted on buying for me. I'll be the best-dressed girl in my class."

"I can't wait for the fashion show. I suppose that means I have to take Mario on another father/son outing into Santiago, or did Mom buy some new school clothes for him as well?"

"Dad, you know better than that. Mario doesn't need school clothes. He gets half a dozen new uniforms at the beginning of the school year. That's all the boys are allowed to wear at Grange School. You are saved. Mom bought him shirts, under-wear, pajamas, and socks. He's all set."

"Gosh. No break for me. Here I thought I could have a happy day with my son in the city. That isn't fair." His mother came to his aid.

"If you want to take a break and take your son into town before he returns to school next week, by all means do so. As a matter of fact, I insist you have a joyful day with him. I'll even give you some extra fun money and let him try his luck at a couple of races at the Hipódromo Chile. I know you are too tight with your money, to spend it on something so frivolous. Mario takes after his grandfather; he used to love horse races. So do it for me, and do it in memory of your father."

Andreas went along. It had been years since he attended any kind of race. In his younger days, he had enjoyed Formula One motor races at the Nürburgring and on the few occasions had been in Monte Carlo. Horse or dog races were not really his thing. But, to appease Gisela and Doretta, he went along with the scheme of joining Fernando and Mario at the Hipódromo Chile.

They arrived just before lunch and enjoyed brats on delectable buns before the races started. Mario had picked up the papers some half-drunken guy had dropped on the ground and began to study the odds, wishing to pick a winning combination. Before long, he made up his mind to put his money on a trifecta in the first, third, and fifth races. It cost him some money; but he was itching to try his luck. Fernando frowned as he was doling out the dough Esmeralda had insisted on giving him for the occasion.

Everyone was thoroughly disgusted with the outcomes of races one and three. Race five was a different story. Mario had picked the right horses for Win, Place, and Show and wished he had invested more heavily at the betting window. Of course, his father never would have gone along with a heftier investment. As it was, he thought it was an absolute waste of money to bet on horses. Mario was thrilled with the outcome and couldn't wait to share his good fortune with Grandma Esmeralda. He had come out way ahead of the money he placed on all of his "big-time" betting.

He piled his money in front of Grandma. "Look Grandma, the money I made at the racetrack. When can I go again? This is fun!"

"Oh no! Don Carlos! This is where I agree with your father. In no way do I want to encourage you to become a gambler. It's an illness that you do not want to have. It's fun once in a blue moon, when you make up your mind you will not spend any more than a fixed amount on what you are willing to lose. Gamblers always brag about their winnings; they never talk about the amounts they lose."

"Grandma, I've never seen a blue moon. How come people talk about it?"

"It means it's something that rarely happens. One speaks of a blue moon when there is a second full moon in a given month. It doesn't happen very often.

"Mario, you listen to me. Your grandfather, Don Carlos, was a wonderful loving man; but in his younger days he lost a lot of money at racetracks. It's not anything I would like you to aspire to. Your father saw some of this when he went to the races with your grandfather, and he swore he would never waste his hard-earned money on gambling. I'm pleased that you had such fun at the races with your father and Andreas. Let's just not make it a habit, okay?"

"Yes, Grandma. I heard you loud and clear." He gathered up his winnings and crumpled them into his jean pockets. Mario rushed off to his room, wanting to count how much money he had. He wasn't about to tell Alona about his good fortune.

# Chapter 48

STILL deep in their sleep, the phone rang at the Garcia Lopez Hacienda at four o'clock on the morning of March second. It was still dark outside. Fernando picked up the receiver, not certain how he wished to address such an untimely caller.

"Garcia Lopez! Fernando speaking. Who the heck calls at this hour?" He caught himself, almost having said hell. There was a certain hesitation before the response came forth.

"This is Lutz Osram. I'm your wife's brother calling from Germany."

"Hallo Lutz; I get the feeling this isn't good news."

"You are correct. It's rather sad. Andreas had a major heart attack on the plane. There were two physicians on board, but they weren't able to revive him. He was dead on arrival in Düsseldorf. He was taken by hearse directly to the cemetery. The funeral will be in three days. Our mother is devastated, although she was quite aware of his serious heart issues when they married."

"Would you like to speak to your sister? She's right here." Before he could answer, Fernando handed the phone to Doretta.

"It's Lutz calling; Andreas had a major heart attack on the plane and died."

"Oh no, Lutz. Fernando just told me. That's so sad. I had hoped for a few happy years for Mother. I guess it wasn't meant to be. I feel badly that it happened on their way home from seeing us. I hope Mother doesn't blame us for Andreas's death?"

"I agree it's too bad he went the way he did. But let me assure you, Mother would never blame you for his death. You had a terrible event in your lives, and Mother and Andreas needed and wanted to be with you. Andreas knew his days on earth were few and numbered, and I believe he died a happy man. He called me the day you and Mother went into town with Alona, and he told me how happy he was to have made the journey and what an enjoyable time he and Mother had with all of you. Please don't lay any guilt trips on yourselves. You've got enough heartache to deal with. I'll write you when all is over. Love you, Sis!" And he was gone.

Doretta debated calling Lenny; he was the more emotional of her two brothers. Her mind was in a total upheaval. *Do I want to fly home to Germany? There was enough money to fly them First Class. How will Mother feel about my not being with her as she buries this man?* She resolved to discuss it with Fernando as soon as he stepped out of the shower.

"What do you think I should do? Would you have a problem with my flying to Germany to be with my mother? It must be a terrible shock for her, losing her second husband and seeing him die in front of her eyes and then on an airplane. I can just imagine what it was like."

"If you feel this is what you want to do, by all means. It certainly isn't any hardship on our finances. The children will be well taken care of. Mario is starting school in two days and Alona will spend a good portion of the day at her school. When she is home, Juanita and Valentina can look after her. And, of course, Mother will be here too. I can guarantee you, I can get a First Class ticket for you on a plane later today."

"I'm not certain about being there for the funeral, but I do have the need to be with my mother, to connect with my brothers, and to see my grandmother one more time. Are you sure you wouldn't mind?"

"Join Mother for breakfast, and ask Valentina to start packing for you. I'll call the travel agent and see what I can do to have you on your way this very day." Esmeralda was shocked to hear what had happened and was fully in agreement with her son that Doretta should make the unplanned journey to Germany to be with her mother.

Fernando and Doretta entered the Santiago airport at one o'clock for a two o'clock departure for Frankfurt with a connecting flight to Düsseldorf. Lenny met her at the airport. He spotted her the moment she came into his visual field. *She looks great considering she'll be forty this year,* thought Lenny. He hugged his sister fiercely, being thankful that she decided to be there for their mother.

"First stop will be Grandma's. She won't make it to the funeral. Not that she didn't like Andreas, but her health is such that a walk from the parking lot to the gravesite would be a real challenge. Grandma is beginning to show her age. She still refuses to be taken anywhere in a wheelchair. She's a stubborn old cuss," spoke Lenny.

"Guess that's where all of us got our spunk. I hate to bring this up, but there's no better time than now. Are you seeing anyone? You and Lutz will be thirty-eight this year. Will I always have to hear from Mother that you've decided to be confirmed bachelors?"

"I've been seeing a woman for a couple of years now, but neither of us is interested in having our relationship blessed by a piece of paper. Furthermore, we are not at all inclined to have any offspring. Anna is forty and feels it's too late for her to have children. I'm in full support and agree. We enjoy each other's company and whatever comes with the territory. Does that do it for you?"

"Surely does. It's your life; and you are a big boy. I have to respect that. I presume Lutz is in a similar boat?"

"Not quite. He's married to his work, taking his law practice very seriously. Frankly speaking, I would hate to be married to someone that dedicated to a job. Life has to be more than just work and accumulating money. To tell you the truth, I know little about my brother's other life and furthermore, I don't care. It's the world he's created, and it's the world in which he must live for better or for worse."

"Boy, you've become quite the philosopher. I'm glad I decided to make this trip. It's really too bad that Andreas had to die for me to come and see my family. But, like your brother, I've transformed my life in another hemisphere. It is indeed my world today. There's no question about it; all of us have moved far beyond from where we started."

Doretta immediately recognized the little house that became home for several years after WWII. Rosebushes had become climbing rose trees that seemed to enclose the house. For a moment, Doretta was taken back to *Hänsel and Gretel.*

"Here we are. Grandma will be excited to see you. She had given up on the idea years ago when you first moved to Switzerland. When you married Fernando and Chile was in your future, she was certain she would never again lay eyes on you. Be prepared; she's changed a lot except for her beautiful smile and her loving personality."

Grandma took in the image of her granddaughter as she crossed the threshold of her home. Her voice wasn't as strong as it used to be. "My, my, child. You haven't changed a bit since I last saw you. How do you manage to keep that slender figure? Don't they feed you in Chile?"

Doretta held her grandmother firmly. "Grandma, you never change. Your vision is still as sharp as it used to be. Put your mind at ease; they do feed me in Chile. I've apparently been blessed with my father's genes. He was never what people might call a big man; I remember him as tall and very slender. Looks to me like all three of us have taken after our father. I gather Lutz looks just like Lenny since they always looked totally alike. Am I right in that assumption, Lenny?"

"Right on; Lutz is a beanpole just like I. It does have its advantages. I can eat anything I choose without gaining any weight. That's a consolation approaching the age of forty. One thing neither Lutz nor I am good at is exercising or any kind of active sport. Andreas tried teaching us about the importance of exercising, but he never got very far with us. And then look, what good did his exercising do him?"

"Leave the man in peace," said Grandma. "Doretta, come and sit by me on the sofa. I want to hear all about your life in Chile. I still cannot accept the fact that someone stole your two boys and no one has been able to find them or the perpetrators who did this. You poor girl."

"Grandma, we are finally learning to accept our fate. Esmeralda, the boys' other grandmother, and I have been daily praying over the matter and are trying to believe that the boys are safe and lovingly cared for by someone who wanted to have children in the worst way and couldn't have them. What leads us to this conclusion is that there was absolutely no evidence of any aggression or any blood shedding in the abduction of Elijah and Eduardo. Mario and Alona are truly the sunshine in all our lives. Thank you for keeping Daddy's amulet for all these years and passing it on to Alona. All of us were deeply touched when Mom shared that story with us just before their return to Germany."

"I was honored to do it for your departed father."

Saying farewell to Grandma wasn't easy for either. Doretta knew this indeed would be the last time she would see her. Lenny was only too happy to drive his sister to their mother's house in Düsseldorf, the home she had moved to when she married Andreas.

"This looks lovely. I'm so glad she is no longer living in the hustle and bustle near the Wasserturm in Essen. It looks like a quiet and pleasant neighborhood."

"Lutz and I were glad she found Andreas and decided to

marry again. It gave her a new outlook on life. We are also thankful they came to see you in Chile, especially this last time when you needed all the family support you could have."

"Thank you for seeing it that way. I'm actually very concerned about facing Mom. How's she taking the sudden loss?"

"Lutz and I believe she handles it well. She knew of his heart condition and was aware something like this heart attack could happen. She'll be okay in time. Andreas left her fairly well off, and we don't need to worry about Mom having to make any major changes in her lifestyle. You'll see."

They rang the doorbell which was promptly answered. Gisela seemed pleased to be able to embrace her daughter. "Thank you for making this trip. I know it wasn't anything you had planned or anticipated; it's not for Andreas but for me that you came. Thank you again. Lutz is here; he's on top of things and has seen to all that needed attention. It will be a simple service day after tomorrow. As per his wishes, Andreas was cremated and the urn with his ashes is to be interred next to his first wife. I suppose, when I go, they might place my urn to the other side of Andreas since I never knew of a final resting place for your father. I don't even want to think of where he might have wound up."

"Mom, please let father rest in peace and don't go there. It's been years since I had those horrible nightmares, each time reliving the day he was beaten half to death in front of our eyes. I've had enough personal trauma lately."

"Sorry, dear, I didn't mean to do that. But let's go upstairs. Lutz is anxious to see you. I can't believe it's more than ten years since you last saw one another." Gisela took Lenny aside. "Let's go to the kitchen, and give those two a chance to talk."

Lutz got out of his chair as he heard his mother and Doretta come up the stairs. They practically ran toward each other when Doretta stepped into the living room.

"My God, you are a sight for these old eyes," was all Lutz could say at first.

"What do you mean, old eyes? Mine are older than yours. Maybe they are not as used to bending over important paperwork every day of the week. Those are some pretty serious eye glasses. I didn't remember you ever wearing any."

"I needed to wear them almost from the time when I started practicing. Must have been all that heavy reading I was doing. That has to be it. Neither you nor Lenny need glasses. But why are we spending time talking about me. How are you holding up?"

"As you see, I'm still here and keep going. Having Elijah and Eduardo taken from us was traumatic for all. But, like I explained to Mom, we've accepted our lot. Who knows, they might be located somewhere yet. I hope and pray they weren't hurt or tortured. That I couldn't stand. I've seen too much blood in my life." Lutz reached out to her and took her in his arms.

"I'm so sorry for your loss. I can't imagine how I would have acted in your and Fernando's place. How are Mario and Alona dealing with it?"

"Mario is having a much harder time than Alona. Obviously, because of being older, he's much more aware of how we are feeling and handling the boys' absence. Like his father, he feels very much guilty of having been on a most exciting journey while the boys were home and abducted in our absence. Personally, I believe it could have happened even had all of us been there. They were literally taken away from our doorstep.

Who would have thought such a thing could happen? None of us and none of the staff taking care of the children imagined such a thing."

"You don't think it was an inside job, do you?"

"That thought never crossed our minds. The people who are working for us on the hacienda have worked for the family for generations. They are part of the family and feel the loss as badly as we do."

"Sorry. Just thinking. My legal mind has to look at all angles. Enough of that; I don't want to add to your sadness. From the little that Mom has said since her return and under the circumstances, it sounded like your situation with Fernando's mother has significantly improved. That was good news. She briefly touched on the adventure with the Wind Angels and what an event it was. For her to leave the warmth of her bed at some ungodly early hour in the morning was a challenge in itself. I was glad to hear she termed the experience rewarding."

"It was a sight for all of us; neither the children nor I had ever seen it before. Fernando and others talked about it; but because there hadn't been any serious threats of frost since I came to Chile, the experience was new to me. It was indeed beautiful, but the best part was that the Wind Angels saved this year's grape harvest. Mushy grapes dripping from vines don't pay the bills."

"I get it. You do have a good head for business. I was very much pleased to learn that Fernando was open-minded enough to let you assume certain responsibilities in the winery, which made sense. What would you do with your time and all the help you have to take care of the house and the children? You couldn't just sit around and read, do needle work, God forbid, or some other things bored women do. Glad to hear that you two have a good relationship. How do you handle the Catholic environment?"

"After I went through the indoctrination in preparation for the marriage ceremony, I made it quite clear to my in-laws and the monsignor what I thought of certain doctrines. What I've learned since is that, in situations such as were laid upon us, having a strong faith like Señora Esmeralda's helps and sustains you through the darkest hours."

"I'm glad to hear that. I don't know if Mom or Lenny have written about it or said anything to you, but I've become a practicing Jew. It's a way of honoring our dead father and what he died for. I don't go to temple every day, but I keep Shabbath and attend and support the synagogue. My practice is closed for Pesach, from Rosh Hashanah until Yom Kippur, and during Hanukkah. I see a Jewish woman and enjoy being with her when she says the Jewish blessings over the candles, wine, and challah every Friday night. We are just good friends; but who knows what might come of it? I'm glad you had children. I doubt there will ever be any forthcoming from Lenny's or my loins."

"Thanks for sharing. I'm proud of you. It's interesting how things in life work out. I thought I would never get over the way Señora Esmeralda reacted when she discovered that I wasn't only German but a Jewish half-breed to boot. One might have thought I was a leper. Needless to say, that has all gone away. We've learned to like and love one another and, more importantly, to respect each other. Our relationship couldn't be better. And you'll never believe what started us out on this road to positivity. When Mom and Andreas came for their first visit, the entire family went to the Teatro to see

*Tosca.* Esmeralda saw how I reacted to the opera and came to the conclusion that I had a "soul" after all. We discovered that very evening we had the love of opera in common. It was that seed that started the positive flowering of our friendship."

"I've really enjoyed this chance to speak with you. We better join Mom in the parlor. She's got the table all set to receive you. I'm sure she's wondering by now what all you and I had to talk about and am glad she allowed us to have this time together. Lord knows when we'll see each other again. My lady friend loves to travel. Perhaps one of these days, she'll convince me to take a vacation. We might just come and see you in Chile. Wouldn't that be great?"

"It would be. And know you and your friend would be more than welcome at our home anytime. There's certainly plenty of space for guests. Let's go see Mom."

"Come in and sit down. I made fresh tea for you and a good, strong cup of coffee for us. I remember, you always liked waffles as a child. That's why I made them instead of getting something from the Konditorei. It was nice that you had a chance to catch up with your brothers. I look at you and can't believe your ages and all that happened since you were born."

"That's what happens when you get older, Mom," dared Lutz to say. She just peeked at him over her stylish glasses. He got the message and dropped speaking any further about getting old. It was not one of Mom's favorite subjects to discuss.

"Before he took off, Lenny told me he is bringing his lady

friend to the service tomorrow. Am I going to meet the mysterious lady in your life on this auspicious occasion?"

"We hadn't talked about it, but if this is what you wish, let me give her a call and see. It's kind of too bad that we all shall be together for the very first time at a funeral service. Lenny doesn't even know that I'm seeing Deborah." He walked out of the parlor to find Mom's phone. Once seated again at the table, we learned that his friend was indeed willing to meet Lutz's family at the funeral of their stepfather.

✕

One couldn't speak of a funeral procession. Other than the minister from Gisela and Andreas's church, there were a total of six mourners in attendance: Doretta, Lenny and Anna, Lutz and Deborah, and Gisela. Grandma was there in spirit. She had arranged for a beautiful wreath, all decked out in white calla lilies, to be placed on the site. Grandma knew Andreas was fond of the color white.

The interment was more or less a formality since neither Gisela nor Andreas had been regular attendees at the church. Gisela thanked the man for his liturgical courtesies and invited her other guests to a nearby restaurant for the wake. She was extremely pleased to meet Anna and Deborah, who were a total surprise to her, although she couldn't hide her disappointment that there would never be any grandchildren in her German family. She drew that conclusion from the discussion between her sons and their respective lady friends.

Doretta was overjoyed she had the opportunities to be with her brothers, to have met the women in their lives, and to have seen her grandmother for a last time. While she made the journey to be with her mother during this time of her emotional need, feeling more connected with her brothers had become even more critical to Doretta's inner well-being. She had been too busy with her own life to experience the need of being close to her siblings. Doretta was particularly touched by her discovery of Lutz's adoption of the Jewish faith. His attachment to the faith of their father gave her an inner peace she'd been lacking for many years.

⚸

The return flight to Santiago was long but uneventful. Doretta was extremely thankful to have First Class accommodations; it made the endless trip more palatable, not that she was seeking or expecting enjoyment out of the event. She was pleased to see Fernando at the gate, holding Alona's hand. She was carrying a pretty bouquet of flowers to welcome her mother home. It was her suggestion to have the flowers; she remembered doing so for Grandmother Gisela.

Doretta ran toward them as soon as she spotted Fernando and Alona. "Thank you for being here with Papa. And thank you for the lovely floral greeting. It's something I've only seen people do in Europe." She hugged her little girl. There was no question in her mind, she had returned to the place she called home at last.

"How was it? How did Gisela handle the shock of losing Andreas?"

"Actually, I thought her acceptance of his death was realistic. It didn't come as a total surprise. She was pleased that I wanted to be with her. I loved seeing my grandmother, although when we kissed goodbye, both of us realized it would be a final farewell.

"Perhaps my favorite memory of this journey was a discussion I had with my brother Lutz. Don't get me wrong, I loved seeing and being with Lenny as well, but Lutz surprised me. He confessed that he's adopted the Jewish faith to honor our dead father. That really touched me. And I believe he isn't being Jewish just in name, but he practices his faith. That meant a lot to me.

"Those two brothers of mine may be identical twins in appearance, but they are two totally different human beings intellectually and emotionally. I would never say this to Lenny; I wouldn't want to hurt his feelings. I feel very close to Lutz. When he hinted, even ever so slightly, that he might be talked into visiting us by his lady friend, Deborah, I didn't hesitate to extend an open invitation. I presume you have no problem with that, right?"

"None whatsoever. I would love to get to know him. I've mentioned this to you before. I always regretted not having met your family before I moved us to Chile in 1963. It was a missed opportunity. I do hope he follows through on the suggestion.

"I've got to get you home. Mom and all at the hacienda are anxiously awaiting your return. I realize you were gone for less than ten days, but your presence has been thoroughly missed."

"That makes me feel doubly good. When I got off the plane earlier, I couldn't help saying to myself: Glad to return to a place I call home."

"You have no idea how it makes me feel, hearing you say that." Alona had just listened quietly, hearing her parents solve the problems of the world. All she could think was that she was happy to have Mommy home safe and sound after being on an airplane for so many hours. She wasn't sure she would like to be caged up for that length of time.

Esmeralda and Pablo were in waiting as Fernando pulled the Jeep up by the front door of the mansion. She had the biggest smile on her face as she held open her arms to greet Doretta. "Bienvenida hija," she kissed her face. Doretta had tears in her eyes, being welcomed as daughter by her mother-in-law. Now she knew she was really home at last.

# Chapter 49

SEASONS had come, and seasons had gone. Mario loved school, and he loved being home with his family and Pablo. Alona matured into a beautiful young lady being eight years of age. Nothing was ever heard again about Elijah and Eduardo. Señora Esmeralda was doing as well as could be expected; she was still the matriarch of the house to all except Doretta. Esmeralda adored the mother of her grandchildren and did all she could to brighten her every day, no matter how sad she would occasionally find her seated at her desk.

And so it was on a very chilly day in July of 1973. "I just received the season schedule for the Teatro. One of my absolute favorites is being performed on opening night. It's *La Damnation de Faust* by Hector Berlioz. Jessye Norman is singing the role of Marguerite. It couldn't get any better. Just imagine her singing 'D'amour l'ardente flame.' I can't wait to see and hear her. You will do me the honor of accompanying me that evening, won't you?"

"I know it's all based on Goethe's famous play. I just find the subject so depressing. And Berlioz's title for the opera gives me the willies. I'm familiar with the play and have seen the various treatments of the story in opera: Gounod's *Faust*, Boito's *Mephistopheles*, and now Berlioz's *La Damnation de Faust*. In some countries, Gounod's *Faust* is offered as *Marguerite*—just to add confusion.

"I'm not trying to be difficult. Of course, I'll attend opening night with you at the Teatro. I just wish it was something more joyful than *La Damnation de Faust*. I agree, Jessye Norman will give an unforgettable performance of 'D'amour l'ardente flame.' For me, it's the highlight of the whole opera."

"Glad you are seeing it my way. I will order the tickets for September 11. I'll make it just for the two of us. Alona is too young to sit through that particular opera, and Fernando couldn't care less. We'll make it an early dinner at Confitería Torres since the opera starts at six o'clock."

"I look forward to it. We'll talk more closer to the night. No need for another shopping spree, especially since we didn't attend the opera for over a year. Lately, I don't feel like leaving this place for anything. I feel sheltered by my surroundings, not wanting to know what's going on outside these walls. I haven't seen you take many trips into the city lately. Am I wrong in my observation?" mused Doretta.

"Not at all. On the other hand, we cannot hide in this place. We do need to get out once in a while. The children have their schools; Fernando has the vineyards and the winery and his periodic flights to business meetings. You and I are confined to the hacienda and the servants. Once in a while, when my bones are not talking to me, I take a stroll down the road with Pablo. He loves to be able to run around without a leash. The road to the vineyards is our private property; I don't have to worry about traffic when I take him off leash. He always barks when I want to turn back at the shed for the angel wings. For whatever reason, he likes to check it out. Haven't you noticed it when you take him for a walk?"

"Now that you mention it, yes; he does seem to have a special interest in what's going on in the gray shed.

"Well, anyway, I look forward to our outing. At the moment, I have a pile of paperwork to handle. Amanda sent over a whole bunch of invoices for companies in Germany, Switzerland, and Austria that I need to process. Fernando called and told me not to wait for dinner. He and the crew are in the middle of finishing bottling the 1971 vintage. Amanda will order food in from one of the vendors nearby. I know he won't go hungry. But when he comes home, he'll be ready for a hot shower, bed—and hopefully—me."

"The last thing for sure. I'm pleased you two have kept your love alive in spite of all that has happened in the ten years since you were married. It's good that you are involved in our business and that you understand what it takes to run it successfully. I often wished Don Carlos had allowed me to know more about day-to-day aspects of the firm. He didn't. To him, I was the "Grande Dame," who needed to be worshipped on a pedestal. It wasn't right, and it wasn't what I really wanted. But, of course, he always had his way.

"I'll leave you to your work. I look forward to having dinner with you and Alona tonight. We'll have a nice time, although I do miss 'my men' at the table." She giggled as she tap-tapped out of Doretta's office—her cane firmly planted with every step she took.

# Chapter 50

JUAN had detailed the limousine and was proudly admiring the great job he had done. The car looked like new. Had it been he going into town with just two people, he would have chosen one of the smaller cars available in the garages. Of course, that would never have done for Señora Esmeralda. Going to the Teatro, it wasn't a matter of choice; it had to be the black Mercedes limousine.

The mansion was bustling with activity. Doretta gave Fernando detailed instructions that morning. He seemed to be off in the clouds, but she opted not to comment on the mood he appeared to be in.

"You remember, Mom and I are off to the Teatro this afternoon. Be sure to pick up Alona at school on your way home from the winery. Juan set up the table for your poker game in the card room. I've asked Cook to fix for supper whatever Alona and you and your buddies prefer."

"Will do."

※

Alona was surprised to see her father waiting for her in his Jeep outside the school building.

"This is neat, Dad. I had expected Juanita to walk me back from school. Now I get to ride with you. Did you have a good and productive day at work?"

"You sound just like your mother and your grandmother; you are much too smart for your age. And to answer your question, I did have a good day at work."

Arriving at the hacienda, he thought he saw a light on in Mario's room. For a moment, he was totally perplexed. Mario was supposed to be at school. Just to make sure the lights hadn't been left on accidentally, he decided to check on the situation and was astounded to see Mario sitting on his bed with his nose in a book.

"What are you doing at home? Aren't you supposed to be at school?"

"The principal suspended me for a week. Someone reported me for having distributed the posters searching for my brothers. Supposedly, I was to seek permission to display such matter and violated school policies. One of my favorite teachers, Señor Alvaraz, who has relatives not too far from here, drove me home. He was sorry to learn of the principal's reaction to my efforts to find Elijah and Eduardo."

"You just wait until Grandma hears about this. She'll have a fit. The way we endowed that establishment, there will be some repercussions. Well, I'm glad to see you anyway. You may want to sit in on our poker game tonight. You know, Mom and Grandma are off to the opera later, don't you?"

"I'd forgotten all about that. Are you sure you want me at the poker table? Grandpa tried teaching me some tricks and how to watch for people's body language and facial expressions and to watch my own."

"Are you trying to tell me you are aware of the finer points of playing the game? I never knew what the old fox was up to. He loved to gamble, and he loved the game of poker."

"I won't play. I'll just kibitz and enjoy watching you. Hopefully, you won't be losing too much money. On a more important matter, what are we having to eat tonight? It will be a nice change for me from my school cuisine."

"Well, what would you like Cook to fix for you?"

"You have to ask? You know me, when first I come home from school, I always request Cook's favorite pizza. She's been watching some Italian chef on TV and makes a pretty mean pizza these days. I'm positive Alona likes it too. What about you and your poker buddies?"

"I'll share a secret with you. They and I like Cook's pizza very much. I learned to like pizza while I studied in Europe. We won't tell Mom, although she told me Cook could fix anything we wanted."

"Pizza it is! Yippie!"

"Did I hear pizza?" asked Doretta as she and Alona walked into Mario's room.

"Did you know he was home from school?" asked Fernando.

"Yes, I saw Señor Alvaraz drop him off. I asked Mario to hide out in his room, not wanting Mom to get upset before we were leaving for Santiago. That principal will get an earful when she finds out about Mario's suspension. In the meantime, I'm thrilled to have him with us for a few days. It's an unexpected pleasure. Come here, give your mom a hug and kiss."

Mario obliged. Not only did he hug his mom and sister; he was in a hugging mood and embraced his father as well.

"You don't know how happy I am to be with all of you for a few days." His dad returned the loving gesture with a bear hug and then picked up Alona, not wanting her to miss out on anything. *You two are growing up much too fast, and I miss my boys!* He turned away from his family, not wanting them to see the tears in his eyes.

"I've got to run. Mom is waiting for me in the foyer. We are off to the opera."

"Have a wonderful time. We'll enjoy the pizza and the game," said Fernando. He was looking forward to spending the evening with his children and his friends.

⋊⋉

It was three o'clock on the afternoon of September 11 when Juan helped the señoras into the limousine. They were idly chatting about the gowns they had chosen for the evening. "Our regulars might think we have nothing else to wear, my dear," said Esmeralda.

"I don't care if they remember that I've worn this dress a few times since that evening five years ago. I've never had it on anywhere else but on the cruise. I doubt there's a person in the Teatro who was on the Antarctic adventure. And as far as your stunning black is concerned, the old dowagers in the booth next to us are just plain jealous of your figure. I like the new scarf you got at Falabella's; that changes the look completely. No fretting about what we are wearing. We are looking great. Those guttersnipes would give their eyeteeth to walk in those shoes of mine."

They arrived at the restaurant by three-forty-five. Juan thought the traffic was unusually heavy but didn't make any comment about the many military vehicles he noted. The ladies wanted to be picked up no later than five-thirty, allowing them adequate time to get to their booth and be comfortably seated.

"As usual, our dinner was excellent. You made good choices," said Doretta as they stepped out of the restaurant. Juan saw them emerge and pulled up to the front of Confitería Torres. He put the car in park and jumped from his seat. He smiled at his happy fare as he opened the back doors for each of the ladies, first seating Señora Esmeralda and then Señora Doretta. They arrived punctually at the Teatro at five-forty-five. Making their way to the bank of elevators, they noted many of the regulars in elegant dress. Some were sipping champagne, and others were excitedly talking about the opera.

When they arrived at their private booth, Doretta noted the old dowagers already seated in the booth next to theirs. They were staring at her as if she was wearing a transparent dress showing off her naked breasts. She wanted to fire back with looks that could kill but opted instead for a condescending smile. They weren't worth any further effort. She had listened to their commentary on other nights and decided long ago that they were interminable snobs.

The conductor appeared promptly, and the exceptionally large orchestra was greeted with extended applause. At last the curtain rose on the first act. In spite of her lamentations of disliking the plot and the title of the opera, Doretta became fully engrossed in the story. It was the powerful music that made her forget all that seemed to bother her. Esmeralda kept watching her intently when her eyes were not directed at the proscenium. The applause was more than generous when the curtain came down after Act II.

"After we powder our noses, let's splurge and have one glass of the wonderful champagne. Juan will get us home safely, not to worry my dear. And you are not pregnant, of that I'm positive."

"Right you are. I'm past childbearing age. Fernando and I decided not to try for other children after our loss. We hoped you would see it our way."

"I do, and I'm thankful for the grandchildren I have. I feel sorry for your mother, being so far away from them. But let's enjoy this evening. Now I'm game for a glass of champagne, aren't you?"

"Yes, Mom. I'm totally agreeing with you. Let's enjoy this very evening in spite of the subject of the opera. I always thought Marguerite got the short end of the stick in this plot. It helps to know that in the end her soul is rescued by the angels."

"Oh, you are kindhearted. I recognized that the first time I attended *Tosca* with you. It was your sincere involvement with the protagonist that revealed to me your true nature. And it was that caring personality that made me like you and subsequently love you." She reached for Doretta's hand.

Neither Esmeralda nor Doretta could wait for the inimitable performance of "D'amour l'ardente flame" in the final act. Jessye Norman brought the house down. The standing ovation lasted close to five minutes. Doretta and Esmeralda were stunned. Both had heard the aria performed by other notable artists; none compared to what they were privy to experience on this night. When the final curtain came down and the lights in the Teatro came up, the audience went wild with applause.

It took a good twenty minutes before the ladies could connect with Juan, who was anxiously waiting for them by the main exit of the theater. He rushed them to the limousine, showing some concern but not wishing to alarm his ladies. He had already decided how he was going to make his way out of the congested downtown area. Juan sensed that there were serious problems in the offing.

Having his ladies safely ensconced in the backseat of the limo, he moved away from the curb in an uncharacteristically speedy manner. "Excuse my maneuvers, Señora Esmeralda, but I have good reason to believe there will be trouble any moment in the city. The place is crawling with uniformed and armed men, and I even heard some gunshots being fired not too far from the Teatro. I was hoping the opera would end before real trouble reared its ugly head."

"That doesn't sound encouraging, Juan. Are you aware of any political issues? I thought our current regime was running the country just fine."

"We don't watch much television and only read what we can glean in the paper." He decided not to say more, not wanting to upset the señoras. About ten minutes out from the Garcia Lopez Hacienda, Juan became seriously alarmed. It was way past sunset, which would have occurred behind him rather than in front of him, and it was obviously not time for sunrise. He accelerated and became increasingly fearful of what he was seeing develop in front of his eyes.

Señora Esmeralda spoke first. "Juan, am I seeing things, or

are we looking at a major fire in front of us?" Doretta's eyes popped open.

"Oh, my God, it's the hacienda fully engulfed in flames. And worse yet, it looks like the vineyards beyond are going up in smoke as well. What is going on?"

"I have no idea, ma'am. All I saw in Santiago were hundreds of armed soldiers combing the streets. I was almost certain they had brought a halt to the opera since there were so many Carabineros standing around the Teatro. I'm driving as fast as the road will allow me."

When Juan pulled up to the garages, he saw many armed soldiers backlit by the flames destroying the hacienda. One of them turned around as he became aware of the limousine. He smashed the window next to Doretta with the butt of his weapon and pointed the machine gun at her chest. He screamed at the passengers to get out of the car and ordered Juan to stand to one side. Another soldier pushed the barrel of his gun into the back of Esmeralda, forcing her to walk east of the hacienda toward the vineyards that were a giant field of flames. A ruthless uniformed man stared at Doretta, demanding her name.

"I'm Señora Doretta Garcia Lopez," said Doretta in her very best Spanish.

"And who are you, if I may ask?" *This is déjà vu. I'm back in 1943!* She didn't know where she had gotten the nerve to challenge the soldier.

"Since you asked, bitch, we march for General Augusto Pinochet and are in the process of eliminating all you goddamn Allende supporters. We've killed him earlier in the day. I'm fully aware of who you are; you and your tribe have been on our radar for a while. There's nothing in your background we don't know about."

"Oh, mein Gott; es waren sie die unsere Jungens gestohlen haben!" [Oh, my God, it was them who stole our boys!]

"What did you say, bitch?" He struck her with the butt of his weapon.

"Sorry, I was saying a prayer in German."

"Who is she?" asked the soldier who had mishandled Esmeralda only seconds ago.

"It's the rich bitch who belongs to the bastard and his kids our compatriots are holding in that shed over there. It's the last poker game he'll ever play. Take her and put her in chains before all of them will go on a long ride. She's athletic enough; she might try to get away. Put the scum on the transport to Valparaiso. The torture chambers on the M.S. Esmeralda are in waiting for their Highnesses. Good riddance, you rich bastards."

He almost struck Doretta in the back with his pointed boot. Doretta began to cry. She had no idea what was happening; all she knew was that she and her loved ones were in serious trouble and in the crossfires of some political upheaval. Her arm ached where the soldier, pushing her toward the drying shack, was grabbing her too firmly.

The servants stood together on one side of the burning mansion. Valentina held firmly onto Juan, wishing to stifle her cries. She couldn't believe what she was seeing and hearing. Watching Señora Esmeralda walking away toward a sea of flames, she caught Pablo out of the corner of her eyes; he was following his mistress, trying very hard to walk next to her cane.

Valentina dared to whisper in Juan's ear. "What are we going to do? They and we have lost everything. The soldiers set everything on fire except the little storage shed. I don't even know what's in there. We hardly ever used it."

"Fernando used to store his old motorbike in the shed. I can't recall if he got rid of it. Once he took delivery of his Jeep, he never used anything else. I saw a couple of the soldiers drive the Jeep away. Let's wait and see what they might do to us. From what I could make out, they were after the wealthy landowners, not us servants. They didn't realize how close we were to the family and that all we owned was in the mansion they firebombed and destroyed. They left us with nothing," voiced Juan.

He gestured to those standing with him to move back. The roof of the hacienda was about to collapse. Once it did, the fire was bound to spread out further and beyond the foundation.

A camouflaged truck pulled up, exposing numerous people sitting and standing on the flatbed. Sounds of crying could be heard faintly. Valentina thought she recognized the face of the neighboring landowner. They didn't believe their eyes. Fernando, Doretta, and both children were pushed and beaten with billy clubs as they were moved toward the truck that had arrived seconds earlier. All of the Garcia Lopez family were blindfolded. They were literally thrown onto the vehicle by those who manhandled the captives.

"Get them out of here. Follow the trucks that are headed southwest. They'll know what to do with these useless creatures on the ship. No stopping along the way! They'll have to piss and shit on the truck. Did you understand me?"

"Yes, sir," said the driver as he pulled the door to the cab shut, leaving Juan and his family watching their maneuvers helplessly. The officer in charge blew a whistle and then resorted to a megaphone.

"Men, clear out of here. Our job at this den of iniquity is done. We've done what we came for. Let's hit the next place ten kilometers down the road. If they give us any trouble, I may just order any prisoners to be shot on the spot or have the bastards hung from their trees. It will save time and money. As it is, the M.S. Esmeralda must be getting packed by now."

The soldiers gathered on the truck that had brought them to the Garcia Lopez Hacienda and drove off. Juan had no idea what the officer meant by the M.S. Esmeralda. He was to learn much later that it was a steel-hulled four-masted barquentine tall ship of the Chilean Navy, used by the Pinochet junta to incarcerate prisoners, torture them, and to dispose of their innocent victims at sea.

As dawn broke, the ashes from the mansion that once was the stately home of the Garcia Lopez family were still glimmering and hot to the touch. The black Mercedes limousine had been torched; all other vehicles were stolen by the invading marauders. Juan found some old quilts in the storage shed, allowing the remaining servants to huddle on the ground. Master Fernando's motorbike was still in the old shed. Not knowing if there was any gas in the tank, Juan was pleased to discover two old bicycles as well. The tires looked in good shape to him.

"I think I'll ride this one over to the winery and see if anything is left standing. You want to come along, Valentina? That second bike is actually one designed for ladies."

"That's a good idea you have. I've been wondering ever since last night what happened to Señora Esmeralda. The poor woman appeared to be in shock. I hope to God someone saw her walking and helped her. Oh Dios mío! Let her not have had another stroke."

Valentina kissed Juanita on both cheeks and hopped on the bike. She hadn't been on a bicycle in years and wasn't sure at first that she could handle it. But she did. As they made their way along the burned-out vineyards, a barking dog approached from a distance. Getting closer, they discovered it was Pablo. Juan jumped off his bike.

"Come here, Pablo. Good dog! You are a sight for sore eyes. Why are you so excited?" The dog stuck his snout in both of his pant pockets.

"You are hungry, and I've got nothing in my pockets to give you. There's nothing left at the house either. You'll have to starve along with us until we get a hold of something. What are you yapping about? Show me!"

Juan and Valentina got back on their bikes and followed Pablo closely. He'd run fifty feet or so and then would turn back toward them, always shaking his head and barking furiously before he'd run ahead again.

"He's trying to tell us something. What? I haven't figured it out yet. But knowing Pablo, we'll discover sooner or later." The gray shed of the Wind Angels came into view. The bottom of the building had been scorched, but the old solid-oak wood and the dampness caused by a broken waterline had saved the structure. The closer they came, the louder Pablo's barking became.

"I see the beam from the gate closure has been removed and thrown on the ground. I wonder if they hurt the keeper of the angel wings?" Juan got off his bike, just laying it on the ground. Valentina followed his example. She held his hand as they entered the old barn. Valentina covered her mouth and burst into tears. Pablo sat at their feet, furiously barking.

"Oh Dios mío!" Esmeralda, dressed in her spectacular black Balenciaga, her shoulders still covered with the dazzling Metha creation, was hanging among the gently swaying angel wings. A sign suspended by a silk rope from her neck read: "Perra."

"Who would do such a thing?" voiced Juan. They were both stunned into a reality they were not prepared to face. Pablo kept barking, always looking up at his silent mistress. She had always been there for him when the others were gone or were otherwise preoccupied. Pablo didn't want to let go.

"Pablo doesn't realize that Esmeralda is dead. I've got to find help. I cannot take her down by myself. You take Pablo with you to what's left of the hacienda. Hopefully, between Cook, Juanita, and whoever else is still there, you'll come up with something to feed this poor creature. Never mind feeding the poor creature, see what you can scrounge up for us," and he was on his bike heading in the direction of the winery.

His hopes were soon to be dashed; all that was standing above ground were the torched remains of the once-proud structure. Three of the workers were checking to see what could be salvaged in the wine cellars. At least the secret storage where the precious bottled vintages were kept had been missed in the haste by those who had come to scorch the land.

"I need your help," said Juan.

"The bastards that did all this hung Señora Esmeralda Garcia Lopez in the Wind Angels' shed. We need to take her down and bury her. I'm sure she would like to be interred next to her husband, Don Carlos, in the family plot at the cemetery in Santiago. How, I don't know right now. I haven't got a clue where to find a coffin."

"Burial in Santiago is out of the question at this moment in time. My men and I will have no problem creating a coffin. We know how to make barrels; we'll have a coffin in short order. I'll send Ramon with you to take down the Señora's body. Take that little flatbed wagon with you. Here's a rope; use it to tie the wagon to your bike. You won't have too much trouble transporting her up here. Señora Esmeralda always was a tiny person but never a tiny personality. We will accord her the final resting place she deserves; Señora Esmeralda will be buried with dignity in the small village cemetery."

Ramon got on his bike and followed Juan to the Wind Angels' shed. Nothing had been disturbed in Juan's absence. There was only silence and the gentle swishing of the wings in the breeze. The two men had little difficulty taking Señora's body down. Juan removed the sign, tore it to pieces, and threw the fragments to the ground. "Undeserved!" was all he could mutter. They folded her dress carefully about her and laid her gently upon the wagon.

"I'm sure Señora Esmeralda never envisioned her funeral hearse to be a simple lorry," Ramon couldn't help observing. "My, how the mighty have fallen." He had at times in his life difficulty swallowing his lot and the difference between those who had everything and those who had little or nothing. But never, in his most deviant wishes, had he sought a fate that had befallen his Chilean masters.

There was no funeral cortege; three vineyard workers and her trusted chauffeur, Juan, accompanied Señora Esmeralda on her last journey on earth. She was buried before sunset on September 12, 1973. In time, Juan would grace the grave with a simple wooden cross bearing the name Señora Esmeralda Garcia Lopez.

Juan was greeted by his wife. "We made three important discoveries since Pablo and I left you this morning. Our vegetable garden is untouched; neither was the smokehouse. I discovered a side of bacon and several dozen smoked sausages that are perfectly edible. Pablo has had two of them and seems to be copacetic. Your ingenious daughter checked out the motorbike; its tank was full and the tires she brought up to snuff using the hand pump she found."

"The news of the vegetable garden and sausages makes my growling stomach burst with joy, but what's so important about the master's motorbike?" asked Juan.

"I didn't think you wanted to ride your bicycle into Santiago, or did you?" inquired Valentina.

"Why would I want to go into Santiago, by bicycle or motorbike?"

"We have to find a place to live, and I intend to explore the possibility of regaining my job in the alteration department at Falabella's. Does that make sense? There's nothing left here;

and with our masters gone, what else can we do? You really don't expect any of them to return and rebuild, do you? You realize we are all that's left? The other servants ran away when they witnessed what happened to the family," said Valentina.

"You are correct. I hadn't even thought that far. You can ride on the tail of the motorbike, Juanita can take one of the bikes, and Cook can ride the other. Pablo will have to walk. I believe he's young enough and could manage walking for a good hour. Let's trust the road hasn't been destroyed. Hopefully, things will have calmed down a bit in the city," Juan concluded.

Checking out the storage shed further, Valentina found an old washbasin, some rags, and strong brown soap. All took a sponge bath before retiring to the smokehouse all wrapped in the old quilts. They weathered the night and were up at sunrise and ready for their venture into the big city.

They quickly discovered they were not alone in seeking relief in Santiago. Others were in a similar fix. If they thought the roads were swarmed with armed military, Santiago greeted them with a sea of soldiers holding machine guns, walking and standing everywhere, looking ready to shoot at anyone who appeared to be threatening their cause.

Riding by the Teatro, Juan pointed to the scorched marquee. "Look at that sign and see what they did to it, but you can still read *La Damnation de Faust*. I'm sure you agree with me, we are the ones who were damned by this uprising."

"Please drop me off at Falabella's, and then take yourself and the others to your brother's home. I've been praying they were not affected by this upheaval. Their place is big enough to accommodate the four of us until we can find our own housing. Plan on coming to fetch me no later than noon."

Ж

Walking into Falabella's, Valentina wasn't exactly a fashion plate, but at least she was clean. She headed straight for the elevators and got off on the second floor. Her prayers were answered when she spotted Frau Flott speaking with a customer on the sales floor. Valentina stood back but made sure she caught Frau Flott's eye as she walked by.

"Excuse me just a second, ma'am," said Frau Flott to her customer. Then she spoke to Valentina.

"Are you okay, dear? Please wait by my desk; we'll speak as soon as I'm free. Just by looking at you, I can tell the news isn't good." Valentina had tears in her eyes. She didn't have to say a word. Frau Flott met Valentina as quickly as possible. The customer whom she was serving was a regular patron in the department.

"Now tell me, what's wrong? What happened? Did anything happen to the Garcia Lopez family? Don't tell me they were among those poor people annihilated by these marauders?"

Valentina related the whole story as it had unfolded on the evening of September 11. When she ended her tale of sorrow with the discovery of Señora Esmeralda's body, Frau Flott broke down in tears.

"What you had to experience is horrendous. And to think of that elegant lady being buried in a pauper's grave. I can't believe what's happening out there. It takes me back home during the days of the 1930s. I never thought anything like that could happen here."

"Our dear masters are gone; their world was destroyed, and so was ours. We have nothing but the clothes on our backs.

Is there any chance I could work with you in the alteration department? I wouldn't have any difficulty doing the work. I've always done all the sewing and mending for the Garcia Lopez family."

"Actually, I might be able to fit you in on a temporary basis to start. One of the seamstresses will go on pregnancy leave by the end of the week. She'll be gone at least four months. Once you are in the system, we'll look further when the time comes. I'm pleased to help you and glad to have you back in the store."

"Thank you. You are my savior. Speaking of saviors, you have one other not-so-happy role to play in this unfolding drama. Frau Flott, I implore you, you must contact Señora Doretta's family and let them know what happened to her and her loved ones. I would write to them if I knew how."

"Thank you for saying that, Valentina. I have every intention of doing so. I'm honored that you asked me."

Valentina rose from her chair. Frau Flott gave her a gentle hug. "I will see you tomorrow then, let's say nine o'clock? The lady who's going on leave would have a chance to familiarize you with her responsibilities."

"That sounds wonderful. Thank you for having me back on staff. It will be a start for my whole family. Thank you again." She bowed, leaving Frau Flott behind, who was stunned by what she had just learned.

Valentina didn't bother with the elevator. She took the steps to the main floor of Falabella's two at a time and was happy to see Juan waiting for her.

"I told Frau Flott the whole story, and I have a job at least for the next four months. And who knows what lies beyond that? We'll live our lives one day at a time."

"Paulo was pleased to see me alive. All of us, including Pablo, can stay with them for as long as we need to. In a few days, when things hopefully will normalize in this town, I'll see if I can find work as a taxi driver. It's what I do best. But for now, let me take you home to my family."

Valentina still was terribly threatened by all the machine guns  held by hundreds of soldiers in the city. As they rode by the Teatro, she read the torched marquee once again and whispered into Juan's ear: "The opera should have been called *La Damnation de Doretta.*"

# Acknowledgments

THE author wishes to express his sincere gratitude to the staff of Wheatmark Publishing for their efforts in bringing this latest novel to fruition. Special recognition is accorded to Wheatmark's Senior Project Manager, Lori Conser, for her dedicated and diligent work leading to the publication of the author's writings. Many thanks are due those who have encouraged the author to write, in particular the members of the Green Valley Writers' Forum and family and friends. The author has learned to appreciate the many helpful comments and suggestions by Beta readers. Last but not least, the writer recognizes his wife, Lynne, with heartfelt thankfulness for her endless hours of reading and providing suggestions during the writing process, critical editorial commentary, and invaluable support throughout the project.

*A Backward Glance at Eden*

A Sequel To

*The Blue Sapphire Amulet*


HARALD LUTZ BRUCKNER

# Prologue

JOCHANAAN celebrated his sixteenth birthday on February 6, 1962. Among his many presents, he found an invitation from his mother, Rachel Adina Salm von Graben von Rondstett Unrat. When he read his mother's distinct handwriting, he was touched by her thoughtful consideration in selecting a special gift. He couldn't wait to sit down with her at the breakfast table.

"Thank you, Mom. I'll treasure our visit to Hamburg—Germany's jewel of the North. I only have to wait a whole three days for our adventure to begin. Didn't Fritz want to come along?"

"I asked him but he thought this was one event he wanted just the two of us to enjoy. He isn't as enchanted with opera, and especially Wagnerian opera, as are we. He won't mind being at home. He'll keep Elsa company. And if he gets too bored, he'll have a couple of brews with Walter. I almost said John. I have no idea why he decided of late to go by his middle name? Well, John or Walter, he's still one of Fritz's closest buddies.

)(

The train for Hamburg left on the morning of February 9. Jochanaan liked the elegance of the first-class compartment, and both he and his mother were pleased to have the space all to themselves. Rachel reached into her purse and retrieved the tickets for the Staatsoper Hamburg.

"I thought you might like to know what opera I've chosen. I realize *Der Fliegende Holländer* [The *Flying Dutchman*] is one of your favorites."

"Oh, Mom, I love it. And to see it at a place that is so close to the stormy North Sea. Have you ever been to Hamburg?"

"I attended a professional meeting four years ago and stayed at the Steigenberger Hotel. Your sister Miriam's father and I would have liked to be in Hamburg while we were still studying in München in the 1930s. That simply wasn't possible at the time because of the political situation in Germany. I can assure you, no one shall question our religion today."

"Let's hope not." Jochanaan looked at his watch and then at the train schedule. "Looks like we'll arrive in time for lunch. Can we go down to the Jungfernstieg and have our meal on one of the boats? We could enjoy a bite to eat and see something of the city at the same time."

"Excellent idea. The performance starts at seven o'clock. We'll have a light dinner at the hotel. You'll look nice in the blue suit you brought. I'll wear a two-piece ensemble and brighten it up with a scarf. We don't have to be formal; it's not opening night."

The Hamburg Express pulled into the station promptly at 12:33. They took a cab to the hotel, checked in, and walked down to the Jungfernstieg. The boat ride was fun and their lunch exactly what they had envisioned. As he was getting dressed for dinner and the theater, Jochanaan was humming a tune.

"Isn't that the overture from *Der Fliegende Holländer?*" asked his mother.

"Yes. It certainly is! You know what inspired Wagner to write the opera, don't you?"

"Vaguely; it's so long since I heard about it when Otto and I studied in München. There was a time I disliked anything Wagnerian because of the composer's blatant anti-Semitism and Hitler's veneration of the man."

"Mom, that happened all so long ago. What's important is the man's creative genius. In 1839, Wagner and his wife fled from creditors under the cloak of darkness and boarded a small vessel in Riga bound for London. The ship was caught in a horrendous storm and nearly sank in a Norwegian fjord. Reading a story by Heinrich Heine and recalling the near-death experience on their voyage through the Baltic and North Seas inspired Wagner to write his first great romantic opera," said Jochanaan.

"I'm surprised you know all those details. I never had the time or inclination to be that well informed." Rachel looked at the passing scene as the train carried them swiftly to their destination.

Jochanaan continued, "Wagner wrote *Der Fliegende Holländer* over one-hundred and twenty-five years ago. Millions have been under the spell of this magical score for all these years. It's the first opera using leitmotifs (the storm motif, the Dutchman and Senta motifs, the redemption through true love motif, and others) that occur in the overture and link the action in this one-act musical drama."

Rachel could tell her son was already listening to the score in his mind. Jochanaan went on with much excitement in his delivery.

"I can't wait to hear it. The overture is such a powerful precursor of what's to come in the opera. When I started attending operas with one of my classmates, I was immediately taken by the tragic story of the Dutchman and Senta, the woman who ultimately rescues him from the curse of sailing the seven seas forever."

"There you go again talking about romance. Why do you insist on wanting to become a monk? It simply makes no sense to me."

"Mom, let's not spoil the evening. Wanting to enter a monastery and enjoying an operatic story are two entirely different things."

Rachel decided to let it go; she was still hoping Jochanaan would come to his senses in the course of the next two years.

The performance was all any devotee of Wagnerian drama could hope for. Senta sang the final words, *"Hier steh' ich, treu dir bis zum Tod"* [Here I stand, faithfully yours until death shall us part]. The audience sat spellbound, listening as the last chords of the opera faded away. As the final curtain fell, a standing ovation rewarded the performers.

Leaving the opera house deep in thought, neither Rachel nor Jochanaan or any of the others envisioned the devastation that would be visited upon the city of Hamburg a week later. Storm Vincinette, blowing off the North Sea, brought the devastating flood of 1962 to Hamburg, killing hundreds and causing thousands to lose their homes and all they treasured. It was one of the great disasters befalling Hamburg, the Pearl of the North.

# Chapter 1

THE sirens at firehouse #3 were blaring at 6:31 a.m. on the morning of February 29, 1976. The crew sleeping in the loft of the station had a rude awakening on this early Sunday morning. No one had expected to leap into the day at this ungodly hour, least of all Matt, who was still sound asleep. Hans, his closest buddy, shook Matt by his right shoulder. "Wake up, Matt! Wake up! I'll catch you at the bottom of the brass pole." Hans was rushing away, grabbing his helmet off the hanging rack. Matt slipped down the pole seconds later.

The engine of the firetruck was running smoothly; Matt was the last to jump onto the vehicle already in motion. "Looks like the Laach Monastery is in flames. It must be some fire; look how the bell towers of the Abbey are lit by the glow of the inferno. Makes me wonder what happened," said Hans.

The fire engine raced through streets totally lacking traffic at dawn on a Sunday morning. Bells from all churches near and far were competing with the sirens of rushing firetrucks, ambulances, and police vehicles. Fire engine #3 was the first on the scene since it was closest to the monastery.

The crew jumped into action before the motion of the truck

had ceased. Hoses rolled off the smoothly functioning spools and connected to the well-marked fire hydrants situated near the target area. Matt stared at the flames emerging from the second-story windows and would have sworn he detected a human figure moving within the room that was ablaze. His suspicions were confirmed by the outcry of a dozen friars watching the burning building. "It's Father Frederick Emanuel. He's trying to reach the marble staircase and escape." Matt and Hans, gushing water hoses in hand, rushed in the direction of the building entrance. From regular fire drills, they knew that the entrance to the staircase led to the main section of the monastery.

Getting closer to the solid wood door, they could hear the desperate yelling. "Flood the door! Break down the damn door!" The priest realized what he had blurted out as he splashed water over Jochanaan and himself. "We are surrounded by flames. Hurry! This holy water won't save us for long. The fires of hell are moving ever so close to us."

Matt raised his hand and signaled for help and the need for a powerful beam to break down the door. His signal was instantly recognized by members of the crew. Within seconds, four of the men rammed a solid oak beam with all their strength into the lock of the door. On their third attempt, the door gave way, allowing Father Frederick Emanuel to emerge. In his arms he held the young friar, Brother Jochanaan.

Neither Father Frederick Emanuel nor Brother Jochanaan spoke a word other than mumbled appreciation of thankfulness for being rescued. Father Emanuel gently laid his charge on the ground. "He needs to be taken to a burn unit at the closest hospital ASAP. The young man has sustained severe burns over much of his body." It was only when Jochanaan's tunic was drawn away from his head that the firemen realized that his face was completely blackened.

Matt spoke first. "Father, can you explain what happened to this guy? You were the one who rescued him. Can you tell us what you saw?"

"I was awakened by a loud noise shortly after five and immediately was aware of something burning in the monastery. As I rushed toward a wall of smoke that traveled down the long hallway of our floor and in my direction, I banged on the doors of sleeping friars while making my way to the source of the problem. I kept yelling 'fire, fire' and 'get out of the building.'

"I realized smoke and flames originated from the cell of Brother Jochanaan. When I entered his room, I saw him standing stark naked next to his work table. He was surrounded by flames. A large blanket and a burned tunic were lying at his bare feet. It appeared he had rolled himself in the blanket to extinguish the embers from his burning garments. He was clearly in shock and didn't say a word as he saw me approach. I believe the chemicals from his photo lab ignited and caused the explosion and the fire. I grabbed one of his other tunics, wanting to cover his body, before I dragged him down to the font where I splashed all available holy water over both of us and rushed down the marble staircase. I knew it would be the only way for us to escape the inferno."

Hans got the attention of the chief and signaled for a stretcher. Father Frederick Emanuel lifted Jochanaan onto the gurney and joined the young friar inside the ambulance. Once the ambulance crew had closed the doors, Father Emanuel bent down to his charge and wiped Jochanaan's blackened brow with a clean handkerchief. "Most of the burns on your body are from the acid that erupted from the exploding canister. You were smart to roll in that blanket. It kept you from becoming a living torch. The bulk of the burns are on your legs and your chest. Your face is merely covered with black smudge, nothing that cannot be solved by soap and water." He pressed Jochanaan's right hand reassuringly.

"Thanks, Father, for coming to my rescue. I have no idea what happened. I know how to handle the chemicals in my photo lab. I've done it since I was a young boy. Feel the back of my head. While I was bent over the table and was reading the emerging images, I was struck by something. Last I remember was the smell of cigarette smoke followed by the explosion. You are fully aware that I don't lock my cell and always abide by the rule of the monastery to never hide behind locked doors. Anyone could have come in and surprised me while I was deeply involved in developing the product of my most recent photo shoot." Jochanaan gasped for air; coughing furiously, he gestured for a tissue. He was shocked to see the black phlegm he'd expelled.

The priest looked on in horror and finally responded. "You realize there will be an investigation since a large portion of the monastery was destroyed by the fire. Do you have any inkling who might have tried to hurt you? All of the friars have been with me for years, except young Anthony who joined us three weeks ago. Most of our brothers know of our relationship. Are you aware of any of them carrying animosity toward you?"

"None" was all Jochanaan said before he succumbed to the heavy sedation he had received from the ambulance crew as soon as he was securely ensconced in the emergency vehicle.

# About the Author

Harald Lutz Bruckner, author of *The Blue Sapphire Amulet, Escape on the Astral Express, A Wanderer on the Earth, The Born-Again Phoenix, Harald's Garland,* and *Lighthouse Mystery,* hails from Germany but has spent his adult life in the United States. His work and educational adventures have taken him from merchandising/retailing, the teaching of German and World Literature, to a career in Audiology and the challenges of working with hard-of-hearing and deaf children and adults. Among his favorite academic subjects to teach were his offerings in sign language. In 1981, he discovered the magic of painting in transparent watercolors and has never stopped painting. Moving to sunny Arizona from the high country of Colorado in 2003 caused a major shift in his subject matter, changing from a primarily realistic orientation to one of total abstraction. Since his retirement from academia, Bruckner has pursued his passions for travel, art, music, and the enjoyment of writing.